The Pass

Drumlummon
Montana Literary Masters Series

Vol. 1 *Food of Gods and Starvelings:*
The Selected Poems of Grace Stone Coates (2007),
edited by Lee Rostad & Rick Newby

Vol. 2. *Notes for a Novel:*
The Selected Poems of Frieda Fligelman (2008),
edited by Alexandra Swaney & Rick Newby

Vol. 3 *The Pass: A Novel* (2009),
by Thomas Savage, with an
introduction by O. Alan Weltzien
(in collaboration with Riverbend Publishing)

Vol. 4 *Clear Title: A Novel* (forthcoming 2009)
by Grace Stone Coates, with an introduction
by Caroline Patterson

The Pass

A Novel

Thomas Savage

With an Introduction by O. Alan Weltzien

RIVERBEND
PUBLISHING

DRUMLUMMON
INSTITUTE

INTRODUCTION

O. Alan Weltzien

In August 1937, Thomas Savage, poised to leave his native state of Montana, published his first story, "The Bronc Stomper," in *Coronet* magazine. He was done with what was then called Montana State College (The University of Montana–Missoula), and in the fall, he travelled by train to Boston, there meeting Elizabeth Fitzgerald, a new friend and daughter of his writing professor in Missoula, Brassil Fitzgerald. Both matriculated at Colby College in Waterville, Maine, and they married two years later. During this time, Savage worked hard on what became his first novel. After seven years' labor, during which time Savage worked a variety of jobs, he sold *The Pass* to Doubleday, who published it in 1944. Savage, who'd gone by Tom Brenner since he was five (his stepfather's family name), had always wanted to be a writer. By the time he published his first novel, he had decided to switch to his birth father's surname, in that way confirming his new professional identity. Savage would go on to publish twelve more novels over the next forty-four years.

After spending his childhood and young adulthood in tiny Horse Prairie, Montana, and Lemhi, Idaho, Savage's interlude in Missoula (and brief employment in Portland, Oregon, and British Columbia) convinced him to put as much distance between his native ground and himself as possible. To this day Horse Prairie and Lemhi are remote locations: the former, a high, dry ranching valley about thirty miles southwest of Dillon and over 6,000 feet in elevation; the latter, no more than a wide spot along Highway 28, over thirty miles southeast of Salmon. The Beaverhead

Mountains—also the Continental Divide and state border—run between them, and Lemhi and Bannock Passes are the only connecting links. It was a long train ride to Butte, the nearest city. The Savages lived in Waltham, Massachusetts, before settling on a rocky point in Georgetown, Maine, in the mid-1950s, where they remained for thirty years. But *The Pass*, and the majority of his fiction, insistently proves that he never left home. In fact Savage, like many writers, lived far away in order to obsessively re-inhabit and imaginatively commemorate his home ground.

Savage not only dedicated *The Pass* to his mother, Elizabeth (Beth) Yearian Brenner; he named his female protagonist, the tragic Beth Bentley, after her. Savage's mother remained a seminal influence in his life, and he recreated her several times in his novels. Beth Bentley was raised a ranch daughter, as was Beth Brenner, and Savage captures certain facets of his mother in this initial fictional portrait. For example, Beth Bentley displays the same sensitivity to, and interest in, local tribes as Beth Brenner: "she knew Shoshone" (Chapter X).

The Pass serves in many ways as an overture to Savage's fiction. It covers an eleven-year period, 1913–1924, one generation removed from his writing it. In seven subsequent novels, Savage writes what I call the near-historical past: a period closer to the writer's present than most of the historical novels of A. B. Guthrie, Jr., and Ivan Doig. He endorsed novelist Willa Cather's credo that the most influential period for a writer occurs between ages eight and sixteen, and that a writer's most memorable work grows out of that span (and geographical setting) of childhood and adolescence. In later novels, Savage often returns to the first three decades, especially, of the 20th century—a period, within memory, of initial white settlement.

And for his first novel, Savage uses his mother's family ranch, in Lemhi, Idaho, as the approximate setting (although "the prairie" is called Horse Prairie and, in Chapter XVIII, he refers to the Bentley's "living room in Montana"). To this day, Bannock Pass, at 7,681 feet—"the Pass" of the novel, which straddles the Continental Divide and hangs ominously above the valley and characters in the novel—remains a remote location near Montana's southern tip. A dirt-gravel road zigzags across it from Horse Prairie south-southwestward, down Canyon Creek to Leadore, Idaho. Arguably, Savage conflated Lemhi Pass (Lewis and Clark's "pass," at 7,373 feet a bit lower than Bannock Pass, and closer to Lemhi, Idaho) with Bannock Pass in his geographical imagination. The Lemhi River Valley—the novel's "prairie"—feels similarly remote as a sparsely settled valley where occasional ranchers run cattle and grow hay. The Lemhi River flows northwest about fifty miles to a junction with the Salmon River at Salmon, Idaho. The novel's "Salmon City," this county seat remains one of Idaho's more remote towns due to topography (particularly to the north and west): it's over 150 miles to Idaho Falls, for example. Driving northwest along Highway 28 towards Salmon, one realizes anew the size of the country and the great distance from cities. The landscape's scale and sparse human population also explain why, in a 1999 interview, Savage remarked, "the difference in Westerners has to do with the fact that they feel it's impossible to look at the Rocky Mountains—or to look at the horizon, which is equally vast—and consider that there is such a thing as Europe or neighbors or anything else."

The primary historical event upon which Savage plots *The Pass* is the construction of the Gilmore and Pittsburgh Railroad (the novel's "Salmon City and Pittsburgh Railroad"), a short-lived line that never made much profit. This railroad was built southwest from Armstead, Montana—the town inundated in 1964 by the waters of Clark Canyon reservoir, about twenty miles south of Dillon—commencing in April, 1909. Thirteen months later it reached Salmon City, and a southern spur served the Gilmore (Idaho) mines. Financed by Pennsylvania mining interests and the Northern Pacific, the Gilmore and Pittsburgh was plagued with track problems, and by 1938, highway construction spelled the end of the line, service ending the following spring. Lasting only one generation, this railroad figured centrally in Savage's childhood, as it proved the primary transportation between his stepfather's cattle ranch and his mother's family's sheep ranch. In old age, Savage retained fond memories of the railroad. For *The Pass*, Savage alters dates slightly, as the railroad reaches Salmon City in 1916, midway through the novel (Chapter XVII).

Joseph Kinsey Howard, in the first anthology of Montana literature, *Montana Margins* (1946), recognized the importance of this railroad, and of Savage as a then-new Montana writer, because he included a section from the novel's middle in the ninth (of ten) sections, "Travel and Transport," of his anthology. In what represents one of the longest excerpts in *Montana Margins*, Howard included the final section of Savage's Chapter XVI, all of Chapters XVII-XVIII, and the first section of Chapter XIX: the arrival of the railroad in Salmon City, and some of the changes it wrought.

Writer Annie Proulx, a friend of Savage's, believes Savage belongs to a golden age of what she calls landscape fiction ("Afterword," *The Power of the Dog*, reprint 2001). Certainly landscape figures as the central presence, if not protagonist, in *The Pass*. The novel's opening paragraph places protagonist Jess Bentley at the pass as though he's a diminutive figure in the front corner of a sprawling Albert Bierstadt canvas. The novel's first spoken words, "'Queer country. . . .'"—"a grizzled prospector's" judgment of the terrain—ominously foreshadow the dominance of pass and prairie over the settlers' lives. Savage begins Chapter IX stating, "The prairie's landmarks were silent and brooding," and he combines altitude, remoteness, and weather (a ferocious, sustained March blizzard after a strange, cold fall and early winter) to climax the novel. Haystacks have disappeared, the big red trucks—another sign of change—are stranded near the pass, but the Little Haytrain That Could plows across the pass, chugs into Salmon City, and saves the ranchers and their starving cattle.

Landscape looms as a force both awesome and, at times, awful. Contrary to *The Power of the Dog*, Savage's best-known novel, for example, Native Americans are conspicuous by their absence in *The Pass*. In Savage's initial novel, it is as though local tribes never existed, though Savage's mother's family befriended local natives repeatedly, and Beth Yearian (Brenner), an amateur ethnographer, compiled a dictionary of Lemhi Shoshone terms. By the time Jess Bentley and his bride join the small community of ranchers on the prairie, these Shoshone have vanished, leaving behind only their judgment, repeated to Jess by an old prospector, that the prairie is "bad medicine." Apparently no tribes ever inhabited "the prairie," though bison were abundant. Such omens not only monumentalize the landscape in Savage's novel, but hint at the eventual fate of Jess's newborn son and, months later, wife. Jess directly identifies himself with his chosen setting, becoming one with "the mountains [that] would never change," and the prairie, "a vast, endless, timeless, isolated thing" (Chapter XIV). But his rootedness comes at a higher cost than he can imagine. Beth Bentley's fragility, an increasingly emphasized thread of her character, is paralleled by the white community's vulnerability, as though the only way out of the Lemhi River valley is Bannock Pass. People in this slightly fictionalized Lemhi County are entirely dependent on one mountain pass over the Continental Divide. To the extent that place and weather figure as primary presences, *The Pass* can be seen as a descendent of the naturalistic novel of Frank Norris, Stephen Crane, and Theodore Dreiser.

If Savage modeled the Bentley spread on his maternal grandparents' Lemhi ranch, he moved the action one generation ahead, as his grandparents, Thomas and Emma Russell, began ranching out of a log cabin in 1889, not 1913. *The Pass* animates some popular Western stereotypes, particularly concerning gender roles, even as it questions the price of progress. Savage deftly writes social scenes governing the Bentley house raising, the "shivaree" (surprise party for newlyweds at their house), the fall roundup with the big chuckwagon, and the completion of the track and arrival of the train in Salmon City. The novel glances over the homesteading boom, Savage's "honyockers" (a term immortalized by Joseph Kinsey Howard in *Montana: High, Wide and Handsome*) being Swedish and Finnish emigrant wheat farmers who arrive with the train and fence with barbed wire. The ranchers grouse about the enclosures: Savage has Jess exclaim, "'Why couldn't they go to a farming country, instead of tearing up the land here? This is no place to— plow'" (Chapter XIX). The drought of the 1920s blows most of the sodbusters away.

The novel notes, more briefly, the sinking of the Lusitania and American entrance into World War I (Chapter XXIII). Savage shifts his focus ahead six years to 1923 within three chapters, lightly sketching the impact of the Roaring 20s into the remote prairie. The remainder of the novel (Chapters XXVI-XXXIX) takes place in the winter and spring of 1924: the very year in which he sets *The Power of the Dog* many years later.

In this community, men are laconic and women, voluble. Men distrust talk and women, at least Mrs. Cooper and especially Amy Pierce, talk too much, as though talk marks one's shallowness. Despite Savage's satiric energy focused on these women—Mrs. Cooper epitomizes the prude, for instance, custodian of a fierce and harsh morality and sister of Carry Nation despite her marriage to a former gambler— both emerge as loving friends, their hearts redeeming their often silly mouths. Further, in the marriage between Jess and Beth, their comparable ranch backgrounds give way to an adult-child relationship wherein Jess hides his dependency under his persona as gruff boss. This is no marriage of equals. Beth loses her gumption, particularly after their dispute about her riding the big bay horse and her subsequent accident and its consequences. *The Pass* does not subvert these threadbare conventions of pop Western culture. It even features an old cowboy named Slim, a fussy bachelor who becomes Jess's foreman and right-hand "hand." As though acknowledging the watershed novel of the popular West, Savage twice refers to Owen Wister's *The Virginian*. *The Virginian* is given by Mrs. Cooper as a "whimsical" wedding present to the Bentleys "because it was about country like the prairie" (Chapter VIII). While that may be true, Savage saw himself writing an entirely different Western novel than the kind Wister initiated at the beginning of the twentieth century. Later, at the Masonic Hall winter dance (Chapter XX), the middle-aged spinster schoolteacher introduces the new, young schoolteacher (from Minneapolis, "just out of Normal School") to Jess, whom she calls "a rancher, but a cowboy also!": "'Miss Hayes has been reading the *Virginian* and wants to know all about cowboys.'"

The Pass separates itself from the popular Western genre through its critical sensibility, one which refuses to glorify cowboys as permanent icons. One discovers no gunslingers or guns in Savage. But in this community, if not climate, there is little tolerance of difference. Jess sees through the ranchers' mockery of old Billy Blair with his sewing machine, two milk cows, and cream separator, as though dairying is no man's business any more than is raising a flower garden, which Mrs. Cooper struggles to do (Chapter XIV). Weather and horses kill Mrs. Cooper's nasturtiums just as a blizzard kills Billy (Chapter XIX). Arguably, Billy's eccentricities, if not questionable masculinity, kill him, not his winter trapping (for beaver pelts, intended for a coat for Beth). As Jess and Beth ride home from Billy's place after burying him, Beth, ironically foreshadowing her own demise, remarks "'The prairie killed him. He loved the prairie and it killed him'." Jess's response—"He said, 'I can't hear you.'"—subtly describes his own inability to control his family's fate in the place they have put down roots.

Later novels expose and critique the formula Westerns' enshrined legacy of rigid gender roles and boundaries. But Savage makes his criticism clear from the beginning. In Chapter XXIII he remarks, "Now on the prairie sex was never discussed with another man, and this was strange because the prairie lived because of sex." "Bull" and "stud" are taboo words, "And so childbirth and sex were not discussed because somehow it insulted your wife."

Savage uses Jess to critique the signs of progress, above all the railroad and the telephone. Excited talk about the coming railroad gusts through the novel like a wind buffeting a hayfield, and Jess stands apart from the community's naïve enthusiasm. At the conclusion of the initial fall roundup scene, Jess broods,

> And they wanted a railroad. When they had everything they wanted a railroad. They wanted to change this land he had found and loved already and had brought Beth to. He stood tense in every muscle. He didn't know it then, but he had begun to resent the future and everything it meant. He, the youngest of them, was already the oldest of them (Chapter VIII).

In a later scene, when Beth accuses him—"'Jess, why are you always talking about how good the railroad is when you know you hate it?'," he denies his resentment (Chapter XIX), but it spreads to the telephone, around which Jess always feels apprehensive (Chapter XXVIII). In fact "the hum of the telephone wires brought a new sound of loneliness to the prairie," and Savage gives to chatterbox Amy Pierce—a natural for the telephone—an awareness of loss as well as gain:

And when they got the wires strung up they talked, but there was no longer an excuse to go to somebody's house to ask how the hay was holding out, or to borrow a magazine and stay all day. The telephone had spoiled all that. It seemed that all the new things, all the new ways, spoiled something (Chapter XXXIII).

Savage judges Jess "the oldest" of the ranchers because Jess intuits some of the negative consequences of denser settlement and technological innovation. He sees into the future, conceding his inability to shape it any more than he shapes weather or his family's fate. It's the old self-pitying story, one captured by A. B. Guthrie, Jr. in *The Big Sky*, published three years after *The Pass*. Guthrie gives to his character, old grizzled Uncle Zeb Calloway, the mournful lamentation of paradise supposedly lost ("She's all gone. The whole shittaree!"). Critic Ken Egan, in *Hope and Dread in Montana Literature* (2003), traces this potent theme of "apocalyptic tragedy" through much subsequent Montana literature. Jess founds a ranch but loses his family. He wants to make his mark in his chosen landscape, bereft of native presence, though he senses he can never live in some static realm colored only by occasional rancher-neighbors and a growing herd. Instead, change swirls around his ranch as it always does, the railroad, telephone, long-haul red trucks, and even automobiles presaging, somehow, Beth's death.

Jess does not surrender to what Egan aptly calls the siren song of apocalyptic tragedy. He bottle-feeds the lone colt, symbol of Beth, just as he successfully predicts the hay train, which he has ordered, will reach the prairie. Always full of resolve, Jess buckles down and toughs it out. Far from the naïve reveries of formula Westerns, *The Pass* recognizes that change is always a mixed bag and that in the new, something is always "spoiled." Like the prologue in Howard Hawks's *Red River*, produced three years later (1947), *The Pass* depicts a foundational scene, though the Bentley cattle herd is tiny compared to the Dunstan herd, naturally. The human price of launching a ranch turns out to be higher than Savage's first protagonist ever imagined. That dark note initiates a theme that Savage's later novels set in his home country insistently present. A ranch dynasty, it turns out, always "spoils something."

I

ON THE PASS the wind howled with a thin high whine, rising and falling on two reedlike notes: a raw monotonous wail bending last year's buffalo grass before it and stunting green shoots of early spring sprouting among brown roots. The wind gnawed restlessly at drifts of snow that still resisted spring, but trickles of ice-blue water gathered in drops and ran off into the rocky soil. A single pine stood against the blast, a gnarled old veteran, its sparse needles humming defiance. Cold gray clouds raced across the sky, screening out the pale sun as they swept on across the canyon and shadowed the prairie below.

The young man in chaps felt a curious shiver move down his spine. He took off his buckskin gloves and pressed one hand against the shoulder of his bay horse. The horse tossed its head, jingling the German-silver curb chains, but the sound was lost in the wind.

Only yesterday the rider in chaps and wide black hat and the bay horse had pushed across the desert country, a country splashed with sun, vivid with color, but up here he felt the shiver and knew it wasn't the cold but something that came over a man when he first saw the place he had dreamed of, he and Beth . . . He seemed to see the prairie through heat waves, as something once real, now distorted. He had heard of the prairie, and during the days—weeks—he had traveled toward it he began to know it. But in his eyes now as he looked down on the silent expanse of the valley and across to the jagged blue peaks there was doubt. Again he heard the words of a grizzled prospector he had met on the trail.

"Queer country . . . "

Down there was the prairie.

Behind him was home, Wyoming, the home he knew.

He could go back. He could step up on the bay horse, rein him around, and go back across the desert country, across the mountains and streams into his father's country, his brother's country. He could go home. There were the streams he knew, the coulees he knew, and the solid log ranch house. He knew the coyotes that sneaked through the sagebrush.

Back there were his neighbors. Yellow lamplight in a cabin window; a door thrown open, a path of light darting out.

"It's Jess Bentley. Come to spend the night." Voices. "Put your horse in the barn. Good to see you, Jess." His neighbors. These were the people who had come to the house when he was born, who watched him grow, who predicted good things and knew his name.

And back home there was a hill. It was brown and bare, maybe not much of a hill. But you could pull up your horse there and watch the sun set. You could watch until the night wind began to whisper, wafting up the scent of sagebrush. Pretty soon a bunch of wild horses would come up the draw, single file. You could watch them, the wind in their manes and tails, and see the stud throw up his head, his nostrils quivering.

Jess never told anybody about the hill, not even Beth. But she knew.

He could go back. He could laugh and tell the neighbors, "It wasn't much of a country. I saw it from the Pass, and it wasn't much." He could take off his hat, slap it against his leg, and when the dust was gone from it, the prairie was gone. He could toss his hat on the set of antlers they used for a hatrack in the ranch house. "I saw it, Bill. It wasn't much." And his brother would smile in a quiet way and say, "I'm glad you came back. There's room here for you and Beth."

For Bill was not the kind to leave what he knew behind. Bill was a part of the low log ranch house, of the coulees and the rocks that blended into the soil. Those were the things.

Those were his life. It would be comfortable to be like Bill. He could say, "I was there, and it wasn't much."

And he would be lying.

For the wind went on whining on the Pass. He cleared his throat; his ears were deafened. The prairie sprawled out below, big and wide, and the hills across were wild and blue. By squinting he could make out a single ranch house far below, a dot there against the shadowy willows. Who lived there, and what would they care for Jess Bentley and for Beth? He could go back.

He stood rigid, and now he heard the whine of the wind in the needles of the old pine. He had said, "We'll live here, Beth." And the words had settled something deep inside.

He had met her in the hot stillness of summer; the sun had drawn the life out of the Bentley ranch, bleached it; the ranch lay silent; the barn, the corrals, the house and the stubble around it blended, one color into another, brown logs into stubble, stubble into dust that powdered the gray-green sagebrush, as the ranch faded into the low foothills, as natural as rocks.

Only in the corral was there movement, and there Jess pretended not to see the girl in the riding outfit who sat on the top pole of the fence. But he swaggered as he carried the saddle over near the sorrel horse that stood blindfolded in the middle of the corral.

The sorrel was not moving a muscle. Jess talked in low, soothing tones and put a gentle hand on the sorrel neck, gradually working back until he rubbed the slick neck. Then, cautiously, he picked up the saddle and slid it into place. He reached for the cinch, slipped the latigo through, and pulled it tight.

And still the sorrel stood, head lowered a little, waiting.

Jess took a stealthy look at the girl and smiled to himself. He'd show her how a good rider handled a bronc. He swung up, reached over and pulled off the blind. For one split second the sorrel stood there, blinking in the sunlight. Then it came.

The sorrel ducked his head and lit to bucking high, wicked jumps that snapped Jess's head and brought a dull throbbing to his ears. Pound-pound, sway and pound. The muscles in his legs ached. Whirl, and off again in another direction. The sorrel dipped to one side as he bucked, sunfishing. And then, while Jess balanced for the dip, the sorrel straightened out and bucked in a beeline for the corner of the corral. But Jess wasn't with him. Jess was sprawled in the dust, dazed. The sorrel was somewhere in the corner in the dust cloud, still bucking. . . .

Jess spit out the dry manure and shoved his hair back out of his eyes. That girl . . .

He waited for her laugh. They laughed high laughter, usually, or they came running and called you a poor boy. He waited. A flash of gray flicked past his head; a little piece of sagebrush dropped just at his side.

He thought, "Wants me to be sure she saw me make a damn fool of myself." He made a wry face. He would be angry in a minute when his head stopped whirling. Women ought to stay in the house where they belonged. He shot a hostile glance the girl's way. "Well," he said, "why don't you laugh?"

The girl was twirling a wisp of hay in her fingers. She glanced up casually. "Laugh? There's nothing to laugh at." Her voice was steady, appraising. "You made a good ride. If you'd pulled leather you could have stayed with him." She hesitated. "I'm glad you didn't pull leather."

"Thanks." He got to his feet and, limping, walked over to her. "You wouldn't like me to pull leather?"

"Because I like to see the horse have a chance."

He looked quizzical. "Who are you, anyway?" He was weaving and steadied himself against the corral, striving to see her.

"I'm Beth Ford. My father is Joe Ford. We've got a ranch." She was pulling off her right glove, the gauntlet vivid with beads in Indian design. "It's a good distance from here."

"Around Powder River?"

She nodded.

"What you doing this far from home?" He noticed her hand extended and took it. It surprised him that the hand without the glove was brown, when her face under the black hat was white. He smiled. "I'm Jess Bentley."

She said, "I heard you had a pinto pony over here, and I came to dicker for him. All your ponies as hard to ride as the sorrel?" She laughed a little, and he liked it. A woman who knew horses. He looked closer at her. Pretty head and dark hair sort of out under her hat . . .

He started. Maybe it was beauty she had. Her mouth was generous, and her lips were red; her cheekbones were high. But it was her eyes that made him fumble for words. There was something in them familiar, something he had wanted to see. He was suddenly awkward.

"I'll show you the pinto."

Gallant, he insisted on riding part way home with her. "If I'm along the pinto acts better. He knows me."

The sun beat down so hot that Jess's horse had drops of sweat running down its shoulders in streaks. Heat waves rose shimmering from the hard-baked earth; the sagebrush was dry and shriveled. In the distance the mountains were vague, miragelike and the step of the horses was measured, beating out time, the time when this dark-haired girl would leave him.

It was cool in the grove of pines where they sat by the spring, eating their lunch of thick meat sandwiches and hard-boiled eggs. The branches over them traced a pattern on the needle-covered earth of sun and shadow, a gently moving, gently changing pattern. Jess had never been much to talk. Bill never talked. His father was quiet. But now Jess talked, trying desperately to hit on some subject that would interest her, something they could have in common. He might never see her again. It would be good if she remembered him as a man who rode with her and said interesting things.

He knew he was awkward; he felt it. But curiously it was not the awkwardness of a man before a stranger but that of someone trying to renew an old acquaintance. He picked up a short length of cotton rope he had used to tie the lunches.

"Look," he said. "Ever see this way to tie a bowline?" He tied the knot seriously and held it out for her to see.

She studied it. "I never saw one tied that way."

"It's not much of a knot. Look at this one. Hackamore knot." He tied it, held it up. "Pretty knot. There's lots of useful knots you can tie." He worked away at another knot. "Maybe sometime you might want to get a hackamore made. Maybe you could let me know someway, and I could tie the knots."

He knew when they left the grove of pines there would be an end of something fine; he stalled for a time, pulling the cinch tight on her horse. "Hope the trip won't be too hot."

"The worst part is over," she said, and laughed. "I don't mean the worst part was your riding with me." She rose. "It was a good picnic. Maybe sometime we can have another." She started to get on her horse. Suddenly she turned to him. "Jess, help me on my horse. Stand close here and hold your hand so I can step up."

He watched her riding away up the slope, and hours later he remembered the feel of her riding boot in the palm of his hand as she got on the horse.

It was a month before he saw her again.

For this was the beginning of the somber pattern that was to thread through most of his life. It was a month before he saw her again because his father died, old man Bentley.

A kind old man who used to sit in the sun in front of the barn, whittling. Perfectly contented, and yet when he spoke it was often of New England and the flash of red and yellow in the elm trees in September. Back home, he called it. "I remember back home. . ."

There was nothing in him of the hardness and vigor native to other ranchers of Wyoming. Had he been well and strong, people would have criticized him openly instead of thinking and saying among themselves, "All right. Why didn't he stay back there, then? Why did he take his young wife and move out here, bag and baggage?"

For it never occurred to anybody that it was the young wife, Isabel Bentley, who wanted to come West. It never occurred to anybody that a woman of the seventies would care to leave home and family behind to face alkali flats and empty spaces. They didn't know Isabel Bentley. She had died when Jess was two. Jess knew her only as a tall woman on a sidesaddle, in a tintype.

"You're like her, Jess," his father once said. And Jess, a puzzled little boy, had stared at the picture and wondered how he could be like this woman.

But as he grew older the woman in the picture came to mean everything to him that the women he knew did not. She was not the women, the quiet, gray little women whose hands were rough, whose faces were curiously reposed, the kind little women who cooked and sat sewing; not the women who trimmed the lampwicks and polished the stoves.

No. His mother was a woman in a hat with plumes, sitting straight in the saddle, her eyes in the distance, her mouth smiling mysteriously.

And at twenty Jess would have looked for such a woman and the things she looked for, but the old man was sick. The old man's eyes thanked him for staying. The old man sat in the sun and thought how loyal were his two sons.

But now the old man was dead. They put him in the black frock coat, and he lay on the bed in his room with the blinds pulled. Bill sat beside him, stiff in his store suit, just sitting. Bill took it hard.

August was hot. All morning the neighbors drove over the dusty roads, dressed in black, driving their teams up to the old barn. Jess couldn't remember what they said. He watched them cross the irrigation ditch and move silently toward the house. Once he said, "There's coffee on the stove. Tell the preacher the Bible's on the organ."

He hadn't expected to feel much when the old man died. Death was natural; a horse got old and lay down beside a fence. A cow hobbled off in the willows. Now, the old man dead, things would go on the same.

But they didn't.

The barn was full of horses, strange, quiet horses. When they moved there was a hollow sound he had not noticed before. Everything was still—that was it. The ranch, as if the tired old man had taken its life with him. Stillness to make a man think. He began to remember when he was a kid, little things.

When he was five; the old man sitting beside his bed when he had the measles—just the old man sitting there, and a lamp. A lamp burning and the old man. They had never had much to say to each other.

Jess felt a lump in his throat and threw an extra fork of hay in the manger where the preacher had his team; the afternoon sun shone through a crack in the barn door, a knifelike blade gleaming in the fine hay dust.

"Jess."

He looked up. "Beth . . ."

Her dark suit was dusty. He could see, as she walked to him, that she was tired. "You should have sent word, Jess. You knew I would come. I thought we'd be—too late. My mother and dad are around front with the buggy." She was smaller than he remembered her. "Will you walk to the house with me?"

He blew his nose and walked with her.

Here in the house were his father's friends, the men, stiff and uncomfortable in suits, sitting straight in their chairs, and the women in the kitchen quietly busy with the coffeepot and cups. There was a curious kind of repose in the house, but Jess felt they were waiting for something. He had known them all his life, but he did not know them now. Even Bill, always dignified, was more silent than ever, and it was to Bill that the women said softly, "Don't know how sorry . . ." and the men said, "All for the best . . ."

And Jess was out of it.

The women put down all the windows when it got dark and pulled the shades. The room was hot, and the thick yellow lamplight hung about. The preacher talked and read from the Bible. He would read a few words, take off his spectacles, peer through them at the lamp, put them on again, look sadly about him, and read a few more words. Before he sat down he said, "A hymn. Let some lady take her place at the organ."

The ladies were nervous. The chording you did on Sundays in the privacy of your own home with only your husband to judge was one thing, but with a preacher, a specialist, you might say . . .

Little Mrs. Ford spoke up proudly. "My Beth," she said, "learned piano at school. Played for commencement."

Beth had been sitting at the back of the room. She got up quietly, walked to the organ, and sat down on the bench.

The preacher hovered over her, pulling the stops on the organ. "Pump," he whispered. Her hands were small on the old keys; she hesitated.

Jess watched her. Now, suddenly, a kind of jubilation seized him. In that moment he forgot the old man and the feeling of singleness. He wanted to call out, "Don't be afraid. Go ahead, play." He half expected her to turn and smile, but she was playing now. The notes of the old hymn came out jerky; the organ sighed and wheezed.

Nearer my God to thee . . .

He could have shouted. He should have recognized her, for as she sat on the bench he knew she was the girl in the plumed hat whose eyes were on something in the distance.

II

AND SO IT was in 1913 that Jess Bentley came to Horse Prairie, in the little-known southwestern part of Montana, and bought the ranch from old man Ames. He'd had money after his father's estate settled, for Bill had bought him out.

"Maybe I'm crazy, Beth. Maybe it's crazy to hit out for a place you've heard of, with only a letter from an old fellow who wants to sell." He watched her. "Maybe if it was a good country he wouldn't want to sell." That was the night she told him she would marry him. They sat on a wagon tongue near the barn, listening to the nighthawks, squinting at the yellow light streaming out from the windows in the ranch house, watching the shadows move and pass across the light, the shadows of her mother, her father, and Bill.

She was silent a moment, then, "There's one thing I know, Jess. There's only one thing I ever need to know, now or ever—it's that you and I can be happy—anywhere."

In the beginning he decided to take a wagon, a bedroll; then it was the buggy and a light team. He rode out of the ranch with only his saddle horse. It would be faster; he could cut across the mountains, and the three hundred miles would not be long.

For a hundred miles it was familiar country. Where he stopped those first three nights people knew the Bentleys; the dogs that ran out of the darkness, yapping, finished by whining greetings, twisting their bodies and wagging their tails. A dark shape, standing silent in an open door, and then, "Oh. It's you. It's Jess Bentley. Put your horse up." Friendly voices in the dark.

And then the strange country. The ranches were few; distances were baffling, landmarks unfamiliar, confusing; streams were nameless. He left the roads, the trails, always riding north. A night he spent in the light timber, his horse grazing on the end of a picket rope. He listened to a coyote across the canyon, built a fire, and slept close, covered with his saddle blanket.

Rough, strange country, and at last a broad valley glutted with sagebrush, a country where it would take twenty acres to raise a cow; flats of alkali dazzling and white under the sun; dried-up horse tracks around a pothole. The land hummed with silence, but always in the distance the mountains loomed, beckoning.

At the ranches where he stopped overnight they wanted news: whom had he seen; what had they said; how did the cattle look down-country? Jess sat in their houses and told them, and their eyes watched his eyes and his lips.

"Met a fellow back a ways said he killed a grizzly bear that big."

He must stay a day or two. "Get rested up." Then, "Hear anything about that horse thief? String him up. Country civilized, seems." They offered news of their own.

"Ed here killed an elk on Tipper Creek, had a spread fifty inches. Never see such."

There was a big family of Mormons, a man, his wife, two young boys, an older daughter, her husband, and the grandmother. The boys, about fifteen, were shy, but Jess taught them to braid rawhide. He and the husband talked about horses. The wife showed her garden plot, two rows of beans, a quarter acre of Indian corn, and dwarfed nasturtiums planted along the north side of the shack.

"Sun's almost too hot for flowers." With her hands she tried to give the thin green plants the life that was in her long, slender hands, brown and calloused.

There were a few frightened chickens, long of neck and leg, that fed nervously around the shack.

"You like chicken," the mother said. "Give you a dinner."

"Best chicken I ever ate," he said.

"Give you the recipe for your wife." They took it for granted he was married.

The grandmother sat in her handmade rocker whose seat was neatly crisscrossed thongs of rawhide. She sat on the porch during the day, watching the chickens, and occasionally calling "Shoo!" at them. In the evening they moved her chair inside. She slept a good deal and always woke with a startled look that gradually faded into a grin. If anyone would listen she told what she had dreamed, or sometimes she would deny having been asleep at all.

Jess told them stories, made up stories, lied, anything to interest them; but at last there seemed to be no more to say. He made a last effort. "Two nights ago I stopped at a place where a lady was making a dress." The mother sat by the dining table, sewing, squinting to see in the lamplight. When Jess spoke she looked up. There was a little silence.

"Making a dress?" the young woman said.

Jess was uneasy. "Yes."

Mother turned to daughter. "Wake Grandmother." The grandmother looked up, dazed, then grinned, showing her gums.

"What's that? What's that?" She looked eagerly about.

The mother shouted: "He says there was a lady making a dress."

"Yes, yes," the old lady shouted. She heaved up in her chair and cupped her ear.

"What kind of dress?" the daughter asked.

Jess squirmed. "It was a long, long dress."

The daughter smiled. "That doesn't tell us much."

"It was kind of slick goods."

"Slick and shiny? Silk?"

"Yes. It was silk."

"Did it rustle?"

"Nobody talks loud enough," the grandmother shouted. "Tell him louder. Did the dress have sleeves?" She grew impatient, color rising in her old cheeks. "Tell him louder!"

"I think it had sleeves," Jess shouted.

"He says it had sleeves," the daughter called. The old lady nodded happily.

The mother tried to draw his attention. "Did the dress rustle, go swish-swish when it moved?"

"Yes. I think it did."

The mother's voice was triumphant. "It was taffeta, and it had sleeves!"

The old lady hitched around in her chair and peered at him. "Leg o' mutton?"

He left the shack and the Mormons. They gave him a canteen filled with spring water, and the mother gave him a package of nasturtium seeds. "Maybe your wife likes a little color."

Now there was a broad river meandering across the thin, hard soil like a silvery snake. Mud hens waded and quarreled along the banks. Jess sang and talked to his horse. He first saw the badlands from a high rocky rim of land; he watched the sun rise across the sharp outlines of weird shapes like medicine gods; there were deep coulees cut by wind and cloudburst in whose depths shadows twisted and emerged gold-tinted. The badlands stretched below him, a frenzied Indian rite turned suddenly to stone. Fifty miles across, and at the edge the Mormons had told him he would find a prospector.

"Funny old coot," they had said. "Half baked."

He first saw the old man in the early evening. By now his horse was tired and let out a quiet nicker when it caught a glimpse of the mule hobbled near the clapboard shack ahead. A grizzled old man stood cautiously for a moment in the door and then walked toward him slowly, turning his head a little to comfort the yellow-eyed dog that slunk at his heels, head and tail lowered.

"Howdy," the old man said with dignity. "Going somewheres or just traveling?"

"Howdy," Jess said. "Going north."

"Hobble your pony. I was just fixing to eat. You wash in the ditch there."

Jess hobbled his horse, turned him loose, and squatted by the sluggish stream. He scooped up mud from the bottom and scrubbed his hands; then, suddenly he began to douse water on his face with both hands, blowing and sputtering. The trail dust was gone from him, the sandy dust of the desert and the powdery dust of the flats; he looked up and grinned at the blue range in the distance and hummed to himself, wiping his face on a gunny sack . . .

After supper they sat with their backs against the north side of the shack and stretched their legs out in front of them, watching their feet. Jess rolled a cigarette and handed tobacco and papers to the prospector. It was comfortable to listen to the horse and the mule clinking their hobble chains somewhere off in the light dusk. Jess yawned.

"That was good stew."

"Good venison in it," the prospector said. "You get good meat up in the hills, across, and the sun down here on the flat dries it out fine and makes good jerky." He stared across at the mountains looming in the half-light. "Guess those old hills are famous for venison."

"Back home," Jess said, feeling a little lonely, "we got good venison."

"Sure you have," the old man agreed, "but I always figure every place you go has got something about it it's famous for. Something that makes a man speak up and say, 'Sure, I know that place. That's where they got good meat,' or, 'That's where they got good wild grass.'" The old man hitched up against the shack. He began to chuckle, settling himself. "This damned desert," he said. "Guess you'll remember it for the way sun bleaches out the bones anything that dies."

"See what you're getting at," Jess admitted. "Take back home. Back there the Arapaho Indians came in '77 and raised hell with the whites. Book in the capital city says right there Indians came through our country. Mentions it right by name. You'd remember back home because the Indians came through."

A kind of excitement went through them at the way the idea was worked out. "Take the Lemhi country. Mormons came in there in the fifties. Think of Lemhi country and you think of Mormons."

"Works with any country," the old man said eagerly. "Take," he said, "where you're going." He chuckled. "Where in Christ are you going? Forgot to ask. Tell me where you're going, and if it's around here, bet I can tell you something about it."

Jess drew on his cigarette; the glow lit his face. "I'm headed for Horse Prairie."

The old man turned his face. "Christ, man." He lowered his voice. "You had a long stick you could touch it. It's right over the range there. Big range you saw out there before dark."

The first stars were out, pale and bluish; the air was suddenly chill, and the shack behind their backs creaked, the old boards shrinking. Loneliness swept over Jess. He could reach out with a long stick and touch the prairie, and back there was home and Beth . . . .

The theory about places slipped from them. He wanted suddenly to talk loud, be companionable. His voice was strange and startling in the dark. "You said you could tell something about the prairie to hitch up with it. I never saw it. I never heard much, except it was big." For the first time he realized how little he really knew about the prairie.

"I'm thinking," the old man said. "I'm thinking a while back you mentioned Indians. I guess Indians is the only thing you can hitch up with the prairie." His voice was quiet. "There's a funny thing. What you hitch up with the prairie is the Indians didn't like it, stayed clear of it, to live in.

"You're going to find out no Indians ever lived there. Hunting parties came in the summer, maybe, but never lived there. Maybe the only country where Indians never lived."

Jess turned to the old man's voice. "What the hell's wrong with it?"

The old man was long in answering. "Talked with an old buck once. Said the prairie was bad medicine."

"Bad medicine?" Maybe it never rained there, or the water holes was poison, or streams dried up?"

In the darkness the old man shook his head. "Nothing like that. No. I guess nothing like that. Bad medicine is something funny, bad and—funny. It's something you know about but you can't tell about because you can't see it or smell it or touch it. It's—it's—I can't tell. It's—" He paused. "You feel that cold damp around here? It's like an old white wolf come sneaking down here from the hills. You see the tracks. Maybe you're a hunter. You know it's up there, someway, but you don't see it. Maybe you're the kind of a fellow feels a white wolf around, always hanging around, but you can't tell about it because you don't see it. Maybe the Indians knew something was around, like an old white wolf."

They sat silent. The stars were now bright points of light, cold and glittering. The clink of hobble chains was almost inaudible. The dog whined and stood close to the old man, licking his hand. "Git, damn you." The old man stretched. "Well, time we turned in." He got to his feet, limping a little as he began to walk away. Jess sat a moment. "You asleep?" the old man asked.

"Thinking," Jess told him.

"Don't you go worrying about them damned Indians. They're dead long ago."

It was curious and a little embarrassing to think, now, how the story had moved him. In the light of that morning as the sun reached out across the peaks, the story seemed fantastic, just as stories he had been told as a child seemed unreal as he grew older. He half expected the old man to say something that morning like, "Well, I sure had you last night about them Indians." But the old man went about washing the tin plates and stacking them against the stovepipe. He did not mention Indians or the prairie. Maybe the yarn in the light of day had embarrassed the old man too.

Why was it that at night, in a strange country, you felt things?

The old man stood by the shack as Jess saddled his horse. "Mighty nice to have company for a time. Stop this way again." Jess said he would. "Good luck," the old man called as he rode away. "So long."

And now on the Pass the wind howled its peculiar whine. He could go back; he could go back to all the familiar things. A kind of homesickness took him. He could say . . .

But there was nothing he could say to Beth. Beth had said, trusting him, in her serious voice, "I know we can be happy—anywhere."

He tightened the cinch on his saddle. He swung up and rode down into the prairie.

Late that afternoon he rode up on a cluster of rough log buildings, gray with age, and found the man he had corresponded with about the ranch sitting on a wagon tongue, a long willow in his gnarled hands, poking at a clump of bunch grass. The old man looked up, puzzled, then smiled; his eyes were sharp and blue.

"You're Jess Bentley," he cackled. "I been sitting here a week, waiting." A kind of impatience in his voice. He felt in his pockets and brought out a plug of tobacco. "Chew?" He looked at the brown chunk, turned it over in his hands, wiped the end of it on his pants leg, bit off a piece. His jaws worked. In a few moments he spoke. "Put your horse in the barn. I'll show you . . . ."

They walked along toward the barn. "I'm Ames," he said. "I've got a sister in Ohio."

Jess mumbled politely.

Ames didn't speak again until they had entered the barn, a long, dry, hay-smelling old building. Dusty sets of harness hung on wooden pegs driven into the log walls; an old slick-forked saddle hung by one stirrup from a peg. Two horses chewed contentedly in their stalls. "My sister in Ohio," Ames said. "Past ten years been writing. 'Come back home.' Thinks I'm old enough to die. Thinks I'd better die in Ohio." He laughed and spat, his sharp eyes always on Jess's face.

"Ohio," Jess said.

"Maybe she's right. Not much for an old man here." He was looking out the barn door across the spring-brown stubble of the field and on up to the mountains. "Not much. I've got two horses, there . . . ." He turned to the stalls. "You'll want to see the place. When you see it you might not want it. There's a cliff upcountry where you can see it all . . . ."

The old man was silent as they rode and kept swinging his halter rope and grunting encouragement at the mealymouthed old mare he rode. On the cliff they stopped. "See it?"

Jess looked and turned slowly to the old man. "Sure you want to sell?"

Maybe Ames didn't hear. He was looking.

Maybe he was thinking, "Well, Ames, there's the prairie," for the last time.

It was isolated, shut out, barred from the world, even from the rest of Montana, by the continental divide. In the summer the divide rose high, jagged and blue, its front scarred by deep gashlike canyons that even during the hottest summers withheld some snow. But in the summer it was less forbidding because of the wagon road that wound painfully up the steep slopes and triumphantly over the top to the outside. The Pass. That road was the escape, and Ames had his eyes on it. Far off, there.

In the winter the divide loomed as a grim white wall. Gone was the road, buried beneath the snow. Those on the prairie shut the rest of the world from their minds; from November till June the prairie was their world, their world a broad valley hemmed in by mountains. Ames's world for fifty years.

And once when the stagecoach had broken down near the ranch an Easterner had said, "Ames, you're lucky. You have everything good and no worries." Yes. No worries. Let's see about that.

Take Ames's nearest neighbors ten miles away. Take Cy and Amy Pierce. Cy had been in the country thirty years and was never out of debt. Every year Cy said, "Next year," and ran his fingers through his bushy hair. But each year the smile was less confident, and now his hair, at fifty, was white. He and Amy used to plan a five-room house with a fireplace. If you had a fireplace you could come in on winter evenings and sit there in front of it with your wife; maybe your friends would come in and sit there with you, looking in at the fire. And around Christmas you could have a hot drink of some kind and look at the fire and think about good things . . . .

In the early nineties Cy had a nice bunch of cattle. It looked like the house and the fireplace—well. And the bank. They could pay the bank. Amy planned ahead twenty years on the strength of the cattle, but Cy was cautious.

"We're not rich, Amy. But I guess we're coming along."

They hadn't counted on the winter of '93, when cattle died in the fields and snow drifted over them, hiding gaunt ribs. Amy had cried at first, but she had looked at Cy and felt small and mean. She laughed now; she told everybody she wouldn't know what to do if her house was bigger, and at Christmas time Cy gave her clothes.

There you are.

Newt Cooper lived fifteen miles away; he was a dreamer. He said when he was young with money in his pockets he would stand on the slope of Gun-Sight Peak and strain his eyes to see farther and farther. Someday he would own all the land he could see. That was his dream, and it came true.

Now, five thousand acres of prairie land is nice to look at from the slope of a peak, but the rains began to come at the wrong time, and the hay in the bottoms withered before it headed out.

Newt always laughed when he told how many cattle he figured he'd have when he was forty. "You think crazy things when you're twenty or so. You sort of forget cattle won't eat sagebrush. You just look out across. It's hard to get the cattle out to sell. If we had a railroad . . ."

That was what the prairie did, made you forget things because you were looking out across.

It worried Mrs. Cooper that the buggy was unpainted, that the house leaked when it rained so she had to put pans on the floor to catch the rain water, the water she used to wash her hair. It made her feel better. A window in the bedroom had been replaced by a piece of canvas tacked neatly into place. Mrs. Cooper wondered if you couldn't paint a picture on the canvas of the view she used to see outside. She often said, "I hope Sister doesn't come. Not for a time." Her sister lived in Boston, Massachusetts, and believed the ranch in Montana was a great domain, feudal and strong. Mrs. Cooper wrote careful letters to her sister. Her dream was to travel to Boston someday in considerable splendor. Someday. In the meantime she fought for causes, for suffrage, for prohibition, for the sick and the wayward.

But if you asked them why they didn't go away they would have looked out across; old man Ames knew. The deer and the coyotes didn't go away.

Old man Ames knew what people thought when they looked out across. He was thinking the same thing. But don't be fooled like the rest of them, Ames. Go on, before you change your mind.

He turned suddenly to Jess. "I'm going, Bentley. Like I told you."

Later Jess remembered the old man standing beside the pole gate, kicking at the bottom pole. "Loose. Can't remember when it wasn't. Got to fix it—squeaks when you open it. See?" Then he smiled oddly, and his eyes were far away. "Forgot. You'll have to fix it."

And that night in the cabin the old man told stories of the

country. Most of them were flat and pointless. He took an hour to tell of a wolf he had trailed and shot; he told of building the cabin, of who had helped him. He talked, but always he himself was the central figure, recalling the past, judging it again, and the prairie.

"Bentley," he said, "you're getting sick of me talking. But you'll do the same when you're old. It's a funny thing, but nothing's worth a damn if you can't talk about it." The old man threw a chunk of wood in the stove, leaned down and closed the draft. "The fire'll keep till morning. I'm leaving tomorrow on the stage. Put your bedroll on the bunk there. I've got me a place fixed up in the barn."

Out the window Jess watched the old man's lantern move in the darkness toward the corral, its light shining on the slick hides of moving horses. Their eyes shone dully for a moment. A dog jumped up on Ames, whining and wagging its tail. The old man stopped to pet it. Old man Ames was saying good-by.

III

Jess's COMING CAUSED excitement on the prairie where amusements and distractions were few. Sociables and community dances furnished what entertainment there was. The nickelodeon had not yet made its appearance in Salmon City, but once people had had a glimpse across the footlights, when the Dahlia Players had arrived by coach "from Chicago" to present *Uncle Tom's Cabin* with a cast of eight and two real dogs.

Those on the prairie were curious; they made early opportunity to call on Jess, and first came Amy and Cy Pierce. They arrived in their Concord buggy, driving the two sleek, jet-black Hambletonians known as "the blacks." They were harnessed only for occasions demanding speed or magnificence. They champed the bit and rolled their eyes. You tiptoed around them. Amy never drove them and eyed them fearfully. "I feel as if I take my life in my hands just to ride with Cy when he drives them. I'd no more think of driving them than of—well, of flying—would I, Cy?"

Cy called them his black babies. They were five years old and descendent from Maude S. The black babies, it was said, could make a mile in two minutes.

And so, because a social call was an occasion, they drove up—or dashed up—with the blacks. Amy, a tiny, pretty little woman, faded at forty, nervous in speech and gesture. Already her soft brown hair was streaked with gray. The ladies of the prairie envied her her clothes, city clothes, soft, expensive duster. "—don't see where Cy gets the money. Wears gloves, white hands, treats her . . . doll . . ."

She gave Jess her gloved hand, which trembled though she smiled. "Those blacks—were fast today," she breathed. "Jess Bentley—what a nice name!" Jess grinned at her and helped her from the buggy. "What dust!" she went on. She brushed herself, straightened her hat and veil. She picked a piece of lint from the cuff of a dark serge sleeve protruding from the sleeve of the duster. "We've been going to come—"

"I'm pleased you did. I like folks to call."

She turned. "This is my husband, Cy. He never says much, do you, Cy? He thinks a lot." She patted her husband's arm. "This is Jess Bentley. Isn't Jess a nice name?"

Cy nodded gravely, gave a warm smile. His white hair made his face, by contrast, almost boyish. He and Jess shook hands. There was strength in Cy's hands, but Jess noticed they were surprisingly soft; they were large hands, wide and blunt of finger, a kind man's hands. You could imagine such hands, working in putty or silver, but not, somehow, with picks and shovels.

"Will you both come inside, ma'am?"

"How nice!" Amy bubbled. "Put the team away, Cy. No—don't help him, Mr. Bentley. He knows where—used to come—Mr. Ames." She put her hand on Jess's arm. "Come in and talk to me. I'm going to call you Jess. Those blacks, Jess. Just let me rest awhile." She led the way.

There were two homemade chairs. Jess sat on an applebox, his feet planted firmly on the uneven plank floor. Amy's chair could have been a throne; the folds of the purplish serge dress hid the hand-hewn pine; she sat straight, glancing bird-like about the room with a quick, interested smile which rested at last on her husband, who sat heavily in the chair near the window, his great arms more than covering the spindly arms of the chair; his eyes had wandered out the window. He seemed to be listening, waiting.

"Please, Cy," Amy said softly. "Don't do that." She turned brightly to Jess. "He thinks. He looks out the window. At what, I don't know. He's always done it. He looks so—calm. And yet—worried. That sounds funny, doesn't it?" She laughed. "I ask him what he's thinking, and he can't tell me."

It is true that Cy Pierce couldn't have told anyone what he was thinking and why he was always vaguely worried, yet stoical. Cy feared failure, but what he meant by failure he didn't know.

He had been twelve when his father and mother came to the prairie, the last of a wagon train headed for Buffalo Gulch and the gold fields. It stood out, vivid, in his mind, the night they had crossed the Pass. Cy was sitting on the bedding in the rear of the covered wagon. His father had called back to him, "We're coming to the prairie . . . ."

His father's voice chilled him. He was a sensitive boy, and stories of the Indians heard along the way terrified him. The Indians hadn't scalped him so far; they were sure to get him now, when the end was in sight. That was the way things worked . . . .

He had untied the canvas flaps of the wagon and looked out. There was no moon, but the stars were bright. The wagon swayed, lurched, and the hoofs of the oxen were sharp on the rocky trail. A hundred yards to the side the boy could make out the rimrock along the Pass, white and silvery in the dark.

He fought to keep back tears of homesickness; scenes were clear before him: the woods at home where he had walked, whose paths he knew. There in the darkness were the faces of children he knew; he thought even of the schoolhouse with longing. The rimrock to the side of the wagon was a wall to him, shutting him in, an animal in a cage. But the trip from the Midwest had already taught him one thing; that to be a man was the most important thing in the world, and a man kept his mouth shut. Already, with a curious bit of childish insight, he could see that his father had not the strength of character of others in the wagon train. In his mind he pitied his father, who paled so in comparison with—say—MacKenzie the Scot, who bossed the train.

His father had a cheerful phrase. "By and by we'll strike it rich." The phrase was used whenever things went wrong, and things were usually wrong, financially, in the Pierce family. One "by and by" drifted into another. Cy's father had started out with the wagon train with a kind of grimness, and "by and by" was no longer said lightly, hopefully.

In those days the town of Buffalo Gulch sprawled along the muddy creek that slithered along snake-like, swollen from cloudbursts in the high country. It was a town of flimsy makeshift things, of flapping tents, of naked pine-board buildings with windows that stared insolently across the flat; tongues and doubletrees of wagons were patched and bound with wire; the jewels the honky-tonkies wore were false. It was a town with a brash kind of confidence in the future, an adolescent confidence that had yet met no defeat. It was the town where Frank Pierce was going to strike it rich.

Within the year his claim began to pay, not handsomely, but enough to buoy his spirits. The very meagerness with which it paid indicated that this was the real thing, for men said a claim got better, little by little, like whiskey. The talk of other men, of lucky strikes and gold, excited him, and he followed the talk into the saloons where the tinkly music, the yellow lamplight, and loud laughter were a pleasant background for his dreams. He began to gamble, modestly at first, and enjoyed the kind of awed admiration that others— the family men—accorded him. He traveled with the single men, the adventurers, and their contempt for small money soon became his. He was unaware that the family men wagged their heads and told their good wives that it was a shame a man with a wife and a son . . .

And the wives were kind to Sadie Pierce at prayer meeting and sent her pies and jelly from wild gooseberries.

Other family men slaved, sweat in the diggings, saw their hands harden and crack deep into the flesh, and took their bits of gold and hoarded, seeing ahead some small business bought, some security, and a comfortable old age. But the bit of gold that Frank Pierce panned went on the red or the black, the odd or the even. Give him credit; he knew when he made the lucky strike he would leave the gulch in glory; his wife and son would want for nothing.

Sadie Pierce took the narrow view.

Frank Pierce was at first angry, then sullen. "You'd think I was following those chippies around. To hear you, you'd think I was taking the bread from your mouth." Like a child he sulked and made the grand gesture. He gave Sadie twenty dollars and for a time sat mournfully at home, avoiding his son's eyes, trying not to hear the tinkly music in the honky-tonk. Perhaps his sacrifice was worth it; his wife could buy some bit of silk, a bonnet, a gown, if she wanted. He sighed.

But Sadie Pierce bought three milk cows. She would flaunt before the gulch the fact that she must support herself. Every fiber in him cried out to him to sink deep in drink and gambling. If she didn't care, if he had failed in providing for her and for their son . . .

But something in Sadie Pierce's manner stopped him, and something in the gray eyes of that hulking, silent son grown suddenly so large and close to his mother. But he refused to milk the cows or to feed them. He had no interest. He worked at his claim late at night and made it a point never to return home until the milking was done and the milk cooling in pans in the ditch.

He was vaguely frightened that fall when the first of the families packed up and pulled away from the gulch. Were they satisfied with their few hundred dollars—had they no vision? For three years he had worked in the gulch, and now, for the first time, he noticed a kind of restlessness take hold of people. That fall the adventurers saddled their ponies and left for new bonanzas; the honky-tonkies were not far behind. Still a few family men labored, cow-like, taking out their pinches of dust.

Frank Pierce was alarmed. He could not sleep, and it seemed that his wife and son crossed him constantly, not in anything they said, but in the way they seemed to follow him with their eyes. It was certain they worked against him. He worked feverishly at his claim and called on God to damn the storm clouds and the cold that would stop work for the winter. He watched the last family leave the gulch and accepted with an absent nod the two lame oxen and the milk cow too heavy with calf to travel.

Frank Pierce had made a decision and was inwardly proud. He would stay in the gulch until he struck it rich. A contempt for those who had left seized him. He could call them shiftless, ne'er-do-well. They didn't see his dream—no, his conviction.

And one spring night a raw wind blew down the gulch, rustling the single slump of cottonwoods, whistling through the abandoned frame buildings. Frank Pierce ran, stumbling over the half-frozen soil, carrying a lantern. His breath whistled in his teeth as he made for the cabin with the light in the window.

His eyes frightened Sadie Pierce. With her hand she beckoned for Cy. She asked, "What is it in God's name?"

He grinned, showing his teeth. His eyes were bright. "I've struck it," he said simply.

He stepped into the cabin, took a second step, and stumbled. He grinned to himself. He stumbled into his chair and then started to rise from it, mumbling, "I've got to get back. I've got to get back." His hand fumbled for the arm of the chair but seemed not to feel it. Roughly he swept aside his son's hand. "Don't touch me. I've got to get back." His mouth seemed permanently pulled to one side in a grin.

He could not get to his feet. He fought them as they undressed him and put him in his bunk. He twisted Sadie's arm and struggled.

Cy said, "You can't work in the dark."

"I'll use a lantern." He tried to sit up.

They watched him. He was quiet suddenly, smiling. His voice was soft and wheedling. "It's for you, Sadie. All that gold. For you and Cy." His eyes were crafty.

Sadie Pierce strangled a sob. "Tomorrow, Frank. Then you can dig."

He was dead before morning.

Cy never forgot his mother's strength. His eyes were on her as she helped put Frank Pierce in the grave on the flat. But he was glad when suddenly, as they stood there, she clutched at him and began to sob. He was fifteen, a man. His body straightened. Her words did not disturb him.

"Cy, my son." He held her closer. "We've got nothing."

He scarcely heard her. His eyes were on the land. He had never seen it before. No one had seen it before, not those who left the gulch, their wagons passing it by. No one had seen the land, alive now in the spring, the land stretching along the creeks and up the slopes of the mountains where cattle could graze in the summer.

He never forgot that the land saved them. But it surprised him that it did. He knew that if you trusted anything too much it turned on you. He watched the land, loving it, expecting it to betray him . . . .

He could not find the words to tell his wife how he felt. He could not tell her now as they sat with young Jess Bentley. He envied Jess his youth. But he envied Jess as he would his son, had he had one . . . .

Jess was trying hard to please, to appear at ease as host. With a friendly smile he handed Cy a navy revolver. "It was my dad's," Jess said. "Never missed with it."

Gravely Cy took the revolver, balanced it, peered critically down the barrel. "Good one," he said slowly. "They always carried two of them in the old days. Want you to come over to our place, see the one I have."

Jess beamed, for these people were going to like him, and they were going to like Beth.

Cy chuckled inwardly when Amy suddenly leaned forward and asked in the peculiar, secretive voice when Jess was going to get married. Amy always spoke of marriage in this way. She said "marry" in a way that hinted of all the intimate things, the rustle of sheets, underthings folded together in the same drawer.

"I'll never forget," she said, "the first time I saw Cy; it was in Salt Lake. He came down with some cattle." She smiled happily, seeing it all again. "I was teaching in Salt Lake. I was engaged to a gentleman. Oh, he really was a gentleman!" She smiled on the memory. "But he was—small. He was a small gentleman. I had always admired large gentlemen. And then in the lobby of this hotel I saw Cy." She paused. "Later there were lots of things about him I admired." She paused again. "But I admit it was his size—he was such a big man." She looked brightly at her husband. She laughed happily. When she moved she left the scent of some mild perfume in her wake. "We have to get back. You saw those horses. I like to get back in time for a rest before dinner."

The three had said nothing of importance. They had sat.

Jess had been embarrassed; the muscles of his legs were strangely stiff from sitting on the apple box. Cy had gazed almost constantly out the window. Amy had chattered and been amused. But she sobered as they drove away. She looked back once at Jess standing beside the log shack. She waved and turned to her husband.

"Cy," she said softly, "I hope nothing ever hurts that young man. He's trying so—hard."

IV

JESS HUMMED ON a late summer evening, riding back to the ranch. That day he had ridden in the close green heat of the timber and on the steep slopes of Black Canyon, pushing his cattle, ranging there, to better feed. He noticed with satisfaction that the few hundred head of cattle he had bought from Ames were, for the most part, young Hereford stuff. He longed now for the first fall, when his cattle would pasture in the fields. His pride of possession rode with him these weeks. Everything he owned he wanted close, where he could see it, his cattle, his land, his house. Fixing a fence, the day before, he had got pleasure in stretching barbed wire and stapling it to the posts, separating, marking his land from his neighbors'. He was working feverishly now, chafing a little because he hadn't yet hired a man. He would not hire one until he heard from Cy Pierce. Cy knew a good man who had worked most of his life on the prairie, an old hand, Slim Edwards. He could break horses and he could shoe them. There was nothing he didn't know about branding calves or colts, or helping a cow have a calf. When you told him how good he was he always said, "For Christ sake, I been at it forty years, for Christ sake."

When Cy had spoken to Jess about him Slim Edwards was gone. He had quit the job he had held for ten years or so with a rancher on the prairie. There had been some argument; Slim had rolled up his bed, gone into the barbershop in Salmon City, taken a bath there, had his hair cut, cashed his check, and left for Salt Lake City to visit his sister.

The prairie said the rancher was at fault, but the rancher said that Slim Edwards was an old woman, finicky. Slim said nothing at all, except that he was going to visit his sister and fix up his gut.

They all knew that in two weeks' time Slim Edwards would be back and looking for a job. He had lived a long time on the prairie.

"Best man ever hit this country," Cy told Jess. "I'd like to see you get him. He can do every damn thing."

"Well, I'd like to get him," Jess said. "I'll go into town to see him."

Cy said, "No, let me talk to him. I know him, and I could talk to him. He's funny."

"Well, that's fine," Jess said. As he worked about the ranch, trying to do two men's work, he was anxious, waiting for Slim Edwards to come back.

Now riding back from Black Canyon, Jess was drawn, almost without purpose, to an outcropping of hard brown rock that formed a little cliff far above but overlooking his ranch. The cliff faced the dying sun.

He swung off his horse and stood there, his hat pushed back, a look in his eyes—gazing off across the gray-greens of the valley, up the sagebrushed foothills, and finally on the rugged blue range, the Pass, where the last slanting rays of sun just touched the top.

He stood there a long time, looking, feeling the wind rushing past him, hurrying on to the Pass, a wind as free and alone as the hawk that soared and swooped above on motionless wings.

He didn't see Cy riding out of a little coulee, wasn't aware of him until a pebble rolled and Cy was there by his side. Jess felt a curious embarrassment. "I was looking for a couple of ponies that got out," he said. "Thought they might be over toward the Pass. Thought—"

Cy interrupted him with a slow, thoughtful drawl. "Might be," he said. He looked out across, too, the lines of his face tense. "Too dark to see much." Then in the dusk Cy smiled. "Makes you feel sort of alone."

"Nice," Jess said, "just looking."

Cy puffed on his pipe. "I been here more than thirty years."

The sun was sinking; a shadow lengthened across the land, and they watched the slow sweep of it. It grew darker; the first pale stars appeared, and a coyote howled.

Jess turned a little out of the breeze and rolled a cigarette. The flame of the match lit up his bronzed face and sharpened his feature. "You see Slim Edwards?"

Cy was silent for a moment. "Hmm? Yes. I saw him. Saw him down at the Saloon. He got back."

Cy puffed at his pipe, his eyes on the prairie.

Jess said, "Well, what did he say?"

Cy glanced at Jess. "Slim? Oh, he said he saw his sister and got his liver looked at."

Jess asked eagerly, "What about working for me? What did he say about that?"

"He's sort of an old woman," Cy said, picking his words. "I don't think he wants to work. He's worked too long, maybe."

"What's he going to do?"

"Hang around town for a while and then pick up a job."

The two men stood in silence and smoked and listened to the night sounds. Suddenly Jess said, "Why won't he work for me?"

Cy was a little awkward. "Well, now, he's sort of an old woman."

"You said he was a crackajack."

Cy blurted it out: "He doesn't much want to work for a young man."

Jess said, "For Christ sakes, I can get along with a man."

"He's an old woman."

"He'll work for me too." It made Jess a little cross the way Cy looked across the dark country.

They always hired their men at the Saloon.

There were two saloons in the little cow town of Salmon City, but only one was known as the Saloon. The other was Brad's place, or just Brad's. Brad's was where the ranchers went to drink, to bargain, to talk. There the drummers, stopping at the Salmon City House, stood at the bar, flashily dressed, and bought mixed drinks, talked of territories covered, and women.

"I remember in Chi once. This baby doll . . ."

Probably it was all talk.

It was different at the other place, at the Saloon. For there a weathered painted sign above a narrow door leading up narrow stairs said, "Rooms." You didn't get a room there. That was where old Kate Kelley had her Girls, where she had Rose or Louise or Becky, usually two of them. The Saloon was at the opposite end of the town from Brad's, and late at night you could look in through the window and see men playing pool beneath the hanging kerosene lamps, cigarettes dangling from their lips, their eyes squinted. Men in work clothes watched, sitting in the stiff hard chairs along the walls beside the pool tables, leaning forward to watch a difficult shot, tense and then laughing and talking again, relaxed. In the pocket or not, they didn't care, but they had to kill time, waiting from someone to come and hire them.

Sometimes there were only a few of them, only one or two, but by the middle of July, when haying was about to begin, the Saloon was crowded, and the bar. The men made brief friendships at the bar, buying drinks on their bedrolls or watches, hocked with Ted Murphy who owned the place.

"Lookit this here guitar I got. She's worth twenty bucks anybody's money. Ought to hear her."

"Loan you a fin."

"Christ, man. Lookit that inlay wood in her. Jesus Christ, a fin!"

"Well, nobody ast ya to hock her."

"Well, Christ, all right. Gimme the fin."

Murphy had you. You had to have a shot, sticking around.

So they made friends at the bar. They were always going to be friends. They went upstairs together to see Rose or Louise or Becky, and they talked together with the girls and had a party. Now they were real pals. They had been to a whore house together. Then maybe they got hired, and one went to one ranch and another to another, and that was the end.

Ted Murphy didn't belong on the prairie. The ranchers used his saloon, but they didn't like it.

It was embarrassing for Jess, because Ted Murphy didn't know him. He might have been a fellow looking for work instead of a rancher.

He got into the city late and first went to Brad's. Slim Edwards had been there, yes, hanging around. Brad reckoned he had gone to the Saloon.

At the Saloon the lights were bright with some of those new gasoline lamps that hissed and threw a hot white light, and everybody inside looked a little pale from them, and their faces had taken on a little of the blue tinge of the thick tobacco smoke, layer on layer. There was laughing and noise, and some of the hay hands were getting drunk and some were plenty drunk. Behind the crowded bar Ted Murphy had the sudden laugh and the quick tense look he always got at night when the place was crowded, when he was making money and there was likely to be a fight. Now he watched, cat-like, two young men shaking dice for drinks and beginning to jaw. In a few minutes they would face each other with fishy drunken stares, and one of them would call the other a liar. And there you were.

Jess easily singled out Slim Edwards from the others in the Saloon.

He was a long, tall man, seated in one of the stiff chairs by the pool table, and on either side of him young men argued and laughed, while he himself sat straight and aloof. His nose was long and a little Roman, sharp of bridge. His leathery tough skin was stretched tight across his cheekbones like old saddle leather. His long thin legs were crossed as easily as a young man's, and he wore polished boots and a high crowned, well-brushed Stetson, creased in Montana style.

He sat very stiff and disapproving of the talk and the talkers, looked down his long nose. None of the young men paid him any attention.

Jess moved down along the row of men in the chairs and stopped near the chair of Slim Edwards. When a young fellow got up and walked over to the bar Jess sat down and watched the pool balls zigzag along the cushions. He rolled a cigarette and put all his attention to it. Luckily he had no match.

He turned to Slim Edwards. "Got a match?"

Slim didn't look at him. "Guess I have." Slim uncrossed his legs and fumbled in his pockets, tight across his lean thighs. He handed out the match and looked away again.

Jess smoked a few minutes. "Guess you're Slim Edwards."

"That's right."

"Cy Pierce told me about you."

"Cy is a nice fellow," Slim said.

"I'm Jess Bentley."

"Pleased to meet you. Thought you were. You're the kid that's on the Ames spread."

Jess stood up. "Like a drink?"

Slim hesitated. "Guess so," he said. "A friend of Pierce's would be a white man."

They went to the bar and found a place there and gravely poured drinks from the bar bottle. Jess said, "I came looking for a hand."

Slim said, "Hard to find these days. Kids or drunks."

Jess looked around the room. "See what you mean."

"No pride in their work," Slim said. "Ain't no real cowhands any more, anyway. Christ." They watched the bottles behind the bar and drank.

"Have another," Jess said. They had another. "You know a fellow would like to come out to my place?"

"Don't know," Slim said. "I don't guess you'll find a good man these days. Kids and drunks." He drained his glass. "Have one on me."

Jess grinned and picked up the bottle, then put it down. "Sorry," he said. "Can't. My kidneys."

"Kidneys," Slim said. "Whoever told you whisky was bad for kidneys?"

"My dad always said—"

"Now listen here," Slim said, bridling. "There's nothing to it. I know kidneys inside out. Beer's bad, not whisky."

"Is that a fact?" Jess said, interested.

"Don't you fool with your kidneys. I went to Salt Lake."

Jess looked puzzled. "I don't get you."

Slim hesitated. "I've got a sister in Salt Lake, a fine woman. She knows a fine kidney doctor there. Her husband had a hell of a kidney, worst he ever saw. I went to see this man."

"You had a bad kidney?"

"Bad?" Slim said. "The kidney man said my kidneys, both of them, were worse than either of my sister's husband's."

"Christ!" Jess said softly.

"This fellow took one look at me. 'Christ,' he said, 'how can you pack a set of kidneys like that?' He put me in a hospital with nurses, and I hate a bunch of women, and by God they don't feed you, neither."

"They take the kidneys out?"

"I don't know what they done, exactly. I guess they did take out a little piece of one." Slim leaned close. "I always blamed it on my old man. He let us eat any damned thing. All my brothers had mean kidneys, and my sister married one. Her husband was up and down all night with his. She's got one of those shiny bathrooms, everything white, everything nice."

"By God," Jess said, "I'm sorry to hear."

Slim took up the bottle. "Forget what your dad said. Say when."

"When."

They drank. "Shame, a young fellow like you with a kidney, and not complaining, either, and always harping on it, like most young fellows, always complaining and talking about their guts. They know it all."

"Fine to run into a fellow got the real dope."

"Proud to," Slim said. "Look here. You was saying you needed a man."

"That's right. I've got a hell of a lot to do out there."

"I'll help you out. Don't usually like to work for a young man. Christ, listen to them." They were silent, listening to the young men at the bar, laughing, boasting, drinking. "All wind and no guts. Know it all. You keep your trap shut. I like a man to keep his trap shut, not always harping and complaining like a bunch of women." He hesitated. "You married, Bentley?"

It would have been easy to duck it, to just say no. Jess was tempted a long moment. Then he gave it to Slim straight. "Next spring," he admitted. And he went the whole hog. "Everything's got to be just right—meals on time. Things all slicked up." Not hopefully, but loyally, then he added. "But she sure can ride."

Slim said nothing, looking down his long nose, moving his empty glass on the bar. He turned slowly to spit in the sawdust, rubbed the wet spot with a careful boot toe.

"A buck wasted," Jess thought. And said politely, "Well, glad I met you."

As if he had not heard him, Slim said crossly, "Bunch of men alone—live like a bunch of pigs." He looked at Jess. "I got to have it clean, goddammit." His smile was meager and embarrassed. "Hold on till I get my bedroll."

V

THEY STILL USED the chuck wagon for roundups in those days, and the great lumbering canvas-topped wagon was followed by a remuda of seventy head of horses and twenty men. Sometimes boys in their early teens came along, sons of prairie ranchers. They watched the cowboys, imitated their mannerisms and tricks of speech.

The chuck wagon made a great circle around the base of

the mountains that hemmed in the prairie, starting near Salmon City, swinging within a few miles of Jess's ranch, and then returning around the opposite rim of the valley to Salmon City again. There were a dozen camps along the way, always near a spring or a creek or the timber where wood was easy to get. Cattle were rounded up at each camp, cut out, and trailed to their owner's ranch for the winter. The ranchers usually accompanied their cowboys on the roundup; it was a chance to be young again.

Jess had not yet seen all his cattle. When he bought the ranch from Ames he had taken Ames's word for the number. In that country you took a man's word.

And for the first time he met all the ranchers.

There was Hank Morgan. They said Hank had once married a squaw on a bet. The present Mrs. Morgan was still touchy about it.

There was white-haired Billy Blair, seventy years old and boastful, whose equipment always included a pony of corn whisky, carried he insisted, for medical purposes.

There was Newt Cooper, once a gambler in the Southwest. He had bought his ranch, the Lazy Z, out of poker winnings. He still carried an old deck of cards in his pocket, but only by way of souvenir, for Newt no longer gambled. He had married a practical rawboned woman sometimes known as the old battle-ax. Mrs. Cooper could not be called a gambling woman.

There were the Fisher brothers, Arthur and Westley, fifty-six and fifty-seven years old. Both of them looked like caricatures of Uncle Sam, and each referred to the other as "that old fool." Back at their ranch their wives kept up a semblance of peace between them, but on the roundup it was open warfare. The feud had started in Illinois in 1870 over a pocketknife. Cy, who was roundup boss, always sent them away from camp in different directions.

All day long they rode, from three in the morning until the moon came up. Rode in the heat and dust, parched when it was dry, drenched when it rained. All day they rode and sweat and roped, swayed, cursed, and laughed. They brought up the old jokes, the time Red put the buffalo skull in Newt's bed. The time Amy, who seldom rode, came thirty miles to the camp to see Cy because she was lonely.

And at night there were campfires and low, lazy talk. Singing. They sang well, most of them, putting all they had into the "Strawberry Roan," "Santa Fe Trail," "Go Tell Aunt Rhody," or "Ta-ra-ra-boom-de-ay." Later there had been interest in railroad songs. There were rumors that an Eastern company was interested in the prairie. For the sake of their mining and ranching interests the company might build a railroad over the divide. It was not a strong enough rumor to put faith in, but the ranchers thought of it hungrily. It was fine, what a railroad would do. There would be money on the prairie. Salmon City would mushroom from a dusty little cow town of saloons and false fronts to a city with sidewalks, street lights, and theaters. You could buy anything you wanted. There would be regular mail. And—if you wanted to—you could escape the prairie in winter . . . .

But it was a crazy dream. Newt Cooper, who had known railroads in his gambling days and had traveled on the Santa Fe many, many times, said that railroad tracks were slick as glass, and so were the wheels. You could only run a railroad on fairly level ground. To get up a slight rise a train had to make a good run at it.

"How're you going to get a train over the Pass?" he asked sarcastically over the cigarette he was rolling. "The thing would keep slipping."

Cy took a stick and poked up the fire. "Maybe they could put sand on the tracks," he said slowly.

"And wear the wheels out!" Newt scoffed.

Jess cleared his throat. "Where my old man had his place there's a branch of the Western."

They turned to Jess. "Are there any mountains there?" Newt asked sternly.

"Sure. Mountains. There's a steep grade, and that old train just whizzes up. And down too. Like the song about the Old Ninety-Seven."

"The Ninety-Seven went ninety miles an hour downgrade."

In the quick silence the pines whispered. "How does anybody stand going ninety? There wouldn't be any air to breathe."

"Well, they stood it on the Ninety-Seven. Till the engine smashed into the—""

"Sing that song," Billy Blair demanded. "About the Old Ninety-Seven."

"Get him Red's guitar out of the wagon . . . . Can you play a guitar?"

Red handed him the battered old instrument, big Red with the carrot top and the big mouth that was always grinning. Red's guitar was a part of the roundup. He was the only one who could play it, if you called playing two chords playing it. He knew the D chord and the A seventh, which, as Arthur Fisher said, was enough for songs like "Buffalo Gals," but not enough for the "Strawberry Roan," where you go down low-like. When the D and A seventh chords were not enough, Red faked a chord by putting his fingers down on the frets anywhere. Arthur said he made awful noises. Westley liked the uncertain chords. Lately Red had stopped playing until the song got around to the two chords he knew. It worked pretty well, they agreed. But Jess—he could play even the G chord, which was enough for any song a man might want to sing.

In those days they considered the "Strawberry Roan" the most exciting song of all. Especially, Hank Morgan said, that place where the buster's about to be bucked off. Here they would stiffen their legs and sit straighter on the ground.

But this "Old Ninety-Seven"—there was a song! You could hear it going over the tracks, click-click. Jess made the sound by running his fingers along the frets. You could see the look on the engineer's face, knowing he'd get killed. And then, toward the last:

> *"She was going down the grade*
> *Making ninety miles an hour*
> *When the whistle broke into a scream . . ."*

Jess let out a screech, like a whistle. It made you shiver. You saw fire, sparks, It went over and over in their minds— when the whistle broke into a scream.

They sat in silence for a long time, and nobody made a move to fix the fire. Only the glowing coals now, and the pines whispering behind them, and the rustle of a canvas tarpaulin. One by one they walked in the darkness to their bedrolls.

"See you in the morning . . . ."

When the mountain lion screamed near camp they sat up in their blankets.

Curious how Jess dreamed after that . . .

He was waiting for a train. It seemed years he waited. "Beth!" he seemed to shout, agonized. "Beth!" Sometimes he turned and looked back at the ranch, stretching on all sides of the railroad station, miles and miles of ranch land, and the thin little line of track lost in the middle of the land. The sight made him feel better . . . .

It was drizzling when they rolled out of their blankets next morning at three. The cook was swearing because the wood was wet and the fire sputtered. He didn't give a damn, he said, if anybody ever ate. Saddle blankets were damp and cold in their hands; the horses were spooky and humped up when the saddle touched them.

Smoke from the fire hung low on the ground, strong smoke, grayish, blending into the half-light. They untied their slickers from the backs of their saddles, yellow slickers cracking and rustling, horses shying at the sound. A bad morning.

Cy said, "You look tough this morning, Jess. Sleep bad?" Jess looked up from his plate. "I had a funny dream. I dreamed I had a bigger ranch than I've got now."

The cook shouted, "Come and get it . . . ."

VI

THE WILLOWS ALONG the creek bottoms turned a rusty red. A blue haze with a smoky smell settled down over the prairie; the mountains grew indistinct against the sky, and it was Indian summer.

Jess had hired a third man for the winter and installed Tommy, a grinning young Chinese, as cook at the ranch. He himself must get out the logs for the new house.

He felled log after log there by himself in the quiet of the timber of Black Canyon, heard the snapping of the small branches and the crash in the silence. It was not a thing you could trust to strange hands, felling logs for a house for the woman you were going to marry. Things would go along all right without him at the ranch. The man he had hired was a good worker; Slim and Pete he could trust; Tommy was a good cook.

Lucky about Tommy. It wasn't often you could pick up a good Chinese. Beth thought she was going to cook after she got married, and Tommy was a surprise. She would go on riding in the hills with her husband. Strange word, husband . . . . Made you feel funny, big and awkward and sheepish.

Must be awful to be a woman and have to cook. Stick around a kitchen all day with flour and stuff and see the country through a pane of glass. Well, Beth wouldn't have to do it. He thought of her getting off her horse, hot and dusty, and going into the kitchen to cook. She would look funny standing over the stove in her little riding boots. Funny to think of.

In the evening he sat in camp, a tent with an open flap pitched deep in the timber near a spring, watching the camp robbers begging for bacon rind, listening to the bells on the team, the faint clink of the hobbles. He thought a lot.

He would build his bride's house with his own hands, his own sweat. He would hew each log as she would want it. He would plan closets—even a bathroom—for her. He would drive the last nail and stand back and look. He would walk with her to the spot where they could see the house together some evening. All this his own thought, his own doing, their house, their life, their prairie.

Newt and Billy and Hank and Cy and the rest were willing that he should get out the logs. They had business of their own right then. There were cattle to be fed, firewood to be hauled, calving and irrigating in the spring. But when they had their hay crews in working order the building of Jess's house became their responsibility too.

At first they arrived on horseback. To borrow a pick, a shovel, they said.

"Well! See you're building you a house!"

They drove up in buggies and brought their wives.

"Missus said she'd have a look."

They came in surreys and brought their families. One family arrived early one morning with a picnic lunch.

"We brought plenty for you, Bentley. Fried chicken." The youngest children played in the pine shavings. Those who could drive nails into logs and planks did so.

Doc Morse drove up with his team of grays. "Said down in the city you were building a house, Jess. Well!" He handed Jess a clipping from the Salmon City *Recorder*.

Ye editor hears rumors that Jess Bentley from up the prairie is building a fine log house on his ranch. Word has it that he is putting in plumbing . . . .

They were lavish with suggestions; they had plans for the perfect house, plans the years had brought to nothing. A bad winter, a dry summer—and the old house would do.

"You've got to have stouter logs. Heavy snow. Roof would fall in."

"Peel those logs. Bedbugs'll get in under the bark. Happened once. Slept in the barn all year, starving them out."

"Women finicky."

They wanted cupolas and gingerbread but admitted it would be hard to do in logs. They wanted one large room—it would be easier to heat, have less space to lose track of things in. The women talked of nothing but closets. It seemed they would be satisfied with a big kitchen, a bathroom, never fully discussed, and a dozen small closets to put away things in.

Billy Blair remarked, "Women are like squirrels."

The women disagreed about the kitchen floor. One group, led by Amy Pierce, held that linoleum was the modern thing. You could mop it easier, and with a dark color the dirt didn't show, anyway.

Mrs. Cooper led the opposition and held out for painted wood floors. She clung to the negative argument that linoleum chipped, and people were certainly getting lazy these days. Amy offered to settle the matter by drawing straws, but Mrs. Cooper refused, feeling that drawing straws hinted darkly of gambling.

The men debated a lighting system. The older men wanted oil lamps. They had no use for electricity, arguing that nobody knew what it was. Stories were told of men laid low by the stuff. The younger men said lamps were bad for the eyes.

Electric lights were the thing. You pumped electricity into bottles, sort of, and let it out a little at a time. You weren't forever having to trim wicks.

"Bad on the eyes!" Billy Blair snorted. "Bosh! Been reading by lamps since '60, and I see as good as anybody."

"Can you read?" They howled with laughter.

Jess was not consulted. No one bothered to ask his opinion. He was young, hadn't thought things out, probably.

"Don't let it bother you," Cy told him. "They're arguing so much all you've got to do is have your say, and it'll swing the vote." And eventually even those with the stoutest opinions gave in graciously. "After all, he's the one that's got to live in it."

Spring, 1914.

They stood at a distance from the house, a little in awe of what they had built—a squat, solid, almost square one-story log house. The logs were unpeeled.

Jess said. "Doesn't seem right to peel logs."

"Know what you mean," Cy said. "And if the bugs come, take a little swab of kerosene on it."

There was a porch with a sloping roof running across the front of the house, supported by four pillars of unpeeled logs. Five rooms, including a bathroom. There would be a big white bathtub selected by the ladies from the mail-order catalogue. Just to look at the picture in the catalogue made you feel warm suds around your neck. The picture was a discreet one allowing only a view of the bather's head and face, a woman's face inviting you to share the bath.

Mrs. Cooper frowned. "If she had to bathe in a washtub, all cramped up, she wouldn't smile.

Amy laughed indulgently. "You ought to see Cy when he gets out of the tub. He's cramped up. He can't straighten up for a few minutes, just squats there in the kitchen."

Mrs. Cooper grew rigid. Baths and men were not mentioned in the same breath. She closed the catalogue with dignity and spoke of gardening.

There would be new chairs and rugs, a bed with springs, a mattress. A heavy golden-oak table with legs like those of some clawed beast. A lion, it looked like in the catalogue. But now the house was almost bare. Everything in Ames's house, the bed, the round-oak stove, even the dusty mounted deer head, the hair beginning to slip, even the bearskin, hardly filled one room.

"It's some house. Fitten for a woman."

They stood there, women in calico, men in heavy boots, overalls, big hats, and they looked with pride and wonder.

"Now you can tear the old one down. Make good firewood."

Jess shook his head. "Use it for a bunkhouse. Got to have some place for the hired men."

They chuckled. "You'll marry that girl now. When you going to bring her?"

He was going after her that month.

They began to leave. They got on their horses and in their buggies and waved to him and called, and as he watched them go it was curiously lonely there. Cy Pierce was beside him.

Jess said, "Back home—back at my dad's place—they liked to see a new house." He looked away and spoke offhand. "When a girl came to live in a new house they always had a shivaree. They always had a surprise party to make her feel at home."

Cy said softly, "Sometimes they have them here too."

Jess flushed. "I was just remembering. It was always a nice thing for the girl. She always liked that."

VII

THE STAGECOACH WENT swaying in the hot afternoon sun down to Salmon City, leaving the young man in the big hat and new store suit standing tall beside a small figure in a gray traveling suit, side hat and veil.

He stood a little stiffly, conscious of his dignity as a husband of more than a week, but the half-smile he fixed on the girl was anxious, and he closed his palms and groped at the cuffs of his coat sleeves. He watched her.

Now she had seen the squat log house and the broken, sagging old gray corrals, the willows that bordered the winding creek just below. She had seen the fields out across, green now, and splotched with the moving, watery blue of camas.

He had wanted her to see it exactly as he had seen it for the first time. The old, sagging fences, the gate that squeaked. Now he felt the sagging fence was just a sagging fence, and the gate should have been replaced, or propped up, anyway.

For her eyes had gone away from these close things and rested again on the Pass, high and blue in the distance, the barrier that shut her in with Jess Bentley, shut her out from everything she had ever known.

There had been the wedding.

The neighbors, her neighbors, had dressed exactly as his neighbors had dressed for his father's funeral, had talked in the same polite tones. There was this difference, that the ladies wore hats with flowers, stuffed birds, or feathers, and some of the gentlemen winked slyly. There was no organ in the Ford ranch house, only an upright piano and no one to play it. Only the bride had "taken piano," and it was a little too much to expect the bride to play at her own wedding.

But her mother had placed an open sheet of music, "Oh, Promise Me," on the rack for the neighbors to see.

The neighbors had mentioned the shivaree, the party, the noisy gay party that followed a wedding by a night or two, for they knew that his own neighbors at his father's place would never have a chance to shivaree them.

He had had to say, "We've got to go. We've got to get on to the prairie tomorrow."

Beth, standing beside him, had smiled proudly. Her husband had spoken. He had work to do, attending to their future.

She had gone upstairs to finish packing. Her mother, crying and smiling, had gone up, too, leaving Jess and her father alone in the living room, for the wedding was over; the last buggy had lurched off down the dusty road.

Jess looked about the room. The chairs were pulled around in a kind of semicircle. The bouquets of Indian paintbrush that Beth had picked and arranged wilted on the upright piano, and the late-afternoon sun streaming in through the fresh-washed windows faded the reddish petals.

On a table was a plate of sandwiches, untouched, piled neatly, the bread drying. There was the black leather-covered sofa and the leather-covered pillow decorated with a bit of pyrographic work, the head of an Indian in war bonnet. Beth had done that at school.

A bookcase with glass doors protected neat piles of women's magazines and a few battered children's books. Beth's. The windows were draped in neat white curtains tied back with white bows. Beth had made them. And beside the far window he looked a moment at the tall, narrow table with spraddled spool legs that held up a healthy green fern. Beth had planted it.

His eyes went again to the photograph on the piano top, a little girl in a crisp white dress seated primly in a fancy wicker chair, but even in that picture, stiff and arranged, her eyes held a gentleness.

It was suddenly wonderful to him that she could leave this house so easily, with such high spirits, with such trust in him. It made him a little afraid, a little humble, and he looked at his hands.

He could hear her now, talking softly upstairs and then laughing, and her mother's tired, gentle voice.

Her father was dignified in his Morris chair. He had talked with Jess of the early days, as a man would to a younger man, nicely avoiding anything personal. He had made no references at all to Beth. Joe Ford was not an old man, but he seemed old now, and tired. He smoked a cigar that a guest had given him and watched the smoke.

Now that the women had gone upstairs he went to his roll-topped desk in the corner and brought out a bottle of good whisky. Jess watched him fill two small glasses, cork the bottle.

Joe Ford said, "Drink?"

Jess was on his dignity too. "Thank you, sir." And rose to take the small glass, not too anxiously, from his father-in-law. They sat down, Jess careful to let Joe Ford get comfortable first. Joe Ford looked across the room, out the window at the sagebrushed foothills.

He said, "She used to ride out there. She was always riding out there."

Jess was respectful. "She rides good. Better than any woman."

"Better than any woman, that's right." Joe Ford drained his glass, his eyes still on the window. "She had a lot of friends here. They was going to give her a shivaree."

That had been discussed before. Jess had explained they had to leave for the prairie immediately. Joe Ford said again, "It's not as if you were going to your father's place, where everybody knows you, where she'd make friends quick."

A sudden fierce loyalty to the prairie he had known only a few months welled up inside Jess. What was his father's, what was Beth's father's meant little now, and only the prairie counted, and the life there with Beth. "She'll make friends quick there. They're friendly there."

Joe Ford poured another drink. "Everybody around here, all the people knew her since she was a kid, was going to have a surprise party tomorrow, a shivaree. But you've got to go, so that's that."

That had been a point, too, for Joe Ford could not easily grasp that a man of Jess's age could have a ranch, a going concern, that required real attention. He was surprised and a little pleased, at first, that Jess was firm in leaving. "But you've got to go, so that's that."

Again the fierce pride in the prairie, in the people whom it seemed he knew better than he really did. He remembered the smile of Cy Pierce and the gentleness of Amy Pierce. He wove a small story. "They're going to have a shivaree for us the night we get there."

Joe Ford gave a broad grin. "That's fine! That's damned nice, Jess." He looked suddenly, levelly, at his son-in-law. "Jess—she's just a kid."

"She's a fine girl."

Joe Ford smiled gently. "You say that and you don't really know her. Don't get me wrong. I know you know her well enough to marry her. But someday, you'll see. Someday you'll see what she is."

"I know. And she's going to be happy."

"I don't say that because I'm her father, Jess."

"I know. She's going to like it there. They're good people."

Joe Ford's eyes went back to the window. "I'm damned glad about that party."

"It'll be fine for her, that party."

"I'm damned glad," Joe Ford said, and he looked out at the low gray foothills where she used to ride.

Her baggage they had sent ahead with the freighters, a hatbox or two, a round-topped trunk. They traveled in the swaying Concord stage with only two suitcases.

As they began the long trip he felt a great relief, for the stage was a link with the prairie, and the prairie was home. He could not tell why he felt that she, too, must feel this satisfaction. In the beginning she talked with the excitement of a child as the stage lurched the first few days over a road she knew, past ranches she knew or remembered, and at the stations where they stopped for a change of teams they knew her people, and some of them remembered her.

"Why, you're Beth Ford! Why, I remember your folks had you along one time . . ."

Then the road forked, and she grew quieter as the country became strange, the foothills higher, the peaks bluer. Then as the stage went toward the prairie he began to talk. Big talk, wonderful talk. He believed it himself. But as the stage drew nearer by the day, by the mile, he felt he was leading her to expect too much, and he tried to prepare her for some disappointment.

"It's a new country, Beth. It's like it used to be, all open, all wild."

"I'm going to like it, Jess. I know. Now tell me again about Mrs. Pierce. What was that you said about Newt Cooper?"

Now he found he couldn't paint so good a picture of these people, and sometimes he almost felt he didn't know them at all. He longed for the stage to pass or overtake someone from the prairie so he could talk and show Beth how fine they were, how well he knew them.

Here again was the desert country, dry and hot when the rest of the West was moist and green with spring, and at the end of it the old prospector's cabin. Here the stage driver stopped to water and rest the horses before the long pull up the canyon to the Pass.

He had not seen the prospector since that first time, and although the old man greeted him as a friend he felt shy before the old fellow and couldn't respond right to his jokes.

"Well," the old man said, "it didn't take you long to find a pretty wife."

"No," Jess said. And then, "Everything all right with you?"

"Not kicking," the old man said, grinned, then: "I'm eating hearty." He laughed. And to Beth, "What you ever get mixed up with this coyote for?"

She smiled easily. "I like him. I'm going to tame him."

The old man turned to Jess, his eyes twinkling. "You tell your wife about them Indians?" His eyes were roguish.

Jess said, "I told her about all that." He turned from the old man. "I stopped here. He gave me a good feed." He turned again to the prospector. "Where's your dog? That was a good dog."

"Died. Too damned old. He got to hearing things."

The team had drunk, for their sides were quiet and the sweat froth around their collars had dried. Jess helped the driver harness up, glancing over his shoulder at Beth, who stood with the prospector. He was grinning but not talking to her.

Jess waved his arm at the old man as the stage lurched away and gave him a friendly smile.

"He's a nice old fellow," Beth said.

"Old desert rat," Jess said, smiling.

"They're nice to talk to." She was rested, and her eyes sparkled. "What was that about the Indians?"

"I told you."

She was puzzled. "I don't remember."

"It was just some story about how the Indians used to hunt." He cleared his throat. "I forget just what it was."

He closed his palms and groped at the cuffs of his coat sleeves. She stood beside him, her veil fluttering in a ripple of breeze. She was only twenty. Her clothes made her older, but her face was a little girl's playing at being a lady. Her eyes moved away from the Pass, back to him, and she smiled and touched his arm with a gloved hand.

They picked their way down from the dusty road, her small high heels twisting on the uneven ground, her hand still on his arm.

"I never knew it could be wonderful like this. A husband like you and a house. It's almost too much to expect. Too good."

The gravel crunched beneath their feet, and now more than ever he was aware of the stillness around the house, lost in the expanse of the prairie. "There are good people here." He told her again of Cy and Amy and Mrs. Cooper. "She's a regular card. You won't be lonely. Newt Cooper was a gambler. He tells stories. You like people like that." The sun was hot, the breeze hot.

She moved slowly, her hand on his arm. "Jess, will they like me?" Anxiously.

"You just say that. You know they will. They'll think you're a crackajack."

"This is my wife, Tommy." Jess put the bags down.

Tommy picked them up and looked at her, his face a yellow mask. "How do?"

She smiled. "How do you do? Thank you for taking the bags." Tommy stood directly in front of her. She could not look around him to see the room.

Jess said, "Dinner ready?"

70

"First-class dinner." Tommy padded away, his blue felt slippers whispering across the new floor. They stood a moment in silence.

The bare plastered walls smelled of moist lime and earth, and old man Ames's deer head and bearskin lay in a heap in the corner, the glass eyes dull with dust, dim in the half-light, for the shades were partly drawn.

Beth pulled at her gloves and looked out into the room, getting her eyes used to the light." But you haven't been living in here!" she cried suddenly, looking at him.

"I thought I'd wait," he faltered. "I thought until you came—things all upset—" He couldn't explain that the room must be unlived in until she came. "It's all bare," he finished. "There's nothing in here."

"But, Jess—they'll be coming tonight."

He looked quickly at her. "Who? Who's coming?"

"For the shivaree. There's no place to sit. The ladies will say I'm a bad housekeeper."

He said, "I don't think they'll come. Not tonight."

She turned to him, a little tense, hesitating. Then she put her arm about his neck, standing close to him. "I'm sorry, Jess. Dad said I wasn't to let on I knew. But he warned me they'd be coming. He said you told him. He thinks so much of you, Jess. He wants me to be a good wife." She smiled up at him. "I'm sorry, darling, but when I saw how bare—and nothing in here—"

He could not bring himself to tell her that he'd, well, that he'd made that up. That he didn't know if they would ever come. That he'd—all right, that he'd lied. That, now, the prairie was a strange place and the people strangers.

He said, "I guess your dad did right." He managed a grin. "We'll get the furniture in this afternoon."

He watched her drive herself, working on nerves alone, and even for a time her eyes danced as each new crate was unpacked, brought in from the shed by the hired men, Slim and Pete. She tore at wrappings and cut string with the butcher knife Tommy brought for her, and even used the claw hammer to pry up slats. She had changed to a house dress, with a towel around her waist, too excited to eat dinner, too excited to rest.

Each time he spoke it was worse. Over and over he said, "They'll come after dark. Nobody knows what time they come. They don't say."

Her eyes were wide. "That makes it more exciting!"

"They're good people," he kept saying. "They came to help build the house. I didn't know they were coming, but they all came and helped. They just came."

She smiled. "Dad said he never heard of a young man getting so friendly with everybody in so little time. He says I'm lucky."

"Your dad's a good fellow."

The sun was low now and slanted into the room, sharp blades of reddish light cutting through the dusty room. She said, "We'll clean up after all this. When will they come, Jess?"

"They'll probably come late. You don't know when. Sometimes you think they won't come, it's so late, and then they come."

Cleaning up took only a short time. Now at suppertime the furniture was in place, and the glass lamp was neat in the middle of a clean handkerchief on the golden-oak table. "They won't expect too much, Jess? They know you can't get table covers and things like that quick. They must know that."

"They know." The shadows grew longer; the sun sank, and dusk came down. A mist rose from the creek below the house and drifted up, heavy with the scent of moist green moss and black earth and roots. Supper was over, and the hired men moved in the bunkhouse, the sound of their clumping boots curiously distinct in the dusk. A killdeer piped in the silence, and across the valley the purple hills faded one into another. A bit of sun still touched the peaks with gentle gold. There was an hour when she walked with him through the new rooms and looked at each one silently. She must remember this first sight of the rooms in the house he had built, this first nightfall, this beginning. Exhausted, she was completely happy.

There was an hour when they sat in the new chairs, smiling across the room at each other until she couldn't see, and then she got up quietly and sat beside him on the wide arm of the Morris chair. "Jess. This is the first evening."

"You worked like the devil," he said.

"You want them to like me, don't you?"

He slipped his arm around her waist. "Don't you worry. They're going to like you." He cleared his throat and made a grin. "Maybe they won't come."

She snuggled close to him and smiled. "Don't tease, Jess." She turned her head and stared silently out the dark window. He felt a little shiver go through her. "It's like Halloween, when you're little. Something going to happen, and you don't know what."

He found himself listening, too, holding her, waiting in the silence of the new house where the new furniture was stiff and awkward, waiting too. There was a fellow in the bunkhouse who played the mouth organ, and he was playing now, a muffled, distant and sad sound, like the only sound in the world.

She said suddenly, "I've got to fix the sandwiches."

He tried to put this off. "Maybe it's too early to make sandwiches. They'll dry up."

"You wrap them in a dish towel, a little damp, then they're nice." She sliced bread thin, and meat. She spread butter and peanut butter, fixing it just so, and the bread didn't crumble that way. She cut the sandwiches from corner to corner and arranged them in a circle on the plates.

"That's nice," he said. "I never saw sandwiches cut like that." He looked away. Tomorrow morning the sandwiches would still be in the kitchen. He wanted to hold her close.

He had to pretend to listen, to stop suddenly and listen for the turn of the wheel, the jingle of harness, or a hoof on a pebble. It was dark now. She had gone with the lamp into the bedroom to change her dress. She had told him about the dress but not the color. "That's a surprise." She looked so small, standing there with the lamp . . . .

Now in the dark living room the fire showed through a hole in the stove and made a red moving spot on the ceiling. He watched it. He was going to tell her as soon as she came out of the bedroom. For there was no reason why a man couldn't tell his wife he had lied a little, and she'd understand too.

He watched the red spot on the new white ceiling, red in the center and circled with orange.

She came out, carrying the lamp high, the soft light on her face, and when he looked at here there was an odd lump in his throat. He watched her, a funny grin on his face, and the lump didn't go away.

She said, "Darling, I'm glad the shivaree is going to be here." She smiled and came to him. "Do you like my dress, Jess?"

He said, "I don't see how you packed that dress. You pack things nice. They don't wrinkle."

"Do you like it? The color? Will the ladies like it?"

"I like it fine. I don't see how you pack things so nice."

She moved about the room, straightened the clean white handkerchief under the lamp. She tugged at the chair and fixed a curtain.

She sat down. "Jess, this is a comfortable chair. Pretty big, but comfortable." She let her head rest against the back. "I could sleep right here." She closed her eyes, smiling. She nodded once, her face relaxed.

She slept only an instant. She opened her eyes and looked at the floor beside her, then raised her eyes, questioning. She spoke a little breathlessly. "Jess—it's late. Jess—what time is it?"

He took out the watch he carried, his father's heavy gold watch. "It's not very late."

"No. But what time?"

There had been no sounds from the bunkhouse for a long time. The stove needed wood. "It's almost eleven. Sometimes they don't come until midnight." He could not quite meet her eyes. "I guess I'd better go out and listen. I'll just go outside. They come quiet. They try to sneak up."

"Yes. Do that. I'll"—she hesitated—"I'll put the coffee on."

"It doesn't take long for coffee."

"No," she said. "But I could measure it out and be all ready." She sat a moment and smoothed the front of her dress and patted her hair. "Well, I'll go in and measure the coffee."

"I'll go out and listen."

"Yes. And, Jess—don't be long."

Clouds flew across the sky, and behind them the moon was pale and sickly; the wind was still. Across from him the barn and the bunkhouse were squat shapes in the darkness. He walked slowly along to the barn, listening, and that was crazy because there was nothing to hear but the water murmuring along over the stones in the creek bed. In the barn he sat on a manger and listened to the wrangle horse chewing, and he heard the whisper of hay as the horse pulled out a mouthful, and then the crunching. He rolled a cigarette, lit it, took a few deep puffs. In about fifteen minutes he came back inside the house.

She was not in the kitchen, but the coffeepot was on the table by the sink and the can of coffee was there, too, and a spoon.

She was sitting very straight in her chair, quietly. She looked up, her eyes a little wide, trying to smile. She said, "They're not coming. You went to listen, and they're not coming."

He could not look at her. He cleared his throat a little and held his voice steady. He felt it, dry and parched in his throat. "Oh, they'll be here. Sometimes it's late. Sometimes—"

Then he looked at her, at her hair she had brushed, a little mussed, and at the crisp dress, a little wrinkled. Her eyes were bright, and her mouth trembled with the smile.

Then suddenly she was crying in his arms, pressed close against him. He said, "Beth," very gently, and the lump was big in his throat, for around him pressed the night and the loneliness, a sadness and a tenderness for her, whom nobody should hurt. Nobody at all, because she didn't deserve to be, ever. "Beth."

She turned her head a little on his shoulder, and her voice was small and tight. "I don't care. I don't care."

He held his mouth firm and held her closer. "Don't cry. Don't, Beth. I talked too much. I said too much about them."

Her shoulders shook a little. "I—just can't stand them to hurt you." She looked up, searching his face. "All I want is you, Jess."

Then he knew he could tell her, for the lie didn't seem big at all. He could tell her anything. "Beth," he began. "I wanted to tell you—that I—"

But of course he never got it said. For then they came.

They came as they always did, with shouts and yells and bangings on pots and pans, shrieking like Indians. They pounded on the door.

"Break it in! Shivaree!"

"Surprise and shivaree!"

They pounded, and the new porch and the joists beneath their feet trembled, and back as far as the barn they shouted and laughed and came forward.

"Shivaree! Shivaree!"

So Jess Bentley looked down at his wife. His voice broke only a little as he whispered, "Oh, damn them. Oh, damn them, they came . . . ."

VIII

WHEN YOU GOT married on the prairie they came and they shivareed you. A shivaree is a surprise party, but they had found that a better shivaree results if the surprised know of it. They said to the husband, "Well, I wouldn't be surprised if there was a shivaree out to your place around nine o'clock." That wasn't exactly telling.

For they never forgot the shivaree they gave Anderson and his bride when be brought her back from Norway. It was too secret. It was January, and some of them drove twenty miles by sleigh. It was snowing and ten below . . . . The lights were out when they drove silently into the yard. Anderson and his bride were in bed; the house was cold. There was nothing to drink. Billy Blair said the thought of whisky was the only thing that kept him alive.

It wasn't exactly Anderson's fault; somebody should have told him. But he might have known. Everybody that got married had a shivaree.

It was part of the game that the bride and groom be surprised. The bride should be flustered or bewildered when they arrived, according to her temperament. She should say, "Well, I never!" take the hats and coats of the surprisers, and go into the kitchen to get out food it had taken her all day to prepare.

The groom should come out in his shirt sleeves, maybe even have his shoes off. Some husbands called from the bedroom, "What's that? What's going on?" It was fun that way.

Jess said, "What's going on out there?" They saw his figure in the doorway. They crowded through the door like sheep. "Surprise!" they shouted. "Shivaree!" they yelled, the women's voices sharp. More than forty of them. Cowboys with hair slicked back and boots shined. Hired girls dressed in their best. Hank Morgan's father, eighty-three, and who for the past ten years had hinted that each shivaree would probably be his last. Brides gave him extra attention.

"Well!" he screeched in his high, cracking voice. "Well! Didn't think I'd see this party. Probably be my last, Jess," he added sadly.

Cy was there, his face flushed with excitement. Amy, who knew the look, clutched his arm and tried to look in his face. "Now, Cy, remember you've got to drive home!" She turned to Mrs. Cooper, who was frowning and peering through the crowd about her. "After one of these things," Amy explained, "he drives all over the road. And you know me." Mrs. Cooper nodded absently. "My," Amy went on, "I'm glad he didn't drive the blacks tonight, like he was going to. I wouldn't enjoy a minute of this if I had to think of driving that pair home."

"Newt's as always at these things," Mrs. Cooper confided, still peering into the crowd. She saw Newt talking and laughing with Cy, slapping his thigh and laughing. "Newt!" she called.

Every woman tried to keep an eye on her husband, and every man tried to elude his wife—it was part of the game. No woman expected her husband to abstain, not even Mrs. Cooper, who belonged to the W.C.T.U. On shivaree nights Mrs. Cooper shut from her mind the teachings of Carrie

Nation, whose grim likeness hung above the organ in the Cooper parlor, chilling even the soberest visitors until they got little twinges of guilt. Mrs. Cooper atoned for Newt's lapses by sitting down to the organ the morning after a shivaree and accompanying herself as she sang loudly certain trusted hymns.

But tonight she only wondered how loud she would have to sing and spoke to Newt with cautious tolerance. "Careful. Don't mix different—spirits." She always referred to whisky as "spirits," a word that had a nice medicinal sound, except for those times when she was seized with desire to reform the prairie. Then whisky was "rum," a word synonymous with "vice" and one to be uttered in a terrible voice.

"Careful, Newt, remember—"

"Here comes the bride!" Cy shouted, and there was Jess, leading Beth by the hand, grinning. He seemed to say, "You can't help liking her." A spasmodic half chant, half song arose. Here comes the bride, here comes the bride, da da da-da da, here comes the bride. A crowd gathered around them. Hands were extended, drawn back when not immediately shaken, extended again. It seemed to Beth that she met them all at once, that they spoke as one voice, that their curiosity was a force. It left her breathless and a little frightened. So glad to meet you. So glad to know. So pleased . . . .

Simple words. And yet she put something in them, as if she were really glad, really pleased to meet . . . . You thought, "Here is somebody who likes me, somebody who will smile when she sees me, somebody who will ask me about the things I know and will listen to what I tell."

You liked her, sensed her nervousness, and were glad the grinning young man beside her was big and capable and smiling. Even Mrs. Cooper liked her, Mrs. Cooper who mentally put brides on probation for a time. Mrs. Cooper had known and could name several brides who hadn't turned out so well.

The men, when they had met Beth, drew back from the ladies and formed a tight shy circle of their own. Somehow Cy was left standing at Amy's side. He wished he had escaped.

"Oh," Amy cried, "I'm glad you're here, Beth! I felt sorry for that boy all alone here. He tried to be happy, but we all knew how he felt!" She shook her head at Jess with smiling relief. Jess looked away. "There's nothing sadder," she went on, "than a big single man. Cy, now." She looked at her husband steadily. "Cy needed someone to *do* for him. Didn't you, Cy? He was lonesome. Tell them, Cy," she said suddenly, "how you needed me and what I did for you!"

Cy grinned helplessly. "Now, Amy—"

"Oh, *you!*" Amy cried. "But he knows well enough. For one thing, I made him stop thinking so much. He thought too much. He thought and worried."

Cy took the conversation from her and handled it badly. "Well, you're married now, Beth," he said seriously. "Most of us get married once in a while—most of us married ones, that is, get married." He stopped in confusion and looked at his big gentle hands.

"That's right, Cy," Beth agreed. And then, "Why don't you all go away now and let us ladies talk?"

The men whooped and moved toward the kitchen. Newt knocked over a chair and drew a steady look from his wife. Jess led them, shouting back at them over his shoulder. The ladies began to talk rapidly and made shrill little sounds as they moved toward the bedroom to do and say those mysterious things ladies do and say there.

"And so I said, 'I wonder what she'll be like . . . .'"

"And I just put half as much sugar with the berries and . . . ."

The little shrill sounds were muffled when the door closed.

When they saw the keg of whisky sitting in the middle of the kitchen floor, a nice squat brown keg like a fat, jolly little man, the men whooped again. Whole keg! Right there on the new, bright, oily-smelling linoleum.

"Brought the keg in from the outside," Cy boasted. "Good thing you was home, Bentley, or we'd-a had to drink it ourselves. Now wait." He went out to the back porch and returned with an ax. "Stand back, men!" They stood back. Deliberately he brought the ax down on the head of the keg, wham! And the odor spicy, heady, spread through the room. They sniffed. "Old enough to walk," Cy said proudly. "Where's the cups?"

It began orderly enough, in a kind of solemn ceremony, a time-honored ceremony. You never rushed at a new keg. You approached it with respect.

Cy said, "A toast, gentlemen, to the bride."

They drank. A toast to the groom. They drank. A toast to the new house. They drank. That was the formula for a shivaree. And then the informal drinking began. A toast to the time Shorty rode the blue outlaw. One to Mother Machree. Loud talk, gay talk, in the bright, warm kitchen, and then suddenly the word "railroad."

The word drew them suddenly together.

"They said in the city . . ."

"Stranger at the hotel . . ."

"Trying to buy . . ."

"Double the profit on beef."

"Triple the price . . ."

"Jess, get your guitar. Do the one where you screech."

Then he watched them as he tuned the instrument more by the feel of the taut strings than by the sound, it seemed. His big fingers touched each string tentatively; the fleshy part of his thumb plucked the bass, and the sound was lost in the talk. His eyes were grave, watching them, watching

Billy Blair waving his hands, an old man as excited as a child. There was Newt Cooper standing by the water bucket, dipper poised in hand, having his say.

Jess began to sing, and for a few minutes some of them listened. But the attention they gave him that night by the campfire, that night when the railroad was vague and dreamy and pleasant, was gone. The word "railroad" was now a concrete thing, as real as the dipper in Newt's hand. The cowboy who had asked for the song kept his eyes on Jess for a few minutes and then began to talk to someone beside him.

"Up to seven cents before you know it."

"Straight through to the coast . . ."

Jess sang almost to himself, his lips moving, his eyes watching his hands pluck the strings. He lost interest in the song himself, slid off the kitchen table, and moved through the crowd.

"Future," someone said. "Making of the country."

The back porch was dark, quiet. Something lonely there. Still and cool. "Shouldn't have left them . . ." He heard the muffled talk that seemed to move away from him. A breeze whispered in the tall rustling rye grass by the steps.

He began to dread the time when he'd go back; be caught up again in the talk and the laughter.

The darkness hid the distance. The fleck of fire high in the distance could have been only a few miles away. It was twenty miles to the top of the mountain where it blinked and flickered. A fire leaping up and somebody sitting there cross-legged, looking into the flames, listening to a horse grazing in the dark, pulling grass. Listening to space, smelling space, feeling it deep inside.

"Beth and me, sitting there." It swept over him, the space and the dark and the quiet.

And they wanted a railroad. When they had everything they wanted a railroad. They wanted to change this land he had found and loved already and had brought Beth to. He stood tense in every muscle. He didn't know it then, but he had begun to resent the future and everything it meant. He, the youngest of them, was already the oldest of them.

The voices, the thumpings inside drifted back, the laughter, the shouting. He thought, lifting the latch, "See—it's all right. I'm back again." And they didn't notice him come in.

The ladies, talking rapidly, advanced. Beth led them. "Jess!" She called happily. "They've got presents! Bring the boys and let's look at them!" Her eyes, bright with pleasure, beckoned him. "Hurry. I can't wait!"

"Wedding presents?" He turned a questioning look on everyone and followed her. The ladies closed in, and the men made up the rear. All but Billy Blair. He had slipped out the back door.

They put the brown paper parcels on the golden-oak dining table, large ones, small ones, most of them tied with stout white cord. Beth made a little ceremony of opening them. She would pick one up, weigh it in her hand, shake it, puzzled. "Now, who could this be from?" she would say slowly.

The ladies would smile at one another. The donor would say, "Well, I wonder."

The men stood aloof, unwilling to take part in ladylike business, but they always had pocketknives ready when a knot proved too complicated.

Practical gifts, something to use around the house, homely gifts, blue-and-gray graniteware, potholders with embroidered verses, "When it is hot, I hold the pot." Serving dishes, silverlike tablespoons. Things for a young bride to use and while using remember the donor.

Scrubbing a pan: "I haven't seen Mrs. Burkes lately."

Measuring coffee in an aluminum cup: "We've got to drive over to the Masons'."

Beth thought fiercely, "I'm going to use these things. These things are mine."

A few gifts were whimsical. Mrs. Morgan's, a set of cast-iron book ends resembling grayish sailing ships poised perilously on rigid waves. Mrs. Cooper, to complement them, gave books, two she had always wanted to read herself: *The Virginian*, because it was about country like the prairie, and *The Call of the Wild*, because she admired dogs. Then, should her taste in literature appear too light, she had added a new book, *Farm Grasses of the United States*, and an old favorite, *Diseases of the Horse*.

"For you, Jess," Mrs. Cooper said.

Mrs. Westley Fisher and Mrs. Arthur Fisher presented a pair of cut-glass candlesticks with prisms, over the protests of both husbands.

"If you've got to give something to read by, give her one of those lamps that hang down from the ceiling on chains." Both brothers felt that lamps were a big improvement over candles. When it occurred to them that they were in agreement, they were uneasy and avoided each other for a time like strange dogs.

But it was Amy's gift that showed utter disregard for utility. A dozen Haviland plates. Later they would remind people of dainty ladies toying with squab, taffetaed ladies, genteel and foolish, and foolish plates. White, gold-encircled disks, thin almost to transparency, and embellished with roses that lacked no shade of pink. They would look ridiculous, those plates, but now they were something to be wrapped carefully, guarded, for to own them was to be known as the lady who had that pretty Haviland, and that was enough . . . .

Beth's throat tightened as she smiled, holding one of the plates carefully. "Amy, how could you do it?"

Even Jess was round-eyed. He saw himself eating from such plates with Tommy's heavy bone-handled knives and forks.

"You like them, Beth?" Amy was breathless. "I'm glad!"

"My mother had plates like these. I—I didn't know you could get them now."

Amy glanced at her husband. He smiled at her. "They were a wedding present. Cy's and mine," she said softly, and hesitated. "We used to think we'd use them sometime. We always used to think"—her mind skimmed over the past, resting here, there—"we used to think we'd be fixed so we could use them—as if they were nothing."

She was silent. Then, "We won't ever use them." She laughed nervously and touched Beth's arm. "You're so young, you two."

"Amy," Beth said. "Cy."

Amy spoke softly. "Cy said nothing was too good for Jess's wife."

"We'll eat off them tonight," Jess said suddenly. "I'll get Tommy to fix the—"

"It's not the time," Beth whispered, and louder, "We've got to dance. We've got to try out the new floor. We've got to—"

There was a banging at the front door and a muffled voice outside. "Jess! Come and help with this damned thing."

"It's Billy." Jess started for the door. "What's he got?"

Billy was wedged between the object and the doorsill. "It's a wedding present for you" he said with dignity, squinting in the sudden light. "It's a sewing machine."

They laughed; everybody laughed, because everybody knew about the sewing machine . . . .

Maybe it wasn't that Billy was glad to get rid of it, but its possession made him uncomfortable, and he argued to himself that it would be selfish to keep it, with a new bride on the prairie.

He had exchanged seven hundred Arbuckle coffee wrappers for the machine. It said on the package to save the wrappers and you'd get a prize. But it wasn't his fault, the machine. It was the prairie's. For when they heard he was saving wrappers they saved theirs for him. They came to his cabin with pocketfuls, came when he was milking, when he was in bed. His cupboard was crammed with wrappers, and once the wind blew in the night and he woke up to find the floor littered with them. In two years there were seven hundred wrappers.

"I'm going to move my bunk to the barn and turn the cabin over to wrappers," he told Newt Cooper with some bitterness when Newt had given him a handful. "I think people are joshing me."

"Why don't you write the company and find out what you get for seven hundred?" Newt had asked.

"Because the company wouldn't believe I had seven hundred. They'd think I was crazy."

Newt wrote the letter. For seven hundred wrappers (and ten dollars) the company had two prizes. Billy could get a baby carriage or a sewing machine.

"You wouldn't want those things," Newt said practically. "You better wait."

"No," Billy said. "People would keep bringing them. I'll send for the machine. And"—Billy glared at Newt—"mind you, don't blab about what I'm getting."

The machine came a few weeks later with the freight wagons. Billy was glad no one was around when he uncrated it. It was a scary thing. He dragged it to one corner of the room and looked it over. It had nice little wheels on the legs, on swivels, so you could move it easily. The machine gave the cabin dignity.

That evening he was late with the milking because he wanted to try it out and broke several needles before he realized you couldn't sew leather with it. But there was some satisfaction in working the pedal and watching the little thingamajig fly back and forth. It had a nice whir.

Newt couldn't keep the secret. They came to see the machine, and Billy defended it stoutly. They found him pleased with it. "Nice piece of furniture," he reminded them. "Look at it shine." He had placed his lamp on the shining surface, and a can of tobacco. He kept his two pipes in the drawers, and matches.

But he was constantly reminded that for him it was useless, a symbol of his foolishness. His eyes began to avoid the machine whenever he came into the cabin; he never spoke of it. At last he took his pipes out of the drawers and put the lamp back on the apple box. He covered the machine with a saddle blanket, but that, somehow, made it worse. Giving it away would only admit defeat. He needed an excuse.

"Hate to part with it," he told Beth loudly. "But a wedding . . ."

"It's wonderful," Beth said cautiously. She touched the pedal with her foot, hoping to show she knew something about sewing machines, wondering how the other ladies would deal with it. Jess opened the top, closed it, and peered into the drawers. Beth watched him.

"It's got real nice drawers," he said, straightening up. "Real nice," he repeated loudly. "It opens and shuts easy."

"Billy," Beth said suddenly, "you get the first dance."

Billy was startled. Unconsciously he put his hand to his string tie. "I couldn't dance with a young woman." He grinned. "You dance with the young ones." He grumbled, but his eyes were pleased. A young woman wanted to dance with him.

"I don't dance till I dance with you," Beth told him.

"Well," Billy said, "if you put it that way." Billy crooked his arm, and Beth placed her hand on the wrinkled old sleeve. The orchestra hurried together, five pieces. A guitar, a five-string banjo, two fiddles, an accordion. The orchestra gathered in a corner and began to tune up. Low, uncertain strumming of the guitar. Pick-pick of the banjo. Sour whine of the fiddles, fiddlers leaning forward to listen to the plucked As. Tentative chords on the accordion, little wheezing moans that died almost before they began.

"Schottische!" someone called.

Billy was glad it would be the schottische. It was a dance he remembered. He warmed up to it. "Now . . ."

One-two-three-skip!

> *Down in de cane brake close by de mill,*
> *Dere lives a colored gal her name is Nancy Dill . . .*

Billy hadn't felt young in years. He stole little glances at Beth and noticed her smile. She liked dancing with him, he decided. Enjoyed it. He skipped higher, whirling, laughing. His heart pounded. He would remember this moment, remember it in the evening in the cabin, building the fire in his stove, remember it at that quiet time before he trimmed the wick of his lamp and lit it. It was a thing to tell in later years, to say, "There was a bride came to the prairie years ago, a little slip of a woman with a smile, trying to please everybody. A little slip of a woman, a young woman, and we danced the schottische. Lord, how we danced . . . ."

They all danced hard, laughed, without care. They smiled at one another, appreciative of each other's dancing. Only Mrs. Cooper danced with a kind of grimness, watching Newt's graceful revolutions with a hired girl. It wasn't the girl she minded. It was Newt's dancing.

> *Come my love, come, won't you come along*
> *with me?*
> *And I'll take you down to Tennessee . . .*

Newt danced too well. Of all the men, young and old, he danced the best. She had often been about to ask him where he had learned those fancy steps, but she was afraid he might tell.

Jess danced only a few times. Twice he began a dance with Beth, and twice somebody tagged him. When a young cowboy tagged him he was angry, and angry at himself for being angry. What had come over him? What had happened to those hours since they sat alone in the living room, about to go to bed? He danced with Mrs. Cooper. Mrs. Cooper danced waltzes at half time, sedately, with perfect time. He danced with Amy, who danced double time to everything and with no rhythm at all, talking constantly.

And after that he stood in the door of the kitchen and watched Beth, following her shining head around the room with his eyes, watching the graceful swirl of her skirt. He hoped she wasn't having a good time. He desperately hoped she was. He tagged Newt, when Newt danced with her, intending to whisper to her how much he loved her—and was unable to say it.

"Jess," she said softly, "you're quiet. What are you thinking?" She was small in his arms, looking up at him.

"I—" There were so many things. "I wish we were alone. Out camping. Something like that. I walked outside, and somebody was camping."

Hank Morgan tagged him. He held her eyes for moments until she was lost in the crowd. Cowboys whooped; girls panted and giggled, dancing around the floor time after time when the music had stopped. Milling around like sheep.

"I couldn't do it again. I never danced so hard." They wished the orchestra would begin again. The men were drawing together, a sign, the ladies knew, that they were getting ready to go to the kitchen again.

But they didn't go.

Afterward Jess remembered it as a picture. The bright colors, the moving crowd suddenly froze in one scene when they heard that pounding of hoofs on the hard earth outside. Somebody driving a buggy, and fast. Beth and Amy stood in the bedroom door. Jess had just started to them. Now he stood motionless while the buggy rattled to a stop. His eyes remained on his wife.

"Whoa!" Doc Morse's voice. Drunk? But when Doc was drunk he drove slowly. Somebody hurt. Doc coming after help.

Doc was on the porch, stomping his heavy boots. The crowd turned, moved toward the sound.

The door flew open, and Doc stood there and looked at them. "Folks!" His voice was harsh, but he was grinning, his eyes bright with excitement.

A question whispered through the room.

"Folks, it's the railroad! Word in the city they start surveying next week!"

They stood motionless while the wealth opened before them, while their cattle and the acres doubled, while a thin line of steel cut through their isolation and loneliness and made them a part of another world, one they had left, they thought, for good. And now they had nothing to say. They had planned so many times what they would say. Newt had meant to get up on something high, a table, with a drink in his hand, and propose a toast. "To the prairie!" he would say. "To the future and the prairie!" Now he thrust his hands into his pockets, his lips parted.

They had said many times that Cy would look up slowly and say, "I always knew it would." But Cy stood with his head raised as if someone had called.

Beth had started across the floor to Jess. She had parted her lips to speak. The words were on her lips as she stood there, startled, questioning. He had never mentioned a railroad. Jess had never told her about that.

Jess saw that picture many times. In a moment Doc would slam the door behind him. They would all move again, and when they moved Jess knew the prairie would be different, that only he and Beth would be the same. He never forgot.

IX

THE PRAIRIE'S LANDMARKS were silent and brooding. A stranger could hear a rancher say, "I saw a bunch of cattle drifting north along the butte," and never know the feeling a man had at evening when he rode across the flats and watched the purple shadows shift across the scarred face of the butte.

The butte crouched alone on the flat, a jagged mass of grayish granite, sloping gradually to lose itself in the barren sagebrush country behind. It was an easy thing to squint your eyes and see out there a great gray cougar resting, paws outstretched, massive head raised slightly, waiting. Seasons came and vanished. Spring made no difference, nor summer. Buffalo grass could not take root in its rocky surface, and fall winds swept it. Snow could not rest on the steep face. And behind the butte the sagebrush grew sparse and stunted, starved. Potholes oozed and stank in sudden dishlike swales; small pools of yellowish mud and water tantalized cattle on parching days. And always around the pools were treacherous crusts of flaking earth: there were no bones around the potholes, only dried-up hoofprints leading to the edge.

Sometimes a rancher said, "I spotted a bunch of horses up Black Canyon, near the Corral."

The Corral was a landmark. No one knew who built it or when, but there it was, suddenly, a tumbled-down pole corral in the thick of the high timber. You could have missed it. But each pole, though now moss-covered and tumbled-down, was notched and pegged by a human hand. The Corral enclosed nothing but sighing pines . . . .

Save her wedding ring, Beth came to the prairie with but two pieces of jewelry. One of these pieces was a gold brooch in the shape of a shamrock, the leaves vivid with green enamel, a tiny seed pearl in the center. The other piece was a tiny gold cross on a thin chain given her with solemn words by the bishop on her graduation from boarding school. She wore it constantly and had become almost superstitious about it.

"It makes me feel safe," she told Jess, smiling. But her eyes were serious. It meant many things to her: the little pipe organ in the dim school chapel that played "Onward, Christian Soldiers." It meant the white organdy dress with the puffed sleeves and pink ribbons at the throat and the grown-up pompadour. All those things . . .

She felt like crying when she missed it. It was gone. Only the thin chain remained around her throat.

"But I couldn't have lost it," she insisted. "I was just walking out there in the sagebrush"—she stood at the door looking out—"and I went back over every step." She was conscious that her voice had a tired, flat sound. Then, "It doesn't matter, really. It was just a little gold cross." She felt her throat tighten because that was not all it was. It was the little pipe organ and the white organdy dress.

He knew he could duplicate it easily, but that wasn't the same. What was behind it would have to be replaced by something else, something that had a great meaning.

"My mother," he began, "when she was young like you, had a little gold chain like that one with a little arrowhead hanging from it. A little black arrowhead. Dad kept it in a box."

She looked at him. He seldom spoke of his mother. Curiously she felt it would please him if she wore an arrowhead. "Why, I'd like that!" she told him. "I could use the old chain and put a band of some kind around the arrowhead to attach it." Standing beside him, she squeezed his arm. "We could look for an arrowhead. We can find one."

"There's one place I know," he said, "Buffalo Flats. We could get one there."

Buffalo Flats was a landmark, a great flat stretch of country near the base of the Pass at the mouth of Buffalo Gulch. On this land the sagebrush grew high, as tall as small trees, and thick; and scattered the length and breadth of this land were buffalo bones and skulls, bleached and yellowed, the remains of hundreds of head of buffalo. The bones were white when Cy came to the country. Even then the dirty gray horns were shedding hard little flakes that curled up in the sun.

Scatterings of buffalo bones were common enough to Jess. Of the Flats they told him that a hunting party of Indians had some time long before slaughtered the animals. It was easy to picture the bronzed Indians, racing along bareback, crowding their skinny ponies in near the great clumsy animals, whooping and hollering, peppering the shaggy beasts with their arrows, leaving the wounded and struggling animals on the ground for squaws to skin and quarter . . . . The picture was in his mind as he and Beth rode up to the Flats.

They had picked a hot day for the ride, and the Flats were a good ten miles from the ranch. The sun shimmered in a washed sky, and the tall sagebrush ahead shimmered like a mirage. The country made them silent, and Jess's voice sounded strange and alien.

"It'd be better if we got off and walked." He pulled up his horse. "We can see the ground better. When we come to a bunch of bones we'll have to kind of kick around, but it'd surprise you how many heads are near the surface in places like this." He grew thoughtful. "When I was a kid I had a dozen I found in a place like this. You could pan them out, like gold."

She liked to think of him as a little boy in overalls stalking along in the sage, scuffing in the dirt with his capped shoes. A serious little boy; gradually she was getting a picture of him then. "What did you do with your arrowheads?" She liked to hear him talk.

"Well," he told her seriously, "I had them in boxes. I had the big ones in the big box and the little ones in a little box. That way it made it easier to pick out the little ones when I wanted them."

"Why did you very specially want the little ones?" Her eyes, under her big hat, were smiling.

"You know how it is," he told her. "Some days you think maybe you'd like to have the little ones handy, and some days the big ones were the best to handle and *have* and sort out. You know. The little ones—"

She laughed. He turned, surprised, then grinned. "I never thought how crazy it would sound."

"No," she told him, "I laughed because I did the same thing. With pebbles. There must be some neat streak in us, like squirrels."

He helped her off her horse, an attention he never forgot. He tied the two dusty horses to a tall sage, and then they both walked silently into the tangle, only their heads showing. They kicked at the dusty earth and stooped down often to examine an exposed bit of flint or quartz. They spoke in serious, hushed tones. It was even hotter in the sagebrush, and the air seemed stagnant, old, trapped in the branches. The dry grayish leaves absorbed and held the heat close to the ground, and a breeze could not push through the labyrinth of stalks. Beth's hair began to straggle out from beneath her hat, but she brushed it aside absently, absorbed. She scarcely felt the scratches she got on her arms.

They hunted for an hour, feeling new hope as they reached a new scattering of bones. But they found no arrowheads.

Now he had as good as promised her arrowheads. "Look," he said suddenly. "You sit down here on the ground. I'll put my hat up here on top of this bush so I'll know where you are when I come back. You rest, and I'll keep looking."

She sat down comfortably. "It's a little cooler here, and nice. Like playing some hiding game."

He was gone an hour; he came back covered with dust, and drops of sweat had run down his face. He seemed tired, puzzled. "I don't know," he said. "I don't know what's wrong. But I can't find any."

"I'm sorry," she said gently. "But it doesn't make much difference." He helped her to her feet, and she smiled.

"But I don't see," he began, "why there weren't any here. I've been at places like this since I was a kid, buffalo traps, and I always—" He grinned. "Well, I guess there just aren't any." He was resigned, but he couldn't forget.

To Beth the sun always seemed to sink rapidly when it had swung around to the west. The shadows of their moving horses were lopsided, grotesque, slipping along.

Jess was silent. When she caught his eye he would smile, and then his eyes would stare absently at the gray velvet folds of the hills.

"Jess," she said suddenly, "you said your mother had an arrowhead." He nodded. "Well, then," she went on, "why don't you ask me to wear that one?"

He turned. "I was going to. I was going to when I first mentioned it. Then I thought you might—want to use the old chain and maybe a new arrowhead." Then, glumly, "And I'm not sure where it is. I think my brother's got it."

"You can write him. He'll find it." She was confident.

He was instantly more cheerful. When they sighted the ranch it was really without caring that he said, "I still wonder why there weren't any arrowheads around those bones . . . ."

X

Jess stood frowning at the window in the living room, watching the rain streak down from the cold October sky and soak the black sod roof of the barn. Slim had wrangled early, before the rain came, and now the horses stood dejectedly in the corral, close against the gray poles, tails pressed to their bodies. Nothing is sadder than saddle horses standing in the rain . . . .

He strained his eyes to find the outlines of mountains that would promise fair weather, but they were shrouded in wet, blanketlike clouds that settled lower and lower, screening away the vastness, leaving Jess alone with a chilly reality.

He hadn't slept the night before. He lay there in bed, worrying his pillow, trying not to toss and wake Beth, his thoughts racing crazily around her. And around the bay horse.

There was so much he hadn't known about her when he married her, the little things that now in the dark living room were so important. Her love of color, for one thing. He remembered the bright beaded belt she wore when he saw her first; red beads, white and green beads in Indian design. The Indians had given it to her when they came through her country hunting.

"Let them hunt, Dad. The country was theirs before it was ours." Once when the Indians were camped in the sagebrush back of old Joe's barn she had taken Jess to visit them. "They're good people, Jess. Jennie and Arthur are old friends."

They sat in the smoke-filled teepee, Jess silent, his eyes smarting from the pungent smoke. Beth talked; she knew Shoshone and sign language. Beth, the fat old squaw, and the young buck in white man's overalls that fitted too tight around his middle. They laughed, the three of them, the old squaw until the tears ran down her cheeks. It made Jess uncomfortable. After a time the squaw reached under a canvas near the rusty camp stove and brought out a pair of tiny moccasins.

"Present," the squaw said, sunken lips twisted in a grin. "For marriage."

"What were you all laughing about, looking at me and laughing?" He was a little cross with the squaw. She had seemed to look through him, she and her too-fat son.

"About you. They said you were a good man and lucky to get me."

Jess was pleased, and after that he always told people what good people the Indians were. "And smart too," he would add. "You wouldn't think it to look at them."

The bright belts Beth wore—and there were the red silk handkerchiefs tied to hold her hair back. Sometimes, he thought, she looked like an Indian herself. It pleased him when Amy got a red handkerchief. "Mrs. Cooper'll be getting one next," he growled to Beth. "They all copy you."

And the pictures. The walls of the new house had been bare except for the bearskin hanging up in the living room.

"It needs pictures, Jess."

"Sure. I'll get some in town at the Emporium."

"I'll paint some." She got out a little shiny black box of paints and painted some mountains and trees on the bottom of shoe boxes. He split willow sticks and framed them.

"Look," he ordered visitors. "She painted that from the hill over there." He stood back to look, as she had taught him. "She's always painting," he would say gruffly.

She's always busy washing things, shaking out things, straightening things. "Why don't you sit down and rest?" he would ask seriously.

"Jess"—she would smile, looking up from her work, a wisp of dark hair in her eyes—"there's so much to do."

"You've got all the time in the world."

She would look up at him and laugh. "You never know . . . ."

She read too. Not very much. On rainy days, or in the evenings, sometimes, but it was a lot to Jess. He liked to watch her as she sat quietly, and at last he would say, "I don't see how you can read so much. I'd go crazy."

He liked having a wife that read. He made a bookcase from an apple box and painted it red. He had never before painted anything more delicate than a buggy wheel, and the finished job made him elated. "This wagon paint," he said. "Too thick. I could have got it on evener." He looked at his paint-covered hands and was proud.

They filled the case with the textbooks she had had at school. He watched her open each one carefully, lovingly, almost, and she would read aloud some spidery script. "Julie Haskell. She was my friend at school." He felt a twinge of jealousy that she had had another life of which he was not part. They filled the case with Whittier, a collection of Lowell, a text on elocution, Holmes, Longfellow. She could recite.

"The day is cold and dark and dreary,
It rains and the wind is never weary."

"That's a gloomy poem," he announced. "I don't like it much." His eyes were on hers. "It's a gloomy poem." And he couldn't forget it.

And she knew "I saw him once before as he passed by the door . . . ."

It ended on a pleasant melancholy note: "Let them smile as I do now, at the old forsaken bough where I cling."

"They were always gloomy," he said, and felt close to her because they were together and belonged to each other and were not gloomy.

There was a book of songs for community singing. Mrs. Cooper's gift books. A leather-covered prayer book and Frazier and Squier's *Elementary French Grammar.*

"Gosh. Can you read that stuff?"

"I used to." She smiled. "I studied it at school."

"You mean you could pick up a book of French writing and read it off like American?"

"If the French wasn't too hard."

He longed to tell someone, to work it into a conversation casually, that his wife read French writing. He got his chance when he rode over to see Newt about a black mare he wanted to buy. He found Mrs. Cooper sitting in the midst of a pile of *Harper's Weeklies,* clipping pertinent articles on drink and general moral slovenliness. She gestured to a seat with the scissors.

He took the seat. "Where's Newt?"

"He rode away this morning after horses. Anyway"—she snipped away at a page—"that's what he said."

"Well," Jess said, settling back. "You read a lot."

Mrs. Cooper looked up, a little preoccupied. "I browse," she admitted. "Just browse. There's a lot of nonsense being written these days, but there's bound to be some wheat in this much chaff." She looked at the stacks of books levelly.

"Beth reads a lot," Jess said blandly. "She's always reading something or other." He paused. "But she reads mostly French books. French this and French that."

"French?" Mrs. Cooper leaned forward, took off her spectacles, and held them in mid-air. "You mean to say she reads the French tongue?"

"Why, yes," he told her. "All the time."

"Does she speak it?"

"Why, yes," he said.

"That's culture," Mrs. Cooper breathed. "I wonder"— she hitched her chair close to him—"I wonder if she'd teach me French? When I go East to visit I could work it in."

"She'd like that," he told her proudly. "She might have been a teacher if she'd kept on at school."

And during the months that followed Mrs. Cooper dipped deep into the old Frazier and Squier.

There was Jess's old dog, the old black dog he got from a neighbor when he was a boy. The dog trembled in the hind legs when he walked and always looked sad. He never left Jess, panting along beside him when he rode, traveling the best he could, his eyes always on Jess. Jess rode slow so he could keep up.

"I can't make him stay home. I try to, and he follows me."

But now the old dog was content to stay at the ranch with Beth. She let the old dog in the house at night and listened to Jess complain, pleased and proud and jealous.

He told around, "Old dog never left my side till Beth came. Makes a man feel not wanted." He'd tell how the dog looked up at Beth when she patted him. "Those old sad eyes."

He asked her, "Why do you want to fool around with an old dog? Look. I'll get you a pup." He waited.

"I like him. He's a good dog. I don't want a pup, Jess."

"He's old. He's so old you've got to let him in the house nights."

"Someday you'll be old. You'll be pretty glad to have someone look after you." And they'd both laughed. He seldom thought about getting old, and when he did he saw himself and Beth old and happy and warm before the fire.

Jess was lonesome when she stayed at the ranch and didn't ride with him, always thinking of that first glimpse of her when he walked into the house, with that red thing around her head. He liked it when she helped him and the boys with the cattle, riding like a man and strangely different than she was in the house. He'd say, laughing, "Thought maybe you'd forgotten how to ride."

He wished she'd spend less time at the ranch talking to the ladies who were always after her to visit or to join their sewing groups. He never knew whose buggy would be tied to the hitching rack before the house and how many ladies would be sitting in the front room. If Beth would always be like that girl in the divided skirt he saw once, sitting on the top pole of the fence . . .

And then suddenly he never wanted to see her on a horse again.

It was Hank Morgan who first spoke of the bay. Hank had a line on every good-looking horse in the country. Hank was that way. "Say," Hank said that morning he stopped in for a cup of coffee, "Anderson down-country's got the prettiest horse I ever laid eyes on. Seventy-five dollars. The missus is crazy to have him, but the missus ain't good enough rider. That pony steps around like a cat on a hot stove. Take a rider like Beth to handle him." He grinned at Beth. The men praised her riding. They got a kick out of it.

They rode down to Anderson's that cold afternoon, and the bay was even prettier than Hank had said.

"I've got to have him," Beth cried. "Rein him over here and let me look at him from the front."

Anderson had just started over to her when a little gust of wind whisked along the ground and flapped a dry cowhide tacked up on the fence.

The bay ducked his head and lit to bucking straight and high across the corral, kicking up a screen of dust. When it cleared Anderson was still on top, but he was panting and grinning sheepishly. "I'm not much of a one to sell a horse," he called across the corral. "I'm too honest. Whenever some funny noise starts, this son of a gun's likely to buck. You couldn't hunt with him. He's worse than gun-shy." Anderson swung down cautiously. "He's no horse for a lady, anyway."

But Beth would not be put off. "He's not broke yet, that's all. He needs lots of riding." She turned, confident, to Jess. He knew her ability. He wouldn't let her down in front of Hank and Anderson. "I'd like to have him, Jess." Anderson was uncinching his saddle, talking to the bay, quiet enough now. Jess watched with narrowed eyes. Beth spoke again, a little louder. "I'd like to have him, Jess."

"No," Jess said.

"But, Jess"—she looked at him, surprised—"he can be gentled."

"It doesn't matter," Jess said softly. "You can't have him."

The late October sun had passed behind a cloud; the air was colder when they rode across the flat, a lonesome, desolate and gray stretch of country that Jess, in his mind, always called the Great Waste. They could hear the faraway roar of Nip and Tuck Creek, its rushing waters already black beneath the storm that hung heavy among the peaks high up, a silent storm that stalked down the distant slopes with no warning lightning, no growling thunder. Quiet storm.

At the ford they stopped a few minutes to watch the ugly waters rush swirling along the banks dragging along jagged roots and stumps. The harsh roar almost drowned Beth's voice.

"Jess, say something." Their horses splashed on, struggling against the swift water. "I don't care about the horse. It doesn't matter at all."

He mumbled, and his words were swept away.

Late dusk had settled in around them when they reached the old gate that led to the ranch. Old man Ames's gate.

The old man had said, "You've got to fix it." Jess never had. Knew he never would. He never went through it without thinking of Ames. Sometimes when he got off his horse to open the gate he asked the old man questions, silent sincere questions that were answered, somehow.

"Well," he would ask, laughing at himself for his nonsense, "will I start haying this week or next?" The answer came from deep inside with a squeak of the old gate.

"Would you let your wife have a bad horse—if she was—like Beth?"

There was no squeak. No answer.

Aloud Jess said, "It's damp out. The damp kills the squeak of the gate."

Yellow lamplight flooded out from the dining-room window. Tommy would pad to the door, grinning. "Missy got new horse?" She always asked so darn little of him. So darn little.

He couldn't sleep. He lay in bed on his right side, on his left, on his face, on his back, and each way made his muscles ache. He would wrench his mind away from the bay, from Beth, and from the change that had come over him since he married her. That was the most nudging, most persistent thought. He would fasten his mind on the night sounds, the creaking of the logs in the house, the tick-tick-tick of the clock, the coyote howling intermittently in the field below the house. But it did no good.

Before he married her he was proud when she rode a bad horse. That was the sort of thing that made him want her, that set her apart from others. He wanted someone to ride with him, to laugh with him, to share everything he had and everything he did. And now he refused her a horse because he was afraid. Beth must never know that. Let her think it was because he was stingy, contrary, maybe. But she must never know that he was afraid.

Then the rain came hammering down on the roof, and a cold dampness drifted in through the window, carrying the smell of wet manure and soil.

"It'll be all right in the morning." In the dark everything seemed bad. Everybody knew that.

He heard Tommy come padding into the kitchen and begin rattling stove lids. Crackling flames. Six o'clock. He fixed the alarm so it wouldn't go off, pulled the blinds down, and stole out of the bedroom. "This morning she's going to sleep."

And after breakfast he stood at the window, staring into the rain that now had begun to drip down from the soaked sod roof of the barn. Except for the rain, he and the boys would be starting out to brand the last of the fall calves. Slim had gathered up the four branding irons and had leaned them against the door of the bunkhouse. Cold and wet snow. Slim was inside the bunkhouse playing poker with Bill and Pete; their loud laughter came to Jess's ears, and for a moment he felt the steamy warmth inside there, the kind of close intimacy that comes in a small room on a rainy day.

Well, you can't brand when calves' hides are wet.

Suddenly he felt the pressure of the four walls. He wanted to get out in the rain, to feel it sting and splash against his face. He would get out without Beth's knowing; she would want to be with him. Her eyes would question his expression. He could tell her nothing.

Today he wanted her in a warm house, reading, fussing around, fiddling with the sewing machine that lately she had begun to use. And he was alone in the rain, soaked, uncomfortable, doing penance.

The prairie was not pleasant in an October rain. It was a small, shut-in prairie; the mountains were gone and dissolved in the mist. Spring rains were different, helped the grass, gave the sagebrush a greenish living tinge. Those were the good rains, and you turned your face to spring rains, breathed deep and tried to drink them down in a gulp. But October rains smelled strange, dead, and wintry. Haystacks looked low and meager through the mist. You began to wonder where you could buy a little hay, just in case. October rains smelled of a dying prairie.

He saw his cattle, like gaunt specters, huddled close to the shadowy willows bent low before the wind, creaking, creaking, telling a mean, cold story.

"Ought to give this country back to the Indians." His lips had moved. The sound of his voice came faint to his ears and somehow comforted him. Like ghostly sentinels, a few heavy log fence posts loomed before him. He rode close to one and pushed it with his hand. It was solid. He had been so sure it would be loose that he chuckled.

"Solid!" And he thought, "As solid as my new house." When he thought of the prairie on a bad day it was easy to see why the neighbors had been anxious to help him build it. "It looks good, that new house," he told himself seriously. And generously, "It's sort of their house too."

Now he thought of his new saddle and looked down at the pommel stamped deep with poppies, a saddle to be proud of. Everyone knew when he had ordered it, waited for it with almost as much eagerness as he. He had been grave and silent as they told him what a fine saddle it was, and he had been proud. It was a good saddle and had cost plenty. Beth said it was a fine saddle. She said . . .

His mind filled with her. There she was, sitting in the house watching the rain streak down the windows, watching the horses in the corral, waiting for them to prick up their ears and look in the direction of the pole gate, a signal that he was coming. Beth, watching the rain and waiting. What had he ever done to deserve her? He gave himself a good talking to.

He hated himself a little. She wanted a bay horse. He said, aloud, "I never told her before she couldn't have something."

Suddenly he reined his horse around and started for the ranch, unaware that the rain had turned to sleet, that his hands were now numb with cold.

For she always wore a bright handkerchief or something around her head, like a gypsy or an Indian, and her smile always brought a lump to his throat. She came about to his shoulder. He grinned.

"I wonder what she'll say when I tell her she can have the bay?"

XI

NEWS WAS ANYTHING that happened outside the prairie. When the freighters skinned their long teams over the divide every word they said was worth repeating again. If the freighters hadn't heard anything worthwhile they invented stories to suit their listeners. What you wanted to hear was something, something to take home to your wife or your hired men. It gave you a kind of standing in their eyes, even to repeat.

"I was talking to one of the freighters came in Friday." Everyone would lean forward. "Says in Madison County looks like a tough winter. Hornet nests built up in the brush high as a man's head."

The story would travel. "Hank Morgan was talking to one of the freighters. Says it's going to be a bad winter outside. Have to get in extra hay for stock."

And again: "—cattle thin. They can't seem to locate any hay, either—hornets got nests twice as high as a man's head."

Important news seeped slowly into the prairie. Wilson was President a month before anyone heard of it. Billy Blair went straight into Salmon City to Brad Skinner's saloon where they had the mirror behind the bar as big as the one in Salt Lake City.

"Democrats!" he said. "No wonder cow prices are awful. Shove that bottle over. You can't have Democrats without something happens." Eagle-eyed, he watched the administration, expecting wars and panics, ready to hold Wilson accountable for terrible things out beyond the Pass. But before his criticism was organized the railroad news came, and his thoughts turned to coal and steam and dynamite.

And it wasn't long before they spoke wisely of throttles and firemen; youngsters who had yearned to be cowpunchers now wanted to be engineers. Their fathers said, "Well, I've got a hundred head of steers to go out on that first train." Their mothers said, "I'm going to get right on it and go somewhere."

Young surveyors, bribed by steak dinners and Indian stories, called on the ranchers. Billy said, "They're a fine bunch." They taught him to multiply on a slide rule. He told them about the hanging of Henry Plummer in 1863. Together they spoke of transits, rolling stock, three-percent grades. There wasn't a crossing built that didn't have some of the prairie for witness, not a charge of dynamite exploded that somebody didn't have to be asked to stand back. The day came to watch the trestle put across Nip and Tuck Creek. They dropped everything else and came. For Nip and Tuck Creek was big in their minds, a treacherous, evil stream that twisted and crawled through the badlands in dry weather like a sleepy rattler but swelled and roared when the storms hung high in the peaks. In other times it had taken its toll of life; they still told stories. Its high waters had stopped a doctor from getting to a woman in time . . . .

Nip and Tuck Creek was going to be beaten, roped, and hog-tied. They were going to build a trestle over it right now in high water. They couldn't help gloating a little, and all the old stories were told.

Jess and Beth had a habit of sitting at the breakfast table for a time after the boys had taken their plates to the kitchen. They sat there drinking coffee, talking over the day. Jess always told her what he planned to do that day, what he planned to have the boys do, and this telling of his plans to her always made them seem more significant. It made him feel pleasantly important when she nodded sagely from time to time. Early-morning darkness had merged into dawn that morning by the time they had their second cup—which was always a little cold and into which they never bothered to put cream or sugar. The lamp in the middle of the table glowed weakly, losing the tussle with the daylight. Tommy pattered around the table, removing cold pancakes and egg plates in which the grayish grease was already hard.

Jess was leaning forward, elbows on the table, coffee cup cupped in his hands. "We can take a pack horse and some grub and stuff, and after we see them get the trestle across we can go on up the canyon and camp overnight."

Beth put down her cup. "That'll be wonderful, Jess!" she cried. "We'll take the Dutch oven, flour, bacon . . . ." She numbered things off on her fingers. It always pleased Jess to see them still brown. "I'm glad you thought of the trip." She walked over behind his chair, stood there, smoothing his hair. "Sort of a honeymoon, Jess . . . . Your hair's so wiry." He looked out of the corner of his eye to be sure no one was near. Once Tommy had seen her smooth his hair, and later he went out to the bunkhouse. There was loud laughter in there that died away when he entered.

"What do you want to do that for?" he asked, reaching up to run his hand through his hair. Touching her hand, he took it and kissed it roughly. Sitting where he was made him feel young and ill at ease. He wanted to get to his feet and, towering over her, to kiss her mouth. He hitched around in the chair with dignity, and his voice was low and commanding. "We'll have a good time there. You put on your riding stuff and take something warm to tie on behind your saddle in case you need it. I'll go catch the ponies. I'll ride Baldy and you take Casey." He watched her draw things with a fork on the checkered cloth. Her face, for a moment, seemed to him childlike. "I thought I'd like to ride the bay, Jess. Letting him run out there's not doing him any good."

He used his logical tone, the tone he planned his days with. "Now, Beth, there's going to be a lot of racket up there, and rocks rolling down off the hill, and if you think I'm going to have that horse pile you, you're crazy. And that's that!" He smiled a little at her.

Her eyes were wide, her lips parted a little in surprise. She seemed afraid of him. Quickly he took her in his arms. She buried her head on his shoulder, her breath warm against him.

"All right," he told her. "Ride the bay. But be damned sure you be careful, or I'll take you off him."

"But if you don't want me to, Jess. If you're afraid—"

"You ride him," Jess said shortly. Tommy stood in the kitchen door, grinning. "Get in there, you!" Jess shouted at him. "Get bacon and stuff ready." He walked with dignity out the front door. In the barn he swore at the horses and threw his new saddle around.

Beth sat on the edge of the bed and pulled on her riding boots. There was a song old Joe used to sing when he was happy . . . .

"*Oh, Susanna, don't you cry for me . . .*"

She was happy and a little frightened of her husband. "Sometimes he acts like a regular devil." A little shiver ran down her spine.

When you ride a horse that's a little skittish and somebody is looking, you can't help showing off a little. Each time your horse shies you sit straight in the saddle; you spur your horse a little on the offside and ride gracefully and well.

Beth held her reins high and easy, leaning forward now and again to watch the bay's front feet as he fox-trotted along, shying often at weird figures he fancied he saw in the tangled roots of the tall sagebrush. "He's got nice action, Jess. I don't know when I ever had a horse that picked up his feet better." With her free hand she pushed back her hat, giving her a jaunty look. "You're wrong, Jess, about him being hard to handle."

Jess took his foot out of the stirrup and kicked aimlessly at the top of a tall sage. His spur jingled. "Maybe," he admitted carelessly. "But you watch him." And suddenly, "Hey, you! I saw you spur him on the off-side. You quit that or you'll take up a homestead right in the sagebrush. You don't have to ride fancy for me." He grinned. "I know you can ride."

Her eyes were innocent. "You saw no such thing. I didn't spur him. That big clump of roots there sort of hit my leg and jammed my leg a little so the spur—That clump of roots," she finished riding close to him. She touched his hand with hers and smiled. They rode in silence then, broken only by the shishing of brush against Jess's chap leg and Beth's skirt. Years later, at the first rodeos, riders like them would lead a parade, smiling down on those who did not ride.

"Look—it must be fine to ride like that. Like a part of their horse." But rodeos were unheard of in those days, and only the low, steadily rising mountains knew they rode to Nip and Tuck Creek. A rugged country, one that called for sure-footed horses, and even the most sure-footed slid across patches of slide-rock not quite hidden beneath the rust-colored blanket of dead pine needles. They had been singing when they rode into the timber, Jess's voice strong and boisterous, Beth's clear.

> "Now I know a gal down by the Border
> That I'd ride to El Paso to sight . . ."

But in the timber they were silent. The moving things were silent: the squirrel that watched them with beady eyes, sunning himself on a dead tree, then whisking away into the silvery jack pine; the clouds floating swiftly across the sun cast shadows, chilly shadows. Old trees stood proud and straight, strong old men, leaders in this silence. Shadows under pines cut sharply across the shapeless chalky rocks, white-shining where the sun bored through the trees.

"They call that big one Camper's Rock," Jess said, his voice low in the silence. "It's because of that spring that comes out underneath, and people stopped for water. Up on the sides there's names carved."

He swung carefully down off his horse and put a cautioning hand on Beth's boot. "Careful getting off. Don't let him jump and throw you into the rock."

She nodded; her smile was slight. "It's so darned quiet here. Almost scary."

They led their horses to a reddish-barked beetle-killed tree and tied them. They drank at the base of the rock, lying flat on their stomachs and pushing their hats back to keep the brims out of the cold, clear bubbling water. At last Beth steadied herself on Jess's arm and they climbed slowly up the incline around the rock. At the upper side they stopped, looking down for a moment on their horses below there. Then Jess stepped near the rock and ran his hand along the chalky surface, feeling for carvings the storms of years had almost erased.

"Here. Here's some carvings. Names. You look close and you'll see them." He scratched a match, lit a pine twig, burned it until one end was charred. With the charred end he outlined a faint impression in the rock until it stood out clearly, the initials of some camper who had been gone a long time.

W. C.—16 coyotes—'82.

"You make it out, Beth? Somebody wanted everybody to know he shot sixteen coyotes. Must have been winter. Nobody would shoot coyotes in the summer." He mused. "He was proud enough of those coyotes to want everybody to know about them."

Beth sat down, her hands clasped around her knees. "Maybe it wasn't the coyotes. Maybe it was his name he wanted everybody to remember." She paused and looked down into the gloom of the timber. "No matter who anybody is, they want people to remember."

"Yes. Guess you're right." Uneasily, with his charred twig, Jess scratched out another set of initials.

B. P.—'71.

"You see?" Beth asked seriously. "Nothing about coyotes or what he did. Just a name. That's what counts."

Jess walked silently back from the chalk rock and sat near her, cross-legged. The bay moved nervously below them, clicked a shod hoof against a pebble.

"Jess." She stirred restlessly. "If anything happened to me— how long would you remember? No," she said as he was about to speak. "Forget that we're just married. Remember that you'd get along somehow without me, because people always do."

He looked at her, his eyes worried. "You don't talk like yourself. You're teasing, playing a game."

"Darling, no." She smiled a little. "I'm just wondering." Below them the spring bubbled out, harsh and metallic against the flecked gray rocks.

"Don't wonder. Don't talk like that." He smiled. "Please."

She laughed suddenly. "You love me, don't you, Jess?"

He nodded solemnly. She held out her hand to him and he pulled her to her feet. They rode again into the heavy timber, twigs snapping.

Nip and Tuck roared down through a great clearing. The wind, no longer hampered by the pines, rushed against them, stage-whispering that winter was not far away, whipping the manes of the horses, flapping Jess's chaps. Beth leaned forward and clutched her hat to her head as they rode near the bank of the creek where everyone was watching, waiting for the first log pile to be driven.

Buggies and saddle horses. Beth and Jess tied their horses to a wheel of Cy's buggy. The blacks, tied to the opposite wheel, snorted and watched suspiciously. They laid back their ears and nipped at the strange horses; their manes were brushed, tails combed. Their harness was soaped, glistening; buckles and hames glittered, for this was an event. Jess, conscious of the fact, took off his hat, dusted it, and put it on again at the better angle. Beth pulled the bright belt in a notch and smoothed out the fringe of her riding skirt.

Amy ran to meet them. "Oh," she shouted against the wind. "I thought you'd never come! I've said to people, 'They'll be along any time,' but I thought you'd never come! I said to the man who works that machine over there, 'You just wait!' and he said, 'We can't hold up the railroad,' and I guess they can't!" She paused, breathed quickly. "You look just lovely!" She looked down her front, dissatisfied with her own clothes. "I thought I'd better wear these old things and these old shoes because I said to Cy, 'When you're going out where there's machines and dynamite and I don't know what, there's no use in wearing good things,' and he said there wasn't a bit of use." She paused to breathe. "Here's Cy. Cy, ask them where they've been this long. They don't say."

The four of them walked along to the high creek bank, nodding hellos. Billy Blair waved his hat at them; Mrs. Cooper yoo-hooed before resuming conversation with Miss Slater, the middle-aged bespectacled teacher from Salmon City.

"We didn't get started early," Beth explained. "Coming this way is hard on the horses. The steep hills." She was about to mention the chalk rock, then didn't. Already the chalk rock was a background for a conversation that somehow must always remain a secret between her and Jess.

"We started late," Jess said quickly. "We didn't think what time it was."

At a distance from them there was a blast of steam, and the driver, a hulking black machine of wheels and beams and smoke, lumbered, elephant-like, near the steep banks of the stream. A team of horses strained to move a giant-sized log beneath the hammer. Shouting from the prairie—and the pounding began.

Now the first log was driven, and the second was being set in place. They smelled the steam and the hot oil. Cy lugged out his heavy gold watch. "It'll be afternoon before they finish. They're going to put in anyway twenty-five piles."

"I expected it would take a long time," Amy said comfortably. "Bridges and that sort of thing always take a long time." She turned to Beth. "Cy laughed when I said I was going to bring a lunch. He pretends he never gets hungry. Why do some men pretend to never get hungry when other people are hungry? I say right out that when I sit around I get hungry. Don't I, Cy? Get the lunch. I would, but those blacks over there act funny today."

Beth scrambled to her feet. "Let me go with you, Cy. I'd like to stretch a little after the ride." She laughed. "I don't ride as much as I used to." She took Cy's arm and, smiling, walked with him.

Watching them go, Amy said, "Jess, what is it about Beth that makes her—belong here more than the rest of us wives?"

"Maybe it's—the clothes she wears."

Amy puckered her mouth in thought. "No, Jess. It's more than that." She smiled. "You know it's more than that, and I think you're proud. Oh, look. There's Mrs. Morgan!"

XII

THEY HAD BEGUN to tire, sitting there on the hillside beside the creek. Fragments of rock beneath them began to press annoyingly, and when they hitched themselves over there were sharper fragments. The sun was hot where the wind was shut out, and coal smoke drifted out lazily and settled down, acrid and strong.

At first they had cheered when each new pile was sunk. They shouted and told one another it was fine. After a while they wished they hadn't begun cheering. The remaining piles seemed limitless. The cheering became sober, more polite than fervent, and that was too bad, because not to cheer was disloyal. The loud blasts of steam were becoming ordinary. Now with great effort they managed to comment on the steam at all.

"Just listen to that steam!" Mrs. Cooper said to Newt, hoping to summon up a little enthusiasm. She leaned forward to show how excited she was and wondered why she felt vaguely responsible for the crowd's waning interest.

"I've been listening to it," Newt said dryly. "I thought it was you."

Mrs. Cooper grew sullen, refused to talk. She gazed with interest out over the pines. Newt, ashamed, observed that it was just like summer. "It's not in the least like summer," she told him. "I don't know why you should say such a stupid thing."

They were like that. Amy kept getting to her feet and walking around, peering down at the ground as if she expected to find some interesting thing. Cy thought of mentioning chores at home that had to be done, but he discarded the idea. To go now would be like walking out on church.

Then a last a feeble wave of excitement passed through the crowd, growing as it passed. Those sitting downstream began to get up, stooping to pick up lunch baskets, hats, gloves. The pile driver had stopped working. No hissing steam now, only the black smoke and heat waves playing around the black boiler.

Jess turned to Cy. "What's up?"

Cy watched the commotion downstream. "I don't know. Wait—I'll ask." Cy went downstream, stumbling over the sagebrush, hurrying. When he came back, "They can't go on driving for a while," he reported. "It's the bank of the stream on this side—they've got to blast out that point where it runs into the creek. They're laying dynamite. We've got to move. They say rocks are going to fly." He paused. "We'd better look after the horses, Jess. They'll break loose."

Jess fumbled for his gloves. "Beth!" He jumped to his feet, his eyes searching the hillside. "Beth . . . . Where is she? We got—to talking, and she's gone. Beth!" People turned to look at him.

"She was right here," Amy said. "She was sitting here just a minute ago."

"She must have heard us say dynamite and moved," Cy said.

Now Jess was running to the horses. He yelled over this shoulder at those he passed. "Have you seen Beth? My wife, have you seen her?" Nothing could happen to her. Nothing could happen.

But he ran faster.

And then he saw her moving around the bay horse, just the top of her black hat in the scramble of horses and buggies. "Beth!" he was hoarse, out of breath. "Get away from the horses!" She gave no sign of hearing him. She led the bay out into the open. Before he could call again she had moved

116

around to the bay's side, tightening up the cinch, and then she swung up and saw him.

"Jess," she called, "I thought I'd better get this outlaw in the open or he'll pull the wheel off Cy's buggy. Better be on top of him when he's nervous."

"Get off, Beth! Get off!" He stumbled toward her, out of breath, trying to smile a little. He was cold now with fear. "Let me take him." He paused. "Beth!"

From down below in the scrub pine came the report of the explosion. It burst out and shot across the creek, crashed against the side of the canyon and back, roaring.

The bay moved. Even down in the pine they heard the bay's hoofs pounding, heard his bellowing. They ran to see. You didn't miss watching a horse buck. Young Easterners come out to work on the road froze there, watching the girl go with the horse, her hat hanging at her back by the thong under her chin. They whistled with admiration, and one of them cheered.

But the prairie didn't cheer, because the prairie knew what she was doing. She was riding clean and easy, but she wasn't showing off. They knew, for they saw her face.

"All white," Mrs. Cooper said. "I saw a dead face like that."

It's the snap of the head that counts. They said you expected to see her head fly off. And her eyes, and the color drained, choked from her face. When the bay hit the ground with one of those bone-shattering poundings she stiffened, sick-looking.

And then she tried to smile. "That's what was awful," Cy said. "Trying to grin."

It seems like hours to a rider, up there on the hurricane deck. But the watchers knew it was only a few seconds before the bay started bucking toward the creek.

It happened too quick for Jess to think. There was the moment he stood there, knowing now why he'd run, foreseeing this. He was standing still when he heard his name in a hoarse whisper. "Jess . . ." Saw her try to smile at him, heard her teeth click as the bay bucked. Jess knew. A bucking horse tries to jam your backbone together.

But he moved when the bay started for the high creek bank. Treacherous. Gravel that caved in when you went near it. He saw the ugly black of the stream now, swirling giddily, flowing in under the hollow banks with a sucking sound.

The bay went for the bank as straight as an arrow, and Jess saw the terror in her face. That was his wife; that was his wife with her face like that, and her lips said, "Jess . . ."

He was on top of Baldy, riding wildly through the sage, unaware that his horse stumbled. If he could only get there. O God, if he could only get there before the bay went in the creek.

They heard the crunching sound of the gravel bank as it sloughed off slowly beneath the bucking horse. The horse and the ground went down lower and lower before their eyes, and there wasn't a word spoken, a movement made. Jess was transfixed in the saddle, hearing the sucking sounds underneath the bank, for he couldn't make it now.

The bay was panic-stricken. It turned and faced solid ground, lunging and pawing, rolling its eyes, Beth trying to spur it to solid footing, fighting it to safety. For every inch the bay made it seemed to slip more toward the surging water that bit in at the edges of the gravel, crumbled it and swirled it on downstream. The bay wheezed, a sound like a dry death rattle, deep, wrenched from the heart.

"Quit him!" Jess cried. "Quit him! Jump for the water. I'll—"

She couldn't have heard, bent close to the bay's head, talking to the bay. Above the rush of the water they heard a word or two, sharp, clipped, and quiet.

And somehow the bay got a foothold in that crumbling mass of gravel. Somehow he stood there, trembling, on land again. Nobody but Beth Bentley could have done it, they said. It was as if what she said did it, what she said to the bay. They turned to each other and said nobody else could have done it, got the bay on land. Nobody else.

It was silent as she rode back to Cy's buggy, her hair tangled, her face tired, drawn. Jess followed, his jaw set, his eyes slits. He sat straight and stiff in the saddle, his hands firm on the reins, the skin stretched white across his knuckles. They both reached the buggy. Beth reined in the bay, turned and smiled a tired, uncertain, frightened little smile.

"Get off that horse," Jess said softly. His lips scarcely moved. She was startled, then defiant, as a tired person is.

"He's all right, Jess. He's too tired and scared—"

"Get off." His words stung. For a second she looked at him, stared, unbelieving. Then slowly, painfully, she swung down and stood beside the bay, avoiding Jess's eyes, patting the bay's shoulder. But she saw him uncinching his saddle. Her hand shook.

He spoke from around the saddle he was slipping off his mount's back. "Unsaddle your horse."

She had to guide her hands to loosen the latigo and pull off the saddle. The effort left her a little sick.

"Now saddle my horse and get on." From Baldy's back she watched Jess slap his saddle on the bay and grab up the halter rope of the pack horse. "Come on." There was finality in his words. An end of a scene. But she knew this wasn't the end. She dreaded the end and feared to face it.

They rode upstream toward the flat country that stretched wide and gray, rising gently to the timbered foothills of the upper prairie.

It was a matter, she told herself, of shutting things from your mind. She took interest in the country, speculated on the distance it was to the foothills. "Must be three miles—no, four." She listened with absorption to the squeak of her saddle. "Needs oiling." Then, "Wonder if Jess remembered to get oil." There was another sound she had never noticed. The clink-clink the chains on the bridle made when the horse's moving body swung them together. "Sounds almost like the tugs on a chain harness, a smaller sound."

In a moment he would speak. She sniffed the sagebrush. In a moment he would speak.

It could have been hours before they reached the spot where Jess said, "We might as well camp here." As if he didn't care where they camped. "We might as well camp here."

We might as well camp here . . . .

"All right, Jess." Her voice broke. Her throat was dry. If he would smile or talk . . . The sun sank down. She was conscious of his eyes watching her. Much as she wanted to, she couldn't bring herself to face him. "Smile," she thought.

Dusk closed down on the edge of the timber, and the sounds of day were muffled, now were evening sounds. The evening star blinked down faintly, silvery-cold. From the timber came the snapping of a twig, the clink of hobble chains as the horses moved, feeding. A nighthawk zoomed. Something about the dusk smells fresh, as if the night were the beginning of life instead of day.

Two figures moved through the sagebrush, stooping frequently. There were cracking sounds as they tore off dead pieces of brush and brought it to an open space, where they piled it for a fire. Silently they sat down cross-legged.

She thought, "This is the honeymoon. This is what we talked about this morning. This is what I've waited for, sitting near the timber, smelling the sagebrush with him." But this silence . . . She had planned gay talk that morning in the dull lamplight, not this silence, and Jess—was he angry? It frightened her.

"We're like a couple of Indians," she murmured. "Sitting like this." It was a question.

He didn't answer. She couldn't see his face in the dusk.

"It's getting pretty cold." She spoke haltingly, and he leaned forward.

"We'll light the fire."

"Not unless you want to, Jess." She wanted to touch him.

"You said you were cold."

"Give me a match too." She held her hand toward him. "Where shall I light it?" He showed her. She picked up twigs from around the heap of brush and crushed them in her hand. "These—will help."

Two matches flared in the half-darkness and moved to the heap of tangled brush.

"Jess"—her voice was small—"mine went out. It just started to burn and then went out." He fumbled in his pockets. "No. Don't bother. Your side is burning. It'll be all right now."

The fire burned. Beth drew up her hand and smelled her palm, fragrant with the sagebrush sap. She pulled a piece of brush from the pile and tossed it at him. He didn't speak. Maybe he didn't notice.

Please, God, I hope he didn't notice.

His silence left her alone, frightened. "Please," she thought. "Speak to me."

Sagebrush crackles and sputters. The smoke curls heavy, redolent of other campfires, mountains at dusk, wild horses grazing peacefully above the timber line. It burns harshly brilliant as the flames leap up, casting objects in bold outline. Orange and black. Shadows dart across the ground, fantastic figures hovering in the background. Then the fire sinks back into ashes; shadows fade; little wisps of smoke die out one by one. The fire is gone, and something more. Something built has crumbled . . . .

You don't sit long staring into dead ashes that stir restless in the night breeze.

Jess cleared his throat, a dry sound. She searched his voice for some sign that they were—like they were. He said, "Might as well turn in, Beth. It's getting chilly." He stood and stretched, a tall shadow.

She stood. "I'll help unroll the bedding." She couldn't let him leave her.

They had a hard time with the knots tied in the rope around the bedroll. Their hands fumbled. Then the smooth rustle of canvas, the smell of smooth woolly blankets.

"Got to get some pine boughs for a mattress."

"Let me get them," she pleaded. "Let me . . . ."

"I'll—get them." Suddenly he pulled her close, so close that his breath was hot against her throat. "Beth. When you were on that horse, Beth. Beth." He swallowed. "I couldn't ever—get along without you."

She looked up, almost sick with happiness. Her fingers found his face and touched it. "Oh, Jess. You'll never have to. Oh, Jess, my darling."

XIII

IT WAS ONE of those senseless jokes people have. When you try to explain it sounds foolish. Jess wouldn't have wanted anyone to know that when he woke up in the morning he sometimes called gently, "Beth—it's time for school."

It was dark at six in the morning, but Jess knew when he heard the bunkhouse door slam and the latch clink that it was morning instead of night. Slim going out to wrangle, whistling softly. The stars were whitish; the air was night air, damp and cold, outdoor-smelling; even the tick of the alarm clock was a night sound. It was strange, Jess thought. He could never remember hearing an alarm clock in the daylight.

Yes. It could have been night, except for the door slamming.

It seemed to him that since he got married the mornings were colder and darker and the bed warmer. He yawned and grinned. Well, of course the bed was warmer, with a wife in it.

"Beth," he said softly, "it's time for school!"

A small stifled voice from beneath the covers. "I guess I'll play hooky this morning, Jess."

Then he moved about the room, his boots stiff with cold. Probably going to storm. He groped about in the darkness for pants, shirt, hat. If she was going to sleep she wouldn't want the lamp lit. He wished she were moving about the room with him. He was a little lonesome.

The clouds hung low around the peaks in the distance; the wind swept behind him, wintry this morning, and the snow smell was sharp in his nostrils. He welcomed winter, somehow. A new season, new tasks to look forward to, new things to think, and long evenings alone with Beth, sitting in the warm living room with Beth, deep in the kind of comfort he felt when she was near.

And trapping for a few weeks, too, and the suspense of waiting to see if your traps were full. Then feeding would begin. It would be pleasant to stand up there on a haystack and look down at the cattle, your own cattle crowding around, tossing their heads, watching you throw hay down on the rack . . . . And the ride home across the rippled, drifted snow—the brown weeds sticking up through, trembling in the icy wind.

He wished Beth were along so he could explain about winter and the new things. There she was, in that warm bed, sleeping these two hours. "Women," he thought indulgently. He turned up the collar of his Mackinaw, scratchy against the back of his neck. A winter thing, the scratchy feeling of a Mackinaw. "That was some answer she gave me this morning."

She had said, "I guess I'll play hooky." It was funny how she could think up a good answer when she had just waked up . . . . He could only have mumbled or grunted. You had to think to make a good answer! You had to . . .

Suddenly he jerked his horse up and the wind rushed on past him. "Wait a minute," he thought, and then he knew she had been awake all the time. He turned his horse and started back to the ranch at a fast walk. Her voice had been strange. It hadn't sounded like her. And it was the voice of someone awake, awake for a long time.

He spurred his horse to a trot. He would have run, but that would have been a bad sign, admitting he knew something was wrong. The ranch lay just below him, the house, and the smoke coming out of the chimney, settling to the ground. Storm sign. He thought about it desperately.

When he walked into the house he felt a little foolish. Felt out of place walking through the kitchen where Tommy was making piecrust and had flour on his hands. Not a time for you to be in the house, in the middle of the morning. What would he tell Beth if she happened to be asleep and he woke her? What would she say? He tiptoed awkwardly.

But she wasn't asleep. Hadn't been.

He found her, small in her white nightgown, supporting her weight on the bureau with both hands, bent forward. Her hair hung in long black braids down her back. Never had he seen her hair so black, her face so white.

She turned her head with difficulty at the sound he made and saw him. For an instant there was something like terror in her face, a shadow that passed across it. Then a kind of timid thankful smile and: "Jess."

For a moment he stared at her. "Beth." He was beside her, almost afraid to touch her, as if his hands would bruise her. "What's wrong?"

She took a careful step nearer the bureau and stood there. "Nothing, Jess. Nothing really. Just a sort of—hurt."

"Where?" He tried to keep his voice down.

"I can't tell—exactly." She hardly moved her lips. "Ever since—that horse bucked."

"Ever since—" He remembered her face that day.

"It'll go away. It goes away."

"It doesn't last—" There was no pit to his stomach. "You mean you've had it before? And you didn't tell?"

"It wasn't—I didn't want—to worry you. It was my fault."

He spoke carefully, conscious of his moving lips, controlling them. "You didn't want to worry me." He lifted her back to the bed and carefully covered her. "Now . . . "

"Jess"—her voice was sharp—"where are you going?"

He managed a grin. "We're going in town, young lady. We'll go see the doc."

Doc Morse had the two drafty half-finished rooms in the rear of the Emporium. The back door was his front door. He slept in the small room; his iron cot and the two chairs for waiting patients just about fitted in there.

The large room was his office. Well, anyway, it was where he kept his books. Months went by when he didn't know where his books were. Didn't make any difference.

"What's the use keeping books?" he would growl. "If people have money they'll pay, and if they haven't they can't, so what's the use keeping books?"

Sometimes he called the large room his operating room. Well, it was. It hadn't been a week since Hayes Williams, sawing firewood for Ma Perkins, had backed into a buzz saw. Not bad, but there were splinters, and stitches to be taken. Hayes's pride had been hurt more than his . . .

Anyway, if that wasn't an operation, what was? Just as much as babies delivered on kitchen tables and legs set in a wagon box.

In lofty moments he spoke of the large room as his laboratory.

"Trouble with most country doctors, they lose sight of research."

Not Doc. He had some white rats sent in. Cute little devils with pink eyes and a way about them. You could do all sorts of things with them. They learned to sit up and beg and multiplied like all get out. One of these days he was going to do some experiments. In the meantime he was so doggoned busy he couldn't even think, it seemed. There were those newspapers in the corner, that pile. He would get at them.

He always expected to get around to cleaning the glass on his framed diploma that hung over the cast-iron sink. It did beat all how the dust accumulated, and then the steam, when he was sterilizing instruments. Well, give a man time, can't you?

The diploma said Charles Lincoln Morse, flanked by Latin script. He knew what it meant too. It meant that on such and such a day of our Lord he was a full-fledged medic, 1881. Those were the days, just before graduation. Big school.

"Best . . ."

Sometimes he got a little sad looking at the diploma.

"Me. Charles Lincoln Morse. Gosh. I remember the fellows. Meredith . . .

"Creepy Hogan, the time he threw the cadaver's leg . . . . J. P. Brown, the stuck-up one.

"Gosh. Tempus fugit . . . ."

He was almost voted the man most likely to succeed. Almost. Just missed by a few votes.

"Look at me now," he often thought, looking around at the disorder, the dingy old highboy where his books were, and the doors that wouldn't shut. "That damned steam warps them." The operating table covered with black leather, the wood of oak, the dust, the drying loaf of bread near the sink.

"I've got to get rid of some stuff!" And, "Damn those mice! Look at me now! What have I got?" If only he'd got those few extra votes!

Nobody minded that Doc drank occasionally. All doctors drank—what they went through. In a little room, alone with a pregnant woman in a little room, seeing her bulging eyes, hearing the shrieks. Knowing the ugly, hurt sound a grown man makes when you cut him and, working on, knowing you've got to do it. Knowing the jerk a man makes when he dies. A doctor's got to drink. The prairie knew a doctor had to drink.

When Doc had too much to drink he liked to tell that there was a story in him, a real story. He never told it because he lost interest in it before he started. And what, my fine friends, had become of the young fellow who was voted the most likely to succeed? *Nobody knew.* His name was never in the *Medical Journal,* but Doc's was. Doc had written a piece about country doctoring. The journal took it and asked for more. Well, he'd write another piece. Maybe today. Give a man *time,* can't you?

There would be more time if it weren't for those damned dishes that pile up in a man's sink. *Tempus fugit!*

He had a towel tied around his middle and had just started on the forks, the worst part first; he hated the forks. Egg got in the tines. And then a buggy drove up and stopped outside the window. He threw the fork down with a clatter into the sink. Well, he'd tried to do the damned dishes.

It was the Bentleys. Nice young couple. Young woman was a picture.

"You make yourself comfortable in here," he told Jess. "There's magazines under the cot there. And get that worried look off your face. Whatever it is, it's going to be fine. No, you can't come in. That's my sanctus sanctorum." He grinned a toothy grin. "I do magic in there. Don't want anybody onto my tricks."

"Thanks, Doc." Jess, who had been tense, relaxed a little. A doctor gave a man confidence.

"And you, young woman," Doc said severely, "come in my office. Here"—he took her arm firmly—"this way."

"I'm really all right now." The long drive had brought color back to her cheeks. Her hair was disheveled from the wind, and she could smile. "It was just a little pain, and it's gone." She smiled back over her shoulder at Jess, a humoring little smile, humoring him and the doctor.

Inside the big bare-looking room Doc said, "Mmm. You say the pain comes and goes?"

"Yes." She flushed a little. "It's like—a stomach-ache."

"And your husband said it was from a bucking horse." He spoke casually. "I like your spirit, young woman." He pulled a chair around in front of his desk and began to clear a space on the desk top, shoving books back, crumpling papers, and watching them intently, dropping them into the big wastebasket. His eyes came around to hers. "Had it ever since, you say?"

"Off and on," she said shyly.

"Well, now, I'll have to make an examination." He smiled. He was good at it. "We'll just see what's wrong."

It took about twenty minutes.

She was frightened when he went to a shelf of books, studied the lettering on them, and at last took one from the shelf. As he thumbed it through she tried to control the trembling in her arms and felt her lips grow dry as she waited, watching him turn the pages.

At last he turned to her. "No harm in just being sure," he said brusquely. "Now." He walked back to the desk, sat down, hitched his chair closer, and cleared this throat. "Now, Mrs. Bentley, it's just a sort of strain." He chuckled. "Women weren't meant to be cowboys, you know. It's easy to—get

things out of arrangement a bit. But you're going to be fine."
He hurried on: "You'll have to rest up for a bit. Keep off
horses for a while." His grin was like cartoons of T. R. "I'm
going to give you a prescription to take if it hurts again, just
so you can rest better. No medicine, you know, will do the
trick like old Mother Nature and a lot of rest. There!"

There was finality in his manner, an air of a problem
examined, found simple, and solved with ease. His
brusqueness returned as he walked with her to the door. "And
by the way," he added casually, "when you go out there, ask
Jess to step in here a minute."

She paused, her hand on the doorknob. Just an instant she
hesitated and then turned slowly to him. "Doctor, there's
something else."

"Something else?" He registered surprise.

"Yes. Something else about—me. Something you wouldn't
tell me, only my husband."

He was gruff. "Now! If there was anything else, don't you
think I'd tell you?"

Her eyes were level on him. "There are some things—it'd
be hard to tell a woman."

"Well, now!" he registered disappointment at her distrust
in him.

"Doctor"—she lowered her voice—"I can't go until you
tell me."

He could have put her off. He didn't have to tell her. But
he looked at her eyes.

"Well . . ." He groped for the right words, phrases. "Come
over here and sit down," he said suddenly. She sat across the
desk, straight, her chin up, watching him. He coughed and
moved the books again, straightened papers. "Well. Hmmm.
You know," he began, "a doctor isn't God. Easy for a doctor
to make mistakes, like another man. Sometimes the things
we say turn out to be wrong. That can happen."

She seemed to dismiss this preface. "You don't have to—do that, Doctor—make things pleasant." But her hands were clenched in her muff, her fingers cold and stiff.

"Mrs. Bentley," he faltered, his eyes tired now, almost an old man's eyes. "Mrs. Bentley, I don't think you should ever—bear children."

She closed her eyes, and her lashes hid the faint purple shadows beneath them. Doc Morse looked away and looked back again, to watch the slight convulsive movement of her mouth. A woman's mouth should never make such an uncontrolled, unrehearsed movement. Sometimes he wished he'd never been a doctor. It seemed an eternity that she sat there, her eyes closed. In the corner of the room the little white rats ran across the bottom of their cage, scurrying, climbing up the screen on the front. Doc's voice was gentle. "I don't say you *couldn't* have a baby. Indeed you could. But cases like this—sometimes you take a chance. Too big a chance."

She started to rise, one hand gripping the arm of the chair, and the knuckles were white across the bone. "Doctor"—her voice was thin—"Doctor, please—don't say anything to my husband about—this. Tell him—what you told me first."

Doc frowned. "Mrs. Bentley, don't you see that it's—his responsibility? He'd understand. He'd want—"

"It's not his responsibility!" She let her voice rise. A kind of panic seized her. "It's mine! I was foolish. I did a foolish thing." Almost instantly she composed herself. "No. I'll tell him." She tucked a lock of hair under her hat, straightened her shoulders, and lifted her chin. "I'll tell him." She set her face in a smile and moved to the door.

Doc heard them in the waiting room, the squeak of the cot as Jess leaped to his feet with a loud question. Doc heard her low voice for a moment and then Jess's voice, softer, quieter. The outside door clicked behind them . . . .

Doc stood beside his desk and watched them through the window, watched Jess help her into the buggy, get in beside her and tuck the blanket around her, his face close to hers, murmuring a word before he sat straight, reins in his hands.

Doc watched Beth, smiling at her husband. The buggy moved. But as it started she turned and looked back at Doc. She raised her gloved hand to him. It was a kind of salute, a salute to the secret between the two of them. And only the two of them.

XIV

IN THE EARLY winter the cattle crowd around the haystacks, tired of the tough, frosted slough grass that grows in among the naked, creaking willows. They crowd around until some wise old cow throws her weight against the pole fence. There is a creaking, a crack, a splintering of wood. They crowd through the break, bawling, trampling good hay, eating, tossing their heads, wasting, whittling down the stack until it resembles a top-heavy mushroom that sometimes falls and suffocates animals feeding beneath it. Other cattle crowd in and eat. Hay is hay . . . .

The ranchers rode early and late in November, anxiously watching the fences around the stacks, repairing those that needed it with a hammer and sack of nails they carried tied to their saddles.

Jess rode up in the darkness just as he heard the cracking and splintering of a fence. He spurred his horse forward at a fast trot, shouting.

"Sooooo-ah! Git, you devils!"

A second of silence after his yell, and then cattle stampeded out of the stackyard, jostling, breathing hard, their hoofs ticking the fence as they jumped out and ran into the cover of darkness, curious. He heard them a short distance away, standing there, their hard hoofs moving restlessly in the crusted snow.

"They sure know they were doing wrong, the way they got away from that yard. You'd think the boys weren't feeding them enough." He swung off his horse. "It's that old cow with one horn. She's the ringleader," he mumbled to himself. He began to repair the damage, fumbling in the darkness for jacks and poles. His cattle . . .

Next year there would be more, just as he had planned. Within the week he would meet Anderson in Salmon City and make a deal . . . .

His hands worked mechanically, dragging a pole into place, twisting wire around a shattered one, hammering, pounding, his thoughts on the deal, and Anderson in Salmon City.

"You've got to expand your business." They all said it now. It bit them like a bug. Expand. Now's the time. It was a funny thing. When he was with Newt or Cy or talked with the Fishers it seemed a good idea to buy more cattle, look to the future. Something within, some herd instinct, drove him on.

"Since the railroad's coming." Sentences began and ended with it. The railroad, symbol of the future, the pot of gold at the end of the rainbow.

Yes. It seemed a good idea when he was with them, but now, alone, it depressed him to think of the railroad, and the moment he had stood on the back porch alone at the shivaree didn't seem as foolish, as unreal, as it usually did.

He scarcely realized that his hands were numb with cold when at last he had the fence fixed to suit him.

The moon had not yet risen, but the stars shed enough light for him to see the clouds flying like fluted spears across the sky to the west, driven by a swift high wind he could hear but not feel. He rode home along the high bench above the field, swaying from side to side as his horse wound its way through the wall sage, smelling the sharp, stinging air.

He saw a yellowish light, flickering, lonesome, out across the valley. It moved when he watched it closely. A lantern. That was Billy Blair's place, and Billy was going out to milk. He reined in his horse to watch the moving light. No hurry. Beth didn't expect him until late. It helped his strange, thoughtful mood to watch the moving lantern.

There were thousands of head of cattle on the prairie, but only Billy kept milk cows. Everyone else used canned milk. Jess couldn't milk. Even if a man could milk, he didn't admit it. Why, Jess wondered, should a man be ashamed of milking? Billy could milk with no shame because he was old. Old men can do anything.

Billy had two cows, both Herefords, white-faced cattle, range cattle. Once they were little bum calves, both born on the same sleeting day in March, in the same clump of creaking willows along the ice-choked creek. They were little and cold and wet. Poor little devils, humped up there beside their mothers who lay struggling on their sides, sick and crippled from giving birth, dying.

Billy named the calves right away. One of them he called Gladys after a girl in a dance hall, years before. The other he called Pansy, because it was a pretty name. Then Billy put them across his saddle and took them home. They lived through those first uncertain days because Billy put a little whisky in their milk.

Now Gladys was tall and bony and long-legged. There was something mournful about her. She gave a quart of milk which Billy said was damned rich.

Pansy was low and heavy on her feet, and while Billy milked she turned her head to watch him lovingly. Her mother love was great and possessive. Each year she adopted Gladys' calf, which was all right with Gladys.

"Gladys ought never be a mother," Billy said each year she became one. "She's so high the calf can't reach up good to eat."

There wasn't much sense in Billy's having two cows, but he couldn't turn them out with the beef to rustle for themselves. "If I did they'd have a lot of trouble with the range cows. They was raised ladies." Even the milk was a problem. Billy gave it to anyone who would come for it; otherwise it soured and filled all the pans in the cabin a man needed to cook with. Visitors complained that the cabin smelled of it.

Then, without warning, Billy got a cream separator, a blue one near the back of the catalogue. It lent as much dignity to the cabin as the sewing machine had, and, unlike the sewing machine, a man could work it without feeling foolish. "I got it," Billy explained, "because a man that lives in a country where's a railroad ought to have one and not be old-fashioned."

It was funny about Billy's cows. Jess, riding along again, laughed to himself. Everybody laughed at Billy's cows. Gladys and Pansy and the cream separator . . .

A thought struck Jess so hard that he spurred his horse forward with an involuntary movement of his leg. Jess knew that he laughed at Billy, not because he was amused, but because everybody else laughed. Think of it—Billy was a young man once, a young man riding a horse along a bench above a field, riding and making plans that couldn't fail. Plans for a big beef herd and wild rolling acres. Even the shadowy pot of gold. The young Billy must have laughed at some old prospector who followed his dreams of gold nuggets into Montana's hills, living on jerked venison and sour dough, with nothing for his dreams but a rusty gold pan.

And now Billy's life was a few head of cattle, a log cabin perched on the bank of a little creek, a smooth-forked saddle left from the old days, and two old milk cows named Gladys and Pansy.

Jess saw himself at seventy, caring for something—maybe an old horse—knowing people laughed and grinned. Old Jess Bentley. Old Jess.

"Let them laugh." He growled, and his horse pricked up its ears. "I've got this country. I'm a part of it. If I want to have two old cows I'll have them."

It disturbed him to realize how swiftly his mind had sped over the years. Maybe the ones who laughed at Billy were the same ones who would laugh at Jess.

They would laugh at Beth as they laughed now at Mrs. Cooper when she knelt, pulling at her persistent weeds in her garden. Why was it a funny thing for a woman to keep flowers? They laughed when the horses ate the nasturtiums and when the sun withered them. They told funny stories. In the fall they said Mrs. Cooper covered the flowers with good bed blankets so the early frost wouldn't get them. Mrs. Cooper always prayed for a late frost as she prayed for the life everlasting. When the flowers froze something went out of Mrs. Cooper. Jess would never laugh at her again.

For in years to come they would laugh at Beth. Maybe they laughed even now because of the way she treated her saddle, the way she soaped and polished it, showing it to people. Maybe they said things about the red piece she wore around her head . . . .

He was planning again, his sure, deliberate plans. "I'm going to see that she has so much that no one can laugh. She's going to have everything. Those cattle . . ." he mused. His horse trudged along, scattering the dustlike snow before it. "Those cattle are going to make money when the railroad comes. My land is going to make money." It was working out, was reduced to simple terms. "She's going to have books to read, places to go, and hats, ten of them, with ostrich feathers."

He wasn't, he argued, the only one who was changing. Look at Billy with a blue cream separator. Look at Newt Cooper, who didn't even use to know where his land ended. "Out there someplace." But now Newt knew where it ended—and began. He had had surveyors come, sharp men who handed a man cold figures he could get his teeth into. Squatters would come in and buy the worthless land, so a man had to know what was his to sell, how to make money.

The last of the long clouds swept away into the west when Jess got off his horse to open old man Ames's gate. He was calm. New things were happening; big things were coming, but the prairie would be the same. The mountains would never change, Billy would be the same comical old fellow. Newt would still sit by the barn, whittling, telling tall stories.

He smiled a little, remembering himself standing there three years before on a cliff, happy because the prairie was a vast, endless, timeless, isolated thing. He was pleased that his hands were young, progressive hands. Not at all like old man Ames's hands, calloused, knotted, stiff with rheumatism. For fifty years old man Ames had sweat in the heat when the springs on the flat were dried mud, cracking in patterns in the sun. Old man Ames's face was like that.

XV

THROUGHOUT THE LONG fall Jess saw nothing unusual in his decision to buy the five hundred head of cattle from

Anderson. It was a business deal, nothing more, nothing to get excited about. He was glad to tell the details but told them casually. Practically anybody, he thought, might have been doing what he was doing.

"Yes. Anderson wants forty dollars. Good white-faced stuff." And then, saddling a horse, harnessing a team, he would change the subject, talk of the possibility of an early winter or, "Fellow came by here saw a wolf prowling around the foothills below Black Canyon."

But one evening he sat with Beth in the front room, Beth in the rocker, the lamp on the table beside her, darning his socks. He liked the quiet peace of a sock-darning evening. She darned well and took infinite pains, happiest when the hole was almost irreparable. The mended part was always woven carefully, and loose threads were always clipped closely. When she had finished a difficult piece of darning she would hand the sock to him silently for inspection, smiling gently, very gently, with only a little triumph in it.

It was fine darning, he knew. "Damned decent," he would think. No doubt about it. He had once taken off his boot to show Cy the darned place in a sock, and Cy inspected the darn closely and said, "My wife can't do that. Amy's not much of a darner."

Jess was generous. "Well, there's other things beside darning, Cy." But at the moment there wasn't, not for him.

When she darned the light was pleasant on her face, making soft high lights he liked so much.

"She just sits there, quiet. And when she looks up—"

He would look at her and marvel. There never was anyone so gentle, so fine. Men fought with their wives. There was unpleasantness, misunderstandings, separations. He had heard ugly things, for the men in the bunkhouse had this to say and that. Homes broken up, misery. He had heard these things and, watching Beth, he felt they must not be true.

They had never quarreled, really. And she had never raised her voice to him. No, not once.

The night she darned, and they sat a long time, and he listened to the wind whip along the side of the house, and to Tommy in his room off the kitchen moving around, getting ready for bed.

"When she looks up she looks—comfortable." Sometimes she would pause, needle in her hand, smile, and then go back to work. He watched the smooth movement of her arm as she darned, an odd tightness in his throat. He could not believe his good fortune.

She said at last, "Jess, you're a great one." She raised her eyes and looked steadily at him, a smile playing about her mouth.

He looked at her and stretched, comfortable. "A great one? Why?" He rolled a cigarette, careful not to get crumbs on the rug. Only recently she had spoken about tobacco on the rug.

Leaning over the side of her chair, she put a rolled-up sock in the light wicker basket piled high now with socks. "I don't see how you can be going to take a big chance, buy five hundred head of cattle—gamble, you might say—and not be a little excited. You act like it was nothing."

"That's not much. Everybody buys cattle sometime."

"But five hundred head! You could go broke, you know." She was not smiling. "Think if you go broke. We'd have to give up the place. You'd have to work for somebody; you'd have to break horses. We'd be very poor, and people would say I was wonderful the way I stood by you, the way you gambled."

"That's crazy," he said uneasily, and that started him thinking.

From then on he thought of buying the cattle as the Big Deal. He grew silent. He talked little at breakfast. Slim and the other men sensed something.

"The boss is worried about the deal." Low tones.

"Hear about the boss going to buy them cattle?"

A great many people began to think about the deal, to weigh it, discuss it.

Jess rode alone often. He wrinkled his brow. Beth said, "You look tired. Let me make you a cup of coffee." She was proud of him. "If there's anything I can do—"

"I'm not tired." He would sigh and accept the coffee, looking out over the cup with a thoughtful, worried expression. He got a pad of paper and several pencils and spent time in the evenings making figures, his hair in his eyes. Beth scanned these figures and put the papers away where they'd be handy when he wanted them. The 500s were clear, bold.

On the first of December he dressed and shaved carefully. From the window he watched Slim and Pete ride away from the ranch to fix a broken panel of fence. He would be riding with them, except for the Big Deal. The Salmon City *Recorder* would say:

Jess Bentley from the upper prairie was in town yesterday transacting business. It is said he bought five hundred head of cows from Anderson. Good luck, Bentley!

The *Recorder* was always snooping around a man's business. So it was better to arrive in town in the buggy instead of horseback.

Salmon City was a friendly group of squat log cabins, frame Victorian houses, and shapeless rough pine store buildings huddled against the base of a rocky, sharply sloping mountain. The great boulders and outcroppings that clung there always seemed about to roll down and bury the town. A landslide was always expected.

Salmon City moved, but with the slow, deliberate movements of a sleepwalker. On quiet summer days when people left their front doors open, spicy odors meant that a lady was baking cinnamon rolls. She would have callers later on that afternoon.

"Why, baking! Cinnamon rolls! Well, I will say they do look good. Had no idea—well, yes, I will. Just that little one there . . . ."

"Little coffee?"

"Well, I don't know . . ."

The area around the two general stores smelled of bolts of gingham. Coal smoke hung around the blacksmith shop, and the smell of horses. Here small boys came and learned to swear and to admire the muscles of old Matthewson, who worked comfortably in shirt sleeves.

Salmon City dozed, contented. Even in the winter when the wind blew down the mountain, shining, drifting snow against the rickety buildings, even then Salmon City pulled her blankets closer and slept.

Ma Perkins sat, as she had for thirty years, in her Victorian parlor, elegant with reddish-brown furniture and potted ferns, talking with ladies, prim in calling clothes in the decent shades of brown and gray. Cooking, sewing, and health were discussed, recent deaths described in detail from the first noticeable signs of illness on through to the deathbed scene, right up to the moment when the coffin was lowered slowly into the ground.

Now the ladies, following Beth's example, had taken up reading. Books were discussed. Each of the group was to read a different book each month and give a report. In this way the meat of a great many books could be enjoyed by all.

No one could forget the afternoon, right in that parlor, that Beth had admitted reading in bed.

"In bed!" Mrs. Cooper had gasped. Her gasp was echoed by others. There was something Roman about reading in bed.

"It's much nicer in winter," Beth told them, "than trying to sit by the fire. The light is bad there, and if I sit by the lamp I freeze."

"I think that's fine," Amy said. "I'm going to try it. I read a lot."

"You read novels," Mrs. Cooper said, "and not good wholesome novels about animals. You read love novels."

"I'd think" Amy murmured pleasantly, "that love novels would be especially nice in bed."

"Amy! If Cy should hear—"

"He reads them too."

"I don't think—" Mrs. Cooper faltered.

"Some love stories are good," Beth said. "*Romeo and Juliet.*"

"Well," Mrs. Cooper said, recovering, "I feel that love in some of its aspects—"

"I'll put the coffee on," Ma Perkins said, getting up heavily. "My rheumatism."

Ma Perkins brought in coffee in her best cups, and Scotch shortbread. Pa Perkins had always liked shortbread. "Think," Ma told the ladies, "that one day Pa was sitting there, rocking like you are." She paused. "Just as chipper. He was a chipper one. And the next day"—here Ma passed her hand over her eyes, recalling—"and the next day— gone." There was an uncomfortable little silence. "Well," Ma said, "here today, gone tomorrow. I admired Mr. Perkins a great, great deal."

"He didn't suffer at the—last?"

"No, he did not. He just—went."

Mrs. Cooper said, "You remember old Mr. Kamer. He suffered dreadfully. Just lay there."

"It was his teeth. Poisoned him."

They agreed he had terrible teeth. It was an exciting afternoon.

Across the street from Ma Perkins', Miss Slater held forth grimly before grades one to eight, a nervous, gray little woman in her late forties. She had come to the country years ago for her health and still had what she referred to as "spells." They were a kind of fainting fit. When Miss Slater had one of her spells school was dismissed until later. Eighth-graders—and alert seventh-graders—had come to know by the look in Miss Slater's eyes when a spell was coming on and could make plans.

Long ago she had given up any hope of having the schoolhouse painted white, but at each meeting of the trustees she asked them, heaven knew. With her pig-tailed pupils she had formed a garden club which struggled to keep the patch of grass growing beside the weathered frame building. Boys failing in arithmetic or spelling were required to remain after school and water the grass with water carried in lard pails from the rusty iron pump.

Ladies sometimes visited the school with protesting husbands and took exquisite pleasure in watching their own perform well and those of others perform badly. Husbands were seated in large seats in the back of the room reserved for a possible overflow of eighth-graders.

It had been Jess's idea, that December day, to keep his mind on the deal all the way in from the ranch. He would think of it all day, all the angles and possibilities, and figure. But as he drove past the schoolhouse, magnificent in his store suit, he remembered with a kind of shudder the day that Miss Slater had invited Beth and him to visit the school. There was no sense to it, but Beth said they had to go.

"Everybody ought to be interested in schools," she said vaguely. "They mean a lot."

"Well, all right."

When school took up that afternoon Miss Slater said to the class in a beaming voice, "We like to have visitors, don't we?"

The little girls shrilled, "Yes!"

The little boys peered evilly at Jess who sat miserably in one of the big seats, his legs cramped, his knees jammed against the seat in front of him. One leg was beginning to go to sleep, and Beth, beside him, looked prim and schoolteacherish. He was a little afraid of her. He whispered, "Do they think I'm going to be a father and send it here?"

She didn't look at him, but he could see the slow smile on her lips. And Miss Slater smiled down, as if she had heard. He was crimson under his tan, and the little boys grinned.

It was a bad afternoon.

Miss Slater had walked with them to the buggy. "And I hope," she said, patting Beth's arm, "that someday you'll have a little boy in my school. I'm sure it will be a little boy."

Jess gritted his teeth. Whatever gave the old fool the idea his child would be a boy? Butting in, like that. And Beth. When Beth was around the ladies she was a lot like them. When they had driven away he said, "Beth—you're not—do you want—a pupil for that old fool?"

"Do you, Jess?" He felt her eyes on him and flushed.

"What would I do with one when I've got you?"

"Then you don't want one."

"I—of course I don't. You're enough for me." Then, "Unless you're going to. Then it would be nice." He grew a little panicky and spoke sharply to the team. Suppose she was going to have one and thought he didn't want one? Suppose she thought he wanted one and she wasn't going to—or suppose he did want one? A son was a nice thing to have. Or suppose . . .

The whole miserable conversation, the confusion came back as he thought of the visit to the schoolhouse, and suddenly it occurred to him that a son was necessary to reap the fruits of the deal and a great many more deals. Musing, he spoke to the team. The buggy jounced past the Emporium.

The Emporium had a high false front faced with sheet iron pressed to resemble brick. There was one show window and inside a display case offering patent medicines. The Emporium was owned by Peter Barrett, the banker. Only a few years ago Peter Barrett had replaced the old frame bank building with a solid-looking stone one. That's the kind of man Barrett was. And the new bank looked like a tomb.

At the edge of the town, nicely apart from lesser structures, stood the church, a small once-white building with a steeple a little off center. In 1890, when the church was being built by faith and contributions, they had meant to have a resident preacher. There was enough money for him. Everybody thought there was, until they began to build the steeple. Steeples cost money, a great deal of money, and the steeple wasn't six feet high before they saw that it would have to be abandoned where it was, or there wouldn't be a resident preacher. Unless the ladies canvassed for extra funds, and everybody had been more than generous, as it was. Brad Skinner, who owned the saloon, had given twice.

So the steeple went on to a triumphant point, topped with an arrow and a fleet iron horse that shone for a few years in the sun. But there was no resident preacher.

Instead, the Reverend Pritchet came from Butte six times a year, during those months when the Pass was free of snow, carrying a little black bag. He arrived by stage on Saturday.

"It was a miserable trip," he always said. "God has devious ways of testing a man."

He spent the night at Ma Perkins' in a room designated as "the reverend's room." Early on Sunday morning, after a breakfast Ma described as "real hearty," he unlocked the church, threw open the windows, built a fire from wood hastily laid out by the men of the parish, dusted off the pews and pulpit, and rang the bell in the steeple at eleven sharp. The flock came.

Everybody liked church. The ladies because it was a place to wear their best, and the men because you could stand out front after service and talk about the prairie. For an hour the reverend spoke darkly of sin out beyond the Pass and compared it to local sin which, the reverend warned, was getting out of hand.

He walked angrily back and forth behind the pulpit, banging his fist, running his hand across his bald, shiny pink scalp. For an hour he shouted. Mrs. Cooper said no one could bring hell's fire closer than the Reverend Pritchet.

So for an hour they would listen—Mrs. Cooper, Newt, Billy, all of them. Beth in the back pew, her hair pompadoured and her lady's-cloth suit smooth and rich. Jess beside her, miserable in a white collar. To turn his head he moved his shoulders. He stared ahead, unblinking, taking the discomfort as a part of Sunday.

Suddenly the reverend would hand down the collection plates to Cy and Billy. They walked stiffly down the aisle, a great dignity on them. Billy would stand by you until you gave at least fifty cents. He had the pews on the right. Once all who could crowded into the left-hand pews, but the shrewd Reverend Pritchet gave Billy the left-hand pews that day, and his sermon dealt with parsimony and hell. He mentioned that it cost him exactly twenty dollars and fifty cents to come from Butte.

On Monday he caught the stage and went away. The prairie was without spiritual guidance for a month. But Mrs. Cooper and a few other ladies did what they could to whip people into line.

Jess drove up and stopped before Brad Skinner's saloon, got slowly out of the buggy, fingering his bow tie, and tied the horses to the log hitching rack. His business would not take long; it was planned well in advance. There was no need to take the buggy to the livery stable. When you had a new Concord buggy, no sense hiding it.

It was a pity, the ladies said, that Brad Skinner's saloon was high at the end of the street where everybody could see it. They forgot that the most important business of the prairie was transacted there, the men leaning heavily on their elbows over the mahogany bar, clinching their deals with a drink of Four Roses. Even with Old Forrester, if the deal was a big one.

Brad's was orderly. "You got to run a saloon like any business. You got to run it square."

Nobody could remember when there was any trouble in Brad's saloon, except for New Year's 1900, when a fellow who punched cows for Anderson shot the Mexican who called himself Jesus Martin. Jesus Martin. It was a kind of name you didn't like to say. And, after all, Anderson's man was drunk, and it was a new year and a new century. That is not a thing that happens often. And then the dead man was a Mexican. It was not good to be named Jesus.

Had Brad not been a husky man, there might have been more trouble during those mad days every year when the roundup was over and the cowboys came to town, those days when Ma Perkins locked her hen house and school was dismissed because of the example set by drunk cowboys and because an elderly cowboy had once lurched into the schoolhouse and insulted Miss Slater in a way. After fifteen years Miss Slater still flushed at the thought.

"You take the nicest man," she repeated now and then, "and give him whisky, and he's just a regular beast. Just beast!"

Brad liked to tell that every board in his saloon had been selected by himself, that the false front was higher than any false front in the state. Back of the bar, running the length of it, was a mirror. A man could stand there all day, looking into it, watching what was going on behind him. You could stand there and see behind you the painting of the naked woman, pink, plump, with golden hair, reclining comfortably on green, green grass under a tree.

In two corners of the long dim beer-smelling room were felt-topped card tables where during the day a few men played halfhearted poker, looking up whenever anyone came in. In a third corner were a roulette table and wheel, covered with oilcloth during the day. But at night, when Brad lit the big shiny brass kerosene lamps overhead, the little white pellet clicked your money away.

At night the mahogany bar was crowded, and from up and down its length came the clinking of shot glasses, squat little glasses with heavy false bottoms. There was the squeak of corks, spicy whisky fumes, fumbling, friendly babbling. At night, Brad, his horseshoe tiepin flashing handsomely, walked among his customers, laughing, joking, buying drinks, his keen eyes alert over the smile.

But when Jess walked in the bar was almost deserted. Both front and back doors were open for a periodic airing out, and a cold draft pushed through the building and along the bar. The beer smell was cold and stale. Not a day for drinking beer.

Anderson stood at one end of the bar, his hat on, a glass in his big rough fingers. He picked the glass up, put it down, watched the moist ring it left on the bar. It was funny for a man to drink alone when a friend was coming. You always waited for your friend.

"Maybe he's going back on the deal," Jess thought. "Maybe he's thought better of it. Doesn't look like he's going to do business."

But when Anderson looked up he smiled. "I been here a long time," he explained. "Brad saw me waiting and set one up." He was embarrassed; his big hand tried to cover the little glass. Anderson didn't have his suit on.

Jess said, "Well, all ready for the signing?"

Anderson nodded and took a worn leather wallet from his pocket. "I got papers here. We'll sign and take them over to the notary. Or do you sign over here?"

"I guess here," Jess said. The saloon was the place to sign things. He had planned on signing in the saloon.

Anderson's hands were unsteady. He'd had more than one drink. It's funny that a Scandinavian's tongue gets tight from drinking when an American's gets loose. "Look the papers over, Jess."

Jess glanced at them quickly and handed them back. You could trust Anderson.

"Five hundred head," Anderson muttered. "The ones you looked at."

Jess was proud of his new fountain pen. He took it out with a gesture, handed it to Anderson. "You sign, then me."

Anderson hesitated, shaking the pen. Then he signed suddenly, watching the point of the pen, his letters shaking a little.

Beth would have been proud of the way Jess signed, easily, forcefully. He even added a flourish. "There," he said. "Brad, give us a drink of the best." To Anderson: "Sure glad to get this off my mind. Makes a man think, getting into something like this."

They drank in silence. Two men came inside, slamming the door shut behind them. They called for Brad and sat at a poker table, talking. Anderson said, "I didn't have to think twice about selling. I thought only once. Glad to get the deal over. Get rid of those cattle." He spoke so loud that Jess looked at him.

"That right?" A man shouldn't talk loud when he talks business.

At the poker table a man laughed loud. Anderson turned and glared, then looked sheepish. "Jumpy, I guess. Brad, bring us another." He turned seriously to Jess. "Guess I didn't tell you I'm trying to get everything sold off. Me and the wife want to get back to the old country."

"To the old country?"

"It's been a long time since we was in the old country," Anderson said. "Twenty years or more." He closed his eyes a moment. "I was born there." He seemed to be remembering. "The wife, she's been sort of not well these days. Sort of wants to go back."

At the poker table the men laughed again and lit cigars. The strong smoke drifted over, a blue haze you could see in the mirror.

"I'm sorry about your missus," Jess said. He thought about old man Ames going back to Ohio to die.

"There's one thing about the old country," Anderson said suddenly. "It's pretty country there." Jess looked doubtful. "You don't believe it. I know. You're like all the rest of them here. You think this is the only pretty country." He stopped abruptly. "Brad, leave the bottle."

They drank, and then Anderson went on: "Tell you something. There's mountains there. There's a stream comes right down where the old folks lived that looks like Nip and Tuck. Prettier, even."

"I guess it's nice back there," Jess said.

"There's fiords," Anderson said. "There aren't any fiords in this country. They're big rough cliffs with water between, blue and deep."

"No." Jess admitted. "There aren't any fiords here."

"You never saw anything like a fiord. Looks like a creek running down the narrows. Like the narrows down from Black Canyon."

"That would be good. Let's have a drink on it."

"You don't believe there could be anything as nice as the mountains back there. I remember. I was twenty. I get to missing them. I'll be glad to sell the ranch and get back there."

Jess set his glass down, startled, incredulous. "Sell the ranch? You're not coming back?"

"No. I'm not coming back." He pushed his hat back. His forehead was wet, creased with a red mark. "You know what I'm going to do? I'm going to take them presents, all of them. I'm going to take my brother a saddle. Back there they ride bareback. I'm going to take them all something. I'm not coming back."

Even as he got in the buggy for the trip home Jess knew that somehow he was going to get Anderson's ranch. "One year I'll have the credit." It would be like this. He would make something on that five hundred head, and then he'd go to Barrett. He wouldn't tell Beth until the right time, and a right time was bound to come up.

Well, suppose he'd had too much to drink? He'd feel the same in the morning, cold sober, rested. He'd still want that ranch. But something disturbed him, something about Anderson and the swiftness of passing years. What had happened to these last years?

The Concord buggy moved along out of town, and the horses held their heads high. Past the Emporium, past the schoolhouse, past Ma Perkins'.

Boothill was at the end of town, where everybody was buried. You passed right by it. Sagebrush grew up between most of the graves. Funny little road winding up to it, dusty and twisty. Sagebrush grew higher on Boothill, and through it the wind chased its tail, howling like a coyote. The wind blows hard in late fall, bringing the faraway smell of the blue peaks beyond.

Funny thoughts come when a man's had a few drinks.

"I wonder if the sagebrush grows up tall in Norway?"

XVI

ONE AUGUST MORNING in 1916 something was happening to the prairie—one morning when Jess and his hay crew were putting up the last stack of the haying season. A brilliant day, and dew that had fallen on the windrows of raked hay was whisked up before the sun that even at nine o'clock scorched like midday. Thick, slick stubble, green-brown, crackled dryly beneath hoofs of horses, and through it grasshoppers snapped and sang.

The last day of haying was a day to celebrate, to look forward to, to reckon by and talk about later. The night before the boss always went into town and brought home kegs of beer and hid them in the creek where the cool willows reached out over the shadowy moist bank. There the kegs waited, cool and secret.

On that last day the boss would pretend he had forgotten the beer or hadn't been able to get any because Brad Skinner had forgotten to order any. All day long the crew would ask questions, because it had always been done that way. The buckrakers would yell up at the men on the stack, and the derrick man would look as if he knew something.

How much beer? What kind? Milwaukee?

"Two more loads, boss, and you'll have to get out that lager," they'd yell, pushing back sweat-soaked hair, dark and shiny in the white sun, licking dry, cracked lips.

"Sorry, boys," the boss would say, looking sheepish, "but I couldn't get to town."

There was a kind of sharp pleasure in believing him for a second. Made it nice when the beer was really there. Why, a man couldn't stand that last day of haying, knowing there wasn't any beer . . . .

"Why, by God," they'd say, "if there's no beer we're going to take a match and we're going to set fire to every goddamned haystack!" The boss would be worried-looking, the old boss would.

And here it was, the last day of Jess's haying, and no one mentioned beer. The stackers didn't come down from the stack between loads to mop their brows with damp red bandanas and to drink deep of the warmish metal-tasting water in the milk can under the wagon. They pitched as fast as they could and called for more hay.

"More hay! Got sleeping sickness, you?"

And it showed in the fields, too, where the teams dragged rakes. Take Joe, the raker. They said around the camp that Joe loved the old mare called Rosie. He said to her when she was slow, and Rosie was slow, "Come on, Rosie," like she was a girl, and was asking for a kiss. But today said, "Hike, damn you, hike!"

At ten o'clock the derrick broke down. The crew worked feverishly to fix it, sweating, cursing their luck. Blue faded shirts and streaked on the backs with sweat, long dark marks. Jess running his horse over the field toward the ranch for tools, hammers, crowbars.

"By God, we've got to get this stack done."

"It'll take two hours anyways to get to the city!"

You don't know what's happened.

It's the tracks. The tracks of the Salmon City and Pittsburgh. They're in the city. The first train—it's coming!

XVII

"At one o'clock in the afternoon," according to the Salmon City *Recorder*, "the crowd assembled at the track, where the speaker's stand had been erected, just above, or below, where the depot is going to be, in Hayes Williams' cow pasture. The Salmon City Band came with a soulful blow of voluptuous music, and the thousand people present felt like the Fourth of July."

The speaker's stand was a rough yellow pine-board affair set high on stilts, a decorated gibbet. Yellow pine two-by-fours showed through where the alternate red-and-white-and-blue strips, wound spirally, had separated.

The steps leading to the platform quivered as a Mr. Clinton (they said) of Pittsburgh, Pennsylvania (they said), ascended. He covered the first few steps with dignity becoming the president of a railroad. Then, near the top, he scurried. But the prairie did not laugh, as the prairie would not laugh if the steps were golden and the climber were God. For Clinton was a kind of god. America, people said, needed his sort. His florid face, his jovial manner covered a shrewd and canny streak, but it pleased him when a venture could be successful and at the same time humanly decent.

He walked erect now to the rear of the platform to straighten one of the flags which served as a backdrop, a neat, patriotic gesture. Then, his voice friendly and intimate, he spoke.

"Friends, we are here"—everybody looked approvingly at one another—"we are here, not to dedicate the railroad, to watch the golden spike driven, not to watch the locomotive—and modern cars—pull in . . ."

A nervous murmur arose from the crowd.

"We are here," Clinton boomed, "to open up"—he paused for breath—"to open up the prairie!"

"That's the same thing," Amy whispered crossly. "I wish Cy would get back from the stable. He was all for keeping the buggy here. Said he wanted the blacks to see the railroad come, like human beings. I said—"

Clinton went on: "Those mountains that loom back of you will today witness the flowering of this country." Clinton gazed heavily at the mountains. The platform creaked, and he took a quick, dignified step forward. "At two o'clock the train will come rolling in, bringing new prosperity—to all."

Loud cheering.

Cy and Billy joined the group near the foot of the platform. Cy was scrubbed, his face shining like a child's. His hair had turned, in the past two years, almost as white as Billy's. He was deep in thought. The whole celebration seemed to rest on his shoulders.

Amy said, "Cy, you missed the first part of the speech. He said the mountains are going to flower. Isn't that nice?"

'Yes," he said absently.

"There you go thinking again! Look—there's Mrs. Cooper. Yoo-hoo! Doesn't she look lovely?"

Mrs. Cooper bore down upon them, Newt trailing, his face cynical. Mrs. Cooper wore a severe black suit which gave her the look of a rather handsome black mare. She clutched at her hat with the waving black plumes that looked bluish in the sun.

"*Mon Dieu!*" she called. "French for goodness. Newt made me late. Must wear his diamond stickpin. Hasn't worn it since—don't know when." She breathed heavily. "Man is vain."

"You look lovely," Amy said.

Mrs. Cooper was pleased. "Nonsense."

"I wish," Amy said wistfully, "I knew exactly what to do about clothes. I love them so. If I could just make up my mind what to wear when—"

154

"That would be a good starting point," Mrs. Cooper admitted.

"The trouble with me is," Amy said, "that I go into the clothes closet to pick out something to wear, and I lose confidence."

"I have a book," Mrs. Cooper confided, "about clothes. Beth had it at her school. 'The safest way is black or gray,' the book says. Black is my type."

"But black and gray are dull!" Amy cried.

"Life is apt to be dull," Mrs. Cooper reminded her.

Clinton's voice was far away. "Jess," Beth said, "can you make sense out of Amy or Clinton, either one?"

"No. Mrs. Cooper doesn't make any more sense than Amy. She didn't used to be like that."

"We're all changing, Jess."

"Not us. Not you and me."

"Shh!" Amy said. "Listen to Mr. Clinton."

" . . . this long-awaited time." Clinton took a glass of water from the table, drained it. "This is an occasion on which I have long wanted to speak. But I wish that one among you, one of you who helped us to realize this dream, would step forward. Step forward and speak—dedicate this road." He took his gold watch from his pocket. "There will be just time." He glanced down in front, and eyes were turned away from the stand. People began to drop behind taller neighbors. The crowd was turning itself inside out.

Jess, suddenly uncomfortable, felt Clinton's eyes on him. He pulled his hat down over his eyes and looked away. He would have been safe, except for Amy.

"Go on up." She laughed, wrinkling her nose. "You handsome! Make him go, Beth!"

Billy yelled, "Get up there, Jess!" His words spread like disease. The crowd had a victim. Get Jess up there. Then nobody would worry.

"Speech! Jess Bentley! Get up there!" Jess turned, almost panic-stricken, to Beth; his eyes pleaded with her to do something, to keep him from getting up there on that damned stand where God knew what could happen to a man. Shamed before his fellows. His knees were watery and his heart pounded. All those people. All those strangers. There was a low, weak feeling in the pit of his stomach.

"Beth!" he said, and felt his voice dry up like a spring on the dry flats. "I can't talk. I can't talk!"

She took his hand. "Go on, Jess. They've got to have a goat, I guess. And I'd like to see my husband speak for all of them. I want you to be—the biggest man on the prairie up there."

It's funny, what a woman can do.

"I'd just as soon go up there," Newt said loudly.

"You can talk big," Mrs. Cooper said. "You're safe as a lamb. He's going."

It was miles to the speaker's stand, a great gaudy platform covered with flags and banners the color of blood. Every step took him farther away from the only one in the world who cared for him, and just when he thought he'd reached the steps the whole damned business shook with heat waves and moved off. All those damned strangers . . .

The steps quivered and shook, like when you dream you're walking a log across a gorge.

You could stand it if there was a breeze, but the sun pressed in on the heavy, moist air and choked you; all you could smell was the sweat of a thousand people and the pitch oozing from the knots of the raw yellow pine.

And down there were people you used to know, just faces now, hundreds of grinning faces, waiting for you to make a damned fool of yourself.

But a little apart from them all Beth stood in her lady's-cloth suit, her hat back a little, her duster over her arm. But Jess saw only her eyes. Years ago she had looked at him like that, two, three years ago, in a hot, dusty corral. A horse quit bucking, and he saw her eyes, gray and quiet. Yes.

He spread his arms and gripped the sides of the table in each hand, steadying himself. Somebody laughed. Jess smiled out. It was going to be all right now.

"I guess you know," he began haltingly, "the only time I made a speech before was when I asked my wife to marry me."

He couldn't have begun better. Men who hadn't thought of their marriage for years remembered the embarrassment and chuckled; their wives made a pleased sound.

"When we got married," Jess went on, "we didn't ever think about a railroad here. We thought everything would just go on like it was, quiet, and nothing big around like a railroad." The fear was gone; the crowd was with him.

"We planned to do just like everybody, work hard and swap horses and visit around, and maybe want to get outside sometime. But we knew we could never get outside. We were a long ways from the market and we couldn't get top prices for our cows because they lost weight on the trail.

"We knew there'd be shivarees when people got married and maybe camping trips, but we'd always know there was something we didn't have—a chance to be big—real big." He found now he could relax his grip on the table.

There was quiet, not a sound, except for the flapping of one of the flags that moved listlessly in a hot little breeze that had sprung up.

Quiet, quiet; then faintly, a sound unknown to the prairie. Far in the distance, but coming nearer. Huh-huh-huh-huh. Louder. Huh-huh-huh-huh. Jess turned, and his eyes moved up the glistening stretch of track, a ribbon of promise, on across the flat lonely fields around the town. A black dot at the end of the track grew bigger and bigger. Huh-huh-huh-huh.

He spoke quietly. "Folks, I can see it now."

He watched them. Watched them go out of their heads in that second. A thousand pairs of staring eyes, then a roar of cheering, and the Salmon City Band began to play.

The train came rolling on down, proud, two flags fluttering on either side of the boiler, and bunting adorned its front from headlight to cowcatcher. It rolled slowly, majestically, forward, and the blast from the whistle sent the crowd cheering.

Mrs. Cooper was startled. She had long expected the railroad to come, but this whistling and clanking and hissing . . .

"Glory!" She gasped. "Don't go near it, Newt. No telling what it might do. Newt!"

But Newt and others were already running alongside the engine, shouting welcome to the fireman and engineer. The engineer grinned and answered by shooting steam out of the pistons, hiding the runners in a moist cloud.

Ladies called out and tried hard not to look at the wheels. No one heard. The band boomed away—"Stars and Stripes"—the cymbals crashed on the down beat. It was minutes before the train stopped and the officials from Pittsburgh, whom nobody noticed, slipped off the train.

There was no describing the engine. It was big and black, and it shone terribly in places. You would do well to stay at a distance unless you were crazy, like Newt and Cy, who had climbed into the cab.

"You ought to see the stuff they've got in there." Newt bragged. Cy smiled silently. Neither mentioned how they'd felt inside the cab, as if the train might suddenly bellow and carry them off.

They sniffed the thick black coal smoke and the hot, oily odor of the boiler.

They had forgotten about Jess. He watched them, let down, tired. Now they had all left the speaker's stand, their shouts moving down the track, sweeping on down . . . .

But Beth stood there, just as she had, a little lost figure in a duster and a big hat. Jess smiled awkwardly. "I guess that wasn't much of a speech," he said.

Somewhere the Salmon City Band was doggedly playing "Stars and Stripes Forever." The sun glittered on the instruments, but Jess didn't hear them; he heard her say, "Jess . . ."

And that was the big moment of his life, that moment when her eyes said, "You are beyond doubt the most magnificent man who ever lived."

XVIII

AFTERWARD BETH REMEMBERED the time before it happened, the uneventful days. Her longing for them was like homesickness and tinged with self-reproach. Because in those tranquil days she had not felt tranquil, only bored.

She remembered the week's blizzard three months after the railroad came. A December blizzard that descended on the prairie like a savage, crushing animal. And she must stay inside the house.

On the second morning Jess came in after he had saddled his horse, hating to work facing the storm. He stood by the stove, his Mackinaw smelling hot and wool-like and of the barn. Mittens, Scotch cap, scarf around his throat. He stood spraddle-legged, rolling a cigarette.

"Please, Jess," she begged. "Take me with you to pitch hay. We can take an extra fork, and I can pitch to keep warm. I can put on trousers. It's not so cold out. I've seen worse. I've seen it really cold." She tugged at his arm. "I hate it here alone, Jess, in the blizzard." She was a little ashamed.

He was bluff. "With this going on you want to go out?" He turned to the window. Hard, dry snow slanted sharply. A hundred feet away the barn was a gray shadow. Jess's saddle horse stood, head down, tied to the fence. "Not a chance. But I'm going to do something for you today."

She was a little appeased. "What, Jess?"

"I'm going to take some traps down, and after I get through feeding I'm going to try for some beavers. There's lots of them down the creek; three places I know of they're damming the stream and flooding things. And there's more over by Billy's on his land. Bet if I go over today and tell him you want some skins he'll get them for you. He likes to trap." He watched her, happy when she smiled. "You can have a long cape made with ten skins. Think of that, Beth!" He snatched up a Navajo blanket from the couch and threw it around her shoulders. "Look! Beaver cape!" He looked at her proudly. His wife walking down—somewhere—with a beaver cape on, and everybody looking. No thought of the drifts that rippled along the creek, the hours of freezing hands, the stumbling, the broken holes through the thick ice, and dark disappointment when a beaver gnawed its foot and got away.

"When Billy and I get ten good skins we'll take them to the city, and old Smith will make them up." He looked at her, musing. "Beth Bentley in a beaver cape. It looks nice on you."

She walked across the room, trailing the blanket, running her fingers across the rough wool. "It's soft, Jess. I'll take it." Laughing, she flung her arms around him. "But where will I wear it?"

"Where?" He gazed out the window at the storm. "London. Maybe New York." She laughed. "But I mean it, Beth." He wondered if she could see the places he could. Strange names, London, New York. Absurd to say them in a living room in Montana, with a blizzard at the windows wanting in. London. New York.

She endured the second day, the third. The fourth, and the storm raged. Calves lay frozen under the willows. The men carried axes with them to keep water holes open, the water only a thin trickle under thick ice. They counted the calves, and the lines deepened in their foreheads as if the wind had etched them there. Axes, frozen stock, storm. It was wrong to fret at her own inactivity. Wasn't it wrong to think of a beaver cape?

But she did think about it, and she did fret at the long hours. It wasn't that she wanted to go out in it. For a moment, perhaps, to get the feel of it, to try to understand it as Jess understood it. For a moment, watching the dry snow drift against the barn, she would wish passionately that she were a man, but not for long. The sixth day, when Jess froze an ear, she rubbed snow and grease on it, glad to be feminine and helpful. It was only that she missed him.

She would turn away from the window again and walk across the room and back again. "I have two beaver skins now. I have. Maybe Billy has two. New York. Oh, *damn*!"

On the fifth day she remembered the magazines. "All these nice magazines," Mrs. Cooper had said. "*National Geographics*. Wonderful. Takes you to faraway places."

"That's what I need," Beth said grimly to herself. "To be taken to faraway places." It was a month ago that Mrs. Cooper had brought them. Now Beth sat with the armchair pulled up to the stove and read and looked. Indian temples, a languid native leaning against an ugly stone torso. South American birds of brilliant plumage posing stiffly against tropical foliage. Tangled leaves and grasses.

" . . . has a peculiar whistle and is found nesting in the higher altitudes of the pampas. Dr. Meade counted no less than six different varieties, each one of them. . . ."

Dr. Meade went on finding birds, and on the prairie the wind blew so hard the house shook and creaked, and in the fields the cattle hugged the willows, waiting for hay. New York . . . There had been a girl at school who had been to New York.

At school they had thought Beth strange, coming from a ranch. She didn't mind. The headmistress had called her the most ladylike of her class. She wondered if the headmistress had known what made her that way, studious, rule-abiding? When you were homesick it didn't help to break rules. When the girls climbed out windows for a dish of ice cream in town she would go to her room and write home, or paint a picture of a hill at home, just as she remembered it.

"That was a long time ago." Now she felt the same homesickness for the prairie in summer. Maybe if she painted the way the barn looked in summer . . .

She sat sketching, blowing against the window to melt the frost so she could see the barn. "I've got to *blow*," she thought, outraged, "even to see it!" Her browns were very brown and dry and hot and her greens bright and vivid. She sketched in a horse and rider, unable as usual to get the hind legs of the horse to resemble anything more horselike than a jackrabbit's. But the picture made her lonesome. She tore it up and dropped the pieces, one by one, into the stove.

"Tommy, those playing cards. Where are they?"

Solitaire at the golden-oak table. Cards slipped on the slick surface so you couldn't make a neat row across. A neat row was tremendously important just now. Calm, orderly neatness was what you needed on a day like this.

"Now, if I beat this game the storm will stop. The wind will die down, and nobody will even know there was a storm." Shuffle, cards slipping. Ten on jack. Three on four. King up. Five on the—All right.

"Two out of three, then. If I win two out of three—"

The front door blew open, and the cards scattered like imps of hell before the iciness.

Beth stood up, furious, walked with deliberate calm to the door, and slammed it. She was about to kick it. "He's got to fix that door!" She almost sobbed. "He's got to fix it so it won't do that!"

If only Mr. Clinton had the telephone in now, instead of six months from now. Call up Amy or Mrs. Cooper and talk about the storm. Just to know that someone else hated it, caught in four walls. Why, it was dangerous not to have a telephone in weather like this. Suppose somebody got sick? Suppose somebody broke a leg?

"Tommy," she called, "do you think he'll be home early?"

The sixth night was the worst of the blizzard. When Jess came in he refused to talk about it and wouldn't look at the thermometer. He sat silent in the lamplight, drumming his fingers, and she, who had waited so long to talk, to be gay, sat silent too. Suppose she should start some conversation— about Dr. Meade and the birds in South America?

That night she lay beside him, aware of his warmth, and crept closer when the wind rattled the windows, drowning out the tick of the alarm clock. When the wind ebbed she heard it again, a comfortable sound. Tick-tick-tick. Tick— and she was asleep.

Suddenly she was sitting bolt upright, her heart pounding. "Jess!"

He turned in bed, grunted. "What, Beth?" He found her hand and took it.

"I don't know. Something. Something I don't like." Her throat was parched. "Listen."

In the darkness he listened intently to please her.

It wasn't that the wind was blowing harder than usual. That wasn't it. Nor the creaking of the house. Those sounds you learned to know, trust even.

It was the pitch of the wind. It moaned. It moaned like a human being. It penetrated the room and froze into something terrifying.

"It's just the wind," Jess said. He felt her hand tremble in his. Patting her shoulder, he got out of bed and put a Mackinaw on over his nightshirt. "I'll get you a cup of coffee." He lit the lamp. The flame flickered, leaped high, smoked, and cast wavering shadows over the room. His figure was enormous in shadow on the wall, and he appeared to lean over the bed. "You stay here and I'll go start a fire."

"I'm going too," she said quickly, and scrambled out of bed. "I'm not going to stay here alone." The floor was cold.

They brought their coffee to the bedroom and got in bed. "This is pretty funny." Jess laughed. "Breakfast in bed. What would the boys say?"

She sipped her coffee absently, looking over her cup. "I don't hear it now."

"I never heard it," he said lightly. "I think you had a nightmare."

"But Jess"—she spoke slowly—"when you have nightmares you dream about something. I wasn't dreaming anything."

He kissed her briefly. "Don't be a crazy one." They put their cups under the bed, and Jess leaned over and blew out the lamp. "I won't let anything get you," he said seriously. "Snuggle up."

He breathed regularly and was asleep.

XIX

THAT MORNING THE snow fell softly from a gauze sky, great lazy flakes drifting down. It was hard to see as they rode away from the barn. The mildness after the blizzard hung like a curtain about them, and Jess's voice was hushed and intimate.

164

"Watch when we come to those willows, Beth. Every morning I go by there there's a coyote runs out." They watched. "See him, Beth?" Jess was triumphant. A grayish, indistinct shadow scurried ahead and disappeared into a clump of brush. "Yesterday I saw two weasels. Cute little devils." He was glad to have her with him again. There seemed a lot to say, as if she'd been gone.

"If the snow would clear up you could see it up on the Pass deeper than I ever saw it. So deep the timber low down is drifted over. Mornings I've watched it drift higher and higher."

"You love it, don't you?" She watched him fondly.

"The Pass?"

"Yes. And the prairie."

"I guess I do, Beth. Sometimes I get to thinking how good it is the railroad's in, how good for the prairie, open it up. That's good, isn't it?"

"It's fine, Jess."

They rode on while the clouds lifted.

"About all those new people that have come in, Jess, since the railroad. Those farmers."

Jess scowled. "Those. Beth, I went over the other day to that big piece of land one of them bought from Newt, and what do you think?" He turned indignantly in his saddle. "I saw a plow leaning against the fence. A plow! And I kicked up the snow and saw underneath where they'd been plowing." He shook his head. "I wasn't going to tell you." His voice was bitter. "Why couldn't they go to a farming country, instead of tearing up the land here? This is no place to—plow." He warmed to his subject.

"That's what the railroad did for the prairie, Jess. That's what it means when they say they're going to open up a country. The railroad's got to have people to ship things— wheat, carrots."

"Well, I knew that—but—"

"Jess, why are you always talking about how good the railroad is when you know you hate it?"

But I don't. I think—"

"Is it because we'll have more?"

"Well, yes."

She watched him closely. "Because *I'll* have more?"

"Well, yes."

She began to hum to herself. She came first with Jess. She came even before the prairie.

She watched him pitching hay into the hayrack, occasionally took up a fork herself until she grew tired, and her feeling, then, for the prairie was that of one woman for another woman who no longer matters. When early in the afternoon the clouds began to lower again and the temperature to drop, she was secretly amused.

"Spite."

Before they swung on the horses again Jess took off a mitten, wet a finger, and held it high above him. His voice was serious. "Think we'd better get right home. Not bother with Billy's today." He wet his finger and lifted it again. "Wind from the northeast."

"But, Jess, we haven't see him for weeks! Look, Jess. I've got warm clothes on. And I've got to thank Billy. Not everybody would bother about beaver in this weather."

"It looks bad." And even then the shadow that means blizzard passed over the country and the wind began to chase the snow before it.

Her hands and feet ached dully with cold when they caught sight of the cabin.

"Hope he's got a good fire," she said through stiff lips.

"He must be out. Can't see any smoke." Closer. "No fire. I wonder—" Suddenly Jess spurred his horse forward.

"What is it, Jess?"

"Nothing." He looked straight ahead.

Billy's old cooking stove with the nickel trimming was icy. A few ashes had blown out through the draft to the floor and scattered wildly as Jess pushed open the door of the cabin. Unwashed dishes. A frying pan with cold hard fat in the bottom. Water frozen in the bucket, milk standing frozen in a pail by the blue separator.

Jess said, "He's been gone awhile. Stay here, Beth." Then, "I'm going down to the barn. Fix a fire." He went out, leaving her to shave kindling with Billy's butcher knife.

Billy's barn was a little log building like the cabin, with a sod roof blown bare of snow, the black cold earth showing through. There were no windows, only a wide doorway and rickety plank door braced with a crisscross. Snow had drifted halfway up the northeast side of the barn. Behind, in the corral, Jess heard Gladys and Pansy moving around, crunching the snow and bawling.

He kicked the snow from around the door and opened it. At last, in the gloom, he made out Billy's old saddle horse. He stood a moment until he could see better, holding the door against the blast of wind that swept the snow inside. And then he saw the old mare leaning against the side of a stall, too weak to stand. She nickered feebly. The rope that held her was chewed at, frayed. Her eyes were bright and feverish, her sides gaunt, the great ribs prominent, and between them the skin sagged. The bark from the top pole of the stall was chewed off. She nickered again.

The stench of the place hit Jess hard. Fetid manure, the heavy breath of a horse dying of thirst, and the raw meaty smell of two beaver skins stretched and tacked to the wall.

Jess's throat closed. He turned and stumbled through the snow, back to the cabin, hurrying, stumbling. For the traps were gone from the spike in the wall of the barn.

She looked up at him, questioning, from the little pile of kindling. "His horse is down there, Beth. Take care of his horse. And let the cows out. They'll need milking. Billy hasn't been here for anyway three days."

The snow was piled high along the creek, and Jess's horse floundered through, shaking, winded; a mile below the cabin the willows huddled together like frightened things, hiding from the searching wind. There by the creek was the beaver dam, but Jess never reached it. The snow-covered mound was between Jess and the dam. Snow skittering over the mound made it seem alive.

He laid Billy on the bunk in the cabin. Beth couldn't look at the face, wouldn't think, refused to feel the frozen flesh beneath the plaid wool shirt. One arm was crooked. Jess didn't tell her he'd had a hard time getting the fingers from around the traps, now that he'd put the traps back in the barn.

They pulled the grayish sheep blanket over him. The crooked arm made a tent over his face.

"We've got to get someone here," he told her. "We've got to ride and get Cy and Doc Morse." The fire roared; the draft sucked, but it was cold in the cabin.

"You go, Jess. We can't both. I'll stay—here."

He spoke softly. "You don't mind—alone?"

"No. I'd mind—not being here." She moved. "I'll just sit here and fix up a cup of coffee." She went to the cupboard, opened it, and stood on tiptoe, searching the shelves.

"The pot's not there. It's on the stove."

"I'll wash it out. Go on. Don't—get lost."

He hesitated. Then he went out. She watched the door for a long time.

There was only a little coffee in the can. She started to put it in the pot but with a quick movement put the can back in the cupboard, pushing it back on the shelf. There was just enough coffee for one cup.

She sat facing the stove, her back to the bunk. The stove went on roaring monotonously, and when a piece of wood snapped she jumped and sat shaking. Dead people should lie peacefully and not have an arm flung back, crooked, so the fingers pressed through the thin blanket—a final gesture, a kind of pointing; she wanted to look at the face and couldn't. She couldn't look behind her.

At five o'clock in the winter it is dark on the prairie, and they wipe out the lamp chimneys with last week's copy of the *Recorder*.

The lamp flickered and flared, and her hands shook a little. The light was like that, flickering and flaring, at the shivaree, and he had said, "Why, I couldn't dance with a young woman like you." He'd wanted to dance. His hands were eager as they clapped one-two-three before they danced.

She turned suddenly from the stove and looked at the bunk. She whispered, "Billy, Billy." And crouching by the bunk, her hands on the rough blanket, she sobbed, her shoulders shaking. It was better that way.

They found her crying quietly. The men stood in the door and moved awkwardly away. She heard the crowbars strike rock outside the cabin, the shovels, scrape. Silences when the men rested a moment, and the wind again . . .

"Billy," she whispered. "Why?" No sense to it. Something wrong. No pattern in Billy's death.

They wrapped the old sheep blankets around him and lowered him down. Beth held the flickering lantern, shielded it from the wind with her body. The icebound chunks of earth rattled down, thudding, but the wind deadened the sound.

Cy said, "Remember how he used to cuss you and then give you the shirt off his back?"

Jess said, "Remember the whisky he took along on the roundup?" He pulled his cap down over this eyes. "He's the last of the old-timers, Cy."

Going home now. Going home. Cy somewhere behind in the sleigh. Sometimes the clank in his harness back there in the black. Beth reined her horse around to Jess's right where the wind would carry her words to him.

"He won't get to see the country change, Jess."

"No."

They rode along, the horses stumbling, lunging in the drifts, in the cold.

"I can't make sense to it, Jess."

"What's that?"

"If a horse had kicked him, or he'd been sick. But like this—just freezing . . ."

"I can't hear you."

"The prairie killed him. He loved the prairie and it killed him."

He said, "I can't hear you."

XX

THE MAIL THAT came for the cowboys on the prairie was generally saddle-and-boot catalogues. Personal letters were looked on with suspicion as containing only bad news, news of death, or requests for loans from forgotten members of a family. But at Christmas time parcels came addressed in pencil with faraway postmarks. Dallas, Texas. Bangor, Maine.

A necktie from Eleanor. A silk shirt from Edith.

"My kid sister . . ."

A box of homemade candy, dry and sugary, to be passed around and then hidden. It would last until February if you were careful.

Or a photograph. To John, with love from Mother. A thin little lady with glasses, steel-rimmed. Letters on ruled paper, rough, blue-lined paper, narrow. It came in pads.

Wish you was with us, John. We are all going to Milwaukee to be with Mother and the kids. The kids are pretty excited. Bobby says he wants his uncle John to send him a picture of a horse.

We was hoping you was with us this year. You are the only one gone except Matt, God rest him. Why don't you write?

Talk flew about the bunkhouse of brothers and businesses, wives, children, brothers-in-law, and sisters. At Christmas the family was close and real and necessary. You were proud to have a family. Mom and the old man, kid brothers who were doing good.

We was hoping you was with us.

No wonder a man got drunk around Christmas and went into the city to dance at the Masonic Hall. When you danced there you were no longer a cowboy but an ordinary man, dancing, having fun.

"Hand over the bay rum, Slim. Got to smell pretty for the girls."

"Take more than bay rum. Have a drink before you wash up?" The spicy whisky in the warm room and a tipped-up bottle.

"Boss and the missus going in?"

"Sure. Had his suit airing on the line."

"Go easy on the bay rum!"

Warm water in the tin washbasin, steam rising. Strong white soap with a good scrubbing on the neck and behind the ears, and humming and laughing because it was Christmas time.

The boss was going all right. Jess couldn't remember when he had so looked forward to a dance.

For one thing, it took his mind off Billy. Three weeks ago Billy had frozen in the snow.

"Look at it straight," he told himself. "Everybody dies." And yet Billy had died trapping, trapping beaver skins for Beth. "But how could a fellow know? He might of frozen getting in kindling." But he hadn't.

Billy had left no will, and Jess had made arrangements with the state to take over the property. Billy owned more than anyone knew—all the land stretching out in the hills, all that unfenced land. Jess and Billy understood unfenced land, free land. He had gone in deep with the bank to buy the land, and the extra responsibility weighed heavy.

"The railroad's got to pull me out." When the winter was gone and the hills were green, things would shape out. Things always had. In the meantime . . .

There was the dance in the city. Beth would like that. She was up to something. Cy had driven over with Amy several times in the past few days, and the two women were up to something. When he came in, one or the other of them would disappear into the bedroom.

"They act funny," Jess told Cy.

"I know the signs," Cy said, smiling. The two men would ride off to look at the cattle.

Jess would never forget that afternoon before Christmas. He had come in from harnessing the team. The buggy was spick and span, and he'd had a drink with the boys in the bunkhouse.

There was only a single lamp burning in the front room, and the heat from the stove brought out the wild smell of the pine branches Beth had tacked up over the door and from the tree where the gold tinsel shone dully in the yellow light. The glow was comfortable and pleasant.

"Jess!" Beth's voice came muffled from the bedroom.

"Yes? About ready to go?"

"Jess, don't come in here. Stay where you are a minute."

The quiet glow from the lamp, the quiet room; then Beth swept out in a dress he hadn't seen before, a dark green dress that rustled and showed her arms and . . .

"Beth." He was suddenly shy. "Beth." She was a vision. She smiled and posed, stepping lightly toward him. She stood in the glow of the lamp, and he spoiled the cigarette he was rolling. "Beth." He had never seen this woman before.

He was tongue-tied driving to the city. He spoke softly to the horses, avoided the snowy ruts. He stole shy glances at her, and pride choked him when they walked into the Masonic Hall. She left her coat in the cloakroom and walked in, her dark head high, and people turned to look. This Mrs. Bentley who could ride like an Indian. This Mrs. Jess Bentley. Jess bowed a little to people he knew very well.

The Masonic Hall was a large, high-ceilinged, rectangular room, and its very vastness made the arriving dancers cluster together in tight little protective groups. An ambitious room, with a hardwood floor over which the brothers had argued bitterly at several meetings. The practical brothers, foreseeing rentals for dances, had triumphed.

The chandeliers that hung high above were not kerosene lamps, mind you, but acetylene. When the big door at the end of the room opened they swung slightly in the draft, and your shadow swayed drunkenly.

High along the walls were great, dark, heavily framed photographs of dead Masons, secure behind their beards, with eyes so keen and cold that younger Masons were uneasy as they danced in the sanctum. One nice thing about the Masons was when you died your picture went up in the space allowed at the south of the hall, and your funeral expenses were paid.

Two great chairs on raised platforms, like thrones, faced each other across the room. Small bad boys sometimes climbed up in these during a dance, but they were shunned by adults who, when they sat, occupied the hard benches along the wall used by ordinary Masons.

Here in the corner by the big door was the ladies' group, a chattering knot, divorced for the time from the men's group a distance away, an uncomfortable knot, dressed in uncomfortable suits. Self-conscious, self-effacing in white shirts and neckties. Talking cattle, or horses, of things that comfortingly had nothing to do with white shirts and neckties, of things that made a man at ease and showed he was no different in a suit than in overalls.

"I said to Al, 'If you use the Thomas rake . . .'"

"I like the Masonic Hall for dances," Amy said. "The floor is slick, and even when you dance with somebody who sort of lopes around, it isn't bad if you sort of hang on and drag your feet."

The Salmon City Band, in full uniform, tried out their instruments, tooting and groaning, and Amy did a thoughtful little dance step. "Another thing about the Masonic Hall. I can't look at those big chairs without thinking of Cy sitting in them. He's Big Chief, or something. He's always thinking. They want men who think. I nearly die at him. I know he's something big because he brought home a long sword one night to polish and strutted around, showing me." She began to laugh.

"Cy with a sword!" She beckoned. "Cy—come over and tell Mrs. Cooper about your sword and what you said!"

There was a shocked silence in the men's group.

Mrs. Cooper lowered her voice to a confidential tone. "As for me, Newt can go and be a Mason all he wants to. After what he's done." She paused significantly.

"What's he done?" Amy drew closer, shutting out possible intruders.

"For my Christmas present. You'd never guess."

But what?" Amy's hands moved in impatient arcs.

"Well, he's gone and bought me a trip to Boston, Massachusetts, where Sister lives!" Mrs. Cooper grew animated and sparkling. She looked almost handsome. "It's that long, the ticket!" She measured the distance with her outstretched arms. "It says Salmon City, Butte, Minneapolis—where the wheat is—Chicago—where Newt's brother lived that time—New York, and then Boston."

Her voice trailed off, and Tremont Street and the Common were just outside the Masonic Hall. "I wasn't going to tell you till tomorrow. But I couldn't wait. And I know something else."

"What? Don't wait forever!"

"I can't tell," Mrs. Cooper said primly. "I promised Jess I'd tell nobody. It's between him and me."

"You can tell me," Amy said sweetly. "I never tell anything."

"Now, see?" Mrs. Cooper said suddenly. "I've forgotten what it was myself! Now!"

"You haven't."

"Yes, I have. *J'ai ouiblié*. That's French for I've forgotten. *J'ai ouiblié, ouiblié, ouiblié!*" She patted Amy's arm.

Turning, she caught sight of Beth sweeping with all the dignity she could muster in through the big door. "Look, Amy!" The ladies stopped chattering.

And talk died in the men's group, leaving the word "horse"

in mid-air. Beth and Jess drew near. Jess stopped with the men, grinning, and Beth moved on to the ladies.

Anywhere they would have turned to look. In the Masonic Hall, Cy said, "Gosh. Beth looks real pretty."

Jess grew red. "She made it herself."

"It's not the dress," Cy said.

"Maybe something about her hair," Jess said, watching her. His wife. Mrs. Jess Bentley.

You remember how it was at the dances. The band started, and for one awful moment everyone stood around avoiding each other's eyes, pretending not to hear the music, going on talking until they had to shout. Then the clerk at the Emporium and that girl who hashed at the Salmon City House walked out brazenly and danced. Then everybody rushed out, afraid, somehow, to be the last. And, confused, you danced with anybody near.

Jess found himself hastily introduced by Miss Slater to Miss Edith Hayes. Miss Slater spoke highly of her as Eadie. The name fitted. Eadie. Recently Miss Hayes, Eadie, was of Minneapolis. She was small, blonde, now vivacious, now shy, just out of Normal School. She did things with her eyes.

"Eadie is our new teacher," Miss Slater bubbled in her middle-aged way. "She's helping me with the lower grades. She's brought a bit of sun into the schoolroom." Miss Hayes dropped her eyes as Miss Slater patted her arm.

Miss Hayes said, "Ooooo!"

"Mr. Bentley," Miss Slater hurried on, "is a big man here. He's a rancher, but a cowboy also!"

"Ooooo!" Miss Hayes said, intrigued.

"Miss Hayes has been reading *The Virginian* and wants to know all about cowboys. They don't have them in Minnesota, she tells me."

Well, a man can't leave a woman standing there when he's been introduced, and when the band plays you ask her to dance, to show no hard feelings. That's how it happened.

"Maybe you'd like to dance this one, miss?" Jess extended his arm gallantly.

"Ooooo!" Miss Hayes said, stepping lightly forward. They swept out into the crowd, Jess looking wildly for Beth.

"You waltz so well," Miss Hayes said. "Most of them don't dance well, specially the waltz." She clung tightly.

"I've not danced for a long time," Jess said. "We don't get out much."

He felt better when he saw Beth dancing with someone he didn't know, a tall man who bent attentively. Lots of people a fellow didn't know, these days. He couldn't see her face. He maneuvered around until Miss Hayes could catch sight of Beth.

"That's my wife," he told her. "There." He had never remembered that Beth was such a good dancer, sweeping and swaying.

"She's very handsome," Miss Hayes admitted brightly. "But I can't—I just can't think of you as married. You're so young, and dancing so!"

"Oh, I'm married all right!" He wanted to laugh. He talked more than usual. The lights were bright and flickering, the company good, the band in tune. There had been a little drink in the cloakroom. But most of all, there was Beth dancing, having a good time. Strange how the sight of her could give him a good solid sense of well-being.

The sound of many feet sliding on the floor was almost deafening, and people called to one another, smiling as they danced by. A flash of color, dark suits, a heavy down beat. *One*-two-three. The waltz made a man feel—sort of grand, sort of gallant, like men in books.

He saw Beth again and smiled, a great smile, but she didn't see. He was sure he had caught her eye, but he saw her laugh gaily at something the tall stranger said, throwing her head back so he could see the white of her throat. Again he tried to catch her eye. He spent the rest of the waltz following her. Miss Hayes followed doggedly, looking up with questioning eyes. Mr. Bentley had long, long legs.

Jess was vaguely uneasy. "I looked all over for you," he told Beth. "When I saw you I tried to catch your eye, but I guess you didn't see me."

"I didn't," she said. "You know, Newt introduced me to a young man here selling things, from Chicago. He was telling me about Chicago, the buildings, the streets and things. And the stores. I was interested." She patted a wisp of hair into place.

The band started "Red Wing," the tuba making a sharp, hopping sound. They had always liked "Red Wing," used to hum it as they danced, and smile as they made the little hop that makes a good two-step. It was their tune.

"Here's our tune, Beth."

She took his arm and smiled at someone across the hall.

There was a barrier. When he squeezed her hand she didn't squeeze back, and she only talked when he asked her questions. She didn't hum. That was the thing. She didn't hum.

> There once was an Indian maid,
> A shy little prairie maid . . .

"You look nice, Beth."

"Do I?" She looked at him. "I didn't—think you thought so."

"You didn't think—Beth, why didn't you think so?"

"I just didn't think you did."

He felt the heat, heard the babble. It made him a little sick. "It's close in here. Stuffy."

He could not tell how long the dance lasted, how many times his friends called to him as they danced past. He remembered the smell of hot coffee and pushing through the crowd for chocolate cake instead of white. She didn't thank him. He offered her one of his sandwiches. She didn't want it. Nobody made any difference; no tune made any difference. Noise, shouts, people bumping into you, and they didn't make any difference. For he had come to the dance, made the long trip with high heart, and now all that was gone. He fled when she began a conversation with the ladies. In the cloakroom Cy gave him two drinks from a quart. He waited to feel them while Cy went on about a new house he was going to build.

When he danced with Beth he was either too gay, he felt, or too morose. He didn't feel like himself but someone trying to be himself. Then the band played "Home, Sweet Home."

Jostling in the cloakroom, and he heard them joke about getting the wrong hats and Mackinaws, and a few told stories, and a few were unsteady on their feet. And then those minutes standing beside the big door, feeling the cold draft, talking loudly and foolishly to cover her silence. Because she wasn't trying now. She was quiet, waiting for him.

"Keep them from knowing something's wrong between us. Make them think things are all right." Because it was a shameful thing for a man and wife not to get along together.

Endlessly the miles stretched, clanking harness, slip of the iron-tired wheels into the snowy ruts, cold woolly smell of the old robe he tucked around Beth. Each time he tucked it he tried to speak, but the words caught. What would he say? Where would he start? How had this happened?

Miles, miles. The moon made the side of her face pale, as white as the snowy prairie alongside.

"Beth, I did something wrong. I don't know what I did. I'd like to make it all right."

Her eyes glistened in the moonlight "Don't you know, Jess?"

"No. No, I don't know." He stared ahead.

"It's such—such a foolish thing." She tried to laugh. "It's hard to tell. It's about the way you feel inside. It's"—she sat straighter—"it's foolish. Foolish."

"Please, Beth."

"It's—you didn't dance with me first." Her lips trembled. "Lots of people thought—I looked nice. And they told me. Right away. But I didn't care what they thought. I wore this dress—for you. And you didn't even—" Her head was on his shoulder and she was crying.

He put his arm tightly around her. "Beth, I'm a damned fool. I didn't know. I haven't been to enough dances to know. But every time I looked at you I thought how—nice you are. I told everybody about you."

Her words were indistinct against his shoulder. "Did you—did you tell the new teacher?"

Jess's heart lifted. It was over. He raised her small tear-stained face with a mittened hand. "Beth, this is Christmas. Merry Christmas to my wife. I've got a present for you."

She sat up, sniffled, and smiled weakly. "What?"

"Wait till we get home."

"If you kiss me."

If you squinted your eyes just right when you looked at a star the light came right down to the ground in a long flash. All the stars did it. He felt very old and wise and comfortable.

It was a big bulky paper-wrapped parcel, not wrapped very well. When packages have been opened and wrapped again they never look very well. The paper rustled . . . .

The cape was rich and brown in the lamplight. She buried her face in it. When she looked up her eyes shone.

"Oh, Jess."

Behind them the stove roared, the sound they knew, and this was their hour. "Put it around me, Jess." It was soft against her neck and arms.

"I couldn't wait," he said shyly. "You should have had it for the dance, but I wanted to wait till Christmas." He looked at his watch. "It's three hours into Christmas now. And there's something else. Something else."

"Something else?" Watching him, her hand brushed the soft fur.

"In the pocket, in the lining."

She wriggled her hand inside. "Jess—there's something in it!" She unfolded a paper in her hand and held it under the lamp, curious. "Oh!"

The ticket reached from her fingers to the floor, unfolding. Butte. Minneapolis. Chicago. New York. Boston.

"We'll have a good time," she whispered. "We'll always remember this night."

He held her tight, smoothing her hair. "Always." He felt an odd lump in his throat, and a kind of sadness came over him as he held her, his wife, who from this moment was one of the great ladies he knew must be. And he would tell her first thing in the morning that he couldn't go. First thing. Wait and see.

XXI

AN HOUR IS a long time when you've never been on a train before. An hour to think how you tried to raise the window of the car . . . .

Beth had tugged at it frantically. There was Jess just outside, a little apart from Cy and Amy and Newt, standing there, waving to her with his hat. Just to call to him, to call, "Good-by, Jess!" once more. But the window wouldn't budge. Then she had leaned close and pressed her nose against it. Her lips moved. "Good-by, my darling."

His lips moved.

An hour to think of that. She saw Amy go to him and take his arm. Because this was the first time they had been apart.

An hour ago.

Before that he had said, "I don't see how I can let you go."

Her heart cried, "Then don't let me! Let's pretend we're just seeing Mrs. Cooper off. Let's pretend that."

But he was proud. That was it. He was proud. He said, "I want you to have things." He would never understand that he was all she wanted. That was clearer now than ever before. But it made him happy, her going. She felt strangely alone. "I'm going to be homesick," she told Mrs. Cooper, who sat opposite, calm, poised.

Mrs. Cooper looked up from her book. She had always wanted to read on a train. The idea of just sitting there, going somewhere and reading at the same time, fascinated her. She, of all people, traveling! With a kind of comfortable grimness, she recalled that for years she had had her own ideas about gadabouts. Had always regarded staying at home as a virtue. Well, heaven knew it was tiresome enough to be a virtue. Now, feeling pleasantly lax, she smiled.

"Have something to eat. I brought a big lunch. It's almost noon." She leaned over and began to untie a string around a shoe box at her feet. "I've always wanted to eat on a train. When we change at Butte there's a train with a dining car. I've always wanted to eat on a dining car."

The stove at the end of the car was hot, and the wall behind it smelled strong of varnish. Beth said, "I remember when we got the stove in the front room the varnish smelled like that. Jess put asbestos behind it."

"Asbestos is good," Mrs. Cooper admitted. "Try this cold ham."

Before another hour Mrs. Cooper had engaged the woman across the aisle in conversation. She was the wife of one of the new people in Salmon City, the new people who had come after the railroad. Newt called them buzzards.

"Yes," the new woman said. "We lived in Butte for years. A real town." She spoke easily of electric lights, of automobiles, which she had seen often. And many a railroad train she had ridden on. Railroad trains were common enough. She was kindly to Mrs. Cooper. "And where are you going? To Butte?"

The conversation could not have taken a better turn for Mrs. Cooper. She leaped into the breach.

"Mrs. Bentley here and I—we're going to Boston, Massachusetts." It amazed her how she had said it, as if it were nothing. The new woman remained silent for some time, and a little sullen, Mrs. Cooper thought. She took up her book and began to read with great unconcern. Then, "Beth— this book is very good." She raised her voice slightly. "As the French say, *c'est bon*."

The train climbed. Twice it stopped near Nip and Tuck Creek, and the crew shoveled snow, the passengers watching and thinking how lucky and useless they were. Higher and higher the train pulled, creeping along. And down there was the prairie.

"If it were only storming, so I couldn't see." If only leaving Jess had been over quickly. Miles off down there, there was a speck in the snow. Her house. Foolishly she thought of the screen door that slammed, tried to remember the exact sound. Tommy in the kitchen rattling the stove lids and . . . "I will not think of Jess. I will not think of Jess."

It was still daylight when they crossed the Pass. The shadow of the train running alongside was dark, cold against the snow, a blue-tinged shadow moving silently. Occasional straggling pines were black, not green, and the silence that must hang around them seemed to enter the car, a silence that Beth felt keenly.

Stuffy in the car, and someone was peeling oranges.

She took one quick look back down on the prairie. The mountains back there loomed, protective, cradling the country in great snowy arms. Home. It was getting dusky in the car, but Mrs. Cooper could see her face.

"Must be six o'clock," she observed. "We've got more lunch. How was that ham?" Again she untied the string around the box. Newt had kept a hammer and nails in it, his odd-job box. Jobs he never got around to, until the railroad came. Funny change in Newt. The way he used to just sit—Newt was a fool. He would never get on, alone, with so much to do. "Beth, have some of these boiled eggs. Newt helped me boil them this morning." She sat back impatiently, brushed off a sleeve of her traveling suit. Why must she think of Newt Cooper, an ordinary and often quite surly man? He probably wasn't thinking about her, she thought crossly.

Somewhere the darkness slipped down, and the conductor came in from the baggage car, swaying up the aisle, to light the kerosene lamps overhead. They gave a weak, yellowish light and weren't good to read by. Faces looked tired and drawn in that light. The new woman complained that the light kept her awake. After an hour the conductor turned them down, and the new woman took off her shoes.

"Take yours off too," she advised Mrs. Cooper. "Easier to sleep with shoes off. Everybody does it on trains. It's all right."

Mrs. Cooper removed hers thoughtfully, wondering if a woman should take her shoes off on a train where there were men passengers. No man but Newt—strange thought—no man but Newt had ever seen her with her shoes off. These were strange times. She and Beth slept covered with their coats, soothed by the clicking wheels underneath. Clickety-clickety, farther and farther.

North Dakota, Beth thought, was endless. They had stumbled around in the lamplight at the main-line station, hardly aware that they were changing trains, that they now had a berth to sleep in. But aware they had left the Salmon City and Pittsburgh, the last link with home. Today North Dakota stretched off into the horizon, a cold white desert. Here the train flicked past a crossing. Wagon tracks weaving drunkenly across the snow, horse tracks, but no wagon, no horses. A solitary windmill off to the right, a gaunt thing starving in the white waste.

"No mountains," Beth said.

"I knew Boston was a long way off, but I didn't know it was this long." An open book lay unnoticed beside Mrs. Cooper. She was in a sort of daze. "We can eat in two hours. They have a dining car." With a determined straightening of her body she thought heavily for a moment. "We'll have some kind of fish."

Chicago. They clutched their bags, trusted no one. Mrs. Cooper shot hostile glances right and left. A late train and cups of lukewarm coffee in a dismal restaurant and the terrifying traffic sounds.

"I never saw so many people," Mrs. Cooper said softly. "I don't think they look very clean."

"How do you feel?" Beth asked, straightening her hat in the wavy mirror. They stood in the ladies' room, distrustful.

"I—don't know." Mrs. Cooper faltered for the first time in her life.

"I always thought a person would feel sort of different when they were in Chicago. I keep saying 'Chicago' over and over, and I don't feel any different. I'm just Beth Bentley. 'Chicago-Chicago-Chicago.' It doesn't mean anything at all."

"I wonder what they're doing at home," Mrs. Cooper said sadly.

"I suppose he'd—be eating supper."

"Yes. He'd be eating. Beth," she said slowly, "I'm sick to death of eating."

They heard their train called.

That winter morning the fog hung drearily over South Station and seeped like smoke through the doors after tired, white-faced commuters. Fish-smelling fog, damp. Lights in the station were diffused and fuzzy. Lost-looking men and women stood about in groups, talking in voices as gloomy as the atmosphere. A tired porter lugged a bag across the expanse of floor, his cap pulled down, limping a little.

Beth and Mrs. Cooper stood uncertainly at the gate of track 15.

"She said she'd be here." Mrs. Cooper's voice was helpless.

"Maybe she didn't get your telegram." Beth was desperate.

"I thought at the time that that man in New York didn't look trustworthy, not the kind of a man to get a telegram through. He was sort of slinky-looking." Mrs. Cooper's voice rose with alarm. "Oh, Beth!" People turned.

"Are you sure you gave him the right address?"

"Heavens! I can't remember. I can't remember!" Mrs. Cooper passed her hand over her eyes. "Beth! I told them the wrong number!"

A woman in furs with an overcoated man in tow bore down on them.

"Sister!" the woman cried.

"Emily!" Mrs. Cooper shrieked.

The couple approached rapidly; wet, quick kisses.

"This is Beth Bentley I wrote you about."

Emily gave Beth a wet kiss.

"This is George," the woman said.

"You're fatter, George," Mrs. Cooper said. "You look older."

"Well, Sister!" George said.

It was five o'clock in the morning.

XXII

WHEN YOUR WIFE went away they chuckled and slyly said you'd probably be flying around until she got back, and why they said this no one knew. Because on the prairie men seldom flew around when their wives were gone, but complained about the untidy house and the cooking to be done and wondered why they didn't feel like flying around.

Newt was determined to enjoy his freedom. He would go down to Brad's saloon for a game of poker. He would gamble.

He wore his diamond stickpin. The old deck of cards he had used in the Southwest felt good in his inside pocket. There was a look in his eyes, a rakish angle to his hat, and a spring in his step.

But something was wrong. He sensed it the minute the cards were dealt. There they were, new slick, shiny, crisp, the bicycles blue and the background white—a familiar old pattern—and they meant nothing to him.

It seemed the rules were not the same. Where had he been that the rules had changed? Since when had a heart flush beat a spade flush? What was this about wild cards—some sort of woman's game? He grunted and lit a cigar.

In the old days he was admired for his poker face. "You watch Newt Cooper's face," they used to say. "You won't see anything." They didn't know that fine feeling in his stomach, that gone feeling that came when the cards were dealt or when he drew one card to a flush or straight.

Yet now as he picked up his cards a great calm came down on him. Even though there were four dollars in the pot and he was drawing to a pair of deuces, his old lucky cards, he was calm. Nothing, nothing wrong with his stomach, none of the old dread.

In the old days he used to have a drink when he got too nervous. Maybe it would work backward now; maybe if he had a drink the old tightness would come back, the old feeling.

He had two drinks. Nothing happened. Flat calm. Poker was suddenly a waste of time.

"You might call this poker," he said sourly. "I call it old maid." He came out on the muddy lamplit street and looked up and down, wondering what had happened. Well, he knew that the only thing that gave him a kick was speculating in land, as he had speculated since the railroad came. Cards would never come up to it.

"When I was a kid, must have been crazy, getting hot over cards." Speculation in land was big gambling, man-sized. It was holding four cards to a royal straight and drawing the fifth. Because damned if he hadn't been drawing the fifth, right off the top of the deck. "I know how to call the fifth card," he told himself. He walked up the street, his leather heels hitting hard on the new cement sidewalks.

Jess was no gambler. His plans for the future were systematic and cautious. They began with the wagon.

The prairie had been openhanded, foolish. When something wore out, a set of harness, a saddle, it never occurred to anybody to patch it up. They sent for new ones. Maybe it was pride.

"See? I can't afford a new house, maybe, but I've got new harness, fine and strong and black . . . ."

It was late in January, one of those strange warm afternoons when the chinook winds breathed a false spring. He rode along with Slim and Pete, his cap pushed back, letting the moist warm air hit his forehead and temples, his Mackinaw open and smelling warm in the sun.

Yearling white-faced calves watched them from openings in the willows, and some of them wandered aimlessly out into the open, content, stopping to throw their heads around and to lick at their backs, a comfortable animal gesture, nice and lazy.

Fat calves, chewing their cuds.

"Calves look nice," Jess said. "You're doing a good feeding job. Never saw better. Fat calves, fat as butterballs."

Slim looked up, his red face grinning.

"Just the same," Jess went on, "no use shoveling too much hay to them. Winter's not over. Hay's got to last. And I want extra for next year."

Something on the boss's mind? Slim dismissed it, cheerful over an immediate problem. "Got to have a new wagon to haul manure this spring for dams. Old one's shot."

"Shot, is it?" Jess was thoughtful. Slim went into detail. Loose spokes, tires sprung, tongue cracked, hounds loose and splitting. And at the ranch they stood looking at the old wagon, Slim oddly uneasy but confident the looks of the wagon would bear him out. Jess frowned, scratched his head, and passed judgment in a slow, deliberate way. "We'll fix her up."

"Well," Slim said doubtfully. "I guess it'll do for this year, we play our cards right. Till June, anyway."

Jess chuckled. "We'll fix her so she'll be rolling five, six years from now."

"But, boss—"

"We'll start on it in the morning." Jess walked through the slushy snow to the house, watching his feet solemnly. Slim watched. Something about the boss's back.

The wagon came out so well that Jess turned his attention to the harness. A harness maker came to the ranch for a two weeks' job, repairing hames, collars, bellybands, pole straps. They began to say that Jess was getting a little stingy.

He hired a blacksmith to repair old rakes, and coal smoke from the roaring forge hung about the buildings, and the anvil rang. Now mowing machines were pulled apart and put together again, tighter. Make things last a little longer, make things do. The results were even better than he had hoped. He wasn't envious when Newt told him of three new mowing machines just arrived by train at the Emporium.

"That's fine, Newt." He knew his made-over machines were as good. What was a new mowing machine but pretty paint and a yellow factory tongue that split the first time a wheel went in a ditch?

He pitched a camp in Black Canyon, and for a month he and the boys worked in the timber, getting out logs for a new fence between his land and a squatter's. He watched the ponderous log fence spread out, a barrier between him and strangers.

"They'll never get in here with their damned plows, Beth," he thought. "This is ours. That's theirs." The fence would last fifty years, and then . . .

Well, somebody would carry on. Somebody must carry on. That was the way things must be. And looking at the fence, he was worried about that time after fifty years, and sad, somehow.

Newt was always busy now, as busy as he had been idle other years. He had new ideas, new schemes. He sold another piece of land and mentally put the money into a new scheme.

"God," he told Jess, "it's getting money for nothing! It's that old brush patch, I call it. They'll never make out there. Swede farmers. If they can make their wheat grow there—" He laughed and winked. "They'll buy anything." But everybody bought and sold and gambled; there was something in the air, and nobody knew what it was. Maybe the war in Europe. But something was satisfied when you bought or sold or gambled.

Jess hated to meddle in a man's business, hated even to be aware of another man's business. A man's business was as personal as nakedness. But Jess worried about Cy.

Cy drove over often with Amy, stopped for supper. The three of them would sit in the evening before the stove, Cy ponderous in his chair, watching his big hands, Amy nervous and smiling. Jess read Beth's letters to them haltingly. After a time Amy would make coffee, come back, and then the three of them would talk about Beth.

"I miss her, Jess. I believe she's my best friend." Amy seemed lonely occasionally, but she had plans for the new house, and of these she talked. The house was as good as built. The room would be like this, the walls like that. And it was going to be big. "It's wonderful, Jess. We've waited— we've waited so long."

Cy would smile at her and shake his head, bewildered but pleased, and his thick thatch of white hair would give a look of saintly tolerance to his smile. What would he do with her, his quiet eyes asked, and what would he do without her?

Impatient, Jess knew that she would have her house, for Cy never spoke of expanding his land or of improving it.

Often he wanted to say, "Look. Buy that piece of state land back of your place before the price goes up. Some stranger might get it . . . ."

And the maddening thing, Jess knew that if a stranger got it Cy wouldn't care. Cy never spoke of new mowing machines, as Newt did, but he never spoke of repairing the old. He never spoke of anything. He was composed, his eyes confident in these fevered, not confident times . . . .

Jess had subscribed to a Boston paper. At night when Tommy had gone into his room, he would take it out. It was good to take his pocketknife and slit the cover, always so tight and brown. He stuffed the stove with wood and closed the draft before he began to read. He wouldn't have to move then. This was something he must give all his attention to, this reading the paper.

A slit of the knife, an unfolding, a rustle and the curious smell of the paper, and he was in another world, a world that in some strange way beckoned to him although he knew he'd never be a part of it. But Beth was a part of it, just as she was a part of the prairie. She was a part of it now.

Shops, streets, bustle. He always read the society pages and was amazed at the amount of print it took to describe a party, a wedding. It made him a little jealous of unknown people to remember that the Salmon City *Recorder* had given only a paragraph in the You-and-Your-Friends column to his and Beth's marriage. "Well, here are the places she goes and the sights she sees."

In the spring the last snow melted and ran in scurrying little rivulets around the roots of the sagebrush, tracing intricate spider-web patterns. The earth was black and wet, fragrant and alive. Slippery going. Once Jess's horse lost its footing and slipped to its knees. Jess, caught unawares, jerked his spine painfully.

"Stand up, damn it!"

For that day he had seen the worst. A farmer had a four-horse team and was turning the prairie sod there where a man could see. "I wish I had a million dollars. I'd buy every damned acre in the country. I'd tear down every barbed-wire fence in the country." He muttered like an old man, glad that Beth couldn't see it.

Yet he wanted her soft voice and her gray eyes that encouraged him, told him everything was going to be all right. He couldn't tell her about it in a letter. She would worry, would think he wanted her back.

Well, he did want her to come back. He must think of some way to get her back without actually telling her. He would think of something.

Thirty-five letters in three months, and the thirty-sixth that afternoon brought news of Old North Church. To them Old North Church was Boston. Before she left she had brought out her old history book, and there on page fifty was a picture, a woodcut.

"I remember," Jess said. "In seventh grade. That's the book I had." It was exciting about Old North Church. "One if by land, two if by sea . . ." The words made a kind of chill go up your spine, and you didn't know why. He had always thought of the British as Indians, ready to swoop down from the timber as they had on the old stockade that still stood not far from the old Bentley ranch. The old man used to tell him about the stockade, and he always saw the old man going up in the tower of the church with two kerosene lanterns. Then Paul Revere, Jess Bentley, started on a wild ride to warn the ranchers on a little sorrel pony.

"I used to call him Banjo."

"I'll write you about it Jess. I'll go there first thing."

But it wasn't till the thirty-sixth letter.

. . . and I saw it. And I went up in the tower, way up. I could see the ocean and the boats. Jess, the ocean makes me homesick for the mountains. Something about the mountains and the ocean is the same. Maybe because you can see so far out and then have to guess what is beyond.

The tower of the church is high, and the steps are rickety.

He got out the history book. Beth had been in that tower. He felt close to her and to the past as he stared at the blurred woodcut. Whoever thought when he studied history there in the log schoolhouse that somebody he married would be in that tower? You would think that even then, when he first saw the picture, he would have felt something, some— warning, sort of. It was creepy.

The letter went on:

I forgot to tell you that the last time I hung up my saddle I left the skirts so they might bend back when I use it again. You'd better fix it . . .

He would fix it as soon as he finished the letter.

It must be spring up there now. It isn't spring here. There are only a few hours when the fog lifts so you can see.

Tommy was airing the house, and the front door and the back door were open, so the barn smells drifted in and hung about. Damp smells, of snow water in deep puddles about the bases of corral posts, of shoots of grass, green now, pushing up through old brown roots. And with them the smell of sagebrush, heady and spicy. Beth's favorite smell, the smell of the country.

He wrote:

Yes. It is spring here. The snow is melting and the ice is gone off the creek back of the barn. The water is muddy so you can't drink it.

One of the mares that had a little colt died, and I am afraid it will die because I can't feed it right. They have to be fed about ten times a day, and I can't be here all the time. There is no one here to take care of it, so I believe it will probably die.

FROM YOUR HUSBAND
JESS BENTLEY

He held the letter up before him, snug in the envelope. The sagebrush he had picked down by the barn made a funny little lump. A tall sagebrush, tall as a man's head.

XXIII

IT WAS EARLY spring on the prairie.

It tried to rain, but the rain turned to sleet, and a man couldn't see as far as the nearest willows. Ranch hands spurred their horses into the sleet, squinting up their eyes to watch cows, thin after a long winter, standing beside newborn calves, little trembling white-faced calves, learning how to suck.

There were thin young heifers, small heifers standing near willow bushes, and these needed help to have their calves. The ranch hands took down their lariats with stiff, cold hands, roped the heifers, helped them.

Nothing had changed about the years. Across the storm in the ranch houses the women peeled potatoes and peered in the oven at browning roasts.

"That sleet'll turn to rain," they said. "Are the men in yet?"

"There's a hundred fifty calves now."

"Well, that's good. You see the men coming yet?"

There was nothing different about the year you could touch or hear or see. A man had his work in the fields with the cattle, the work he began when his cheeks were smooth and his voice cracked, the work he had now when he was married, with a wife and kids somewhere.

But on the ocean a great ship had gone down.

At night the young ranch hands lay in their blankets in the bunkhouse and felt the roughness against their skins. They figured and wondered how a fellow could run a bayonet into another fellow's guts; they lay quietly and listened to the snoring of the older men, and they knew the sleet had turned to rain. You could hear it against the dark window.

It rained on the prairie, and there was the smell of winter-killed roots in the earth. They read the calm, confident words: ". . . that a state of War exists between the Imperial German Government and the Government and the People of the United States . . . ."

They had planned a hurried celebration in the street to cheer the United States and President Wilson. The Salmon City Band was going to play "Stars and Stripes Forever" at the end of the street near the church, but the rain continued and the man who worked the drum said you couldn't take a drum out in the rain.

They held the celebration in the Masonic Hall on a dark, stormy April afternoon with thunder crashing over Black Canyon. They jammed in the door, steam rising from their clothes, talking loudly, curiously friendly with neighbors. Streamers of red, white, and blue were tacked up over the end of the hall where the biggest throne chair stood, and the portrait of the potentate came down and a lithograph of President Wilson went up.

One of Miss Slater's eighth-graders gave the Gettysburg Address. A pig-tailed young lady in a nightgown-like garment recited *America*, with gestures, in a trembling voice.

They remembered the rain.

For it had rained and the thunder crashed on the day the first draftees went away on the train. While the engine shunted cars in the yards the young men walked in straggling groups up the muddy street to Brad's saloon, coat collars pulled up, trudging along in the mud that splashed on the legs of suits they had worn to dances.

A crowd came out and stood on the roofless platform at the station, waving as the train pulled away into the mist. The young men leaned out the windows and grinned as the train moved away.

The train disappeared around the curve. The crowd stood alone, and there were a few mothers sobbing, and a few sisters, and a few fathers saying gentle things and looking about, embarrassed.

It was the first time in months that the whole prairie had gathered at the station to see something, to listen to the band. It was a changed prairie. The war had made young men go away, and there were new people in their place, Swedes and Finns, big men in bib overalls who had read in pamphlets about cheap land and big crops, maybe.

That late summer of 1917 they saw yellow waves of wheat toss and roll across the land that only yesterday was sagebrush. It billowed and swelled. When the ranchers rode beside it they said their horses shied at the sight of the yellow wheat, as alien as the men who grew it. Stooped, big-footed men with earth in the cracks of their hands, big calloused hands with short wide nails. The prairie was no longer "we," but "we and they." The ranchers laughed at the stooped, strong men who grew the wheat. No one knew why this was.

"What do you think they've done now? They've got *chickens!*"

It was incredible.

"I rode by yesterday. I was watching them. They've got barbed wire. They're putting it around every place."

"I ran into one of them in town. He was buying seeds. They've got seeds for cabbages in the store down there, and they buy them."

And there was nothing you could do.

Mrs. Cooper found Beth in front of the barn leading a three-month-old colt around and around in a circle. The June sun glistened against its sorrel hide; its ears pricked forward, and it lifted its hard round hoofs high.

"Well," Mrs. Cooper cried. "So here you are." She advanced. The colt stopped, trembled, snorted a little.

"I'm teaching him to lead," Beth said. She patted the colt's neck. "Jess made me a halter out of horsehair for him. Look at it."

Mrs. Cooper came forward cautiously, held a coaxing hand out timidly. "A very pretty halter," she said nervously. "Why, Beth!" She stopped. "You've got pants—trousers—on!"

Beth laughed. "They were Jess's. Tommy washed them and—"

Mrs. Cooper was solemn. "I never thought I'd see women wear pants. But they look comfortable. And the way you have your sleeves rolled up—cool. My"—she laughed—"when I think of you in Boston—silks and satins." She thought a moment. "It's funny about you, Beth."

"Funny?" Beth unsnapped the halter. The colt stood a moment, then ran, bucking, to the barn, shying at its shadow.

"Yes, funny," Mrs. Cooper insisted. "How you wear pants. They don't look improper—on you. It never made any difference what you wear—or do. I think—" She paused, uncertain, "Now, I don't want you to take offense—but I think you could—smoke cigarettes, and it wouldn't make any difference."

Beth laughed. They walked toward the house, Mrs. Cooper slapping viciously at the mosquitoes that buzzed in a gray swarm about her. "Anyway," Beth said, "I'm glad to be home. It was nice back there, but—"

"I know," Mrs. Cooper said shortly. "I'm glad too. I found I hadn't enough room in Boston. I felt shut in. I kept saying to myself, 'You're shut in.' It was not good."

"The only thing I remember now were the lobsters we ate. Remember?"

"I shall always remember. Those little black eyes they had. Daring you to eat them. And those claws." She shuddered. "Creatures of the sea."

"That was the last day there."

"It was the night you got the letter with the sagebrush. I suspect Jess. The look on your face." She sighed. "I wish Newt had thought of it."

The front porch was cool. Beth brought another chair, and they sat silent for a while, looking out at the Pass, its peaks still white. "You know," Mrs. Cooper said at last, "I found Easterners provincial. They lacked that—how do you say?—*joie de vivre*. No spunk. Emily was cross when I told her she had no spunk. Her husband also lacked spunk. George is an unfortunate name, isn't it? Newt has a lot of spunk. All of us here have it."

They watched the shadows move across the face of the Pass. "I'll never leave again," Beth said.

"Nor will I." They sat back comfortably, everything settled, slapping idly at the mosquitoes. At last Mrs. Cooper cleared her throat, to indicate she was now ready for the real business of the day. "As I drove over here I went by one of those farms." She paused to let the fact sink deep. "You never saw such people." She rocked nervously in her chair. The bird-of-paradise feather fluttered. "The other day I thought to myself, 'Well, after all, they are neighbors.' I decided to call with the buggy. I have now learned to drive rather well."

"Well, the woman's name was Peterson. Her husband bought all that dry land from Newt, that land back of the Butte. He's got things growing on it too. Well, what do you think?" She stopped rocking, and the feather was still, expectant. "They're Swedish!" She clutched the chair arms with her hands.

"That's not so bad," Beth said. "Anderson was Norwegian. That's about the same."

"That's not it," Mrs. Cooper insisted. "It's all right to *be* Swedish. Heaven knows, maybe a lot of us have Swedish somewhere. But it's not all right to *talk* Swedish when people call. This is America, you know," she said sarcastically. "And Beth"—Mrs. Cooper lowered her voice, as she did when about to speak of some ugly subject—"that woman was out there splitting wood."

Beth said, "Oh, Swedish women don't think anything of doing man's work. They're strong. And look at me—sometimes I do a man's work."

Mrs. Cooper was triumphant. "There! You see? You're different! But those Swedish women—if they're so strong they ought to stay in Sweden or Minnesota and not come here with their wheat." The feather bobbed.

"I'll get some tea," Beth said suddenly.

"Tea is good," Mrs. Cooper admitted.

The tea was iced in water glasses, a cool moistness on the outside that showed the prints of their fingers. They watched the prints lazily and stirred and sipped.

"Have you seen Amy lately?" Beth asked. "She doesn't come around like she used to."

Mrs. Cooper set her glass down beside the rocker. "That's what I came about," she said. "I don't know how I got off on those Swedish people. I came to ask if you knew anything about Amy."

"Jess and I drove over last week, but they weren't home."

"My foot!" Mrs. Cooper snorted. "Weren't home my foot! It's just that Amy won't see anyone. Newt and I called, too, and no one answered." Her voice dropped. "But I saw the window curtains move." She pondered. "Good tea!"

"But that's not like Amy," Beth said slowly.

"Mmmm," Mrs. Cooper said. "I noticed something peculiar last time I saw her." She thought. "I think she was quieter. Sort of reserved. And the house. Tidy. No dust. No old magazines. Something funny going on." Mrs. Cooper grew mysterious. "She's in hiding, Beth."

"But why?" In spite of herself, Beth caught a gossipy note in her voice. The ladies' traits were contagious.

"Well, Cy came over and stood around like he does. Then he asked me if we'd come over for a little 'get-together,' as he called it. I've never been to a 'get-together.' Either a person has a party or a person has somebody over, and none of this 'get-together.' I wouldn't miss it. Eight o'clock. Sunday."

She was off down the dusty road, her back straight and important.

Amy had only one lamp lit in her front room, and that was in the corner where you couldn't see anything. If it was a party, it was a strange one. The men stood around wondering what to do with their hands and feet, and that was strange because there were no strangers. The ladies wandered, talking halfheartedly, for not one subject that had yet come up interested them. Why had Amy avoided everybody and now suddenly invited everybody over? Cy was even quieter than usual. Beth always had good luck talking to him. She would ask him about Indians and the early days and make him say a lot. But tonight he avoided her questions. He fixed a fire in the kitchen to make coffee and left the men huddled like lost sheep, afraid to sit down until the ladies did. The ladies made no move because the hostess stood, even more confused than they. Occasionally she picked nervously at the corners of the big silk scarf she had flung about her shoulders, low-hanging, covering her.

"What a pretty scarf!" Mrs. Cooper boomed. She had not meant to boom. It wasn't important. The ladies, seeing an opening, crowded around to see the scarf and to feel it.

There was a quick silence. A woman giggled. Another whispered, and the ladies made a circle around Amy, moving her, unprotesting, into the bedroom. The door closed behind them. The men, staring, shifted their eyes and pretended they hadn't noticed and groped for something to say or do.

"Heard you got a new saddle horse down at your place, Newt," Jess said suddenly.

"Ought to see him. Steps around like a cat." Encouraged, Newt stepped out in front of the men, lifting his legs high. "Look. Walks like this."

But he had no chance to walk back. The bedroom door opened and the ladies surged out, led by Mrs. Cooper. She had something in her hands. She beamed. Stunned, Newt saw that it was a baby's sweater. With thumb and forefinger she held out each tiny sleeve. With arms extended she advanced on her husband.

"Oooooo!" she cried sharply. "Look what we've got!"

She came closer and closer. She held up the garment to Newt, and it was lost in the expanse of his shirt front. She brought it up coyly and rubbed it against his cheek, where a few bits of fluff stuck to his whiskers. Newt fell back, but his wife was firm. "See how soft! Oooo!" She rubbed the sweater against her own cheek. Like wolves the men pounced on Newt.

"Little sweater looks pretty good on him!" They laughed loud, dry laughter.

Cy stood, crimson, beside Amy. Her hand touched his arm. She smiled up at him, happy. "Cy held the yarn right on his hands while I wound it, didn't you, Cy?"

He muttered something.

"What's that, Cy? Oh, he's pretending he didn't want you over tonight! He's pretending it was my idea, aren't you, Cy? Well, it was then! It was all my idea." She patted him. "You put on some coffee and I'll take care of all these mean laughing people." She looked after him, then turned. "Now!" she said. "You all sit down." She looked around happily. "Surprised?"

"Frankly," Mrs. Cooper said, "I was surprised." She steered Amy into a far corner of the room.

"It was funny," Amy said. "I didn't want anyone to know— until I was—sure. I'm sure now."

"Yes," Mrs. Cooper admitted, glancing at the scarf. "I see you are sure."

"Cy calls me 'little mother,'" Amy said. "He wouldn't want anyone to know that."

"No. He wouldn't want anyone to know that. Now, tell me about it."

"At first," Amy began, "I felt awful. I'm almost fifty. I didn't want anyone to know. You don't think anything about young people—you know. But older people—you know. But Cy was glad. Wanted to tell everybody, and I kept telling him not to. I wouldn't go out of the house, and then one morning I was glad to." She was serious. "I accepted it."

"You might as well," Mrs. Cooper advised.

"So we decided to have you over. We knew you'd all have to know sometime."

"Sooner or later we all would have known," Mrs. Cooper said.

The coffee smell seeped about the house, steaming cups, plates of sandwiches made of thick slices of beef. Now it was a proper party, and men disappeared into the pantry for a second, and women disappeared into rooms.

Jess found Cy alone in the kitchen. The two men moved in the lamplight, their shadows tall and stooping. Cups clicked; stove lids rattled. Jess and Cy were silent and uneasy, because in both their minds was a forbidden subject, childbirth.

Now on the prairie sex was never discussed with another man, and this was strange because the prairie lived because of sex, the breeding of cattle and horses. A man would buy a bull and refer to it—sometimes even to another man—as a "gentleman cow." Both men would avert their eyes as the bull went about his business. The word "bull" was terse and lewd and brought to mind a kind of purposeful wandering.

Nor was "stud" used, for this word brought up a low, throaty neighing, insistent, and feverish eyes. And although it was ignored, a man was an animal and lived with a female. And so childbirth and sex were not discussed because somehow it insulted your wife. When a man spoke to a friend who was going to be a father he was very careful.

"Reach down that pie, will you, Jess?"

"Mmmm," Jess said. "Apple."

They leaned against the table, chewing, watching the ceiling.

Jess said, "Congratulations. Sure is fine."

Cy still looked at the ceiling. "I don't know. Kids are squawky. Trouble all the time."

Jess stared at the sandwich in his hand. "Not much trouble." Then he blundered on, ashamed of what he was saying, afraid of the bigness of it. "You've got everything, Cy. You've got everything a man would want."

Cy stood straight and stretched, nonchalant. Jess turned his head and felt as though he were caught stealing, or cheating, doing something ugly. For Beth stood in the door.

She smiled. "Hello." And briskly she gathered up some loose sandwiches and arranged them neatly on a platter.

XXIV

IT WAS A late fall morning and the peaks in the distance were orange with sun; the cattle wandered slowly out of the timber to feel the warmth against their hides and to lie down and twist their necks and lick themselves. Buffalo grass glistened with moisture where the slanting red rays fell, but in the shadow of the timber the frost lay thick. A meadowlark piped, piercing the early silence.

Cy stood in the door of the barn, hatless, watching the sun until he was blinded. It was that hour when the prairie was close to a man, intimate with silences. But Cy felt nothing. Now he had worried too long, and the chill in the air did not touch him. He scarcely heard Doc Morse call from the porch.

"Cy!" Doc's voice was loud in the frosty air. The forced heartiness of a man who has worked all night.

Cy turned. "Doc?"

"It's a girl. A regular little girl!"

Cy grinned and walked blindly to the house, and his eyes were hot. His step was the step of a young man.

Doc said again, "It's a girl. A regular girl!"

The chore boy pushed open the kitchen door with his boot, his arms piled high with wood. He found Doc and Cy sitting at the kitchen table, a bottle between them. Cy's white hair was tousled above his eager eyes. "You want to see the prettiest little lady?" A vertical finger against his lips as he rose unsteadily. "Sh."

Amy slept, smiling, and beside her was Adele Pierce, swaddled in blankets, with a small red face and a snub nose. She was four hours old and very ugly.

"Pretty?" Cy whispered hoarsely. "My two girls."

"You've got two girls!" Doc agreed. They were struck with the idea.

"You know what?" Cy demanded of the chore boy. "I came in here and put my finger down by the baby, and that little cuss took its hand and touched my finger!" Cy brought his right hand up and clutched at the long finger of the left hand.

"That's pretty good," the chore boy admitted. "Smart for the age of it." He began to back around the corner of the wall.

"Smart!" Cy repeated. "Opens and closes her eyes!" Cy opened and closed his eyes.

The chore boy said the boss and Doc were lit up like Christmas trees. "No breakfast," he announced gloomily.

They joined the boss in the kitchen, shy awkward men who knew what the boss expected. They had a few drinks and then a few more. They got a kind of breakfast, but the cattle in the hills took care of themselves that day.

Mrs. Cooper explained that she had brought beef tea to no one since ten years before when a friend up the creek died after a lingering illness.

"You remember her, Amy. Too frail to visit. She just lay back there suffering."

"It's nice," Amy said, taking a hand out from under the quilt and patting Mrs. Cooper's arm, "but I don't need beef tea. Beef tea is something you've got to *need*. I never felt better." She turned to look at the sleeping baby in the clothesbasket beside the bed.

"You're a brave little woman," Mrs. Cooper announced throatily. "A brave little woman."

"I'm not," Amy insisted a little crossly. "I never felt better. I'll be up in a day or so. They say Chinese women work in the field soon after."

"And look where it gets them," Mrs. Cooper said. "You're a brave little woman. Having a baby is a great undertaking, even for a Chinese woman." She swished the beef tea around in the jar, looking a little distastefully at the reddish-brown liquid. "And you must remember that you're almost fifty."

"I'm going to be up." Amy sat up in bed, squaring her thin shoulders. "Cy's going to let me drive the buggy. He's going to let me take the gentle team and drive around the ranch here, and later I can visit.

"But, Amy," Mrs. Cooper said coldly, "you never have."

"Cy says a woman who can have a baby can do anything. He says having a baby is difficult. He'll be gone on the roundup for a couple of weeks, and I'm not going to sit around here until he gets back. I'm going visiting. I've got something to show off." She beamed down at the baby.

Mrs. Cooper leaned over the baby, her great spare figure almost witchlike. She grinned. "Itchy-kitchy!"

When she had been up a week Cy went into the city to sign papers.

"Men are always signing papers," Amy said. "Everything you do, you sign papers. Don't men do anything else in town? What do you sign? Why do you sign?"

Cy smiled. "I guess it makes us feel important. Signing a paper is something no other man can do in exactly the same way. I wish I didn't have to go in. Wish you could come with me. Amy, maybe you could wrap the baby up—" He knew it was impossible.

"No. I'll be all right. I won't even be lonesome."

He smiled at that. For twenty years she had been lonesome when he went away. He used to bring her presents. Gloves. She had always liked gloves, small white gloves with long sleevelike cuffs. A box of chocolates. He would say, "Did you get along all right, Amy?" She had never gotten along all right. She had been miserable. Couldn't read, couldn't think. It was a cruel thing that it pleased him.

She would ask, "Did you bring me something?"

He would say, "I was going to, but I forgot," and would follow a long story of why he forgot. Then he would bring out the gloves or the chocolates.

When the papers were signed Cy went to the Emporium. He knew what he wanted. An Edison phonograph with several cylinders. She need never be lonesome again. She could listen to "Casey Jones."

He came home whistling. He had a plan all worked out. "What I'll do," he told himself, "is I'll have the contraption rigged up in the front room with a string on it to start it, and when she asks me what I brought I'll pull the string." He laughed aloud, startling the blacks so they lunged, wild-eyed. "Easy, babies!"

In the kitchen he smiled to himself, pulling off his driving gloves. "And did you get along all right, Amy?" Chuckling.

"Wait," she called from the front of the house, "until I tell you!" She came to him, talking around a safety pin she held in her teeth, lisping. "The baby has gained. Three ounces." Mrs. Cooper's book on babies—some new book—said you mix water with milk. "But that's nonsense, Cy." She had been too busy to think.

She didn't mention the present. For the first time in twenty years she didn't mention a present. The routine they had built, guarded and cherished, had vanished in one afternoon. She had not been lonely.

He sighed wearily and slumped down heavily in his leather chair, legs stretched out before him. Sadly he watched his feet, noticing that his shoes were worn and old. "Don't know when I've been so damned tired," he said.

She was a little concerned. "What did you do today? No trouble about signing papers?" She laughed a little. She began to sew busily, glancing up brightly now and then.

"No more than usual. Just getting old," he said slowly. "Then I had to do an errand."

"What errand?" She stopped for a second, needle poised. "I didn't know you had anything else to do."

"Something to do at the Emporium."

"My present!"

"I didn't get a present," he said crossly. "Didn't have time to think."

She smiled. "I was busy, too, but I had time to think of you. I didn't forget you." She rose, came to him, and sat on the arm of the big chair.

"It isn't much, what I got," he told her. "It's an Edison phonograph." He remembered happily that she was dumbfounded. He set it up, feeling clever. No trouble at all to slip the cylinder on, to secure it, to lower the needle. "Casey Jones" filled the room, the high notes sharp and fine in the ears. It was funny how the baby could lie quietly in the clothesbasket. Someday he would say to her, "You lay there as if nothing was going on. And all the time we had a phonograph playing, the first phonograph we ever had."

XXV

Now Cy Pierce had everything he wanted.

There was his wife and his child, his land, and now his new house, Amy's new house. It was a big brown house of logs, bigger even than they had planned, and it had been ready to move into not a month after the baby was born.

It had been funny, watching the new house rise, log by log, and living in the old house. It was as if he were two men. He would stand in the bare plastered rooms of the new house, looking through raw-pine glassless sills at the old house, and it made him sad. He would stand in the house looking out through the small panes of wavy glass at the new house, and that made him sad too. They had had a party, had danced and admired the new house and the electric lights. But the party was not like Jess's, because there were many new houses now.

Late that August he stood inside the barn. It was not cool even there. Horseflies zoomed in through the big door. A horse stamped, swished its tail, and hung its head again.

A dog lay before the door of the harness room, tongue lolling out. Regularly a drop of saliva dripped off and fell in the powdery dust. Only when a fly buzzed too close would the dog become suddenly alert, raise its head and snap viciously, and collapse again, head in paws.

The chore boy trundled a wheelbarrow piled high with sour hay and manure the length of the barn and dumped it somewhere out back. Cy stood beside his saddled horse, pulling at the saddle strings.

He knew exactly where he was going to ride.

The chore boy dropped the wheelbarrow handles, rubbed his palms together, and smelled them. "Christ, a barn smells! What you want to ride in this heat for?"

"I've got a little business," Cy said.

"What you going to do? Let me take old Bess and go."

Cy said, "You finish up the barn. You got your work to do."

"Hell," the chore boy said, "I could finish this evening. You let me go. You don't got to do it."

"You finish up the barn," Cy said.

He led his horse out the door into the blinding, burning sun. The sun blended all colors. The gray road trailed off at the sides of the greenish gray of the sage, and that trailed off into tannish gray toward the fields where the grass lay scorched. At last the brown stubble fading into the foothills. Even the blue of the sky was bleached, washed out. The pommel of the saddle was hot to his touch, sun-baked.

The field lay across the dry bench, a stretch of little gray hills jammed together like biscuits in a pan, little gray hills eroded and cut by cloudbursts. Up and down you had to ride, through this badland where a few farmers had come, had gambled and plowed up the ground.

Here below him was a house, the shack of clapboards and tar paper, squatting to one side of the shallow gulch. Across from the house the lean-to barn covered with dry willow branches brought up from the distant creek. There was no clear-flowing water here, only a deep well and bitter, yellow water.

A young man with big hands had lived on the land in the shack, and a young woman with a brown, lined face. She wore a man's shoes. They had plowed up the ground and sat in their shack looking out at the dry furrows, waiting for the rain to fall on the slanty roof, praying for rain, thinking of the ranchers and the good green land along the creeks.

At last they went away with their roll of gray bedding and their brown cardboard suitcase. The ranchers hadn't driven them away. The sun and the cloudburst that dissolved the powdery soil in the furrows had done it.

Cy rode down to the shack conscious of a curious silence. The door with the cracked black leather hinges sagged at an angle against the doorsill and scraped across the floor when he pushed it in. His footsteps were ghostly.

For a moment he stood just inside, getting his eyes used to the bit of yellowish light that filtered in through weathered cracks in the roof and the dirt-glazed windows.

Grime, trash covered the floor and filled the wide cracks. In one corner the stove was rusting.

"*We got to take the stove. We got to cook on something.*"

"*How we gonna take it? Heavy. Charge you a hundred dollars, ship it. Where we gonna—? We get new stove, when we know . . .*"

The bedstead made of rough slats. Apple-box slats. The boards they use to crate machinery, farm machinery paid for with a piece of paper and a man's signature. From the mattress rose a mustiness that filled the room.

"*Terrible to leave a bed and mattress. Funny, first thing we buy we move somewheres, a bed and mattress. Pretty soft, that mattress.*"

"*You wait. When we get where we're going we buy a mattress that thick!*"

Cy walked across the floor. Underneath something scurried. Mouse and rat leavings crunched beneath his feet. And there was a child's doll, a pretty china face, the head cracked off at the top. The body had been of white muslin stuffed with sawdust. A leg was missing, and a china hand.

"*Willa, why you want to take that old doll? It's all broke. You leave it here. Now you stop crying! You see. Mamma'll buy a doll big as that one of these days! You see!*"

Once the table had been covered with oilcloth. The rusty tacks around the edges held frayed bits.

"*Here. I rip off this oilcloth; you use it wrap round the lunch.*"

Cy walked to the window. Flies in the cobwebs were dusty dry shells, quivering in the faintest movement of air. The spiders had gone. A dead bird on the sill, its body shrunk in the heat, its feet curled, withered, only the sharp little talons intact. A bird can live a long time without food or water. A bird can fly blindly about the room and beat its wings and foolish head against a window for a long time.

On the floor lay a newspaper, stained with round brown spots from rain leaking in. Cy picked it up.

Ye editor was in the crowd that welcomed back our boys. The Salmon City Band came and played a French tune, "Madelon." . . .

There had been no time in this shack since that day five years before. When the tired young woman and her man shut the door behind them time stopped and began to rot.

Cy let the paper fall to the floor.

The prairie had been good to him. He had everything he wanted. A wife and a little girl almost two. He had land and a new house.

And he wished that he had had a chance to speak to the big-handed young man, to smile at the young woman in the man's shoes.

XXVI

SO THE WAR was over and forgotten. President Harding was dead. Coolidge was President, and Mrs. Cooper said the trouble with him was that he'd lived in Vermont as a child where nobody had enough to eat. Mrs. Cooper admired Mrs. Coolidge a great deal, and a picture of Mrs. Coolidge had taken the place of Carrie Nation over the organ. "She's active in Girl Scouts," Mrs. Cooper said. "She's very kind-looking, and I think she's suffered."

The twenties were beginning to roll. There was a restlessness in the country, a fever, and some of it had seeped into the prairie from the outside. Young men of the prairie talked as they talked outside of radios: Fadas, Freed-Eisemanns, and Atwater-Kents; of automobiles: of Maxwells, of Overlands, and Willys-Knights.

"Them Willys-Knights. They got sleeve valves. Old motor gets better and better." And now nobody called automobiles "machines."

Gray choking clouds of dust rolled up once more behind the lumbering chuck wagon, and they swore because farmers had come and thrown up barbed-wire fences on the open range.

"They should of took the wire with them when they went."

"Country's not what it used to be, not what it was."

They rode again, day after day, dust in their throats. Bellowing, milling cattle. A horse fell; a leg was broken. Dust and sun and miles. They told the oldest jokes because these belonged to them.

At night there were the same campfires, but some of those who used to sit around were missing.

"He was a nice fellow. Remember . . ."

They sat on their haunches and leaned forward in the darkness to poke at the fire with sticks.

"He would give you the shirt off his back."

The coals of the fire would die, and the smoke would curl away. They sang softly, the oldest songs. They sang the "Old Ninety-Seven." Like the train, that song had once been new and strange. Now it belonged to them, as the trucks, the big red trucks that were crowding the train out, would never belong to them.

Down on the prairie the women waited, missing the heavy thump of men's boots and the loud voices.

Amy drove up proudly before Jess's house and called: "Beth! Here I am! I mean, here we are. I keep forgetting my daughter. You have to get used to them." She climbed out of the buggy. "Take the baby. She walks now. I've got to take the team in. No—don't come. I know about a team, a gentle team, anyway. Cy's taught me about teams. He says I can do anything now. He said someday when he was along he'd let me drive the blacks!"

Beth watched, amazed, as Amy, awkward but game, led the gentle bay team to the barn.

Amy hedged. She talked of nothing. Several times she looked sharply at the baby toddling about the room. "They do grow, Beth. A baby's a wonderful thing to watch growing." She sighed. "I suppose you miss Jess, now he's on the roundup."

"Yes, I miss him. But I read, and I paint—"

"I know what it is to be lonely. That is, I did know. You get used to a man. They have a strong smell. I don't mean they smell bad. I mean in the house you're aware of them and it seems much safer."

"That's the way it is." Beth wandered to the window and stood looking out at the mountains.

Amy watched her. "If you had someone to be with you—when he's away. Someone to keep you busy. If only—"

Beth turned and smiled, her eyes vague. "If only I had a baby, you mean."

Amy flushed. "I just meant you do get lonely and—" She picked a thread from her sleeve. "All right." Her voice was direct. "Of course you ought to have a baby. They're wonderful, even"—and she smiled—"even when you wonder what to do with them." She sighed. "I knew that people laughed at me for sticking close to Cy. I enjoyed the way they talked and tried to seem more dependent than I was. But not now. I love him, but he's not all I've got." She laughed self-consciously. "Listen to me arranging things."

Beth turned again to the window. Somewhere out there in the mountains Jess was. She turned slowly to Amy. Her eyes were still and gray and deep.

"I'm going to have a baby. This fall, Amy."

It was hard to tell with Jess not there. Hard to tell.

The blue haze of fall lay like a mantle along the divide, enveloping the peaks, folding along the ridges. Smoke from distant forest fires hung heavy and fragrant on clear days, and the sun, when it set, was blood-red.

They rounded up their cattle and held them in the corners of the fall-bronzed fields. Lariats snapped out and caught the hind feet of fat calves. Here branding irons were pulled from the fire, and the heavy yellow smoke of scorched hide and burning hair curled around, acrid in nostrils. Twenty thousand head of calves were branded that fall, and almost a thousand of them were Jess Bentley's.

He was glad when branding was over. He missed Beth beside him, admiring him when he made a good throw with the lariat, missed admiring her when she took a hand with the roping herself. But she couldn't ride now. He fretted.

"It's my fault. It makes a slave out of you."

"It's not your fault. And it's fair to give up something you like for something you'll love." He liked the sound of that so well he often repeated it to himself, but he wasn't convinced.

From the cluttered pages of the fall and winter catalogues the prairie picked its Mackinaws and replaced round-oak stoves, puzzling as usual over the tricky problems of shipping weights.

"How you figure this? Ten pounds eight ounces to here?"

"Which zone we in?"

"Says here fifth zone."

"Well, you figure it. You know which zone."

They bought mittens and long woolen underwear and Scotch caps. They got ready for winter. Now the sun was up two hours before the last of the tinsellike frost disappeared from the buffalo grass on the sidehills. The shadows were long all day, and winter's chill came at four o'clock.

But it was pleasant, Jess thought, to drive out on crisp fall afternoons when the wind whipped against your cheeks and to stop with neighbors for coffee and cinnamon rolls.

Beth did most of the talking. Jess preferred to remain in the background, to bring a cup of coffee, to carry away an empty cup. He was quiet and reserved and thoughtful, as becomes the head of a family. He complimented people on their babies, nodding his head and smiling. But his own would be better.

"Boy, it'll be, too."

Sometimes he thought of the old days when he had found fun at a dance and occasionally in a bottle, when his ambition had been to ride any bronco in the country. "I must have been crazy."

One day they drove along the narrow winding road that ran along Anderson's land, a dusty road, bumpy with round gray cobblestones, high with sagebrush. Foothills on one side, meadow on the other. He drove carefully, creeping along. Man couldn't afford to jounce his wife now. He hoped Beth would ask where they were going.

She did.

"You'll see," he told her. It was pretty, the way the breeze brought color to her cheeks, the way it blew the soft hair under her broad hat. She had never looked better than she did now.

He drew the horses up directly above Anderson's biggest field, fall brown now, dotted with hay stacks. Far across the valley Anderson's house was a neat white speck. Anderson's biggest field was more than a thousand acres; along the far end reddish-brown willows grew along the meandering creek, good shelter for cattle from the winter wind, nice warm parks that the sun could warm in the spring and melt the snow around the willow roots where a cow could have her calf in a nice dry place. These were the things to look for in a field.

"He must have five hundred tons of hay there, Jess."

Jess moved his lips, multiplying, adding. "Near that. Anderson says six hundred. He says he's got the water rights to get seven hundred. Matter of work. Fellow could work. Fellow could work hard to a piece of land like that."

She turned to him. "It's not like Anderson to tell you all that. He's closemouthed. He doesn't talk about his business."

Still looking across the field, Jess said, "I've made a deal with him. He and the missus want to go back to the old country."

She looked at him, amazed. "Jess," she faltered. "You're not going to buy him out? The money—"

"I've bought him out. No farmer's going to get hold of this. No farmer's going to take a plow and rip up the land and put in wheat. There's not going to be combines where a chuck wagon belongs. It's going to be like it always was." He spoke directly out to the field. "If the sun wants to parch hell out of it, that's all right." He paused for breath and grinned, a little embarrassed. "And it'll make us money."

Beth put her head on his shoulder and looked up at him. "What is it, Beth?"

"I was thinking. More of us—more land for us." She was so serious that he laughed.

"If you had twins you'd break me."

That was pretty good.

He went on. "Anderson's going next month. Then it's ours." He looked out across. "I guess," he said lightly, "it'll be a girl."

"It will be a boy."

"How do you know?"

"I know." He knew she knew. They could say all they wanted to that a woman didn't know what she was going to have, but Beth knew.

From somewhere a gust of wind swept over them. Beth shivered a little and drew her coat collar tight. "Jess—I was thinking about Anderson. He's been here a long time."

"And he's been wanting to go for a long time. He'll be all right. Sure he will."

"I can't help thinking how it would be if you had to go."

"That's crazy."

"I guess it is." Then, cheerfully, "Tuck the blanket around me. It's getting chilly." The wind had come up. "And, Jess, I'm glad about the deal with Anderson. I can't help thinking sometimes. You know. Sometimes you can't help thinking."

Yesterday was fall.

XXVII

DOC MORSE CAME far more often to see Beth than he had to see Amy, Jess knew. It worried him. But Doc stormed and growled and insulted him until the extra attention seemed flattery.

"Remember back, Jess. When Amy was heavy I was busy as all get out. I wouldn't be around so much if I was busy; don't forget it." He groused. "I'm so damned tired. Every woman on the prairie's had a baby this year. Couldn't get my own work done. Doing some experiments with white rats; see if I couldn't control the male's feeling for the female—matter of diet. No success. *Sic transit gloria mundi.* Take my rig to the barn, Jess. I'm too damned old."

Jess, grinning again, would help the old man out. "Sure appreciate the care you're taking of her."

"Bosh. Always interested in a first baby. After that it's hack work." Doc would hurry into the house, and when Jess came back from the barn, any advice he had given Beth was given, anything said was said. They isolated him.

"Now see here, Jess," Doc said. "I'm an old man. I'm not going to deliver this baby. You're going to send her to Butte. They've got a fine hospital there, great big new place. I've written them, got a private room Two weeks from today. Going to be hard for you to get away? You've got to brand calves?"

Jess, frowning, looked at the old man. "Amy's going with her. Should I go?"

Doc was silent a moment, filling his stubby pipe. He spoke suddenly to cover the silence. "No. Of course not. Don't butt into women's business." They looked at each other, understanding well enough about women and women's business.

In October the sun rose late. Now in the deep shadow of the cliff above the house the frost tinsel on the browning stubble lingered late until the reddish rays bronzed and melted it. The sun moved lazily across the sky, and on these Indian-summer days Jess walked with Beth in the upper field; he, tall, gangling, awkward on foot, and she beside him, her hand on his arm, walking slowly. If she had been handsome before, now she was beautiful, for her eyes, always soft and smiling, now held something that brought a lump to his throat.

"Lean a little on my arm."

"Your son's so heavy. He thumps."

"Thumps?"

"Thumps."

"That would mean a good strong one."

"I would say so." Smiling.

"Doc said so. You say they're good strong thumps?" He flushed when her eyes caught his, for they had been through this many times before. He was obsessed with the idea that she should be in the sun, that her face and hands should tan a little. They sat where the breeze could not reach them, against the willows along the winding creek. Below was the comforting sight of their house, and above them the blue velvet folds of the mountains.

"Has Doc said any more about—when?"

"He still says two weeks—less now."

"Less." He was silent awhile, his face bronze in the sun. He reached to one side and caught a still-green willow branch and watched it. He reached suddenly into his pocket, moving his long legs. The pocketknife he drew out was small in his big hands. He opened it slowly. "When I was a kid I used to make whistles out of willow branches.

"Well"—he cut the willow, then made a six-inch piece of it—"you cut the bark around here. Then here. And notch it." He laughed softly. "There's not enough sap to get the bark off this one. But"—and his eyes were deeply serious—"it's a good thing for a kid to do in the spring when the sap's running."

She watched him.

Behind them there was a faint scurrying, rustle of drying leaves and stubble, the creaking of twigs. Then a brush rabbit, small brown puff of fur, no bigger than Jess's fist, crept out into the sun, its nose wriggling, its ears flat against its head, beady eyes bright. It raised its ears cautiously, then lowered them and crept back into the underbrush.

"When I was a kid," he said, "my dad brought me a little brush rabbit. He was always bringing me things like that."

"What did you do with it, Jess?"

"I made a box with a screen on top. Even a kid can do that if you help him a little."

She bit her lip. "What did you feed it?"

He glanced at her, then away. "I—made a derrick, a little toy one like we used in the fields. I put up hay from grass around the house, cut it with shears, and made a stack. Then I gave it to the rabbit, and water in a dish." He was looking out at the cliff, remembering. Then softly, "But the rabbit didn't do very good. It wouldn't eat the grass. It sat in a corner against the boards."

The silence was deep.

She cleared her throat. "What happened to the rabbit?"

"I was just a kid," he said. "I took the box down to the willows, like here, and I took the screen off. I took the rabbit out and set it down in the tall grass. It—hopped off." He looked at her. "I was just a kid."

She raised her eyes to his. Even then his hands must have been big, his legs long, awkward. "Jess . . ."

He said, "It was going to die, that rabbit."

Her lips parted in a little smile, and her eyes were moist.

Now everything was upset. Suitcases in the living room, clothes on chairs. Tommy packed a lunch for Beth on the train.

"Move, boss." And Jess shaving at the little mirror in the kitchen, would step to one side. He puffed out his cheek to shave better. He grimaced. He stopped the razor and hummed.

"Now, where's the bay rum?" he called loudly.

"In the bedroom here," Beth called. "Just a minute, I'll bring it."

He began to wipe the lather on the roller towel. "No. I'll get it," he mumbled.

Before he had finished she stood beside him, the big square bottle in her hands. "It seems to me" he said, "that you're pretty spry."

"I feel wonderful." He went back to his shaving, the lump in his throat.

Doc had called the night before and had talked with her in the bedroom while Jess stood in the kitchen and fidgeted as Tommy fixed coffee. "You never got married, Tommy?"

Tommy looked up shrewdly. "No. Never had sons." He measured coffee. "My brother had many sons. My brother never sick over one son. Velly good woman. Not one daughter, seven sons."

"Was his—the woman—sick after the sons?"

Tommy grinned. "She bring in stovewood right away."

Jess was cross. "Your brother could have brought in the wood for the—woman." But his mind was at ease about Beth. There was Amy who, at almost fifty, had had an easy time, and now this Chinese woman.

He wore a white shirt, whiter against the swarthiness of his skin, but the back of his neck was white under his hat, for Tommy had shaved his neck. His hat was carefully brushed, his suit pressed. He sat rigid, proud and tall in the top buggy, the reins taut in his gloved hands. "I'm not jouncing you?"

"No, Jess." She looked almost childish in the old-fashioned full skirt. Her face was tranquil under her big hat, the veil up over the brim.

"We've got to get an automobile," he said, "like everybody else. We—wouldn't want anybody thinking they had old-fashioned folks, would we?" He grinned at his little joke. There was a cloud of dust on the foothills on one side. "See up there?"

She shaded her eyes.

"Cattle."

"Cows and calves. We'll brand tomorrow. In a little while, when you come back, you can ride again and rope, like before."

"Who'll take care of the baby?"

"Why, by gosh!" He turned to her. "I forgot! I forgot all about him!"

There ahead at last, on the edge of town, was the little low station, the sun glaring down on it, the train beside it, waiting. There were two buggies there and an automobile.

"I sort of wanted nobody to be there today, Beth."

"It's still the prairie, Jess. They've got to come."

"They've got to fuss and fuss," Jess grumbled.

She put her hand on his arm. "Amy had to come; Cy had to bring her. And Doc wanted to be here."

"And, good lord," he said, "there's the Coopers. She always stirs up everything."

Regardless of the heat, Mrs. Cooper wore a dark wool suit, for the calendar said fall. She came forward, the heavy skirts billowing. "A fine one you are, Jess Bentley, keeping your wife out in the sun! Here, Beth, take my arm."

"Jess and I are glad you remembered today was the day." Beth laughed. "We hoped you hadn't forgotten."

"Nobody forgets friends," Mrs. Cooper said. "At any rate, not old ones. I was about to drive up to the Fishers' yesterday and warn them that today was the day, and then I thought, no, it would be better to have the going away quiet. Mrs. Westley Fisher is a great one for butting in and arranging things, and I just thought it would be easier this way."

"A trip in a buggy is tiring now," Beth said.

"Of course it is," Mrs. Cooper said. "Newt, help Jess out with the bags. Don't stand there. Call Cy and Amy. They're around the station."

Amy came around the corner of the station carrying her baby. "Yoo-hoo!" She laughed. "My, you do look happy and expectant."

Mrs. Cooper turned to Amy. "I shouldn't say she looked expectant especially. She kept active until the last, which is more than you did, Amy. You never exercised. You sat."

"But see what an easy time I had!"

"My dear woman," Mrs. Cooper said gently, "you suffered a good deal more than you let on. Beth is wiser, moving about. She never sat."

"But I had a wonderful little girl!" Amy insisted.

"Now, see!" Mrs. Cooper triumphed. "My mother always said active women have sons; inactive women have daughters. I remember distinctly."

Jess said, "What's that you said?"

Mrs. Cooper repeated. Jess said, "Doc said something like that." He laughed, pulling down the leather suitcases from the buggy, thumping them down on the board platform.

"You made that up, that saying!" Amy cried.

"I did not," Mrs. Cooper said coldly. "Jess remembers the old saying. Dr. Morse told him, didn't you, Doctor?"

She had called inside the open door of the station, where the old doctor had gone to buy tickets. He came toward them. "What was that?"

"I was reminding Amy what you said about women who didn't get about. My mother remembered the saying too. My mother was a wonderful woman, and my father too."

No one stirred in the little town, but a breeze, high up, creaked the old windmill beside the Salmon City House. A horse tied at the rack in front swished at flies with its tail and hung its head.

There was a moment before the train pulled away, a moment when Beth and Jess were alone, time enough for her to lean close.

"Darling," she whispered, "I'll be back soon." He squeezed her hand. "I'll bring a boy back with me."

"Sure you will," he whispered. "Sure," and flushed.

Now the little train puffed away. Mrs. Cooper stood tall, correct, and waved, and the two figures on the platform waved, Beth and Amy. Newt slouched near his wife. He turned to Jess. "Your real troubles are beginning now."

"They sure are, all right." And he laughed.

Cy said, "This is the day, Jess."

Jess said, "This is the day, all right."

Newt said, "We ought to go up and have a drink. We ought to go up to Brad's and have a drink."

Jess shook his head. "I got to get home. Got to brand tomorrow." It wasn't right to drink and talk loud now. He'd drive home alone in the buggy. And plan.

XXVIII

EVEN AFTER FIVE years the telephone was a strange thing. Nobody used it without self-consciousness. They still said, "I was talking with so-and-so *on the telephone*, and I said—"

High on the wall in a little brown box, the mouthpiece placed so that the average man stood straight talking into it and a woman stood on tiptoe, the telephone gave a man a strained feeling, and his words were awkward. Jess was always aware of how foolish he must look, talking into nothing. When he rode horseback across the sagebrush flats where the thin gray poles straggled off into the distance, the wires sagging, he marveled.

"What won't they think of next?"

He had heard that in other places, in cities, the telephone was always working. You could, they said, call long distances and hear and be heard. But on the prairie the buzzing and clicking and humming that clouded an outside call reduced conversations to simple, short sentences, and anything important was always confirmed by letter.

"I'll write you a letter."

Jess always hung up the receiver with a feeling of apprehension, never of satisfaction. He hoped that the telephone would be "working" within the next week or ten days. Amy was to telephone when the baby was born.

"At least that ought to come through," she had told him.

He did foolish things. He had recorded a brand that fall and had an iron made up, differing from his own, and with it he had branded a dozen calves. He said something vague about needing a second brand for his cattle, but Slim and the rest of the boys knew well enough what the brand was for.

An irrigation ditch ran past the house, clear and swift, and a dam near the house could divert water into a little vegetable garden near the kitchen where Tommy spent his spare time pulling weeds and mumbling at the rocky soil.

He cut picketlike stakes and fenced the deep portion of the ditch off, made a little corral. Then it occurred to him that while the baby was learning to walk he ought to be in a little corral of his own, a kind of pen you could pull in and out of the sun, with rungs around the top so the baby could pull himself up.

"I'm going to make him a corral," Jess told Cy. Cy was enthusiastic, took the idea for his own, and made his daughter one. But Jess held back. He would make his pen when the call came, something to keep busy with while he waited for Beth and her son.

He had a kind of hunch one Friday after supper. One dark, dismal Friday when the rain had started in the afternoon and the thunder roared down from Black Canyon. Lonely, he had gone into the bunkhouse and sat with the men in the rickety chairs there, listening to their talk of other places, other times. They rolled cigarettes and talked while they rolled them, looking out into the warm little room. The rain on the roof made the older men think.

They talked of their brothers and their brothers' wives, and how fine their old man was, and their old lady. You were to understand you couldn't judge their families by them.

The young cowboy was silent. The Kid, they called him. For in the past of the older men in the room was the freedom and the wildness now his. And it led to nothing. Now they were lonely, middle-aged men sitting in chairs in a room that belonged to somebody else.

"Oh hell," the Kid said at last, yawning. "Say Boss, you heard on the phone yet?"

They all came back to the present. "Not yet. Maybe tomorrow."

The Kid laughed. "It's a night like this, raining, when it's hard to hear on a phone, that a call comes through."

It disturbed Jess a little. He walked through the rain to the house. He'd just call.

He rang twice, a short and a long ring, loud in the silent room, and he heard the crack of distant lightning in the receiver, and a hum.

"There's been no call tonight," Central said.

He still had the hunch.

He went to the kitchen and made a fire, quietly, for he heard Tommy snoring in his little room. The silence and the excitement that mounted in him made him deliberate, secretive, and he grinned and hummed softly. He made a big pot of coffee and drank it standing, listening to the rain and the growing storm.

Then the sudden peal of the telephone filled the house.

He heard very few of Amy's words, but—enough. It came through.

"A boy," Amy said.

He kept shouting: "Are they all right? Are they *all right?*"

Amy's voice was distant, thin. "Yes. She's all right . . . ."

He sat in his chair and looked at the telephone, that little oak box with the crank, silent now, as lifeless as the chair he sat in. And over it had come—this happiness, this warmth.

He savored what was his in the silence. The lightning behind the windows never reached his eyes; the thunder rolling down from the canyon never reached his ears. He walked bareheaded to the bunkhouse and found it dark, but as he stood just inside the door he heard the beds creak.

"What's that?" Slim called crossly and struck a match so Jess saw his gaunt frame and lined old face. "Oh. You, boss."

The other man and the Kid leaned on their elbows and waited.

"I got the call on the telephone," Jess said stiffly and looked at them.

Slim said, "Well, I'll be damned!"

They got out of bed. They stood around him in their long underwear and shook his hand. "A boy!" they said, and they looked from one to the other. "Well, what do you think of that?"

For a moment Jess stood, stiff with pride. "I've got a bottle inside," he said. Then he began to chuckle a little, softly, then louder. Then he laughed, his face flushed. "A boy!" he said. "Oh, I'll be damned!"

High up in the peaks the wind howled and hummed in the rocky crags and bent the spindly pines and rushed down on the prairie. A bunch of wild horses grazed on the barren gray foothills, picking at the sparse dry buffalo grass, their tails to the wind. The big bay stud that led them had a tangled mane, ropelike tangles they called witches' halters.

Ranchers told their young sons, "That tangled mane. They call that witches' halters. The witches twist up the mane that way to hang on."

The big bay stud looked nervously at his bunch of lean mares and sniffed into the wind that rushed on down. Below, in the fields, the cold wind sneaked through the willows and made creaking sounds. Clouds flew swift overhead, and snow flurries came and went, leaving thin, short-lasting skifts of hard dry snow on the close-cropped stubble.

Now Jess rode with his men, rounding up a bunch of beef cows, and their saddle horses slipped on the snow. The Kid's horse fell. He was thrown clear, but his horse bumped his mouth on the frozen earth, and the heavy silver bit cut deep into the tongue. Nothing bleeds like the cut tongue of a horse.

But all this had happened before. This was early November.

Jess did not look for a letter from Amy or from Beth during those two weeks. He was completely happy, and part of each afternoon he spent alone in the blacksmith shop where he had his tools, making a pen for his son. Each picketlike little stake he worked over, sandpapered with his big hands, and when he finished one he went to the big door and looked out on the prairie and the high-flying clouds. There was an odd smile on his lips. Then he would pick up the saw or hammer and go to work again.

Cy came and admired his work. "That's a fine piece of work, Jess," Cy said. "You're good with your hands."

"There's not much to it," Jess said, grinning. He had never been good with his hands at work like this. But this piece of work *was* good. "I've got a can of red paint. I'm going to paint it."

Cy shook his head slowly. "I wouldn't do it, Jess. A baby chews everything, and paint wouldn't be good."

Jess looked gratefully at Cy and stored away this new knowledge. There was so much you had to get to know . . . . That night he took the can of paint and put it high on the cupboard shelf in the kitchen.

Newt and Mrs. Cooper came for supper, and even at his age there was still something of the dandy about Newt, tall, lean, and his eyes were a little cynical. "Newt always is elegant in a suit." Mrs. Cooper regarded him. "His stomach's been upset all week. He gets that gas."

Newt looked levelly at his wife. "That's why I said come here for supper tonight, for a change. And it's not gas I get."

"My cooking has nothing to do with the condition of your stomach." She turned to Jess. "He didn't take care of himself as a young man. Fried foods and irregular hours." She dismissed the subject. "Cy told us about the pen you made."

Newt said, "Cy said you did a fine job with your hands."

Jess said, "Cy does fine work with his hands too." He had the pen in the room behind the blacksmith shop, the storage room where he kept old saddles and harness, an old heating stove and rolled-up tents. Hiding it, to surprise Beth.

"Well," Newt drawled, "that's a job."

They exclaimed over the fine fitting of the pickets and the braces. "You can't paint it," Jess said. "A baby chews everything."

He was to meet the train alone.

"We're not going to be there because I know how you feel and, besides, it would excite Beth. I'll bring beef tea Wednesday," Mrs. Cooper said. The arrangement was that Cy would not meet the train either. Amy would go directly home with Beth, to help out.

Tommy set up the ironing board and sponged his serge suit with tea water. They both hummed in the kitchen while Jess shaved, peering at himself in the mirror, very serious, then grinning, then very serious. He had harnessed the team, polished the harness, and scraped the mud from the buggy early that morning, and now he walked proud and straight to the barn, his dark suit pressed, his blue shirt starched. He had great dignity, and his father's heavy gold watch chain flashed in the red afternoon sun.

He glanced at the empty seat beside him and the two lap robes freshly shaken out and folded neatly there. It wouldn't be an empty seat long. He thought deeply of the wonderful things that had happened to him, of the big decisions he had made while driving in a buggy. For a long time the road ran along beside his land, and he could not worry that the haystacks on it were fewer, smaller than usual.

He approached and passed a neighbor on horseback. While they talked he took out the heavy gold watch and glanced at it. "Well," he said heavily, "I've got to get on. I'm meeting my wife on the train." He laughed a little. "She's bringing my son home now."

He had no time for the neighbor's gloom. "He's always been gloomy about the winter. I don't notice the fall's so dry and cold."

But how fine it had been that the neighbor hadn't heard about his son. The neighbor got down off his horse and shook his hand . . . .

He drove into the city at least an hour early and tied the buggy and team to a hitching rack behind the station. Walking soberly up the dusty road to the town, he went, through habit, to the post office. Everybody was there around traintime. Women stood at the breast-high tables and scratched at post cards with the old pens. People stood near their boxes and waited for the train and exchanged words with the plump, smiling postmistress. An official-looking sign told the loiterers, "No Loitering."

The ranchers of the prairie came to the post office to talk about the prairie. They talked about diseases that cattle got; they talked about how low streams were, or how dry the summer was. They talked about hay.

Jess smiled absently at those he knew and pushed through the crowd to his letter box. He hadn't had mail for a week. He looked in through the little glass door. A paper, some letters. He twirled the little knobs. He held in his hands his mail, the tight-rolled paper, two letters from outside ranches that had bulls for sale, a letter from a mail-order house.

And a letter from Amy.

He started to open it. Then a rancher spoke, standing just behind him. "How's the hay look up your way, Bentley?"

Jess turned. "So-so."

The rancher spoke crossly. "We been talking around. There don't seem to be much hay in the whole damned country. We get a hard winter . . . "

They always said that in the post office in the fall, Jess thought. Working up worries for themselves. And he said what he always did in the fall: "Well, winter's not here yet."

The rancher said, "It's a damn funny fall. Don't like the cold, dry kind of fall."

Jess was conscious of passing time, and the crowd in the post office was heavier now. Through the window he saw men and women walking down toward the depot. "Oh, we'll make out," he said heartily, a little impatient. Damned if he had much interest in the winter, or even the letter in his hand. Knowing, anyway, what it would say, he shoved it in his coat pocket.

He walked back to the station swiftly, breathing the fine fall air. It would be good for Beth, that air. She would get good and brown, too, in the warm sun. Sometimes sunny November weather lasted until Thanksgiving . . . .

They'd have people over for Thanksgiving dinner. Beth couldn't do much, but Tommy would fix the turkey, and Amy and Mrs. Cooper could come and help. They'd have everybody to dinner. Even a lot of the new people.

Everybody would be there, in his house, in Beth's house. There would be so many that the place would be crowded, and everybody laughing and the baby there, asleep, probably in his basket, and not even waking up with all those people there too.

He walked toward the station in a kind of daze, his eyes serious, building up, step by step, scene by scene, the dinner they would have, their Thanksgiving. He came to suddenly when he walked inside the deserted station and shook his head a little as if he'd been sleeping.

In the dry-smelling, dark station the hard benches were ranged along the wall, and few people ever sat on them. A big wall clock ticked away, and you could see just the brass pendulum swinging lazily to and fro behind the dirty little glass door.

An hour before traintime . . .

He heard steps behind the closed ticket window, and the click of the telegraph key began. He sat on one of the hard benches, and at last the sound of the clock and the clicking of the key died away and he thought again, his eyes looking vacantly at the gaudy sign, a lurid scene of a train bearing down on a low black touring car. "Cross Crossings Cautiously," the sign advised.

"We'll have everybody there," he thought. Then there was a scraping of the ticket window, and it was raised. The ticket agent, a thin, stooped little man, said, "Hello, Mr. Bentley . . . ."

The ticket agent and his wife had been in the city ten years. They were poor. They were thin. They had two children, a little girl of four, blonde and red-lidded like the mother, stooped a little like the father. And there was a little boy.

They lived upstairs in the station and you could see the thin wife going up and down the scaffold-like stairs on the outside of the weathered brown-painted station carrying water from the rusty old pump below. She looked small on the end of the pump handle. You heard her thin sharp voice raised, calling the little girl and quarreling with her husband, for her voice carried through the thin ceiling of the station.

She must sometimes have gone into the town to buy groceries or to talk with someone. But you never remembered, for she and her husband seemed never to leave the station, afraid to leave, afraid of the prairie. They belonged to a different world, a world that lived near the railroad tracks, knew intimately the wail of train whistles and the stench of soft-coal smoke.

The woman dressed untidily, and the little girl was untidy too. They were all too thin . . . .

They had been in the city ten years, and nobody knew them. Late at night you came in the station to buy a ticket, and there was the husband sitting under the lamp, a green eyeshade protecting his weak eyes. He hunched over the telegraph key. And it was funny. Because you saw him, and no matter who you were or how little you'd seen of the outside world you knew that his kind of man worked too hard in crowded places and ate too little and slept in crowded dingy places and tried to be decent in frayed white shirts . . . .

As he worked over the key he had a pot of coffee simmering on the low potbellied stove. They said it was a shame the way the little girl stayed up late. She stayed with her father, inside there, while he worked, close to him, and then the mother would call in the high, thin voice that matched her thin, plain hair in the knot behind.

The little man smiled his thin, ingratiating smile. "Hello, Mr. Bentley."

Jess had been staring at the window as it scraped open, and the sudden look at the ticket agent embarrassed him. "Hello . . . ."

"You expecting the train?" And he went on importantly: "Because it's a little late. They telephoned me from the main line. They always telephone me when it's going to be late." The telegraph key began to click, and he stiffened a little, listening. He laughed a little, offhand. "That's just Idaho Falls . . . ."

The little girl peered up over the window, her eyes wide. Jess smiled at her and she looked soberly at him. He said, "You've got a fine girl there."

The ticket agent looked down at the child. "She's Daddy's girl." He went on, "I've got a boy too. Little fellow, months old. He's just a little fellow. Bobby, we call him. You see, my name's Robert, and you call a little fellow Bobby."

"Matter of fact," Jess said, "I came down here to meet my wife. She's bringing my boy home from the hospital."

"Is that right! Congratulations! Well, now, I did hear talk. Say, Bentley, that's fine!"

Jess held his dignity, but the color flooded his face and he coughed a little. "A kid's mighty funny-looking, new."

"All red," the ticket agent said. "It'd surprise you, Bentley, how red they are!" The little man laughed, remembering. "I'm not one to forget how I felt when my wife gave the little fellow to me to hold, first time. Didn't know how to hold him, thought I'd drop him, first time. Didn't want to squeeze him, hurt him."

"I guess you get used to it, though," Jess said. "You must get the hang of it."

The little girl stood on tiptoe to whisper to her father. He held his ear close to her moving lips. He looked up, smiling. "She wants to see your baby, Bentley, when he comes. She likes a baby. And I'd like a look too."

"You'll see him, all right. He'll probably be squalling." Then Jess said, "I don't hear your boy crying."

"No, he don't cry much. Never did."

"Well, they say most of them cry all the time. Friend of mine, Mrs. Pierce, says it develops their lungs, crying."

The two were deeply serious, and the old clock ticked above them. "Well," the little man said, "Bobby, he don't cry."

Jess was silent a moment, then, "Maybe he don't get in the sun enough."

The two looked at each other. Jess repeated. "You ought to get him more in the sun."

The little man doubted. "My wife says—"

"You must get him in the sun." Jess thought. "Listen," he said. "I've made a sort of pen for mine you can move around outside. Kind of a little corral. You just pick up your family one Sunday soon and drive out to the ranch. I'll show you how to make a pen and fix it right."

Then Jess knew someone was behind him, wanting a ticket. He moved aside, but before he turned to go he smiled at the ticket agent.

People walked down from the town to watch the train come in. They came and looked at the wall clock and set their watches by it and then stood in groups and talked in low tones. Soon they would feel the weight of the train shake the earth and the floor beneath their feet. They would watch to see who got off. Then they would go back to the town, satisfied.

There were signs that the townspeople came to know. They knew there was no use to watch up the track for the train, to get set until the ticket agent opened the big double doors of the express room and trundled his express cart out, tugging at it until it rolled along over the broad platform.

The big doors rolled back. The express truck rolled.

They came out of the station then and looked down the track at the point where the rails, ever-thinning and narrowing, swept around the sharp hill.

Jess stood on the platform, his eyes fastened on the sharp point of the hill. He didn't look about him. Somehow he didn't want his eyes to meet others', but he smiled at the ticket agent pulling the truck because they had a bond. The ticket agent smiled back.

It was funny—it sure was—how nervous it made you to think of holding a baby. It wasn't a joke, this holding a baby the first time. Complicated. You had to hold your hand behind the baby's head.

A little sweat broke out on his forehead.

Eyes cast down, he went around behind the station and looked at his buggy and team, just to kill time. Then he was walking swiftly around again to watch the point of the hill, and though he knew well enough that the whistle of the train always shrieked a warning just before it came in sight, he'd just be sure . . . .

Maybe he'd better not hold the baby at all. Not until its neck got a little stronger. There would be all the baggage to attend to, and the women to help in the buggy, and a lot of people would be around, probably.

He stood very still and watched the point down the track. Then for a moment his eyes went beyond it, out across the prairie to the mountains, hazy in the late smoke of Indian summer. From behind him, up in the town, the comfortable sounds came, the clear barking of a dog, and shouting children playing at some game . . . .

There was a creak, then the heavy clank of the semaphore brought him back. The faded red plank arm slammed down. At almost the same instant the whistle shrieked, and the train swept around the sharp curve of the hill at a giddy angle.

Those on the platform fell silent and watched. Jess felt the tremor in the earth, and it crept inside his body, mounting and mounting. He braced himself for the second blast of the whistle.

It came.

Then the sound surged ahead in waves, hissing, pounding, surging forward, crushing, drowning thought, movement, speech. The black hulk of the engine ground past; the cars swished along. Brakes grated. The train jerked to a stop, and ahead the engine sighed and throbbed, resting. A brakeman swung down.

Then the people moved and talked bravely and loudly above the noise. The ticket agent piled the gray canvas mailbags one on top of the other on the truck, like cordwood. The little man worked importantly at this business, this work was his. He tugged at the truck, heavy now, got it moving, and hurried with it inside the wide doors. Then he came out and stood at a distance on the platform, craning his neck a little.

Jess grinned at him, and the little man grinned back.

There was quite a crowd on the train. One after another they got off, women in sturdy traveling suits and flashily dressed drummers. Women ran forward and kissed other women, and men stood aside and then picked up luggage.

The little ticket agent moved a step forward, watching.

The crowd had thinned.

Jess held his dignity. Beth and Amy would be the last to get off. They would need time. Their bags . . .

And the *baby*. Jess Bentley's son . . .

He wiped his forehead, pushing his big hat back a little.

The last of the crowd had gone away. The ticket agent looked about him. Only he and Jess Bentley stood on the platform.

The little man looked up at the wavy panes of glass in the windows of the car, and behind there were indistinct shapes moving to the door of the car.

Mrs. Pierce came out on the rear platform, her little girl in her arms. She didn't look down at Jess Bentley, just stood aside.

The engine was quiet up ahead, only a low throbbing sound, and the platform was still. The agent listened, keeping out of the way, the little girl beside him still and staring.

A great grin cracked Jess Bentley's face. He stood big and proud, his hat shoved back, all his dignity gone.

"Where's my boy?" he shouted. "Where have you got my boy?" Now Jess Bentley was not worrying about how to hold a baby.

Then the agent could see the young woman too. She leaned against the iron rail of the car, looking down at her man with dead eyes.

Jess Bentley began again: "Where's my—" Then he stopped.

The little girl stood on tiptoe and tugged at the agent's sleeve, whispering. He put his hand down, groping, touched the child, found her hand. He whispered, too, and began to lead her away.

For there was nothing in the young woman's arms. Nothing at all.

XXIX

HIS SUIT OF dark serge and the coat with the letter in the pocket were hung neatly in the dark little closet off their bedroom, and in there on the floor were her two suitcases. The house that had been confused and cluttered with her going was orderly, neat. Only the rocker had been moved to the window where she could sit quietly, looking out. She did not want the chair on the porch or beside the barn, sheltered from the wind, in the sun.

That first late evening he had helped her from the buggy anxiously. She had leaned on his arm as they walked slowly into the house, and only then did he realize how weak, how ill she was. She seemed to weigh no more than a child.

At the door of their bedroom she had hesitated and spoke to him. And it was Amy who went with her into the bedroom.

How like a stranger's voice hers sounded, muffled there in the bedroom. How strange and cold the room was. Then Amy, a quiet Amy, came out. "She's asleep, Jess."

He said suddenly, "Amy . . ."

She looked at him, standing with her hand on the knob of the bedroom door. "Yes?"

"Amy—I've got to know something."

"Yes, Jess."

He looked at her, started to speak, stopped. Then, quietly, "Amy, did he—live at all?"

She nodded. "A day."

He said softly, wonderingly, "Then I—then we really had a boy, didn't we, Amy?"

Amy left within the week, leaving instructions. "She's to be built up. You've got to make her well. She's got to rest . . . ."

He looked at her. Of course. Nothing else but to make her well mattered, nothing but to make her smile at him in a way he knew, not the strange, polite smile.

He got up quietly in the mornings, tiptoed in the bedroom, but before he got out of the room she always stirred, and her voice when she spoke was never thick with sleep.

"I'm getting up now, Jess."

He couldn't see her in the cold darkness of the room, but he knew she was sitting up, wide-eyed. "Beth, please sleep."

"I've go to get up. I've got to fix the house."

Slowly, deliberately, she ate the oatmeal and the boiled egg he insisted on. He was jovial, gruff with her. "Eat all that egg, now!" And he would add, trying to grin, "Or I'll have to lick you!" She made a smile, but not the smile he knew. She was pale and gaining no color, thin and gaining no weight.

Before he left the house she would walk slowly around the room, arrange the curtains, move a book in the bookcase. Yet he felt when he left that she sat in her chair by the window.

The child was never mentioned.

Sometimes as they sat together in the lamplight he wondered if that wasn't the trouble. If only they could talk out—if she could tell him a little about the boy. For the child had lived a little. She had seen him, touched him, maybe even given him a name . . . .

She sat darning. The shadows were sharp on her thin face. He couldn't risk speaking, startling the strange calm from her face. He dreaded what might take its place. Now he knew the child would never be mentioned.

That was the evening he went to their closet, took out the letter he had never opened, and burned it, one of the two things that linked him with his son. The other thing was in the room behind the blacksmith shop. He knew it was foolish, but he couldn't destroy it yet.

The late-fall work had to go on. He was in the fields with his men, and flocks of wild geese flew through the cold November skies, their distant honking sad, unworldly.

"Looks like snow . . . ."

"It's funny the snow doesn't come," they said.

With his men he cut out cattle, shifting young heifers into this field, that field, cows and calves into that; steers he drove to the upper ranch. He tried to remember little things about the day to interest her.

"I saw a coyote. It had its winter coat, a fine coat. Funny it doesn't snow, Beth . . . ."

The last of the cattle trailed down from the range, down the bare November hills, five at a time, an old cow trailed by a calf, six at a time, then a lone, gaunt old bull following the old trails down, past the timber, the gullies, down the wide bare flats to the narrow deep trails along the fences, down and down to the ranch, to the fields. Thin cattle, because the summer had been dry, waiting near the gates. Winter was near.

He would have spent every hour with her. More than anything else he wanted to say, "Let me stay here with you. The boys will get along without me." She wouldn't have it. He began to feel she was more comfortable alone, as if she did something in the house she didn't want him to see. "I've got to get up. I've got to fix the house."

He worked and tried to think it was worth while.

In one bunch of cattle he found a half dozen dogies, calves whose mothers had died or been lost in the hills that summer. No one knew how they lived, for they'd had no milk since they were a month or two old, little, weazened, wise-looking calves with coarse matted hair and bloated bellies.

He drove them to the ranch and put them in the pen behind the barn. He worked with tools to make a trough for them and bought ground oats to put in it, for ground oats, a little each day, would make the swollen bellies well, and the tight, weazened look would go.

"I've got some calves out back," he told her. "They're coming along nice. Maybe you'd like to look at them."

"I was going out today to look," she told him. "But I was busy here."

She had had her supper in the front room, for now she avoided Slim and the other men. The plate was beside her on the little table where she played solitaire. The cards were laid out, and she sat back and smiled as he came into the room.

"Finish your game," he said.

"No. I'm already beaten." She said, "I did some cleaning." The dress she wore was clean, fresh, and her hair was done up neatly. The yellow light from the lamp made sharp shadows on her face. "I cleaned out that cupboard in the kitchen."

That wasn't hard work. He nodded wisely and praised her. He picked up a newspaper, unfolded it. "What's the paper say?"

"I didn't have time to read it." She was silent a moment. "Jess . . ."

He looked up quickly. There was something in her tone. Her smile didn't betray it. "Yes, Beth?"

She spoke in a flat, conversational tone. "When I was cleaning the cupboard I found the funniest thing." Her eyes were on him, smiling. "I found a little can of bright red paint. When did you get that?"

His mouth was dry. He stammered a little, not daring to shift his eyes from hers. "Oh, that can—of paint. I—" He finished quickly, "I got it to paint something."

It was the next night, when he rode alone in the fields long after supper, watching the cattle to see they didn't break inside the fences around the haystacks. The moon was high and cold, a winter moon, and the cattle were ghostly against the black willows. The haystacks, fewer this year, were black mounds casting squat shadows in the moonlight. The fences were spindly. He rode home at last and pulled up his horse at the gate. Suddenly he looked up.

He saw her then, standing near the blacksmith shop, her cape pulled about her. She seemed to be looking toward him. He couldn't tell. He started to call. Something kept him silent. Silently he watched her turn and move almost swiftly to the house and inside.

He hurried to the barn with his horse, unsaddled, hung up the saddle, and dropped the bridle on the floor. He walked swiftly toward the house. He paid no attention to the dogs that jumped and whined at him.

He stood inside the kitchen door, strangely weak, breathless, and went on in the living room. She was sitting in her chair. She had her coat off, but her hair was a little rumpled, her cheeks flushed.

"Hello, Jess?"

He felt a kind of dread creeping over him. "Hello," he said, "Well, I got back."

"I've been waiting for you. I've been sitting here."

"You feel all right—tonight? You didn't go outside—to get a little air?"

"No. But I feel pretty good tonight." She yawned. "Now, you're home, I guess I'll go to bed. I was just waiting."

"The rest will do you good." He reached down, kissed her, then crossed to his chair, sat down, and began rolling a cigarette, waiting.

She got up quietly, lighted a candle, and went with it to the bedroom. He waited. He waited until he heard her get into bed, until the candlelight was gone.

Then he got up. He went to the kitchen. Beside the door he had a kerosene lantern, the chimney black with soot. He lit it, put on his Mackinaw, and slipped out the back door, pushing it shut easily so the latch wouldn't clink.

He walked, almost ran, toward the blacksmith shop, went inside the big wide doors, and the pine shavings whispered beneath his feet. He went around the big anvil and the sawhorse, back to the little door in the rear, and opened it. It creaked a little. He held the lantern high.

It was nothing, nothing that he saw, really nothing at all. Just a little corral, a little pen he had made with stuff he had found on the ranch, a few pickets, a few nails, a little pen. It was too awkward to hide. A few blows of the hammer, a twist of his wrists—it wouldn't be a pen any more, just so much wood for kindling.

He put the lamp down and stood a moment, looking. Then he stooped. There was the hammer in his hands.

And then he felt eyes on his neck, something behind him, and a chill ran down his spine. He turned slowly. She had thrown her cape over her nightgown. Her long hair hung at her sides. She was pale, but she stood straight, straight, chin up, and her eyes frightened him. Her voice was strangely high and sharp.

"Don't touch that!" she said. "Don't touch it. It's *his* . . . ."

XXX

Mrs. Cooper walked among her dozen chickens, the eleven hens and the rooster. They were young hens, for only that spring she had decided to raise a few chickens.

She had seen, clipped out, and sent away an advertisement for baby chicks, and when the literature came she sent a check for two dozen. They came some weeks later in their cardboard carton, peeping and pecking.

Newt had been against chickens from the first, as he was against pigs and alfalfa and sheep, anything that belonged to a farm. "It will look like a farm around here, all those chickens. This is a cattle ranch."

"Pooh-pooh," Mrs. Cooper said. "We're paying good money for eggs when we could raise our own."

"What do you expect to feed them? We've got no grain."

"We'll buy a few sacks. Besides," Mrs. Cooper said, "they eat all sorts of things. Scraps, and they pick around the yard, eat seeds and things."

"I'm not going to have chickens on the place," Newt said and scowled.

"Pooh-pooh," Mrs. Cooper said.

Mrs. Cooper felt now that Newt should have taken a stronger stand on the matter. The chickens were a mistake.

They were strong and white and small, more like birds than chickens. She had seen them fly, like grouse, from the barn to the back door when they were frightened. She had always liked to think of herself as going out among her chickens quietly, feeding them as they clucked, gathering up the eggs in the apron.

They never laid.

They were incredibly wild, always forming a cautious circle around her when she fed them, rushing forward to pick up the grain she threw at them, then darting back.

"Here, chicky-chick," she would call, but when she stepped toward them they rushed back, squawking. At the end of each feeding Mrs. Cooper would shout at them and wave her apron, which never contained eggs.

"Shoo! Go away, then!" and they would fly crazily, stupidly. It was satisfying to see them in such confusion.

And the rooster, small, white, impertinent bird, was the most disgusting thing she'd ever seen.

She was a little ashamed of something she had done, although as she told herself, the chickens had driven her to it.

She had cooked some prunes, as she did occasionally. She felt that prunes were good for a person because of the iron they contained, and other things. She always ate a few herself, since they were cooked, but, like Newt, she never cared for them. When they spoiled she threw them out. She could tell easily enough when they spoiled because of the whiskylike smell they had and the froth on top.

She wondered, she just wondered what would happen if she gave the prunes to the chickens.

"Newt," she had said, "I think I know why those chickens don't lay."

"Who," Newt drawled acidly, "ever told you those things were chickens?"

She didn't look at him. "Those chickens need iron. I think they need a tonic of iron."

"Give them iron, then," Newt said.

"I intend to," Mrs. Cooper said primly.

She got out the prunes, frothy and smelling strong. She called the chickens, and they came flying from the barn, running in their stupid way. They jumped back when she threw the prunes and then began to gorge themselves. Mrs. Cooper went inside the kitchen and watched out the window.

The chickens began to grow quieter. They picked up their long yellow legs slowly and deliberately put them down. She had never seen them so quiet, with such a foolish dignity. She watched, fascinated as the rooster finally folded his legs under him and sank down. When he turned on his side Mrs. Cooper gasped.

"I've poisoned him . . . ."

Then the rooster stretched his neck out, feathers fluffed up. The rooster pecked slowly at a prune beside him.

Mrs. Cooper spoke softly. "Disgusting, drunken, evil thing . . ."

Now this morning, late November, Mrs. Cooper went down in the pale fall sun among her chickens, curbing her will to frighten them, for she was fattening them.

She wore her sunbonnet and loose wool coat. She looked up suddenly as the gate beside the house creaked. "Hello, Jess." Mrs. Cooper looked closely at him. She said suddenly, "Is Beth all right?"

"Yes. She's all right."

"Well, you looked so quiet," Mrs. Cooper said, and threw the remaining wheat to the chickens. "Come inside the house. Newt's below fixing fence. He'll be up directly. If you want, you can take the car and drive down along the fence and see him there."

"No," Jess said. "I don't want to see him."

Puzzled, Mrs. Cooper walked ahead of him through the kitchen and into the parlor. She snapped the blinds up, and the sun filtered through the starched lace curtains.

Mrs. Cooper sat down. She kept on the loose wool coat, for the room was cold. Jess sat down and held his hat and gloves in his hands.

"I can't stay long," he said. "I've got to get back."

Mrs. Cooper straightened the loose wool coat. "You certainly caught me in a state. This coat is warm, though. I bought it in 1913. Wasn't 1913 a wonderful year, though? I've never known such peace as 1913!"

"It's been mighty cold, and no snow." Jess smiled and looked uncomfortably about.

"Nineteen-thirteen cold? No, I don't believe it was."

"I mean now," Jess said. "Cold and no snow now."

"Well, some years are cold," Mrs. Cooper admitted, "and some are warmer." They sat silent for a few moments, and Mrs. Cooper rearranged the loose wool coat. Jess moved his hat in his hands.

"I've got to be going." He started to rise.

Mrs. Cooper stirred. Then she sat back and looked levelly at him. "Jess, what did you come for?"

"I just stopped by."

"You didn't just stop by. Why should you want to chitchat with a middle-aged woman in the middle of the morning? What do you want?"

"I feel like—I'm butting in."

"Don't be childish. It's Beth. I knew it when you came."

He looked at his hat and his hands. "It's been a little lonely for her." He looked up, grinned. "I'm not very good company."

"Well, good heavens! I'll take the buggy this afternoon—"

He broke in: "I wondered if you could have a little party and ask us over."

"Well, I should say I could! I've been wanting a party all fall. We might as well be strangers lately. We had a wonderful party in 1913."

"We could come any time you say."

Mrs. Cooper settled back in her chair and looked thoughtful. "I never had any children, Jess, but I think I know how I'd feel if—I lost a child."

"She's a little like she was lost."

"I think I'd feel lost, that everything had changed, that maybe everybody had changed. I think we've got to show her nothing has changed. That we're all the same." Jess looked up, grateful, and started to speak, but Mrs. Cooper went on: "We've got to have a party. Better than any party we've had. We've got to say the things we did and laugh the way we did, and she's going to watch and listen. I'll play records on my phonograph, the old tunes." She thought. "Jess—is there any song or tune that belongs to you and Beth? Any tune you heard or danced to when you were both very happy?"

He looked up, and his forehead wrinkled. "There was 'Red Wing.' We used to dance to it."

"I still have it somewhere." Mrs. Cooper nodded. "At the end of the party I'll play 'Red Wing' on my phonograph, and you and Beth will dance."

"I couldn't have figured that out," Jess said shyly. "It's all the little things she doesn't do now."

Mrs. Cooper sat up straight and straightened the collar of the loose wool coat. "When do you want to come, Jess?"

"I don't know. Any time you say. If you're not busy . . ."

"You'll come soon. Right away. Thanksgiving is next week. We'll have a fine dinner." Mrs. Cooper thought and spoke suddenly, triumphantly. "We'll have chicken. I'll gladly—have Newt do away with the rooster and certain of the hens. And Cy and Amy. That's it."

Jess broke in: "And after we'll all be in there and we'll talk, and Beth there, and you'll play 'Red Wing.'"

"That's right." Mrs. Cooper nodded wisely. "I'll discuss the—chickens—with Newt this evening. Now," she said, rising, "go away and do your work and forget about all this. I'm busy and you've interrupted me in the middle of the morning."

There was a column in the Salmon City *Recorder* known as the "Legals," and in it were notices dealing with deaths, bankrupts, auctions, and straying animals. The words were stiff, businesslike. When old Hayes Williams died there was a notice that began:

In the matter of the estate of Hayes Williams, also known as "Tick" Williams, deceased . . .

His estate was his cabin behind the station and four hundred dollars in bills that Doc Morse found in a Prince Albert tobacco can. The column urged that creditors "come forward." Nobody came forward. Not even old Mrs. Higgley, chambermaid at the Salmon City House. She should have come forward, they said.

The following articles will be held for sale at a sheriff's auction at the Peterson ranch: one cast-iron stove, one cast-iron bed and mattress in fine shape, one set harness . . .

Once a year, in the spring, Ma Perkins listed her milk cow as "strayed."

And once a year, in the fall, always late fall, there was this:

The last railroad train of the Salmon City and Pittsburgh for the season will leave the depot in the city at the usual time on November 25.

Passengers and freight will be accommodated. Weather permitting, the railroad train will resume service May 1 . . . .

Five years before, when the first notice appeared, the readers of the *Recorder* shook their heads. What about getting cattle out; what about mail?

The trucks solved that, the big red trucks that ran all winter, growling and plowing through the snow, their heavy chains slapping against the fenders. The trucks and the men who drove them were the new prairie, as the railroad train was the old.

Any other day than Thanksgiving, Jess thought, would have been a better day for the last train of the year to leave. For he and Beth saw it that day.

He had spoken casually to her about the party one morning shortly after breakfast and just before he went out to catch up his horse and ride away for the day. He had reasoned that it would give her something nice to think about, something to plan for.

"Oh," he said, "and Mrs. Cooper has invited us over for dinner Thanksgiving."

She was busy at one of the little tasks she had taken to so suddenly, cleaning out drawers of the table in the front room. She glanced at old letters and stubs of pencils, at rolls of string and photographs. She had two piles and hesitated before putting an article in one or the other.

She hesitated, leaning over a drawer. She turned and looked at him, then her eyes went quickly about the room, resting on each article in it. Then, smiling, she said, "That's nice of Mrs. Cooper. It will be nice to get out."

As the time came to drive away in the buggy she seemed to be her old self. She was long in the bedroom, dressing. He waited in the living room, listening to her move about in the bedroom, and he heard the familiar clink of the lid on her powder jar, a part of the painted china dresser set he had given her for Christmas. "Fixing up," he said softly. "Fixing all up." He called out gruffly: "I'm ready. I'm not waiting for you to pretty up, young lady!"

"You wait!" she called. "You wait!"

It was like old times . . . .

Then the door of the bedroom opened, and she stood in the door for him to see. Of course, he thought, it was the dark suit she wore that made her face and hands pale, and naturally the circles under her eyes were dark. But the suit that looked so nice once hung loosely from her shoulders, and the little pose she made hurt him. "You look just fine," he said. And again: "Just fine."

He drove slowly over the frozen ruts and tried to shake off the feeling of afternoon about the morning. The sun was low and red.

"Forest fires someplace."

"I see, Jess. Funny to have fires this time this year. This is almost winter."

"We're going to have chicken," he said. "She's got a rooster and some young hens." Then, "Talking about chicken makes me hungry. Does it you?"

"Yes it does, Jess. And the air smells good."

He said suddenly, "Would you like to drive a little? Like you used to?"

She hesitated. "No—not now. Maybe later. Coming back."

"Yes. Maybe coming back, after you eat." He laughed again, and the wind whipped away the sound. But she had laughed too.

The buggy creaked along the road, deep-rutted now, that ran beside his land, beside the old jack fences, splintered and gray, that staggered crazily along the inner rim of the sagebrush. The color was gone from the country, and only frosted brown stubble and gray of the foothills remained. Even the peaks in the distance were faded in the dull red disk of the sun that lay in the prairie, and the haystacks, once green, were the color of straw. Cattle moved near the ice-crusted creek near the willows and hunted there for long dry grass. The stubble in the fields was short.

"Look out there at the cattle, Beth."

She looked where he pointed. "Jess—there aren't so many haystacks this year."

"Oh, enough," he said. "Enough. Newt butchered a cow and looked at the spleen. You know how you tell weather by the size of a cow's spleen. Well, the spleen's wrong. Here it is December almost and no snow, and cattle doing all right." He spoke to the horses, and they trotted a little. "Remember, Beth, when we drove along here the first time?"

"I remember. I felt very grand riding with you. Do you remember I had new shoes, Jess? Kid shoes, and they hurt me."

"You took them off, unlaced them and took them off. Remember? We met Mrs. Cooper on the road, and before you could get your shoes on she saw us, and you covered your feet with the robe, right in summer . . . ."

Beth laughed, and a little color came to her face. "I told her I was very cold-blooded and had bad circulation. She was puzzled."

He said, "Nothing's changed, is it?" He laughed. "Except your shoes don't hurt now, do they? The shoes you've got on don't pinch."

Before they got to the Coopers' they drove around a hill, and the wide view of the prairie came suddenly, and seeing it again, they were silent.

Around the hill the road was narrow and sidling. The buggy tipped a little, and Beth caught his arm. It was then that they looked out across and saw the train. There across the valley the little train puffed along. It was strange how the distance swallowed sound and the power of it, how the train seemed to crawl silently.

She still held his arm. "Jess, stop a minute."

He pulled up the horses. "What's wrong?"

"I want to see the train." She gazed off across the space. "It's going for the winter."

He spoke loud against the wind. "It'll be back in the spring."

"Yes. Of course. It will be back in the spring."

The distance did not swallow the shrill whistle off there, nor the echo, a phantom whistle trying to be real.

Mrs. Cooper met them at the kitchen door. "Beth!" she cried. "Come inside and sit on the comfortable chair." She held open the door and pointed to the flour on her apron. "I'm making biscuits. I wonder why it started you've got to have biscuits when people come. They're not very good for the stomach."

Jess said proudly, "Beth made biscuits last week."

"They were pretty heavy," Beth said.

"It makes little difference, light or heavy," Mrs. Cooper said, "once they get in the stomach."

They moved into the neat parlor. Cy stood up, grinning, the color rushing to his face, and they shook hands. "Amy," Mrs. Cooper called. "Come out! Beth's here!"

The bedroom door opened, and Amy ran out, dressed in something light and flowered. She kissed Beth. "You look wonderful, Beth." Beth smoothed the sleeve of her suit and fingered the carved brooch at her throat.

Mrs. Cooper said, "She made biscuits last week for Jess."

"They weren't very good." Beth smiled shyly.

"I thought they were fine," Jess said.

"Hot breads are lovely!" Amy said. "You remember my cousin Millie Noble from Texas? She ate hot breads all the time, she said."

"I remember Millie Noble," Mrs. Cooper said, "and I also remember that she had a sallow complexion."

"Oh, she didn't!" Amy cried. "She had a lovely complexion, like cream. She was lovely, no matter what you say."

"They get hookworm down there," Mrs. Cooper announced darkly. "They go barefooted and they get hookworm."

"Millie Noble never went barefooted either here or there!" Amy cried. "John Noble was cashier at that bank and lovely to Millie."

"Let me take your coat, Beth," Mrs. Cooper said.

"Let *me* take your coat," Amy said.

"Jess and I can't thank you—enough. Such a nice party." She looked from one woman to the other.

"It's scarcely begun," Mrs. Cooper said mysteriously. "You wait."

They sat down and nodded and smiled at one another silently, thinking of something to say.

"Mighty cold today," Cy offered, "and dark even with the sun out."

"I hope you're dressed warm, Beth," Amy said. "Your undergarments should be warm."

"I have on the warmest I own, down to my ankles."

"I have some of the silk and wool—you'd never know, really—that sort of tie around. The silk takes the curse off the wool. I sometimes wonder about men's skin—so tough. Cy wears the two-piece in winter."

Beth laughed. "Ugly things, but the one-piece Jess has—"

Mrs. Cooper broke in: "I'll not remain in the room

discussing men's undergarments except to say," she added stiffly, "that Newt cannot stand wool near his skin."

"That's wonderful!" Amy cried. "I supposed all men—"

Beth said, "Why, Jess—"

Mrs. Cooper looked levelly at her husband. "Can you look at Newt Cooper now and realize that this morning he sulked like a child because I insisted on his dressing in garments that contain no more than fifteen percent wool—at the most? 'No wool!' he said. 'No wool at all!'"

Beth turned to Amy. "You had to dress your little girl warm today. They kick out of things."

Amy was startled. "The baby? I left her with the Fishers. I thought—the noise—and not sleeping—"

Beth said, "I know with a baby it's got to be quiet. In the hospital it was quiet. You could hear every sound."

"Well, it's not quiet in this room," Mrs. Cooper said. "Beth, come help me with the biscuits. You grease the pan."

Jess rose to help her from the chair, but she had already risen, smiling her thanks to him. "I'd like to help with the biscuits." They left the room, and Mrs. Cooper was telling her, "No wool. No wool at all."

Amy turned to Jess. "She's taking her capsules, isn't she? She's getting sun when there is any, and not getting chilled? Don't let her get a cold. Get her in the sun . . . ."

Jess spoke quickly, curiously ashamed. "She's doing the right things."

"Does she often talk about—?"

"Yes. Oh yes. She talks about—she's all over that."

"She seems happy today. Almost gay. I'm surprised. I thought—would take longer."

"She's all over that," Jess repeated.

Mrs. Cooper leaned over and opened the oven door. "Beth, tell Jess to come here a minute and you stay away. I've got a secret. I want to ask him if it's all right to do. Jess is wise. We'd do well to follow his advice."

"Of course I'll tell him." She paused and smiled. "You won't talk about underwear?" And went to get Jess.

Jess leaned against the sink. Mrs. Cooper bustled about. "I'm very happy," she told him. "Beth seems fine. A little quiet, maybe, but fine."

"Amy says almost gay."

"But we'll still play 'Red Wing' at the last."

"Yes. It will be even better."

"We're pretty wise, aren't we, Jess?"

They grinned at each other. Then Mrs. Cooper said, "I want to do something today. I want you to tell me frankly."

"What's that?"

"Well"—Mrs. Cooper bustled—"the wine. I bought a little port wine for Beth. A little before the meal. I'd take a little, for appearance sake, and Amy."

"That's a fine idea. Give you all an appetite."

"For the appetite, and what good spirits might follow would be purely medicinal." Mrs. Cooper frowned. "I wanted to be sure. Last night I took a small glass when Newt had gone to bed. I sat right down in my chair and waited for the—effects. You couldn't say they were harmful. I simply felt warm and rather encouraged."

"And a little wine builds you up, they say."

"Yes, it does, so the doctor says. And so she wouldn't feel strange sitting there drinking with just Amy and me, I had the doctor buy some spirits—whisky—for you men. Doctor wouldn't say anything about buying it because doctors are under oath not to say anything."

Mrs. Cooper brought the glasses in on a tray. There was an inch of wine in three of the water glasses. The other three were filled with whisky.

"For the love of God," Newt growled, "why didn't you bring a big drink?"

"There's no need to blaspheme," Mrs. Cooper said gently. "There's another quart in the cupboard. You must understand this is purely for the appetite's sake."

The men worked away on their whisky. Newt went to the kitchen and brought back three glasses of water. Mrs. Cooper smiled and laughed a gay little laugh. "We don't need water with our wine, do we, Beth?"

Beth took a sip of the wine. A faint glow had come to her cheeks. "He's not used to so much. He wants it weaker. Newt is a sensitive person."

Mrs. Cooper laughed again. "I thought he liked it better." She looked at her husband and said seriously, "Another bit of whisky, Newt? . . . No? Another glass, Cy? . . . No? Well!"

"It's a wonderful color, the wine," Beth said. "A nice red."

"Now see how it's brought color to her cheeks!" Mrs. Cooper said. "They say wine is very clean and nice."

Amy said, "It's just so nice and clean I think I'll have another tiny glass."

Mrs. Cooper poured Beth's glass full and Amy's. "I've got to deal with those biscuits. I never felt less like a good flaky biscuit."

"You could have a little wine instead," Beth said.

"If you'd feel better about it, Beth," Mrs. Cooper said, "I will." She poured herself a drink. "I thought the oven quite cool. Hot breads that are underdone are dangerous."

"Doughy," Beth said. "Tough."

Amy leaned forward and said gently, "My cousin Millie Noble—"

Mrs. Cooper turned. "Why must you keep referring to your cousin? You've talked about nothing but Millie and the rest of them all afternoon."

"It's simply that Millie is lovely," Amy said.

Beth said, "She was reminded by the dough, the biscuit dough. Millie was fond of it."

"I can't recall," Mrs. Cooper said. "How odd your cousins are, Amy."

Amy said, "Frank Noble—"

"I know all about *him*," Mrs. Cooper said.

Newt glowered and Cy nodded his head. Jess's eyes were on Beth, and he smiled and winked at Mrs. Cooper. She winked back archly.

Newt said, "Somebody's got to attend to dinner."

Mrs. Cooper looked at a point just below her husband's chin. "Perhaps my husband will serve dinner for a change."

They made a great deal of noise at dinner.

"Oh, I couldn't eat any more," Beth would say, and to please them she did eat more. Mrs. Cooper kept glancing at her and then at Jess. Once when her eyes met his her lips formed the words: "See—two helpings." Then at last Mrs. Cooper got up from her chair.

"We'll have music now."

Dusk had fallen. Outside the dining-room window the buildings—the barn, the blacksmith shop—and the corrals were blurred against the cold fall sky on the horizon. One of Newt's hired men moved across the yard carrying two milk buckets, and his mournful whistle came inside.

Mrs. Cooper said, "You'd better light the lamp now, Newt."

It was a gasoline lamp, shadeless, and Newt pumped it up soberly, lit several matches, and held them under the generator. They watched him, for they distrusted the lamp. It made them nervous. The flames shot up wildly before the mantels caught and hissed out the garish white light. Mrs. Cooper lowered the blinds. "Arrange the chairs, Newt."

He fixed the chairs in a semicircle. "Take the rug away." She caught Jess's eye. "In case anybody wants to dance."

It was an Edison phonograph, a large one of fumed oak, like an elaborately carved coffin stood on end. Mrs. Cooper said it was much more complicated to work than those victrolas, and told how, on the one occasion that Newt had operated it, a cog in the winding mechanism had slipped and the handle had flown around crazily and rapped him painfully on the hand. "He was about to play 'Yacka-Hoola-Hicky-Doola,'" Mrs. Cooper explained.

She approached the machine with dignity, and the others sat attentive, stiff in their chairs that Newt had arranged nicely in a semicircle.

"First," Mrs. Cooper announced, "we will hear 'Smiles.'" She wound the machine slowly, started the motor. "Everybody smile!"

They smiled, and then the record ended, and Amy said, "Remember the time . . ." While Mrs. Cooper sorted through her records the friends remembered, their faces thoughtful, vague. Beth still wore the smile Mrs. Cooper had ordered, sitting rather stiffly in her chair; Mrs. Cooper again caught Jess's eye and looked archly at him, nodding.

Mrs. Cooper played a second record and hurried back to her chair when she had put the tone arm down so she would be well seated when the music began.

Jada, jada, jada-jada jing-jing-jing . . .

It was clear now what she was doing. Each tune went back a year or two. Each record recalled a time when they said this and that. They remembered years, complete rounded periods of time when life was good and they'd been friends together. And of each good year a fragment remained, recalled now. A word spoken, the smell of a sagebrush fire, the friendly yellow light of a lantern flooding through a window, and a smile . . .

Amy cried a little, and Cy touched her hand.

There was a prewar tune, "Cecile," a waltz hesitation. They were silent now, and only the hissing of the lamp came through it when the music stopped each time.

Beth was sitting quietly, her hands folded in her lap, listening. Her hands were thin, and her wrists. The white light was cruel on her face. The smile was gone. Jess was awkward in the chair across from her.

Now Mrs. Cooper caught his eye and gave him a knowing, silent look and nodded her head again. She was near, very near, to playing "Red Wing." Jess must be ready. He must rise in a few moments, make a little bow, and ask Beth to dance. He must not be shy before his friends.

The little half-smile he gave her in answer was her cue. She got up slowly and went to the phonograph. She took a long time getting that last record out. She blew on it, chasing the dust. No one must speak now.

She wound the machine. She dropped the record down. She lowered the tone arm, touched the lever, and turned to smile at Jess. He shifted in his chair. She noticed the beads of sweat on his brow. She sat down.

The little two-step began, and the plunk of the banjo was sharp.

> There once was an Indian maid,
> A shy little Indian maid . . .

Mrs. Cooper watched, a triumphant little smile on her lips.

Jess sat uneasy. He counted on this small thing, this tune, this "Red Wing." They had danced to it those years before in the Masonic Hall. This tune must say, "Let's begin again, all over again . . . ."

He looked at Beth. He must get up. He must go to her and make a funny bow and ask her for the dance. She held her handkerchief in her tight-closed fist, watching it.

He must get up. For he knew exactly when the record ended, when the needle ran around and around in the last groove, silent.

It was that time now. Only a few bars left, only a few bars of the thin, tinny music.

He got up.

He looked across the room at Beth.

She was already standing. "Jess," she whispered. "Jess—remember?"

Mrs. Cooper did not smile now. The needle ran around and around in the last groove. Beth's eyes wavered and rested on the handkerchief she held in her hand.

It was too late, Mrs. Cooper knew, to start the record again. The tune was gone.

Behind them the white glare of the gasoline lamp came around the drawn shades and the buggy jounced over the deep ruts. Carefully he had tucked the carriage robe about her, for there was snow in the air, cold and sharp-smelling. As the buggy moved the night closed in behind until the light from the Coopers' was gone.

"Are you warm, Beth?" He tucked the robe about her again. "I can't see you in the dark."

"Yes, Jess. But tired. I'm very tired, Jess."

"I won't talk then. But that was a fine dinner, wasn't it? That was fine chicken. You ate a lot of it, didn't you?"

There was a strange silence, and he hurried, tucking the robe better about her.

She said, "Jess—I don't want to leave home again."

He was quickly, "No. Not till you feel better." He held his breath until he knew she wouldn't speak of it again. He said, "People have a nice time with the Coopers. It picks you up to go to the Coopers'. It—" He chuckled and explained: "At the Coopers' you re-Cooperate. You see, Beth? You re-Cooperate."

She stirred, then the silence came again, and beside them the old jack fences were shadowy, the sagebrush black masses. "Jess . . ."

"Yes, Beth?"

She spoke softly. "It hurt when she played the music, when she played, 'Red Wing.'" He could scarcely hear her above the rattle of the buggy. "A song reminds you of things that—can't be again."

"She didn't—she didn't mean like that." He spoke haltingly.

"No. She couldn't. I know that song was a mistake."

The minutes went by. A cold breeze stirred, and through a break in the clouds the stars came. "Beth, I told her to play that song."

She echoed his words in a strange, tight voice. "You told her?" He couldn't see her. He knew she pulled the robe about her. "Why do you try, Jess?"

"Try?"

"Why do you go on pretending?"

"Pretending? What—?"

Her voice was husky. "We can't be like we were. That's gone. I rode that horse. I spoiled—"

"Beth . . ."

Her voice was a whisper. "I saw you in the blacksmith shop. I knew you went there. I knew what was there. I knew you stood there."

He said, "You've got to stop. We'll be home—"

She went on: "We'll be home. And it will be empty. We'll go in that room, and it will be empty. There's nothing there for us. There never will be."

He took her arm. "Beth!" She strained from him and pressed against the side of the buggy.

"You never saw him. You never held him. He was little. I held him. He looked like—"

264

He began to shake her hard. "You don't talk. See? You don't talk. I don't care about him."

He felt her shudder. "You don't care about him . . . ."

"I don't care about him. I can't talk about things. I say wrong things. It's not wrong when I say I don't care about him." He held her. "I'm going to talk now and try to tell." He swallowed. "When you get married you don't think about babies. You think about who you marry. You don't care about anything else. A baby doesn't mean anything. It's something nice, extra. And that's all. You get married because you love a person. See, Beth? I married you, and I love you."

He released her. She relaxed suddenly, sobbing, and sank back against the seat, trembling. He took the reins tightly in his hands, spoke to the team, and stared ahead. The buggy jounced on, and the minutes passed. At last he said, "I'm sorry. I hurt you."

He thought she wouldn't speak. She said, "I'm very tired, Jess."

"We'll be home in a little."

She said softly, "Did you bank the fire, Jess?"

He stared ahead. "Yes."

She said, "Then it will be warm in the room." She took her hand out from under the robe and found his.

He turned his eyes to her. He couldn't see her. He could only touch her. But he knew she was smiling. And he knew she was smiling as she used to, the smile that made a lump come into his throat.

Now it was a funny thing that she should smile at him so in the buggy. So many wonderful things had happened to him when he drove a buggy.

265

XXXI

It was a week after the party.

Cy harnessed a team in the barn, a pair of squat bay mares, and as he adjusted the collars and buckled straps with numbed fingers he talked to them, told them how fine they were and how much he thought of them.

It was eerie there in the barn that winter morning, and dark. The sun had not yet risen. The lantern gave only a little light and outlined dimly the old pole mangers and a saddle hanging by a stirrup from a peg. The lantern shone on the sleek rumps of a second team in the double stall, the blacks. They moved their feet and chewed at the hay in the manger.

"Don't mind them," Cy told the gentle bay mares. "They're tough. I'd rather have a couple of mares." He patted the thick bay necks, picked up the halter ropes, and turned to lead them out the big door to the hayrack.

He stood for a moment facing the hill that rose a short distance before the barn door. He saw only the black outline of the hill, but its top was tinged with red, for the sun was rising behind it. And there in the sky were deep red clouds like puffs of smoke moving slowly along the horizon.

He had never before seen the sun rise red. Late in the morning he had seen red suns, but they did not rise red. He stood very still and listened to the chewing of the blacks in the double stall.

December had begun, and no snow that had come had lain on the prairie. Even now he was hitching a team to a wagon, not a set of sled runners. No winter that came so late could hurt the prairie. He was still hitching his team to a wagon . . . .

His mind wandered.

He turned and tied the bay team to the stall beside him. He walked out into the still red dawn and into the house. He surprised Amy having a second cup of coffee, sitting comfortably near the heater in the living room.

She looked up, startled. "I thought you'd gone. I heard the men drive away with their racks long ago."

He looked a little sheepish. "I thought I'd have another cup of coffee."

She rose. "I'll get it. Sit down. It's nice to talk a little in the morning."

He sat down and looked at the stove and waited for his wife. She came with the coffee and sat down, smiling. "This is nice and comfortable, Cy. I can't remember—"

"I felt like another cup of coffee," Cy said. The few pieces of furniture seemed lost in the room, a room as strange and uncomfortable as when they had moved into it.

Amy sipped her coffee. "It's good and hot."

"I think we're going to have snow," Cy said.

"Do you think so? This is a funny winter. I love snow for Christmas. I think Beth is going to have us over for Christmas, and remember you promised you'd use the sleigh bells. They sound lovely."

Cy gulped his coffee and set the saucer and cup on the floor beside him. "I've got to go to work."

"You just came in!" Amy cried. "I thought we'd talk a little. And the baby would be glad to see you . . ."

"I felt like a cup of coffee, that's all," Cy said.

Mrs. Cooper looked out her east window. Newt and the men had long since gone out, horseback, and her Swedish hired girl fussed in the kitchen. Mrs. Cooper heard a roast of meat go into a hot pan and begin to sizzle. The odor came into the living room shortly after, and the smell of the seared meat in the morning, she thought, was a little sickening.

Mrs. Cooper felt small, childish, useless, and stared out the window.

"Red skies in the morning, sailors take warning."

Hadn't thought of it since she was a child! Dealt with the weather.

She went to the organ and sat down. She pumped the pedals until the old instrument wheezed. She played a few mournful chords that brought Anna, the hired girl, to the door.

"Anything wrong, missus?"

Mrs. Cooper turned. "No, of course not! Can't a body play a little? Go back to your meat! It smells terrible!"

"All right, missus," Anna went cheerfully into the kitchen.

On a table with a fringed throw Mrs. Cooper kept an album of photographs and a Bible. She stood over the table, and her hands moved nervously. "Anna," she called. "How long has the weather been good?"

Anna came and stood in the door again. "Oh, missus. Since last Sunday, anyways."

"I don't mean that! I mean how long since we've had a mean winter?"

Anna laughed, and it irritated Mrs. Cooper. "I don't know, missus."

"Well, I know!" Mrs. Cooper said, and was a little ashamed, her voice had been so loud. "Go back to your meat, Anna!" She waited until Anna was in the kitchen banging pots and pans. "Seven years." She picked up the Bible and turned quickly to a verse that spoke of kine and of corn. It ended: " . . . and they shall be very grievous."

It was still on the slopes in the gullies of the sagebrushed foothills, and high on one bare slope a bunch of horses grazed, picking along the roots of the brush for short dry grass. The mares grazed quietly, the red of the dawn dull on their long winter coats. The stud lingered behind them, herding them. Suddenly he raised his head and sniffed . . . .

In the timber a gray pine squirrel sat alert on the trunk of a fallen pine, its beady eyes glistening. The sun made pink patterns on the dead pine needles beneath the trees, and the patterns inched along and grew. There was a quick movement, and a buck deer staggered stiffly to his feet, stood uncertainly, stretched his back. His mulelike ears pricked up, then he moved gracefully into the timber, and a twig snapped behind him. The squirrel disappeared.

Above the timber line the gray rocks were thick and the sun outlined their sharp edges for a few moments. A cloud passed over, and suddenly there it was dark, and the first rustle of the wind wound through the crags, whispered, moving on down to the timber, down to the foothills and the prairie.

The snow fell softly.

For three days the snow fell without stopping, soft and deep. It fell along the steep banks of the iced-over creeks and made little ledges of itself out over the creek bed that fell softly of their own weight. Under the banks the mink waited, peering out, and the weasels made desperate little plunges to find shelter.

White-faced cattle crowded close to the brown willows, and a little steam rose from their backs. They watched a coyote move awkwardly with high steps, his eyes straight ahead, looking for rabbits, but there were no tracks to follow.

Then after three days the snow stopped. The sun was brilliant, glaring on the white prairie, and beneath the warmth the snow settled. Then there were tracks: the dot-dot-dash of rabbits, the neat, narrow prints of coyotes, and the tiny rhythmic patterns of weasels and mink, edging along the creek banks. The cattle moved single file across the white fields and stood bawling before the fenced-in haystacks.

People laughed on the prairie.

They put on their overshoes and made tracks to the barn, the criss-cross patterns of overshoes. They laughed and took shovels and made paths to the barn, to the meat house.

"Why, there's snow; you can't open the barn door!"

They stood in the warm kitchens, the last flakes of snow melting and glistening on their shoulders.

"Sit down now. Have this fresh-baked bread, like you like, with butter."

"Well, no. I got to shovel."

"Just one piece, with butter melting. You shoveling and not eating!"

"Well, just one piece then. Just the heel then."

"Little coffee?"

"Well . . ."

Men met other men on horseback, theirs the first tracks. They pulled in their horses and grinned and squinted their eyes in the sun.

There was something awkward about them. "Well, winter's here, all right."

"I'd say it was."

"Seen Cy Pierce going up with a sleigh above his place, get wood."

The snow had stopped. The sun shone. Men looked at each other and grinned.

"You can't go out," Jess said. "You'll get snow in your shoes, and then you'll get a cold."

"It's a beautiful afternoon, Jess," she pleaded with him. "You can make a path."

"When the snow settles. Stay inside."

"I haven't seen the calves since this started, this snow. I wish you'd let me feed them the oats. I like to see them come up from the creek, running and bucking."

"You can feed them one day."

He went through the snow, whistling. She wanted to feed the calves. She was weak, pale. "She's picking up, though," he told himself. "She wants to feed the calves. I'll be damned!"

In the barn he made a careful measure of the oats and spilled it in the bucket. He went to the back door of the barn and called, rattling the oats in the bucket: "Come on, calves!"

It was fine to see them run out from the willows, the four little scrubs, stunted calves, but fat now, lively. He remembered their bloated bellies, thin necks and old, old faces.

"Spry little devils now." He chuckled. "She wants to feed them." Well, she could soon. Keep her busy.

"Come on, calves!"

They crowded along the trough he had made, shoving, eating, raising their heads, and sticking their long tongues out to lick their moist noses where oats had stuck. He threw the bucket down beside the trough and, breathing deeply, he wandered down near the creek where the water rushed roaring beneath the now-thick ice. He had an ax cached in a clump of willows. They'd need a new water hole, those calves, for the old one was already iced over . . . .

Behind the willows where the ax was, there was a track.

He stopped, stared down at it. "Jesus . . ."

More tracks. They went toward the fence. An animal had sniffed at the fence and crawled under, out of the pasture and into the open country that vanished into the white hills.

Not a coyote. No mincing, narrow doglike tracks. These tracks were as big as saucers, fresh, two toes missing.

Wolf. Been in a trap. Old lobo lost two toes—old renegade. One of the breed that walks boldly down in the dusk and kills for the love of it.

Fresh tracks. He felt prickles in his spine. That wolf had watched from around that bush when he called the calves, watching there.

"He was watching there," he told Beth.

"You'll get him," she said, smiling.

He picked up his rifle from the rack in the bedroom, peered through the barrel, grunted, got out cleaning fluid. You couldn't beat a .30-Government. He worked away with swab and ramrod, sniffing the banana odor of the fluid.

"I wish you could go, Beth."

"I can soon. Can I do anything while you're gone?" she teased. "Feed the calves tonight, or anything?"

He smiled. "When you feed the calves you'll be well," he told her.

"Kiss me before you go," she ordered. "And again for good luck . . . ."

When he left the flat, the brown bare willows along the creek that cracked and sighed in the cold, the country was white, cold, and glistening. But the tracks were easy to follow. Sometimes the wind whipped new snow over them, covered them, but he found them easily. He began to climb up from the floor of the valley. The ranch was lost, shut out by the low foothills rising smooth and white around him. His ears tingled, listening to the soft brush of the bay's feet kicking snow.

His mind was filled with wolf.

Into the foothills for an hour, up and up, always climbing, when he noticed the distance between the front and hind tracks was shortening. "He's getting tired, old lobo." He patted his rifle thoughtfully.

The going was hard now. The bay began to lunge, its tough muscles knotting and relaxing, hard under the rough winter coat. Miles traveled, and the snow deepened. White, white everywhere.

Then suddenly the tracks were made by only three feet, and there were places where a bushy tail had dragged in the snow.

"Lame, packing a leg . . . ."

It wouldn't be long now.

"Can't be more than just over that rise." He rode down the draw. The bay floundered, recovered, breathing deep in the barrellike chest. "Catch him! Catch him!" Over the hill.

A frightened rabbit crossed before him, bounding lightly over the snow, and stopped in the draw, its long ears flat against its head, watching from the corners of its bright eyes.

His blood tingled, and there was a trembling in the pit of his stomach. In that brief moment he seemed to have caught the past. He could have touched it with his hand . . . .

Already the sun was low, shooting red paths across the snow, tingeing the shadows in the coulee with pink. The wind was still, and the snow the bay loosed lay quiet beside the tracks, like dust.

Suddenly he pulled the bay short. There on the crest of the rise ahead, not twenty yards away, was the wolf. Jess whistled softly and blinked.

For the wolf was white.

An arctic wolf, lean, old, tongue lolling out, sides heaving, defiant old yellow eyes watching him. "Must be the last in the country." The last one.

He reached for his rifle, his eyes steady on the wolf. Then he hesitated. He might miss at this distance.

The wolf moved again, slowly, limping down the ridge, one hind leg dangling, useless, swinging in and out. It sank deep in the fresh snow, tried to hold its chest up, and glanced back, its shoulder humping along, tail dragging. A long gray shadow glided along beside.

"I'll get him this time. Soon's I get to the ridge."

He slipped the rifle back into the scabbard. The bay plunged. A spurt of speed. The wolf limped faster and no longer looked back. Its shoulders hunched painfully.

He reached the ridge, and the wolf was just below. Right in line, right *there*. No hurry to shoot. It was fine to watch from the ridge, knowing the old devil couldn't get away no matter how fast it limped. No cover, nothing to right or left but the low white hills.

The wolf floundered, tail dragging, its cold yellow eyes desperate.

"Well . . ." He slipped the rifle out. It made a slick, slipping, sure sound. No hurry. He raised it slowly, the butt snug against his shoulder. He sighted down the barrel. "I'll just get this bead on him. There." He squinted one eye. "And I'll—"

The wolf turned its head slowly and looked back. It stopped in the snow, too tired to try, tongue limp, dry, hanging out the side of its mouth.

"I'll just—"

He didn't know what happened. Some tiring force, some weight dragged at his hands, his elbows. He struggled. Almost physically he struggled against the force, his arms aching, his fingers cold and stiff. But the rifle came down, an inch at a time. He slipped it back into his scabbard.

He dropped his eyes and rested them on the bay's neck. He spoke to the bay. "Well . . ." The bay moved its ears and lifted a front foot. "What's the matter with you?" Crossly. "Can't you stand up?"

He swung off slowly. He took a long time untying the stiff saddle strings that held his lunch wrapped in a blue jumper.

He tramped and kicked a clearing in the snow and squatted down on his heels and began to chew the sandwich, stuffing his mouth. He gulped down the last.

He looked over his shoulder.

But the wolf was still there, sitting on its haunches, looking at him, grinning like an old dog.

XXXII

THE LITHOGRAPHED CALENDAR said March.

Jess was disturbed. In the first place, he knew that the years had almost proved a strange thing, that a man could say, "Well, spring's about here because the hay's about gone." Or he could say, "Well, hay's about gone. We're in for spring."

Either way.

And one gray cloudy morning, pitching hay from one of his last stacks, Jess thought, "Well—"

But where was spring? The snow was deep. It was still cold. The cattle began to have the lean, hungry look of winter's end, their hipbones a little prominent, their necks a little thin. Old cows were sharp-faced, the weak ones hobbled, the points of their hoofs dragging across the snow's crust. The oldest cows died. "Stacked up in the brush," they said.

And where was spring?

It was not that the winter was hard. Only long.

There had not been one blizzard, not one wild, shrieking storm a man felt in his bones and fought as he would a living thing. All winter they had spoken of it, he and Beth.

"There hasn't been a real storm, Beth. And here it is March!"

He always grinned when he said it, but their eyes met in an uneasy way.

In the second place, Beth worried him. That was funny too. She had been well. She had almost no color, and there was nothing she was able to do outside, but she was well enough.

Doc Morse said, "You can't expect any real change in her until spring, when the weather's warm and dry, when everything around her's changed." Doc said she'd probably get a cold.

"Let me know," Doc said, "if she gets one. They're dangerous in the winter."

Jess himself had had a series of bad colds, when his eyes watered and his nose was almost too sore to blow. For nights on end before bedtime he had drunk a glass of sugared water with eucalyptus drops in it, shuddering and sneezing.

She had even laughed at him. "You are always so miserable with a cold, Jess."

"They're bad to have. I feel terrible."

"You go to pieces." He always felt ashamed when he had a cold. He had a martyred look; his eyes watered, and his nose grew red. He used a phrase Doc had used. He explained that he was "subject to colds." And she wasn't.

He was happy she was well, but uneasy. Doc had said . . .

It was the damnedest winter, anyway, long, and no real winter storms. Each month had a hundred days.

In March he decided to buy a little hay, enough for a few weeks. He smiled at his thoughts. "What will happen is, I'll trouble to get some cash from Barrett and trouble buying and hauling feed, and then spring will break and there I'll be!"

He'd buy from Newt, for Newt didn't have so many cattle now. He'd have extra hay.

It was a bright day, almost warm, and Beth pleaded with him to let her go along. He was gruff and pleased that she wanted to. "When I need any help I'll let you know. You stay inside. Doc said—"

She laughed.

"I can't help it," he said, "if I'm subject to colds."

He and his horse cast a long dark shadow on the snow, and he rode slowly, thoughtfully, to Newt Cooper's place.

Newt hedged.

He was beside the house on his knees in the packed snow, hands bloody, skinning a coyote. The coyote smelled musky, and Newt worked fast, for the cold stiffened his bare fingers. His pocketknife flashed in the bright winter light. "Other day I said to myself, 'Time for spring. Hay's low.'" He rolled the half-skinned carcass over, and the pelt fell back from the mottled blue flesh. "Coyote's fat, anyway. Hear them howl down your way?"

"I won't need more than a few tons," Jess said chuckling. "Sure as I get hay spring will break, and—"

Newt had found a tough place to skin. His face was serious. "Where you going to get hay?"

Jess squatted down on his haunches. "Thought maybe you'd have a few tons."

"Me?" Newt let the stiffening pelt drop "Me?" He spit. "Listen. I was coming over to your place, see you." Their eyes met, and there was a silence, and then the sound of a horse chewing in the barn.

"How about Cy?" Jess asked suddenly.

Newt rose slowly and stood straight. "We'll just ride over there," he drawled.

Cy drew on his pipe. "Damn a pipe in winter," he said softly. "Freezes up. I've got exactly enough hay to last a week, barring blizzards. I said to myself last week—"

The eyes of the three met. A week's hay. Not enough to do

anybody any good. They shifted their eyes. Newt put his hands in his pockets. Jess shuffled his feet. Cy looked out at the white hills a second, then at his pipe.

Jess laughed. "Well—has anybody got any hay?"

"I've asked around," Cy said. "Nobody's got any." He looked levelly at them. "They were saying down-country that they're putting in an order for the trucking company to bring in hay—baled hay."

Newt and Jess stared. "Bring hay in? *Baled* hay?"

"That's what I heard," Cy said, uneasy.

"That's the craziest thing ever heard of," Newt said. "Why, for Christ sake, for a hundred years nobody brought hay in here. For a thousand years—"

"I didn't say it," Cy said. "I'm only telling you."

"Well," Jess said, "what are we going to do? What are we going to do then?"

"When I was twenty," Newt said, "there was so damned much hay you didn't bother to cut it summers. Why, it was up to a horse's belly, belly-deep! Wavy green hay. I said to my wife—"

"But what are we going to do?"

Newt opened his mouth.

In the end Newt was to put in the order for hay. He would ride down-country and they would tell the trucking company.

"Best thing," they said.

"Safety first."

"Why, there hasn't even been a blizzard . . . ."

Jess was almost gay, riding home. He thought of the things that belonged to him. He thought of Beth, comfortable in the warm house, reading a little, sitting there. He thought of the calves out behind the barn, the little bum calves now doing nicely. "Why," he said half aloud, "I didn't even have to put them in the barn this winter—no blizzards!" and spring would come.

For the years had almost proved a funny thing.

Newt said the trucking company would get hay in in three-four days. They were busy, those trucks, and what could you expect, roads like these?

"What can you expect?"

Jess told Slim to cut down on the hay he fed out to the cattle. Now Slim's bunch of cattle, like those he fed himself, were getting only enough to live. But it wasn't the first time they had lived on short rations. No, it wasn't . . . .

But still the weak old cows wandered off in the willows.

And then it was the fifteenth of March.

Mrs. Cooper said she felt it at eight o'clock that morning. She was standing at the east window, looking out through the dawn, watching the men harness their teams, happy she was a woman with work in the house.

She told Newt, "It was all of a sudden the whole country was still—still." The more she thought about of it, the more it seemed to be eight o'clock, and eight o'clock took on a sinister meaning.

The sky grew overcast, and gradually the country began to darken. And the darkness settled down like a cloak over the peaks and the foothills, over the flats and the fields.

Cattle know things. Jess had seen them come out of the willows that morning, trudging along single file, their noses in the wind, the old thin ones hobbling alone behind, but now some of the hobbling ones were not old.

At four in the afternoon the prairie was dim in the half-light. Jess moved about his remaining stacks like a shadow, strengthening the pole fences, twisting wire in his freezing hands to make an upright secure. He shouted to the cattle standing close, crowding in: "Get back there!" His voice traveled a short distance, but the sound kept his spirits up, a natural voice in a strange gloom.

"We ordered hay," he muttered to himself. But his uneasiness increased, and he worked faster. "Get *back* there!" And the moving shapes of the cattle were stubborn and crowded closer with a hard, dumb stubbornness.

He rode away at five o'clock, keeping his eyes off the cattle. They knew something, something he didn't. It turned colder as his horse trudged along.

"We've sent for hay." He spoke aloud. The sound of his voice covered the slow steps of the cattle behind him, step-step, step-step, fainter and fainter.

He spurred his horse up a little.

The wind was rising when he put his horse away. He threw his saddle on the floor of the barn, a muffled sound, turned his horse out behind the barn where the bum calves were, and started for the house.

He couldn't see the bunkhouse or the kitchen lights until he was almost on them, and the dogs barked at him from their place under the woodshed. They barked, yap-yap-yap, and didn't come out. Somehow even the wind was a relief after the silence.

He lifted the latch of the kitchen door, and the warmth from inside covered his face, and the good smell of frying steak, the smoke heavy and blue.

Tommy said, "Hello, boss."

"Where's the missus?"

Tommy pointed to the closed living-room door. "Inside."

He opened the door.

It was icy-cold in the living room. He walked carefully through the gloom and found the lamp, lit it. He noticed the draft of the heating stove open, but the stove was cold, and it sucked up cold air, gasping.

"Beth . . ."

She was lying on the sofa. There was the afghan Amy had made her beside her, as if she'd thrown it off. But the room was cold.

He tiptoed over beside her, covered her over with the afghan. "Beth?"

He touched her arm. It was cold. He shook her a little, and her eyes opened slowly. She looked at him, the calm of sleep in her eyes, unrecognizing. She looked at the lamp, and her eyes squinted a little as she smiled.

"Oh, Jess. I must have gone to sleep. I was tired."

"It's cold in here." He kept very calm.

"I put this afghan over me. This one Amy—"

"You'd kicked it off."

She sat up, awake now. "Oh yes. I remember. I had a big fire going, draft open. It got so hot. It was cold, so I opened the draft."

He took the afghan and put it around her shoulders. "Lie back again until I build the fire."

He took kindling from the wood box beside the stove, squatted before the door of the stove and laid a fire. The draft began to suck, and the wind began to creak the house.

She said, "It's a terrible night, Jess."

"It's not bad yet. I was down in the field working with the stackyards."

"Could I get up now?"

"When the room gets warm. You were cold."

"All right, Jess." She lay back and smiled at him.

He said, "You were sound asleep."

"I was sleepy all day. I'm glad I slept and didn't hear the storm coming. I hate to hear a storm coming."

"It came quick."

She sat up on the sofa and the light from the lamp was soft

on her face. She locked her arms around her knees and talked to him. "I always feel sorry for the cattle in a storm."

"They're used to storms."

"They've got enough hay, haven't they? If they've got enough hay they're all right. And they can get shelter in the willows. They've got to have shelter."

"They're all right."

The fire in the living room began to roar. The sides of the stove glowed red, and the varnish on the walls smelled, and the wood crackled inside.

He drew a chair up beside the fire and made her sit down. "Now you warm up. I'll go in and see how near supper's ready."

She sat down and settled herself comfortably. "I thought about you all day, Jess. Out in the storm."

"Well," he said, warming his back, "we know how to handle a storm. You take a big storm now, spring will break right after."

"That happens, Jess. Remember the year we had the blizzard two days in a row? The mail didn't come, the roads were that bad."

"Yes. I remember. The wind blew worse then." They listened. "It blew worse then."

"I believe it did." She pulled the robe about her, snuggled down into it. "What if the roads got blocked? We'd be alone on the prairie." She laughed. "It's sort of comfortable thinking about it." She looked at the glowing stove.

"The wind blew worse that year," Jess said.

"Remember—" She grew tense. She sneezed.

He looked at her. Their eyes met, and she wrinkled her nose and began to laugh.

He said, "You've got a cold. You threw that blanket off and got a cold."

"And I've been laughing at you. I thought I was smart not to get one, and then I get one."

He got up, walked to her. "You're going to bed, young lady."

"But, Jess—I'm hungry, and supper—"

"I'll bring your supper in."

She pouted a little. "I don't like eating alone and hearing everybody in the kitchen, laughing, and being alone."

"I'll eat with you, beside the bed."

She sneezed again. "That will be sort of fun, Jess." She walked beside him into the bedroom. "It's the funniest thing. I feel like a child, having to go to bed."

She sat in bed, propped up with two pillows, the afghan about her shoulders, and ate awkwardly. At last she handed her plate to him, and they talked quietly, and it seemed there was nothing in the world but that small room in the lamplight, and the two of them there listening a little to the voices of the men in the kitchen, the clatter of plates and the scraping of their chairs on the linoleum when they got up. There was the sudden rush of wind under the living-room door when they went outside.

"You sleep now, Beth."

He left her sleeping and walked with the lamp out into the living room and sat down. The wind was rising. His hands were steady as he rolled a cigarette, the shadows of his moving hands and arms sharp on the wall. Something was going on outside. Something bigger than himself. He glanced at his hands again and heard the gasping of the stove.

The days that followed were like nights. The snow flew and swirled ahead of him as he rode in the fields, and he could not see but a few feet ahead. Into his short vision nothing ever came but a slinking coyote on some business of its own, or a thin cow standing alone near a willow bush. There was still a little hay. The cattle that didn't come to get it were those that stood alone by the willow bushes.

"Old ones. The old ones stood there . . . ."

Another night.

Beth was up and about the house. He found he couldn't argue about it. She was well enough. She was nervous. "I've got to do something."

"Everything's all right, Beth."

She would not be put off. "This storm's gone on for days." She watched him reading an old newspaper. "I don't see how you can sit there."

"We know how to beat a blizzard," he said. "Be tougher than it is."

"Yes. That's the way."

She had, he noticed, put on the heavy wool trousers he had given her. He chuckled. "You look like you were going to do something about the blizzard yourself."

She looked at him. "Don't laugh. I like to feel I could do something if I had to." She was a little self-conscious.

"Don't worry. The trucks will be in in a few days."

She stared at him. "The trucks?"

"I sent for hay. We sent for hay."

She said softly, "You didn't tell me."

"Yes. I did. I told you. You forgot."

The next day Jess rode along the creeks, winding in and out of the willows, his cap pulled low, his Mackinaw collar pulled up around his neck. He turned his eyes from the cattle that began to bawl when they saw him and tried to follow. They stumbled along, trying to make their legs work, and pretty soon they were far behind, bawling. He wouldn't look back. This was a time when a man needed all his hardness.

He was always counting. Two more dead horses, three more dead cows—white mounds along the willows. He turned his eyes from the little newborn calves with old weazened faces that seemed to wonder why their mothers lay so still.

And he had turned his eyes from the little colt.

It was black. He remembered that its legs trembled as it stood beside a white mound. He looked away and went on through the willows, counting. Once he got off his horse, built a fire of twigs snapped off with stiff fingers from a willow. The smoke rose heavily and hovered over the willow tops, and he crouched over the thin sputtering flame, thinking.

His anger had been deep that morning.

It wasn't the first time, for to get good and mad helped, deadening the whistling of the wind, and it lifted a little the clouds that cut off the future like walls in a tight little room. But that morning his anger had been another thing.

His head had ached from a sleepless night. Beth lay beside him, breathing evenly, and he schemed of a way to get up so quietly and dress so quickly that he'd be out of the bedroom without waking her. It hurt to see in her again the wanting to do things, the wanting to help, and no outlet.

He longed for a cup of coffee and managed a smile when he stumbled into the kitchen, sniffing coffee and hot sputtering grease in the frying pans.

"Morning," he said. Slim mumbled, and the two younger men. One of them—the Kid, what's-his-name—had heavy sleepy eyes; his hair was tousled, his young face lined and tired. He couldn't have been more than twenty, but Slim said the Kid could pitch hay with the best of them. But there was no hardness in the Kid. None at all. He couldn't look at a weak old cow or a slab-sided horse and be hard and know an animal was born to butcher.

Jess had said to Slim, "Tell him to watch how much hay he pitches out."

Lamplight in the early morning is different from that at night. That morning it made their faces as yellow as Tommy's, and they ate silently, blew on their coffee, felt the warmth of the heavy white cups in their hands. They reached across the table for fried eggs and grunted.

Silence, and something heavy, stifling, about the light. Jess said, "Go easy on the hay today, you fellows. What's left has got to last—"

No one looked up. No one but the Kid, his sleepy eyes red. "Has got to last till what?" and he held his fork in his hand, looking straight at Jess. "You think the trucks—"

"The trucks are coming. You can't expect—"

The Kid laughed a funny laugh. "You think those trucks—"

Jess pushed back his chair slowly. The scrape of it went on a long time. He put his cup down in the saucer and looked up, his eyes on the Kid. "Listen. This is man's country, Kid. If you can't get along here—"

The Kid's face got red, and he dropped his eyes, watching his plate.

Slim said, "Hell. The Kid didn't mean—"

Jess moved his eyes to Slim. "And that goes for you too."

Slim's eyes narrowed, and his mouth opened, but he looked away.

Crouched over the feeble flame in the willows, Jess was not ashamed of what he'd said. Hardness would see them through. The trucks would see them through. The big trucks, the big red trucks that roared and beat at the snow, their big chains slapping at the fenders. The sound of them . . .

He'd seen those trucks. Heard them. Great big red trucks.

He got stiffly to his feet, stamped out the little fire, and the few soft ashes were black in the snow. "I'll take another look in the willows."

Darkness was settling down on the prairie when Jess rode homeward, his hands, feet, face numb with cold. He was almost unaware that he had been through the same willows before.

And the little black colt was still there, humped up, its eyes closed now, ears against its head, tail pressed against its thin, bony little body. It hadn't moved. It still stood beside the white mound, shivering a little.

His horse nickered. The colt lifted its ears, opened its eyes. It nickered weakly in answer, swayed, took an uncertain step, its long legs wobbling.

"Now go back," Jess said. "Don't try to follow me." This was a time when a man needed all his hardness. He couldn't stop. He had to get back to the ranch. He had to feed the bum calves and put them in the barn, for the men would be late tonight.

And you couldn't raise a colt that young.

He started to ride away.

The colt nickered again. Jess struggled against a weakness that swept over him. "Now don't you follow me. I'm sorry as hell your ma's dead. But I can't raise you. Nobody every raised a colt little as you."

Be hard. That was it.

But the colt hobbled closer, its legs long and weak, like broom handles, its knees like knobs.

"Now you—"

Suddenly the colt stumbled and fell in a heap on the snow, its legs sprawled out before it. "Now you—" Desperately.

Then it looked at him.

"Damn!" Jess muttered. He hesitated just a second. Then he swung off his horse, stooped down, and gently picked up the colt. He laid it across his saddle. "It's so damned little," he grumbled. "So damn *little*."

Tommy was outraged and spoke in quick, sharp Chinese when Jess came in the kitchen door. What kind of place he working? Horse in kitchen? Cook in barn!

"There's no place else," Jess faltered. "No warm place." He put a layer of gunny sacks on the floor behind the kitchen stove. "You watch he doesn't get burned. I'll go and get the missus."

Tommy softened a little. "Missy take care of horse? She good with little horses."

"Yes. She can take care of him . . . ." That was it. Something she could do in the house, keep her busy. "Beth!" he called and went into the living room.

She was lying on the bed, asleep. It was cold in the bedroom, but he knew when he touched her arm that she had been there only a little while. Her arm was very warm to his touch. She wore her trousers and a shrunk-up denim shirt of his. He watched her a moment, smiling. She looked more like a slight boy than a woman, and her cheeks were flushed a little.

He shook her several times before he woke her.

She opened her eyes slowly, looked at him a moment with a languid expression. Then her eyes changed, and she looked a little guilty. She sat up on the bed, shook her head a little.

"I shouldn't have slept."

"Get up, Beth. I've got a surprise."

She got up. "Hand me my coat out of the closet."

"The surprise is in the kitchen. You won't need—"

"I'm a little chilly."

He walked importantly ahead of her, and she followed, still a little drugged.

At the stove he stood aside. "Look at that."

The colt was down, its knees folded under it. Its ears pricked up. They looked at it a long time. Jess said, "It's got no mother."

Beth knelt beside it, touched it. "It's the sweetest thing."

"I don't know," Jess said. "You can't raise a colt that young."

She took his arm, reaching up to him. "Look, Jess. I've got that rubber nipple. Get a whisky bottle out of the bunkhouse. The colt's going to live. Nothing's going to happen to this colt."

"Beth—could you really raise him, Beth? He was all alone. Standing there all alone."

She smiled. "I know I can."

He smiled, seeing her eyes shine as they hadn't for months. "Good girl, Beth."

She put her hand against the wall and rose to her feet. "I'll fix some canned milk with water and some sugar. Bring the bottle, Jess."

He stood with his hand on the latch of the back door, his cap pulled low. "I'll be right back. Twenty minutes, maybe. I forgot the calves behind the barn. They ought to be in tonight. Hell of a storm."

She looked away from him at the colt. "It's not so bad out. Bring the bottle right back. The calves are all right."

"It's worse than you think, Beth. Wind goes right through you. The calves ought to be in. I'll come right back."

He carried the lantern, walking swiftly through the snow, and the wind beat against him, taking his breath, seeping in through his Mackinaw, chilling him, making a crazy sound, howling through the poles of the corral. He leaned forward against the wind, and the snow, dry as sand, cut his face.

He passed the bunkhouse, squat and black in the storm, and there were no friendly lights there, for the men still had not come in. There to one side he made out the black patches of willows along the ditch, drifted full. When at last he stumbled and groped near the wide dark opening that was the door of the barn he felt the house must be far behind him. The night was unnaturally lonely.

He stood inside the barn. There was a strange quiet there, a little core of silence broken only when the old logs sighed and strained against the wind. Drifting snow flew in through the door and whispered across the old board floor.

Holding the lantern high, he walked down the middle of the barn, past the high-walled box stall where he would put the calves. At the far end of the barn he touched the big wooden latch that held the door leading to the pen at the back. He tugged at it, strained. The suction through the barn snatched the door from his grasp and it banged outward, trembling on its hinges.

For a moment the flame inside the lantern failed. Then, holding the lantern high again, he began to stagger through the deep snow of the pen toward the black outline of the willows where the calves would find shelter.

They were not where they usually were, snug against the big wide pocket in the willows. Well, God knew where the storm had driven them. Maybe to the corner of the pen. Leaning forward again, he struggled on. The snow sifted down his neck, and he felt it, clammy, on his ankles.

He began to get a little anxious.

"Come on, calves!" he called. They couldn't have heard. The wind whipped his voice away. "Come on, calves!" He couldn't hear his own words . . . .

Suddenly he stopped. Had the calves got out? What about the fence around the pen? Was it tight? He walked along it, stooping over to see tracks. Twice he circled the fence and stooped again.

Where were the calves?

He stood, holding the lantern high, listening. Then the hair rose on his head, and a shiver crept down his spine.

There were no calves in that pen. He could almost feel a wolf's eyes on him, the white wolf's eyes, and they were grinning.

He turned suddenly and trudged back to the barn.

Again he stood inside, in the silence.

He laughed to himself. He'd been scared out there in the pen. Like a kid.

Suddenly the wind was silent.

And through it he heard breathing. He turned slowly.

The breathing was coming from inside the high-walled box stall. He pulled the bolt of the stall. The door creaked outward.

The calves were lying down. The lantern light shone dully on their eyes as they lay there. One got to its feet and stretched, arching up its back.

He felt his hair rise again, as if eyes were on him.

He knew how the calves got inside.

When she had got up from the bed she had seemed drugged. Her eyes had shone; her skin was flushed and hot.

XXXIII

AMY PIERCE WAS living in a fool's paradise her husband had fashioned and made real for her. The winter had been long, lonely. The snow drifted deep around the ranch houses and swept across the flat places, leveling the land.

The storm that had begun a week before touched her in no way at all, and the howling outside only heightened the pleasure she felt in the living room as she sat in her big chair near the wood heater.

The wind, she knew, would have rocked a lesser house than hers, this new one, and the worst gusts did no more than whistle under the doors that closed off the main part of the house from the warm dining room, living room, and kitchen.

She was safe in her house.

She liked to tease herself, to imagine she was in the midst of danger. She would stand close to her husband when he left in the early morning to feed the cattle.

"It's really a terrible storm, Cy. Really terrible." She would take his arm, tiny beside him. "Everything's all right. We've plenty of hay, and the cattle are fine, aren't they, Cy?"

He would smile. "We've got hay to last till the trucks come in."

A little shudder would go through her. "And if the hay doesn't come, Cy—if the cattle die—"

"The trucks will come. Those big red trucks. Don't you worry."

"Well . . ."

She recognized the game she played with herself. She knew her husband was strong, and she knew the big red trucks.

But that afternoon Amy Pierce was nervous. She was alone in the house; there was no cook, no hired girl. "We can't afford it," she would tell her friends. "This house cost I don't know what, and I've bought so much—the washing machine and the electric lights and all. We can't afford— sometimes it worries me. Then I got all these clothes, and we can't afford . . ."

Earlier that afternoon, when she put her daughter in the crib for a nap, she had fixed herself a cup of strong hot tea and had cut a piece of cake. Cy had always commented on how little she ate at meals. She had never told him about the numerous little lunches she had throughout the day because he had never asked her.

This afternoon she made a little party of it. The empty cup, now, and the plate with a few crumbs were beside her on a low table. She leaned forward and opened the draft of the stove a little.

"It's a terrible storm. I wish Cy were here . . . ."

Amy looked beside her at the telephone and frowned.

She remembered how they used to say, "When the telephone comes we can talk. We can talk back and forth . . . ."

And when they got the wires strung up they talked, but there was no longer an excuse to go to somebody's house to ask how the hay was holding out, or to borrow a magazine and stay all day. The telephone had spoiled all that. It seemed that all the new things, all the new ways, spoiled something.

The hum of the telephone wires brought a new sound of loneliness to the prairie. The poles teetered along the canyon wall down from the Pass, held up in places by piles of flat gray shale around their bases, and at last marched triumphantly toward the city, a lonely file of them, vanishing to the horizon.

Amy had enjoyed the telephone. Cy had placed hers quite low on the wall, near the chair. She could seat herself and, baby on lap, listen for hours to conversations. "Like having people right in the room . . . ."

Amy frowned at the telephone.

It was not working right, hadn't been working right for more than a week. When it rang she could listen in on the chance, she told herself, that it was for her. But she could ring no one. When she twisted the crank there was only a grinding sound, no ring at all. Something about the batteries, Cy said.

She leaned forward in her chair, stared out into the room, and, without looking, drained the last drop from the teacup. She tried to summon up the pleasant semi-isolation the phone gave her when it was working properly. But it wasn't working properly.

She sat back in her chair and controlled the odd little sense of panic that sneaked over her.

She could listen on the telephone, could sit for hours, one palm tight over the mouthpiece so her baby's occasional wails wouldn't fly over the wires and give her away. But she could call no one.

She wanted very much to call Beth Bentley.

The last news she had had, a week before, was that Beth had a cold and then a fever. Nobody had been very worried, so far as she could tell.

"Somebody," she told herself, "would have called me if it wasn't all right."

Nobody had called her. Mrs. Cooper had called once a few days before and said Jess had told her over the telephone that Beth was resting. Mrs. Cooper hadn't been able to get out in her buggy because of the snow, and the cutter had one runner loose. Mrs. Cooper could not ride a horse.

Amy could not leave the house because Cy used the gentle team to haul hay, and there were only those blacks . . . .

Surely Mrs. Cooper, whose telephone was working, would keep in touch and call . . . .

Amy got up and walked across the room. She looked out the window at the storm.

"You can't even see the barn!" she said aloud, and the wind whistled beneath the door. The abrupt silence unnerved her. She walked into the bedroom and looked at her sleeping daughter, tried to worry about her own problems. She walked back to her chair and fussed with the draft on the stove again.

"Somebody would have *called* me," she told herself. After all, it was a week ago that Beth had had a fever. Dr. Morse had been there, she understood, watching things.

Early that afternoon, right after Cy had gone away, the telephone had rung. Amy listened. She learned that Dr. Morse had gone to a farmer's house a few miles distant to treat something that looked over the telephone like measles. He would stay there all night because the snow was too deep to return after dark. Those who spoke on the telephone had said peevishly that no doctor ought to go and stay all night at a farmer's where there was no telephone, way up there in the hills . . . .

Amy, listening guiltily, had silently agreed.

Still, the fact that Dr. Morse would go up there in the hills, with Beth sick, seemed as if . . .

And a doctor had to go where he was called . . . .

Again Amy struggled against the little panic inside her. She knew so much more about Beth than anyone else. She'd been at the hospital. She knew how unnatural it was that Beth had seemed so well. For Beth Bentley had almost died in childbirth. She had never told Jess, Amy knew, and if anybody was to tell him, it must be Beth. And Beth never would.

The afternoon grew darker. She turned on the electric lights and stood a moment in the unnatural light, feeling the oddness of lights on before it was night. She turned them off again.

She bustled. She took out a basket of Cy's socks, each one rolled neatly in a ball. She arranged herself in her chair, put her feet on the footstool, and spread the socks out in her lap.

She couldn't thread the needle in the light. "It's yellowish out. Yellowish."

She put the basket away in the closet.

She sat by the telephone again and jumped when it rang: Mrs. Cooper calling from the Emporium. Mrs. Cooper's voice was raised, for she always shouted over the telephone. As soon as Mrs. Cooper had done with the Emporium, Amy intended to cut in and ask a question or two.

Mrs. Cooper wanted to know what in the name of heaven had happened that all the hams Newt bought some weeks before were moldy.

"Green!" Mrs. Cooper shouted across the wires. "Green and fuzzy all over!"

The Emporium offered to do anything.

"Don't send me green hams is all!" Mrs. Cooper said and hung up abruptly. Amy was left holding the receiver to her ear, looking a little stupid, she knew. Mrs. Cooper had been too quick for her. Now she must wait until someone else called. She listened at the receiver a moment, heard the humming of the wires in the storm, and thought of the swaying wires, stretching on and on.

It was the storm. That was it. That was why she was nervous. Cy must fix that phone. Somebody must come and visit. Soon. She could stand this loneliness no longer. Not a minute longer.

But the afternoon stretched ahead.

The storm outside moaned in a rhythmic way. It made her a little sleepy, drugged her. It was not the sound of the storms in other years, storms in the old house when the windows rattled and the old logs creaked. This was a dull beating, a thudding. It did strange things to her eardrums and made her a little deaf.

"The baby will be waking up. I've got to feed her."

She had spoken aloud. The sound of her own voice was comforting. "I've got to feed the baby. I've got to feed the baby." She stopped. Then, "I'm going crazy. I'm going crazy."

It was imbecilic, and she sat silent, a little ashamed of herself.

The doctor never would have gone to the farmer's up in the hills if he thought—if he thought . . . and the farmer's was away up in the hills, and the drifts . . .

She'd seen them. She knew.

Farmers up there. Four or five children, strange, silent children, and they worked too hard, like grownups. Measles running through them. Of course a doctor . . .

The storm lulled her. She nodded. Supper. Fix those potatoes. Cy in late. Cy . . .

She started, sat bolt upright, her hand at her throat.

The telephone had rung. It was more than a ring. It was stark appeal, a sudden cry in the room. One short, one long, insistent ring. That was Salmon City. Central in Salmon City.

Amy's hand trembled, went to the receiver. She went cold at the sound of Jess's voice.

"Get Doc Morse. Quick." She could hear him breathing.

A buzzing at the other end. Central trying. Then silence.

The calm voice of Central: "I'm sorry. He doesn't answer. I'll try again."

Another buzzing, and silence. Jess said, "Can't you—can't you—?"

"I'm sorry. He doesn't answer."

"My wife," Jess said, and Amy saw the swaying wires in the storm. "My wife is—"

"I'm sorry. He doesn't answer." A kind of sing-song. "He does-n't ans-wer."

Amy opened her mouth. Closed it. Opened it, and a kind of whisper came.

"Jess, this is Amy. I know—where the doctor is."

She heard his breath again, rasping above the sing of the wires. "Where?"

"Near here. At a farmer's. He's there for the—night." She swallowed. "Jess, what's wrong?"

"It's Beth. Something's wrong. Get Cy to ride over and get the doc." A silence, and the wires hummed. "Beth's bad. I"—she could see his face—"I can't leave her."

Amy couldn't think. Her brain pounded, and the blackness of the room closed in about her. She hated what she must

297

say. "Cy's not here." She heard his breath suck in. It would take hours for him to ride through. "Jess, let me think. Let—me think." And the wires hummed. She stared at the telephone, quivering there before her, moving from her. She shut her eyes and there was Beth's face, young and afraid. Young, terribly young, and afraid. "Jess . . ."

"Yes. Amy—" It was like a sob.

"Jess, I'll get him. I'll get the doctor. I'll go. I'll take"—she faltered, and her throat closed—"I'll take the blacks."

Her feet stumbled as she went to the bedroom. She stood only an instant over the crib of the sleeping baby and pinned the blankets. "I won't be gone long, baby. Not long." She turned, hesitated. "Please, God," Amy said.

The wind moaned and tugged at her heavy coat; the lantern in her hand flickered and smoked, casting a weak yellow glow before her. Once she fell sprawling, and the snow against the hot lamp chimney cracked it. She struggled to her feet, clutching at her open coat. The barn was low and black before her, far away in a nightmare. The blacks sensed something wrong. They raised their heads, snorted.

Amy moved toward them.

This was not the man. This was the woman, the tiny woman who stepped out of their way and cringed when they snorted. They circled twice around the pen, their eyes gleaming in the lamplight. She was small, standing there, lantern in one hand, the breath rasping in her throat, halters dangling awkwardly from the other.

"Quiet!" she shouted against the wind. "Come here."

They snorted when she touched their necks, but she held her hands steady though the muscles in her arms ached dully. Sick deep inside, she stretched on tiptoe to get the halters in place, working with stiff fingers at the fasteners. "Now!" They trotted mincingly behind her to the barn, crowding her. Their feet rumbled across the rough board floor of the barn.

Cy had said, "In winter you blow on the bit before you put it in their mouths. Frost keeps it from sticking to their tongues." She blew until she was faint and a little sick.

The harness was stiff and cold and tangled. She fumbled with the icy buckles, removing her gloves. The cold made her hands ache deep in the bones. Once, with a single side movement, the team threw her against the log wall of the barn. She cowered there, trembling, her arm numb where it had struck, the breath knocked out of her. "Quiet, you devils!" she wailed.

With her whip she flicked the sleek black hides, and the blacks ran in the darkness out into the open country, over the drifts. For a time they ran along the telephone line, and then they turned off. More like wolves they ran, than horses. But the little woman who rode behind them in the hurtling sleigh held the lines tight, crouching there in the seat. "Go it, you devils! Go it!"

XXXIV

THIS WAS THE house where they had all come out one night for the shivaree, when the new-cut logs had given off an odor, a clean new beginning odor that seeped into every room, and everybody felt at home.

She had smiled at his friends, and they had loved her.

He had been proud.

This was the bedroom where the ladies had rustled and whispered, admiring her new clothes and the small dressing table, because they had never seen a dressing table and didn't know they made it of two apple boxes covered with cloth.

Some of the ladies had plumped down on the fine new bed.

Now in the quiet room Jess knelt beside that bed, holding Beth's limp hand, his eyes on her face, but her eyes were closed. There was no fever now.

And the night of the shivaree the ladies had said, "You're a mighty lucky man," and the men had said, "You're some picker." They had said it, not even knowing the touch of her hand, the glance she gave him, the tenderness of her, the smallness, the way her hand felt now in his.

Doc Morse had stepped out.

They were alone in the room.

The room was dim with only the one lamp, but high on the ceiling there was a circle of yellow light, round, the shape of the lamp chimney. Jess looked up at it. His lips moved.

His eyes came back to her hands, whiter than he had ever known them. He remembered brown hands, strong little hands that held tight the reins of a team.

She used to sit straight in the buggy, and she drove proudly.

He had an ugly old dog. She was good to that ugly old dog. An old, old dog.

She did wonderful things with her hands. She took a box of paints and painted green trees and mountains with snow on them, and she gave them to him to hang in the living room. They were there now.

He looked up at the circle of light.

She was good. She had a little black prayer book—remember?—and she read it, not just had it around. And she had a cross, a little gold cross she wore on a chain, and she always wore it until she lost it, and that wasn't her fault.

She was good. She took little small things in and made them well. Remember? Little sick things that nobody would bother with, that didn't amount to much. She took them and made them well . . . .

Her face was white against the pillow, but she wasn't sleeping. He would wait . . . .

He held her hand and didn't press too hard. She knew he was there.

Then she opened her eyes. "Jess . . ."

"Beth . . ."

He waited, watching, breathing as she breathed, counting each breath.

"You're right here with me, Jess."

He nodded.

"Jess, I'm happy when you're right here." A thin, wondering voice. "I knew, Jess. I knew I'd be happy with you. You were riding a sorrel."

"Beth, don't talk." She tried to smile. "Rest a little."

"Let me talk. Remember? Then it was spring and we came home. There was snow on the Pass."

Her eyes wandered to the window and the storm behind it. "You built this house. For me." She was silent. She closed her eyes. "We'll never leave this house again." She didn't stir. "My darling Jess. I love you."

You could hardly see the friends standing there in the opening in the sagebrush. The wind had let up a little, but the snow fell straight down and blurred them like rain.

There were more than a hundred there, huddled together, but they were only a handful, and in the storm they all were shabby. They were in a semicircle, standing back a little from Jess and his four friends. Only Jess and his four friends were near enough to see how black the frozen clods of new-dug earth looked on the drifted snow. The little crowd was silent and motionless. They looked at one another, and then looked away into the falling snow that veiled even the town at the bottom of the hill.

They wanted to do right, and they hadn't known what to do.

It was Cy who called outside to get the preacher at the Main Line.

"When the trucks start," Cy had shouted over the telephone. "When the trucks start with the hay, send the preacher along."

But the trucks had gone hours before, had started out across the flats, and from the Main Line people saw them begin to climb up the face of the Pass until the storm came down and hid them.

The trucks were the last to go. No car could get across the flat even now.

He hated to tell Jess.

They didn't know what to do without a preacher.

Well, they had the church.

Newt got the key from Ma Perkins and opened the doors and aired the place out. Then he shut the doors and laid a fire in the big round stove. He took the sheetlike cover off the pulpit and dusted it off before he remembered there was no preacher. But the pulpit looked better with the cover off.

Then he built the fire in the little kitchen off the vestry where the ladies cooked church suppers, and Mrs. Cooper moved slowly along the pews and dusted them. She bit her lip and dabbed at her eyes.

Miss Slater came across from the school with a bunch of pink flowers the seventh-graders had made from crepe paper and put them in the brass vase on the altar. She arranged them carefully, and Mrs. Cooper watched, holding the dustcloth in her hand.

No matter how hot the fire in the round stove got, the church would not get warm. The ladies kept their coats and hats on, and the men sat stiffly beside them in coats and Mackinaws, hats in their hands, staring straight ahead.

Jess sat on the front pew. His big shoulders sagged. Amy sat beside him, and Cy beside her.

They had put the coffin up beside the altar. Jess stared at it, unblinking. Around him and beside him his friends sat, silent. They didn't know what to do.

The smell of black coffee came out from the kitchen, and at last Newt came out with a tray of steaming tin cups. He went down the aisle with the tray.

There was a rack on the back of each pew holding a prayer book and a hymnal. Cy put his hand over the back of the pew where he sat and picked up the prayer book, small in his hands.

He opened it, glanced at his wife, and got to his feet. He turned and faced the people, standing just below the pulpit.

He began to read:

"'The Lord is my Shepherd . . .'"

High above them in the belfry the wind moved and creaked. The people looked up there. The storm beat against the windows and found chinks to sneak through.

"'The Lord is my Shepherd . . .'" And then the people began to take it up, one by one.

Their voices rose. They were praying now. They didn't need the Book. They were praying for the wife of the man hunched alone in the front pew. And they were praying for the trucks. Their voices rose and rose against the storm, against the moaning in the little church, and soared above it.

"'The Lord is my Shepherd. I shall not want . . .'"

XXXV

THE HIRED MEN had just left the living room. They had sat stiffly, like wooden figures, in the three straight chairs along the wall.

Slim was older, knew the boss better. He did the talking. He glanced now and again at the two men beside him.

They had filed in solemnly, the three of them. Slim had knocked softly at the living-room door before coming in the cold, dimly lit living room. The wind was crazy out, Slim said. He spoke loud.

"We thought we'd just come in and say howdy," Slim said. "Mean night out." He glanced at the other two men. They nodded and looked at their hands. It seemed like a long silence, and through it came the sound of the dogs howling, the sound battered and twisted by the wind. Slim glanced at his companions.

"Dogs carrying on all evening," Slim said. "Barking all evening. Must be coyotes out."

The Kid said, "Them dogs howling." Slim glared at the Kid, for it had been decided who was to do the talking.

"Coyotes out, dogs always barking," Slim said.

Tonelessly Jess said, "That's right."

Slim moved in his chair. It creaked. "Well, boss," Slim said heartily, "I guess you're pretty glad the trucks are coming. This has been bad. Trucks coming must make you feel pretty good, anyway."

The Kid said, "Hell of a storm—creepy. Saw the wind on the Pass—drifting—"

"Well . . ." Slim got to his feet and stretched casually, yawning, and the others got up at the same time, and they watched him stretch, his arms reaching up toward the ceiling. "Boss," Slim said suddenly, "we come"—he looked helplessly at the other two men—"we come to say we was—awful sorry." Slim turned and walked swiftly from the room, and the other two men followed, single file . . . .

After a little while Jess stirred, reached in his pocket, pulled out his father's gold watch. He held it in his palm, weighing it.

It was nine o'clock.

The wind still rose.

The dogs kept howling. It must be coyotes. Coyotes down in the field where you can't hear them, but dogs can.

A blast of wind shook the house, sudden, heavy. The lamp flame leaped wildly, and the kitchen door slammed. The latch clinked. There was something living in the room, some presence.

Then the silence again, and even the dogs were quiet.

"Jess!" Clear.

Jess jerked his head and stared at the door. The lamp blinded him. In a moment he distinguished Cy's big shape in the doorway. His dark red Mackinaw was brushed with snow, and the visor of his cap was pulled low.

"I didn't want to come," Cy said, "after—"

"It's all right. I'm glad . . . ."

"It's storming bad. I never saw it like this."

"I'm glad you came. I'd like to talk a little. Maybe a little talk . . ."

Cy took off his cap, and his thick thatch of white hair fell a little in his face. He pushed it back. "I feel bad, Jess. I don't like to come now. It's selfish."

Jess looked away, then back. "The trucks . . ."

Cy's voice was soft in the small room. "They're stuck on the Pass. I didn't want to come now, after —"

Jess said quietly. "I knew they wouldn't come."

"You knew? Somebody called you and said—?"

"No. I saw the storm on the Pass."

"You knew? And you didn't do—anything?" Cy flushed. "I don't mean—" The calm on Jess's face made Cy uneasy. He began again: "I didn't want to come because of—and then I thought you'd see."

Jess looked at him. "I don't get you, Cy."

Cy stirred in his chair and stood up. "I got to thinking there must be some way out, that the cattle wouldn't die and we could keep our places, someway." Cy's face was contorted, thinking, trying to speak. "I got to thinking—maybe you could think—of something."

Jess walked to the blank, dark window and stood there, hands behind him, his back to Cy. "What could I think of?"

Cy said, "I don't know. I got to thinking."

Jess said, "I can't do anything."

Cy took a step, hesitated. He put his cap back on and pulled it low. "Jess, I didn't mean to come now."

Jess stood at the window. "That's all right. There's just—nothing." His hands clenched behind him. He heard Cy turn and walk slowly out through the kitchen, lift the latch of the door. The wind swept through; the lamp flame leaped, and then the curious silence fell again.

He stood there at the window a moment.

No. Of course there was nothing he could do. Why should they come to him? Nothing he could do.

It didn't matter.

He walked slowly out into the kitchen. There was only a little light there, a dull little patch of light out from the sitting room along the once-bright checks and squares of the linoleum. The stove was a black hulk against one wall, and the wind made the draft throb and suck away. Beside the stove was a stove table with the water bucket and the dipper in it. He'd drink a little water.

There was a stirring, a scrambling behind the stove. It startled him. A scraping, a scrambling.

He looked where the scraping came from.

Funny. He'd forgotten the colt, a little wobbly shape, scrambling to its feet . . . .

He stood by the water bucket. The colt stood a moment, still, trying to balance on the bare floor. Then its stiff legs began to work.

Softly Jess said, "Didn't they feed you? Did they forget?"

It nuzzled him on the knee, wobbling. But bold, confident.

Well, of course they'd forgotten, Tommy and the men in the bunkhouse.

Beth never had.

The colt nuzzled him on the knee again. Well, somebody had to feed it. Things—had to go on. Beth would have fed the colt.

She had loved Cy and Amy . . . . Things had to go on.

Suddenly he strode to the outside door, lifted the latch. Out there the storm howled and took away his breath. The wind cut. He called loudly:

"Cy!" He waited, watching the shape not far away at the gate. "Get down off your horse," he shouted. "Come back in."

Puzzled, a little dazed, Cy stood in the kitchen.

Jess said, "Come in the living room."

They sat down. Jess reached over and turned up the lamp. "I know what, Cy." His voice was different. He began to roll a cigarette.

"You know—what to do?"

"In the morning go to the bank. Borrow every cent you can. And tell the others; get money. Then call outside. Contract for every ton of hay you can get."

Cy looked away, shifted in his chair. "Trucks get stuck. We'll go broke."

Jess lit his cigarette, drew deeply on it. "To hell with trucks. The train will get through."

"The train?" Cy stared. "The train hasn't run for months. Those drifts—you're crazy. We can't—" Cy laughed strangely. "You don't—believe it yourself."

Jess spoke quietly. "I believe it. So much that I'm going to mortgage this place." He got up, stood tall. Then his face was gentle, and his voice. "I got to feed that colt."

XXXVI

IT WAS A long train that left the Main Line yards for Salmon City and went chugging across the great flat country toward the Pass. The car wheels made a cold, lonesome whine on the rails, and a suction between the cars drew up dry snow and scattered it at the couplings.

In the caboose the brakeman sat sullenly on the bench along one side, listening to the coffeepot simmer on the stove. He'd need more than coffee before he got back to the Main Line. What was the old man thinking of—sending out a train this weather, this time of year? Somebody had more money than brains . . . .

He stood up and walked unsteadily to the end of the swaying car, took a tin cup from the cupboard. He poured himself strong black coffee and climbed with it to the cupola, where he sat on the hard black cushions and idly looked up ahead at the twenty moving cars crammed with baled hay, tons of it.

The hay would never get to the prairie. Not that year. Even the old man knew it, and the old man had made somebody pay through the nose.

He stared gloomily at the Pass ahead, a great white wall, solid except for the track zigzagging up the side. And halfway up a storm raged; snow blew off into space like clouds. He shivered and looked at the warm stove. The train slowed, jerked to a stop. He climbed down from the cupola, picked up his mittens. Snowplow already—wanted the snowplow already, and not yet to the foot of the Pass.

The brakeman edged out the door at the end of the car. No use letting the cold in. Cold get in soon enough. He walked along the side of the train, squinting his eyes. Nothing but white. Not another damned thing. He could have been in town, in the beanery, eating pie, drinking coffee with cream, chinning the pretty hasher.

The train moved again. Whir, the great revolving blades of the plow flew, bit deep into the snow, and flung it to the sides. Slower now. The engine saved its strength. Whir, more coal, more coal.

The brakeman came back into the caboose, threw his mittens down on the bench, blew on his hands. The train lurched. The door of the cupboard flew open, and a can of milk bumped onto the floor. Enough food in that cupboard for three days. The old man said, "If you don't make it in three days . . ."

On the prairie they waited. And until now they had faced it. Pioneer blood.

"Grampaw knew what blizzards was."

"Look at him there in the picture. Tough as a grizzly bear."

"Wasn't scared. Tough one. Remember?"

They sat in their houses and talked. No use going out. Nothing to feed the cattle. It was ugly to ride through the fields and see the cattle starving, the cows on their sides struggling weakly, and the stronger ones staying in the willows.

The ranchers stayed in their houses, and the hired men stayed in the bunkhouses and tried to read magazines. Reading magazines in the middle of the day, when they should have been out . . . .

The wind began to work on their minds, and their hope was fading. Why didn't the wind go down?

"I tell you I hear it all day, and in the willows. In the willows I hear it, and then in the house I hear it rattle the windows, and all night, and then I keep hearing—"

Why had they listened to Cy Pierce? It was better to sit tight, to let the cattle die. There would be a little left, the land, and they could start again. Someplace else.

They had been led, had listened; they were angry and ashamed.

Jess Bentley had got them into it. He was crazy. He'd lost his wife and didn't care what happened.

"I tell you I hear the wind . . ."

Coyotes slunk out of the willows, gray shadows, bellies close to the snow, circling around a cow struggling weakly in a drift, waiting. The boldest didn't wait. And at night they would howl, the wind whipping the sound along until they heard it in their houses.

"His wife died, and he doesn't care . . . ."

XXXVII

IT WAS THE night that Cy had called for the train.

Saturday night.

In the bunkhouse they had gone to bed. Now in the darkness there were sharp creakings as the stove cooled. A faint odor of kerosene smoke hung about, for a kerosene lamp smokes awhile after you blow it out. A cigarette glowed weakly in the box of earth in which the stove rested. It was handy to have your stove sitting in a box of dirt. You could throw cigarettes there and spit in the box and keep the floor clean.

As Slim got older he got neater. He would say to a new man, "When you spit, spit in the box. This ain't no pigpen." There were other rules. You had to remember to empty the tin basin after you got through washing.

The Kid, the young fellow, broke most of the rules. Tonight he had left his boots in the middle of the floor where a man would trip. He had gone into Salmon City that morning to see the girls. He said there was no use sitting on his tail at the ranch because it was gloomy there. His job was to feed out hay to the cattle, and there was no hay now, and it was like a graveyard. Worse. He had come back late to the ranch, sober enough because the storm was bad and the cold wore the whisky off.

He had a lot to tell. He had seen a lot of ranch hands at the bar, fellows like him. He knew what they said now about Jess Bentley and his idea about the train.

He lay in bed and figured.

Slim was the last to bed. Slim slept badly, said if he went to bed before nine he woke up at three. No one knew for sure if this was true, but you always heard about how an old man can't sleep and prowls around at night in his underwear. You'd think when a man got old he'd sleep more, like an old dog does.

Slim lay wrapped in the gray blankets, the fuzz worn off them. Blankets warmed up quickly. Slim had visited his sister in Salt Lake City and she had sheets. You had to pull your knees up to your belly to keep warm until you got too stiff to move. Slim's sister always did things nice, but lots of times nice things are uncomfortable. Anyway, blankets smelled of hay in the mattress and the bunkhouse and you, good smells that made it easier to sleep.

Slim listened. The bunkhouse was well built and almost cut out the sound of the wind, except for the crack where the window was open. He could hear the other fellow in the bunk across the room snoring softly—a new fellow, older than the Kid. A fellow who thought you ought to have the window open at night. Slim knew the night air was bad, poisonous, especially in winter, and gave you pneumonia. He knew a fellow died from pneumonia in the night air. Slim himself was proof that night air was bad. He never let the night air strike him and he was almost seventy. Did a young man's work too.

Slim got up stealthily and shut the window. Already the floor was cold to his bare feet.

The Kid, in the other bunk, did not snore. Slim listened. The Kid's breathing was not regular. He wasn't asleep, probably staring up at the ceiling. The Kid needed sleep. A young fellow would ride fifteen-twenty miles to get drunk and see the girls, and he needed sleep. Nervous sort of kid. He shouldn't of sounded off about the boss. Not in the boss's bunkhouse.

You had no right to question anything the boss did unless you were on the ranch a long time.

It was a funny thing. Hired men came and went, and he, Slim, stayed on, settled. All his life he wanted to be settled, and Jess Bentley gave him the chance. Hired men stayed a week or a month or a year and then drifted, like tumbleweeds. There was the Mexican and the fellow with the harelip who was always cranky, like he was afraid you would laugh at his lip and the way he talked. But when he was alone with Slim he talked—nice fellow. Slim felt sorry and told him when he was a kid he stuttered. Slim told the fellow he stuttered so bad he was cranky to keep people from laughing. And after that the harelipped man talked to Slim in his funny, breathy voice because Slim understood when a man had something wrong with him.

There was the red-haired fellow with the scar on his right cheek, and he told everybody he got the scar over a woman.

And the fellow with the battleship *Maine* tattooed on his back in red and blue.

And the nice old fellow from the circus who used to feed the most famous hippopotamus in the world. The hippopotamus was named Lotus, but Slim couldn't think of the man's name.

All these men drifted on and left nothing behind but a whisky bottle or an old pair of overalls hung on a nail. When you looked at the overalls gathering dust over the faded blue, you remembered a fellow and sort of held back before you tore them up to make a rag to swab oil on your saddle or clean the lamp chimney.

Sometimes a man left his name on things, on magazines. Slim had seen men write their names over and over again on a scrap of paper, putting in curlicues and stuff, real fancy writing. They never wrote anything but their names. A few of them had their names on the wall of the toilet out back, and when you sat there you thought about the men. Maybe that's why they wrote them.

They had no neckties. Every Christmas the boss's wife gave Slim a fine-looking tie in a Christmasy box. Mrs. Pierce and Mrs. Cooper gave socks. These were things a man got when he was settled. When he was settled he could have a cigar box with his letters in it and snapshots. Slim had letters from his sister, and he meant to answer them, too, and one that Pete— poor old Pete—had written from Butte when he was drunk. That was a long time ago.

A cigar box had a good smell, and the letters smelled the same, like tobacco and cedar.

You had pictures tacked on the wall that you cut out of magazines—pictures of girls and ships, and one of an apple orchard in the Wenatchee Valley, all the red apples, and a girl standing there, and underneath it said: "The Apple of Your Eye."

Men who came to work could complain about your pictures, but when you had them up they were yours. And a stranger couldn't touch them any more than he could read letters in the cedar box. They were your *things*.

Tonight Slim had his things. He called them all up before him. He could almost feel the silk of the neckties and the hard cool feel of the bronze livestock convention medal—in the shape of a steer—that Jess had given him. It hung on the end of a blue silk ribbon, and you could pin it on when you went to a convention. His things were real, and he clung to them.

They couldn't take his things away from him, like they could take a man's land and his cattle.

For maybe the Kid was right. Maybe those men in the bar were right. They were saying the train would not come. It was ugly to think of those men at the bar saying that. They said Jess Bentley got everybody into it. The Kid had blurted out what they said, like some dirty thing.

Slim stirred restlessly. "Kid," he whispered. "You asleep?"

In the dark the Kid answered in a sharp whisper. "Christ, no." The Kid moved, and his bunk squeaked. "How can a fellow sleep with the wind out?"

The still-warm room was pierced by an icy blade of air, and the wind filled the room and seemed to die there, moaning. The other fellow across the room went on snoring. Slim fumbled for his shirt on the floor, felt in his pocket for the bulge, and drew out his sack of tobacco and papers. The papers made a thin rustle. A match flared. A cigarette glowed. Slim held the cigarette carefully, for when you smoke in bed sometimes sparks and ashes fall off and burn little holes in the front of your underwear.

Slim decided he didn't want to talk. He just wanted somebody else there when his thinking got him down. But the Kid had to talk. Slim could picture the Kid leaning out on one elbow.

"I feel like hell," the Kid said.

Slim whispered hoarsely. "You shouldn't of gone in town. You shouldn't of drank."

The Kid said, "You can't sit on your tail."

Slim puffed deeply on his cigarette. The glow lit his drawn face and probed deeply into the wrinkles around his eyes. He cleared his throat. "What was it they said in town?"

"I told you." The Kid fumbled for his shirt, and Slim heard the rustle of a cigarette paper. "A fellow said Bentley could take a chance with everything he owned. He didn't have a kid or a wife to think of."

Sleet tapped at the window. The Kid was settling himself, yawning and groaning. The other fellow snored softly. In the far distance the wind mocked and made a mean laugh.

Slim spoke in the dark. "That was dirty to say. That fellow was drunk."

XXXVIII

ALL DAY JESS rode along the creeks, winding in and out of the willows, his cap pulled low. The cattle stayed out of the wind, close to the willows, but when they saw him they tried to follow, stumbling along, legs working jerkily.

That morning he had hitched a team to the hay rack and pulled it around beside the barn. He had cleaned the barn out of every forkful of hay, old hay, years old, and all of it didn't fill the basket of the rack. He had driven the team through the fields, pitching a little off, a mouthful at a time. He wondered how long a cow could live on a mouthful of hay.

Where he got the strength he felt inside he didn't know.

He didn't fool himself. He knew when the storm was gone, forgotten when the country was green again and warm and silent, then it would all come back. He'd remember.

But now—now he was needed.

They had looked to him. The prairie had followed him.

Slim had said nothing.

It didn't matter. His friends trusted him. Newt and Cy trusted him, and the men in the bunkhouse.

He was strong. He was strong enough to push through the willows when the others stayed in their houses. He looked at what was there and did what he could on the first day, on the second.

At night he needed to be with people. After supper he went with Slim and the two others to the bunkhouse and sat talking. They talked of guns and cattle and horses, all the things they knew, and the new man told of places he'd worked: of Oregon, Texas. The new man told about Denver, Colorado, and the Brown Palace Hotel there when the livestock convention was on. He told about rodeos at Pendleton and Cheyenne. The new man had talked with the bronc-stomper who rode the horse called Midnight, and the new man's brother-in-law knew this bronc-stomper very well.

Sometimes they almost forgot the prairie and the dying cattle and the wind.

Only the Kid was silent. While they talked he sat on the edge of the big table, his head down a little, his hair in his eyes, braiding rawhide strands to make a halter.

Then one night Jess had come into the bunkhouse after supper to talk again. He had heard somebody playing the mouth organ, and it sounded fine and gay.

When he came in, Slim and the new fellow greeted him silently, and Slim motioned to an empty chair. The Kid didn't look up but kept on playing, hands cupped closely around the mouth organ. He played a little louder and switched to another tune, not a gay tune, a sad, lonesome tune.

Bury me not on the lone prairie . . .

Jess sat and listened, smiling, for maybe in a little the Kid would play "The Camptown Races," or "The Fiddler's Ball."

The Kid kept playing the lonesome tune, cupping his hands around the mouth organ so it sobbed.

Slim sat forward in his chair. "For Christ sake, can that tune!"

The Kid stopped right in the middle of a phrase and glanced toward the dark window.

Jess laughed a little. "Let him go on, Slim. It's damned fine music."

The Kid pushed the hair out of his eyes. He wiped the mouth organ on his sleeve and shoved it into his pocket. Then he slid down off the table and, without looking back, he went into the other room, where the bunks were. In a minute his boots dropped to the floor.

The next day, the third day after Cy had called for the train, Jess rode over to Cy's.

There was not even a dog to meet him in the yard as he walked from the fence, where he had tied his saddle horse. The snow had drifted around the steps of the house and covered the low windows of the cellar. There was a deep silence around the house in spite of the wind.

He wished a friendly dog would run out from the barn, barking, and jump on him, give him a chance to speak. He had a queer feeling walking up the icy steps.

He had never before knocked at the door of Cy Pierce's house. He had always rattled the latch a moment and walked in, talking loud, calling to Cy or to Amy. Not this time. After the silence of the knocking he heard footsteps moving toward him inside. He grinned when the door opened.

Amy was nervous. She stared when she saw him, a funny little movement of her hands to her throat. Then she smiled. "You scared me, Jess. I didn't expect—"

She left him sitting in the front room to put on coffee, and he looked about the new room at the new furniture and the new rugs. Not like the old stuff, not a part of Cy and Amy.

She came back into the room while the coffee heated.

"I thought Cy would be here," he said.

"Cy went out this morning. He wanted to see—" She sat down. "It's bad, isn't it, Jess?"

"It's a bad storm."

"The cattle are dying, and the —" She looked at the new room and she laughed a little. "I don't know why I'm laughing, Jess."

He shifted in his chair. "The train will come today. Maybe tonight."

She looked at him, then away. She said tonelessly, "Will it, Jess?"

He nodded.

"I'll get the coffee, Jess." She went out and came back with two full cups, balancing them carefully. Her face was set in a smile. "I always slop coffee." She sat down and looked at the coffee. "I—know all about it, Jess. Cy never said anything about the ranch to me before, but I know now." She made another little laugh. "I wouldn't care—" She stopped and took a sip of coffee.

He was gentle. "Amy, don't worry. It's all—a part of raising beef critters. We've got to stand up—"

"Yes. I know. We always did." She looked at her cup.

"Just keep—going."

Her mouth trembled as she looked at him. "It's all right for you, Jess. But—we've got—a baby."

He just looked at her.

She flushed. "We'd planned—it wasn't quite fair—" She stopped, her eyes on his face. "Jess, I didn't mean—"

Quietly: "I know you didn't, Amy." He got to his feet.

"But don't go now till I try—" Her voice was tired.

He didn't look at her now. His voice was very gentle. "I just wanted to see Cy."

She stood helplessly, watching him go out the door.

Somewhere in the storm, somewhere on the face of the Pass, the train moved. Ahead, the snowplow groaned, shook, ground, tunneled. The top of the tunnel caved in; back the train went, back a little. Sand run out on the tracks to keep the wheels from spinning. Sparks. Make a run, make a run. Steam gauges high, hissing. Drive, pistons!

Behind, the snow drifted. Hard to back up. Then forward, crawling up the face of the great white wall. The wind rushed across from Black Canyon, across the ridges, across from Nip and Tuck Creek and Grizzly Mountain, roaring, shouting. Keep the train back; keep it back . . . .

But the train had long since passed the fleet of abandoned trucks, lonesome white mounds down there where the highway ran.

Fifty feet forward, forty feet back. The engine groaned deep in its bowels and quivered, made ten feet. Hit the drifts hard. Not too hard. Don't—throw the engine off the track. Not off the track—not too hard . . . .

The pony truck slipped off. It took hours to right it, the crew stumbling around in the blinding snow, high on some bare ridge.

Then, Huh! Huh-huh-huh, screamed the engine. Hoarse. Huh-huh-huh! The pistons, great steel arms, strained, moved; the wheels spun. Sand did no good. Forward, back. More coal. High pressure in the boilers. Could the boilers stand up? A long time now since the boilers were strong and tight. If only the gauges wouldn't jump drunkenly, if the connections wouldn't hiss. Steam and heat and oil, the red fire reflecting on the fireman's face. He heaved coal, panted. The engineer sat rigid, his hand on the throttle, steady, steady.

The snow flew and cut. Darkness settled down, cold, thick, darkness the headlights couldn't cut, and ahead the flying flakes, the distance, the emptiness. And the wind rushed down from Black Canyon.

The strange half-darkness of the past weeks settled down when Jess rode home from Cy's. His hands, feet, and face were numb with cold. He wound down again through the willows. There was no use looking now. He knew what was there.

He fixed his mind on the colt.

It was dark when he rode into the ranch, but the light from the bunkhouse and the kitchen blinked out and made yellow paths across the snow. The creak of frozen willows across the creek was distinct. A dog whined, and there was the clunking step of men moving in the bunkhouse. He walked around the end of the path of light. They could have seen him in the light, might have called. He didn't want to talk.

The dogs ran out from the darkness and whined and jumped at him, and he spoke softly, reassuring them, so they wouldn't bark.

He put his mind to the colt.

"Legs like stilts." He tried to grin.

He stamped his feet on the icy porch, so the colt could hear, and rattled the latch.

He pushed the door open slowly.

There was no tramping of small hoofs when he stepped inside.

He had lost track of time. Supper was over, the kitchen dim, the stove creaking and cooling. The dishes were done, the table set for breakfast.

He walked across the kitchen, his stomach tight inside. His eyes moved swiftly about, resting in this corner, that corner, on the brown case of canned milk.

The stove creaked. "That's where—behind the stove, where it's warm . . . ."

The colt was there.

He knelt down on his knees, and his hands touched the colt's slick hide. It was lying on its side, its long legs stretched out, its eyes glazed, staring.

He knelt there; minutes he knelt there, his hand stroking the cold hide, feeling the hard little ribs. Then his hand was still. He stared at the wall, seeing again—seeing once more the white mounds in the willows, the hundreds of mounds on the prairie, and the colt stumbling toward him.

The picture was not strange. He had seen it—somewhere— before. And while he knelt there it came back.

Now he knew why the Indians shunned the prairie in winter. He saw skinny horses lunging in drifts, Indians beating them until they dropped. He heard the wailing of squaws and the moaning of old men and strong young men passing them without looking back.

He saw buffalo staggering upcountry, cows and thin calves trailing, blundering into drifts near the gulch, crowding in, lunging, trying to get up the gulch and out. They died on the flat, and the timber wolves sneaked down . . . .

He stood up. He big shoulders sagged under his Mackinaw.

Now he knew. The train would not get through. It was not in the cards. It had never been. It was all there for a man to see.

This was the end of trying.

The living room had been shut off from the rest of the house. The air was cold and stale. The cold was one with the silence, a silence only disturbed now when the wind rose and the faint ticking of the alarm clock crept through from the bedroom.

That winter the settling of the house and the warping of the front door sill at last began to tell, for on windy nights the door rattled on its hinges. It rattled only when the wind was in the north. He had lain awake nights, listening.

Only when the wind was in the north.

Jess now sat in the living room, his hands resting on the arms of the chair. His hands made the old movement to roll a cigarette.

He watched his hands. The tick of the alarm clock seeped in when the wind sank. He touched his fingers together and then stared over his hands into the empty room. Suddenly the flame of the lamp leaped in the chimney. For a moment there was a point of light on the motionless brass pendulum of the wall clock, and the shadows of the bold, still hands showed a phantom hour.

A blast of wind shook the house to its foundation and whipped over the corner of the rag rug. The fringe whipped fitfully, then lay still. Then again the small, persistent night sounds.

But the kitchen was silent. The last chunk was burning feebly in the stove there. Weak coals glowed in the ashpan, winking like eyes.

Outside the wind moaned, its voice rising and falling, telling an old story of elements, of sharp things, of the keen-bladed cold that searched the secret places of the willows, stalking with an awful patience. Of moving things, the mad sweep of snow down the Pass, and the stiff, foolish walk of starving animals.

It whispered of forgotten things.

Then suddenly the door began to rattle.

A soft, tentative, questioning sound, like a stranger at the door that stopped for an answer.

The lamp began to smoke. Soot moved up the sides of the chimney, grasping, clutching up and up, waving black fingers.

Jess sat a moment, his eyes on the smoking lamp.

He got up slowly, then walked into the bedroom and sat down on the bed. He took off his cap and tossed it behind him. He struggled with his Mackinaw and let it fall. The buttons tapped against the foot of the bed. He started to lie down, drawing his feet up on the blanket.

The door began to rattle softly. Again the moment of silence, the waiting . . .

The rattle.

Ought to fix that . . . .

No use. It didn't matter.

He lay down.

The lamp still burned in the living room, at the far wall, and when the flame leaped in the chimney the rods of the brass bed cast vertical shadows on the bedroom wall. They moved a little from side to side, grew fainter, and disappeared when the wind sank, then vivid and sharp as the flame leaped again.

The rattle . . .

Softly, then again, again. The vibration rose, died down, and rose higher. The room swelled with the harshness, and the windows caught up the sound and hummed in their sills.

He heard. He turned to the wall.

Then the wind screamed. The door beat and beat against the catch, and underneath the wind sneaked, blundering through the room. Snow sifted across the floor, hid in the corners; the lamp glowed blue; the shadows in the bedroom were black against the wall.

He lay listening, hearing the storm triumphant, exultant. No man could win.

He got up and strode out of the bedroom. "But I'll fix that god-damned door . . . ."

He had the bolt in the table drawer, and a screw driver.

He tried the door. He opened it against the blast outside, closed it, drew the bolt, and listened. It didn't rattle.

He stood still a moment, his chin up, listening again. He drew the bolt, stepped out onto the porch, and closed the door behind him.

He stood blinking there on the front porch, listening. The barn stood out black and hulking behind a moving curtain of sleet. He heard the hum of the wind on the barbed wire in the pasture, a low, mournful tune, a throbbing like an Indian drum, setting the tempo for the storm. He leaned forward. Huh-huh-huh, the wind went, laughing, mocking.

He used to know the wind, could hear it and know things. A storm wind, a clearing wind. But this . . .

This gibberish. Unfamiliar. No meaning.

He turned at last to go inside, conscious of the numbing cold, but as he turned he faced for a moment in the direction of the Pass. Only a second he looked there. His heart leaped in his throat. It was *clearing!*

The moon shone bright that instant, high in the night, a crazy glow through a clearing in the clouds. He stood still. Then suddenly the glow was gone. Gone.

It had never been there.

His hands touched the icy doorknob but his eyes for a moment more rested there in the distance. And again the glow, crazy, like the moon. He blinked.

Then he saw it. Not a glow, but a flash—a flash of light. It was gone, then there again, boring, ripping through the darkness. Flashing. Flashing . . .

He watched it, rigid. His lips moved.

He knew it now.

His shoulders shook. He stumbled into the house. He stood before the telephone, fumbled at the receiver. It clicked. He rang. A short ring, a long ring. Calling Salmon City. Central at Salmon City. He waited, his breath loud in the room.

Central answered, sleepy.

He cleared this throat. He said, "This is—Jess Bentley. Ring up everybody. Tell them—" He steadied his voice. "Tell them the train is coming."

He hung up.

He turned away and stood for a moment looking out into the room. His step was steady as he walked to the table beside his chair, leaned down and turned down the smoking lamp. He sat down slowly and put his head in his hands.

There was a moment of silence, and then the phone began to ring, filling the room with the sharp triumphant sound.

Calling Cyrus Pierce. Calling Cyrus Pierce. Calling Cyrus Pierce . . . .

XXXIX

AT THE STATION the high potbellied old black heating stove should have roared louder and glowed redder. The yellow lamplight in the nickel reflectors should have been brighter.

Jess Bentley should have been there.

Dimly lighted, shadowy, here was where they had waited countless times for the train to be made up, waiting with their wives and children in the dark early morning, sleepy, suitcases beside them, sitting on the hard varnished benches, waiting and waiting.

The train would take a wife to her family outside.

She had talked. She had planned; she had sewed. A coat out of moth balls, hung on the line, waving in the wind.

"I saw her coat on the line, airing. She will be going to see her folks . . . ."

"I'll see Mary and Ed. I'll tell them what you said to tell."

A feverish, excited day, hands fumbling, almost on the verge of tears. Last good-bys. Eggs boiled after supper, after the dishes are done and put away. The eggs are cooled outside and wrapped in brown paper. A little packet of salt and pepper. Bread buttered, ham sliced. Put away in a shoe box, tied with a stout string. Nice lunch.

To bed. Lying there in the dark looking up. Wild dreams of travel. "I'll see Mary and Ed. I'll tell them what you said to tell. I won't forget now."

The awful tight excitement that can't get out. The husband, lying beside her, feels it and touches her. "You have a good time," he says.

Good, generous husband.

Tomorrow before daylight.

They had sat on the hard varnished benches in the early-morning darkness, remembering the odd stillness of the land and the night quiet around the dark ranch houses. Maybe a dog barked.

But let down now. Excitement gone. Tired, sleepy in this real thing. Children, already hungry, cry for the lunch.

You got to wait. *We'll eat going over the Pass.*

Trying to catch the excitement again.

The long bench is hard. The Seth-Thomas clock grinds out the minutes. Get up and stretch, walk to the stove, back again. Tired faces, waiting. It suddenly made no difference. You could see your folks any time. The lunch could dry up in the shoe box.

Then a guilty feeling comes.

"I ought to be home. Looking after things."

The station did that to you. The soft-coal smoke and the hard old bench.

When they heard the news of the train they hurried to the city. When they got there they stood in silent groups, watching the clock, glancing up when neighbors came in.

Midnight.

They did not speak except among themselves, man to wife, family to family. Silent and tight inside. And always new figures came in the door out of the dark, and snowflakes blew in and melted. The station was filled, but each group was alone.

They gathered outside, their voices low as they moved to keep warm, slapping their mittened hands against their thighs. Somewhere off in the darkness sled runners whispered across the snow. Then new people came and stood near the track. They talked as they did at funerals.

It was cold, still and cold. The snow fell softly; flakes fell, tiny shadows against a bobbing lantern. Somebody had an idea.

Somebody dragged an apple box out of the dark clearing and lit it. It flared, and those around were warm. They turned and smiled shyly.

"Come on over by the fire. Get warm." They smiled and stood aside.

Each suddenly knew that this man beside him was a good man. All these people were good people.

"Come on over and get warm." They turned their backs to the warmth and talked, hands clasped behind them, rocking on heel and toe.

"Go find another box. This one's about gone."

Somebody brought two boxes, threw them on the flames. A few more shapes moved into this new circle of light.

"Well, now, if we're going to have a fire, let's have a fire!"

That did it.

The good feeling spread. They hurried off into the darkness and came back with posts and rubbish, boxes from the Emporium's storeroom. People dragged things. Middle-aged men tugged and dragged posts, foolish and happy. They were destructive. They happened on neat woodpiles behind houses. They brought back white slats.

"You shouldn't ought to of done that. That's somebody's picket fence."

"Burns good, though. Good and dry."

"Well, you shouldn't ought to of. My, look at it burn!"

Flames leaped, red, orange, swirling, crackling, yellow tongues licking at the wood, and excitement mounting with the flames.

Their voices grew loud. Small boys dragged an old Christmas tree still covered with bits of tinsel that caught the light. Old chairs. Tires—there was something that really burned. Black, curling smoke, yellow with sulphur. The fire began to whine.

Mrs. Cooper's voice rose strongly. "Remember, Newt!" She turned to the small figure in the man's fur coat. "The Indians called it firewater."

"Cy still calls it firewater. Says it burns." Amy's voice was muffled.

"But the Indians *first* called it firewater. I've been thinking of Indians since I saw this fire. Here," she said, "Here are two boxes they haven't burned. Let's sit."

They sat. They were silent for a time as they watched, drinking in the noise and color. The fire lit up Mrs. Cooper's old hawklike face.

Amy said, "Cy said he would get drunk."

"Newt didn't say, but he will. I cautioned him. He's come to expect it. I would lose face if I didn't." She paused. "I am still thinking of Indians. When I was a little girl the Indians built their fires. My father knew the Indians well. He used to say he knew the Indians better than he knew my mother. I would sit with him and watch them dance. My father would dance with them. This distressed my mother. She was not a dancing woman.

"She would say to my father, 'How can I hold up my head?'

"When my father danced I sat with the squaws and beat with a stick on my tom-tom." She glanced about her, saw a stick at her feet, and leaned over to pick it up. "We beat like this." She began to tap with the stick on the side of the apple box. "See how it goes? Imagine those young people there are Indians. They are the dancers. I am a squaw." She glanced at Amy. "The squaws wailed, Amy." She began to chant with the tapping, a thin mournful sound, rising and falling. "Wee-ooo-wee-ooo," she wailed. "See, Amy? Try it."

Amy tried and was embarrassed. She pulled the big coat about her.

"That is not right," Mrs. Cooper said. "You are too cheerful. Indians were always sad about their singing. They saw sadness in happiness."

"But I can't be sad!"

"Take heart! The Indians certainly knew what to do about their own dancing!" She began to chant again, tapping. "Look. Those small boys are watching. Call them over. I'll tell them about the Indians."

"Oh no!" Amy cried.

"Newt has a disgusting phrase," Mrs. Cooper said suddenly. "He says this is our night to howl." She put her mittened hand on Amy's arm. Her voice was quiet. "I was afraid. I told myself I was a foolish old woman, but I was afraid."

Newt had said, "Now, the minute you see it for sure, toot the horn on the car. Me and Cy here's going—"

"To get firewater," Mrs. Cooper had finished. "Remember!" she turned to Amy. "Something happens to him. At times like this he says things like 'me and Cy.'" She watched the two men walk across the clearing.

Now the two men stood at the end of the bar, fiddling with their glasses. They had made a big show of having the bottle in front of them. Not two little glasses for them. The bottle right there, where they could get their hands on it.

But now they fiddled with their glasses, watching the crowd about them, watching the light on the amber-colored bottles along the back bar. They turned to look whenever anyone came in.

Lights, spicy smell of whisky, talk rising and falling. Laughter. Remember this saloon and tell about the gurgle of a drink that was poured by a good friend, and the sharp clink of glasses. There was a knot of young ranchers, some of them unsteady now.

"No place like it." Insistent. "No place like this country."

"You take the fellows in this country. A hell of a lot different. Different from other places." They pondered this.

A belligerent face. "Different kind of fellows here. Nobody can say different."

Looking around for somebody who said different.

"You got it exactly right. Ask that fellow there."

They bought him a drink. He was a good fellow. He said the country was different and the fellows were different.

"You got it exactly right." They poured a drink. They celebrated. They had come across something big.

"Here's how," Newt said stiffly.

They licked their lips because they always had and put their glasses down.

"It's funny," Cy said, "I don't feel much like drinking here."

Newt shuffled his feet. "Too damn noisy." The bottle before them was almost full, and it made them ashamed.

"Maybe—" Cy said.

"Maybe he's not coming?"

Their eyes met. "Oh, he'll be here."

Newt capped the bottle suddenly and tucked it under his arm. "Let's—round up the women. We'll look."

And the train whistled.

Jess had drawn up his team in the darkness, just out of the circle of light. Snow far up on the runners of the sleigh. He stood up in the seat to get a good look. He wanted to see.

He knew it would hurt.

There were the young men—as he had been—leaving the fire, walking away in the darkness, out of the circle of light, lost for a moment and coming into the light again near the saloon. Lost for a moment, though.

He thought about them.

They lived on the prairie, had their land, and could sit in their living rooms at night.

"I'll get to know them," he thought suddenly. Before the night was over he'd go into the saloon. He would say something, something to make them like him. Something more than "Have a drink on me." They must know how he felt, that they were a part of the country, and he must know them, must say something. Then he could say, "Have a drink on me." He would not be awkward or silent, for they had been in the country a long time.

The shout seemed to come from far away. It burst on him.

"The band's coming." *The band's coming* . . . .

The band joined the crowd out of the darkness. Firelight on the tuba and the two cornets. The Salmon City Band. The tuba began to grumble like an old man. It had always grumbled so, and the light had always caught on the brass. He had put a wall of silence around himself, and the tuba grumbled like an old man.

He looked up the track, and the train was there. There was the gleam of the headlight. In a minute the whistle . . .

It whistled.

It came rolling down the track, proud, triumphant, a dignified old warrior, pistons moving slowly, cowcatcher covered with snow. It grumbled, huh-huh-huh. Steam hissed; smoke floated down, a red cloud in the firelight.

The smoke had always smelled like that.

They shouted up to the engineer. "Right on time," they shouted. "Right on time."

Then the band began to work hard.

They didn't have much to offer, but they had the band, and it played "Auld Lang Syne." *Should auld acquaintance be forgot, and never brought to mind . . . .*

And then Jess saw them, the four figures moving toward him in the darkness, leaving the light, coming to him.

"Jess! What are you doing there?" Amy cried. "I said to Cy, 'I can't see Jess anywhere,' and I said, 'I'm going to look.' Mrs. Cooper said she was having trouble catching the spirit—"

"Jess—I was having trouble catching the spirit," Mrs. Cooper panted, trudging along, "and I mean to catch it. This snow is deep." She paused to rest. "I thought—all of us together. First time—train came." She began to trudge on again. "We're about the only ones—"

He couldn't trust himself to speak. He had never been very good at being hard.

But it didn't matter. He lifted his chin, happy and proud.

For this was the moment. This was the moment he knew must come.

He could see her plain as he saw his friends standing there, almost beneath him now. She was a little way back, in her lady's-cloth suit, and her duster over her arm.

But it was her eyes that mattered, her gray eyes. A little lost figure in a big hat and a duster over her arm. And her eyes said, "You are beyond doubt the most magnificent man who ever lived . . . ."

The End

THOMAS SAVAGE was born in Salt Lake City in 1915 and spent his youngest years at the sheep and cattle ranch of his maternal grandparents, Thomas and Emma Russall Yearian, in Lemhi, Idaho. His mother, Elizabeth Yearian, divorced his father while Savage was an infant. In 1920 she remarried, this time to Charles Brenner, youngest son of the Brenner ranch family in Horse Prairie, Montana. Savage spent his boyhood between these two ranches, on the west and east side of the Continental Divide, and in Dillon, Montana, where he boarded out for school.

A loner during his school years, Savage—known as Tom Brenner until he published his first novel—graduated from Beaverhead County High School in 1932. He headed for Missoula where, at Montana State College (today The University of Montana), he studied writing under Brassil Fitzgerald. Savage left college for a couple of years, working at a riding academy and a dude ranch in the Pacific Northwest. After he returned to school, he became acquainted with Fitzgerald's daughter, Elizabeth, who had departed for Colby College, in Waterville, Maine. Savage followed her by train, meeting Elizabeth and her mother at the station in Boston.

Both enrolled at Colby College, where they got married in 1939 and graduated the following year. Savage was already at work on what became his first novel, *The Pass*. During the war years, he worked a variety of jobs: the Savages lived briefly in Chicago and returned to Horse Prairie, Montana, to help with the ranch because of the manpower shortage. Two sons, Robert Brassil and Richard Yearian, were born in 1942 and 1943, respectively; in 1949, they were joined by a sister, Elizabeth St. Mark. Savage taught writing at Suffolk University and then worked at Brandeis University for a few years, as a liaison between administration and the public and as a fundraiser. The Savages lived in Waltham, Massachusetts.

In 1955 the Savages had bought a ramshackle house on a rocky point in Georgetown, Maine, and they moved there, husband and wife remaining for the next thirty years. By then, Savage had published his first three novels, the third novel, *A Bargain with God,* proving his biggest commercial success. They took cross-country trips to southwestern Montana and the Lemhi River valley of Idaho to visit family. Tom liked showing off his newest sports car. After 1956, the year his mother died, the trips became much less frequent.

Savage published only one novel between 1953 and 1967, but after *The Power of the Dog* (1967), he published five more novels within a decade. His novelist wife, Betty, published a total of nine novels, eight of them between 1970 and 1980. Savage published his final two novels in 1983 and 1988. Betty died of lung cancer the following year; thereafter, Savage lived in Seattle and San Francisco before settling, in old age, in Virginia Beach, Virginia, near his daughter. He died in the summer of 2003, at age eighty-eight.

O. ALAN WELTZIEN is a longtime Professor of English at The University of Montana-Western, in Dillon. He has been obsessed with Thomas Savage for years, and the winter (2008) issue of *Montana The Magazine of Western History* features his article, "Thomas Savage, Forgotten Novelist." Weltzien's most recent books are *The Norman Maclean Reader* (editor), from the University of Chicago Press (2008), and a memoir, *A Father and an Island: Reflections on Loss,* published by Lewis-Clark Press (2008). In addition, he has recently published articles on Annie Proulx in *Rethinking Regionalism: The Geographical Imagination of Annie Proulx* (Lexington Books, 2008), and Savage in *All Our Stories Are Here: Critical Perspectives on Montana Literature* (University of Nebraska Press, 2009). Weltzien is proud to help restore Thomas Savage to his rightful place in Montana letters.